TREASON

BOOK ONE

DON BROWN

THE NAVY

JUSTICE SERIES

TREASON

ZONDERVAN™

GRAND RAPIDS, MICHIGAN 49530 USA

ZONDERVAN™

Treason
Copyright © 2005 by Don Brown

Requests for information should be addressed to:
Zondervan, *Grand Rapids, Michigan 49530*

Cataloging-in-Publication Data available from the Library of Congress.

ISBN-10: 0-310-25933-9
ISBN-13: 978-0-310-25933-6

Interior design by Michelle Espinoza

Printed in the United States of America

05 06 07 08 09 10 /❖ DCI/ 10 9 8 7 6 5 4 3 2 1

PROLOGUE

Black Forest Café
Near the Limmat River
Zurich, Switzerland

Abdur Rahman Ibn Auf checked his watch as the meeting adjourned. *Quarter to twelve. Good.*

Enough time for a little walk, maybe some sightseeing, and perhaps even lunch and a couple of drinks before summoning his pilot for the return flight to Riyadh.

He donned the jacket of his Armani business suit and stepped from the front door of Barclays onto the sidewalk beside Zurich's world-famous, charming Bahnhofstrasse. Squinting into the bright sunlight, he slipped on a pair of designer sunglasses. Around him bustled serious-looking businessmen speaking into cellular phones, young mothers—or perhaps au pairs; he could not tell the difference—pushing prams, laughing young lovers, and groups of beautiful women carrying smart bags from expensive clothing boutiques. On either side of the street, flower vendors displayed profusions of colorful bouquets, and halfway to the corner, a group of students crowded around a bakery window.

A cool breeze hit his face, and he closed his eyes, drawing the pristine Swiss air into his lungs. He breathed in, almost smiling at the invigorating result.

Why did Allah place the great cities of the faith in the middle of a scorching, God-forsaken desert rather than in a place like Zurich? At home, survival was impossible without air-conditioning. Here, nature provided it. But the Great Faith had spawned where it had, and Allah had his purposes. Perhaps to avoid distractions, which abounded here.

Abdur headed south down the Bahnhofstrasse by foot in the direction of the Arboretum and Bürlki Plaza on Lake Zurich. A traffic light stopped him just before he reached the Swiss National Bank Building, and he turned left toward Stathausquai, on the east bank of the Limmat River.

The deep blue waters of the river, fed by the melting snow from the Alps, flowed into Lake Zurich a few blocks to his right. Abdur never grew tired of this view. If paradise was like any city in the world, surely Zurich would be at the top of the list. He watched two tour boats churning south toward the lake.

The sounds of laughter—young and feminine—broke into his thoughts. He turned toward a sidewalk café across the street, on the bank of the river.

There were four in the quartet—or perhaps he might say the *bouquet*—of exquisite Swiss fräuleins. They sat giggling under an umbrella at a white wrought-iron table. He did not need to blink even twice to see they were blond, well figured, and perhaps in their midtwenties. They were all blue-eyed. They were Swiss; how could they not have eyes the color of a summer alpine sky?

One of the fräuleins, the prettiest, with shoulder-length hair and wearing a navy business suit, seemed to sense his gaze. She shot him a coquettish smile, tilting her head slightly toward an empty table next to hers.

The outdoor café on the riverbank would make a perfect spot for lunch and a cocktail. And who knew? Perhaps this was his lucky day. A successful business session in the morning. An unanticipated rendezvous in the afternoon before leaving the country?

Blond European women seemed to be inordinately attracted to clean-shaven Arab men in expensive business suits. This trend had been established, luckily for him, by the late Princess Diana of Great Britain and Dodi al-Fayed. Or so he had been told when he studied at Oxford.

Abdur sat at the table next to the foursome. They spoke German, which was no impediment to his eavesdropping. He was fluent in the three official languages of Switzerland—German, French, and Italian—in addition to having mastered English and, of course, his native Arabic.

Such were the privileges of an educational pedigree for which money had been no object.

He inched his chair closer to the pretty one, and now she was only a stone's throw from him. When the wind shifted, he caught a whiff of exquisite perfume. *Is it hers?* He couldn't tell.

As he listened, he heard her speak in a low, velvety tone as she announced she had ended her relationship with her boyfriend. She sighed deeply—for his sake, perhaps?—then went on to tell her friends she would have to take holiday this year in Monaco without him. "He deserved it. Such an unfaithful dog."

An unfaithful dog.

Was that a calculated message, intended not only for her attractive fräulein companions, but also for his ears? Or merely coincidence?

Nothing is coincidental. Everything is calculated.

Abdur ordered a cocktail and contemplated his next move. Perhaps a round of complimentary cocktails for the fräuleins would attract their attention. Or maybe he would trail her home when she left.

"Ahff wun, yah eff." The sudden deep sound of a man's voice over his shoulder distracted Abdur. "Excuse me, mister," the man repeated in Arabic. "Her name is Marta."

Abdur turned, frowning. The man was handsome, Middle Eastern, and perhaps in his early thirties. He wore an expensive suit, tie, and shoes, all of which were white.

"You contemplate luring her to your hotel." The man's Arabic was flawless. "Except you did not reserve a room, because you had planned on flying back in your Cessna Citation this afternoon to report to Riyadh. But now, with the bat of her eyes, the scent of her perfume, the crossing of her legs, you are contemplating, shall we say, a slight change of plan?"

Abdur rose to his feet and met the man's black eyes. The penetrating quality of the man's gaze was instantly gripping, as if he had the power to hypnotize. Abdur felt a chill shoot down his spine.

"Do not fear, my brother," the man continued. "And I assure you, my sudden intrusion has not compromised your opportunity with this Swiss maiden. You will have your opportunity, if it is what you want. She will cooperate. Trust me."

"Do I know you?"

"I have been searching for you, my brother."

"You look familiar." Abdur frowned again, trying to read the other man's expression. He was unsuccessful.

"I am Hussein al-Akhma of Kuwait."

"Un hum del Allah. Praise be to God." Abdur had seen Hussein's picture in Arab newspapers. But this was the first time he had seen the man in person. "Of you I have heard much, Brother Hussein."

"And I, of you." Hussein inclined his head. "But then, we are a small brotherhood, are we not?" Hussein gave Abdur a friendly pat on the shoulder, and Abdur relaxed. But not much.

"When I was at Oxford, you were at the London School of Economics. But we never met." Abdur was getting his voice back.

"An unfortunate crossing in the night. But Allah has his purposes *and* his timing. And this moment has to do with the latter."

Abdur pointed to the chair across the table. "Please, be seated."

He studied the mysterious man, rumored to be both a billionaire playboy and a stalwart man of the faith. Was this an oxymoronic combination? Perhaps not. Abdur felt the same tug-of-war within. The prophet Muhammad himself—*Peace be upon him*—certainly had felt the same struggles.

"Brother Abdur, though we have never met personally until now, I have known you for some time." Again, a fiery, magnetic flash lit Hussein's eyes.

"What do you mean?"

"You are searching for the purpose of life. I believe Allah has called you. Like me, you have been entrusted with much at a young age. But it is all meaningless unless we are called to a higher purpose." Hussein's voice was smooth, hypnotic . . . as if he saw through the windows of Abdur's soul.

How can he see my struggles? My demons?

"Next to the prophet Muhammad—Peace be upon him—there had been no greater Muslim to walk the earth than the servant of Allah, Osama bin Laden," said al-Akhma. "Not since the British burned the White House in the War of 1812 has a foreign enemy struck the heart of America. But one man on September 11, 2001, carried out what the Japanese, the Germans, and the mighty Soviets did not.

"Drew American blood.

"On American soil."

"He was so bold. So daring, was he not?"

"Yes, he was, my brother." Hussein smiled. "But even Osama was not perfect. The brilliant hero of 9/11 failed to realize that to defeat our great enemy, one must become invisible, blend in with their forces."

Abdur studied his companion. "I do not follow you."

"That was Osama's Achilles' heel. He and his cronies all looked and spoke Arabic. Of course, our Arabic heritage is glorious and to be embraced. But Al Qaida cast the perfect stereotype for the Zionist media to beam over the airwaves into American homes and plaster on the front pages of the *New York Times* and the *Washington Post*.

"Al Qaida," he continued, "gave the world the image of bearded-looking, turban-wearing 'terrorists' firing AK-47s into the air in frenzied jubilation whenever a bomb went off in Israel. Meaningless. What did we ever accomplish by blowing up a civilian bus on the streets of Tel Aviv? Nothing. Yet all this fueled the Zionist propaganda machine around which Christians and Jews wrapped their anger. It caused them to turn their political and military power against Islam."

"It does make sense," Abdur said.

"I am recruiting a new, more sophisticated breed of Islamic fighter. A fighter who can blend into the Western landscape with fluency in English, with the ability to instantly ditch his turban for a business suit . . ." Hussein's black eyes glinted, drawing Abdur in. "A fighter with the willingness to don a U.S. military uniform for the cause of Allah. These characteristics will epitomize Council of Ishmael operatives.

"'Know thine enemy,'" Hussein quoted in Arabic. "Allah has laid it upon my heart, Brother Abdur, to assemble a council of twenty rulers to govern this new breed of fighter and to advance this unprecedented worldwide organization."

Goose bumps crept up Abdur's neck, and he sat forward.

"All who have been called to this council are wealthy beyond earthly measure—among the wealthiest men in the various Islamic nations they represent. All are British- or American-educated. All are fluent in English and fervent in their devotion to Islam. All loathe the three great enemies of Allah—Israel, America, and Christianity."

Hussein put his hand on Abdur's shoulder, paused, then met Abdur's eyes. Something supernatural seemed to hold Abdur in his chair.

"Allah has told me, Brother Abdur, that you are one of the chosen twenty."

Chills shot down Abdur's spine.

"One of his coveted Council of Ishmael." Hussein seemed to caress each word as it passed from his lips. And then he stared at Abdur, silent.

The sounds of summer in a busy European city returned to Abdur's ears: car horns honking, birds chirping, trolley bells ringing, the wind blowing off Lake Zurich. All provided a surreal backdrop that Abdur felt was somehow divine.

His gaze wandered to the table next to them that was now empty. Sometime within the last few minutes, Marta had left, and he had not even noticed. He turned again to his companion. "I feel, Brother Hussein, that this is a divine moment. An appointment with destiny preordained by Allah himself. Beyond that, my words have left me."

Hussein's smile was gentle. Abdur noticed his teeth were nearly as white as his suit.

"Abdur, you need not give up your lifestyle. You are not called to poverty. Only to glory. To use all you have been blessed with—your language abilities, your educational background, your resources—for the glory of Allah. You were born for this day. You were blessed for this reason. Very few Muslims the world over possess your combination of talent, skill, and resources.

"Say only this: that you will come, that you will follow me. That you will say yes to Allah's call. That you will become an adopted son of the Council of Ishmael."

Femme du Monde *School of Modeling*
International Headquarters
North American Division
Madison Avenue, New York City

Diane Colcernian ran her hand through her hair and took a swig of bottled water. She was standing near the elevated runway down the center of a mirrored room that served as a combination lecture hall and practice studio. Four other models lolled against the runway, listening to Monica, the agency's artistic coach, deliver another of her dull lectures on the importance of runway posture.

Angelica, a long-legged blond, rolled her eyes toward Diane, and dark-haired, gamine Corrine snickered. This brought a glare from Monica, who then continued her delivery in her pseudo French accent.

"Next she'll show us an example of her runway work in Paris," whispered Sybil. A moment later, Monica, dressed in designer warm-ups, did exactly that. She floated up the runway stairs and signaled the technician to start the strobe lights and music. Then, head back, body thrust forward, she moved along the runway, her long legs in a fashionable strut. She snapped into a turn and returned to where her young students waited by the runway.

"Now, your turn," Monica said above the music. The women lined up at the stairs, and Diane, who was first in line, climbed up, ignoring the snickers of "Teacher's pet."

Monica made no secret that she was grooming Diane to step onto the runway as a world-class supermodel, just as Monica herself had done twenty years earlier. Diane suspected it was her wavy, flame-colored hair—which, according to photos she'd seen, was much like Monica's in her youth—that endeared her to the artistic coach. Their physiques were similar: tall, lithe, long-limbed, with an almost liquid manner of movement. Because Monica had chosen Diane as heir apparent, she was often harder on her than on all the others; her expectations were greater.

Modeling had been Diane's dream since she was a teenager. She'd thought it would be glamorous—bright lights, public adulation, photographs on the cover of *Glamour* and *Vogue*. But in reality, it was excruciatingly hard work. Monica monitored every bite she and the other girls ate. If she gained even a half pound, lunches and dinners consisted of iceberg lettuce and low-fat yogurt. She spent hours with studio makeup artists, still more hours with the studio hairdresser as he twisted her tresses into extreme—and sometimes painful—designs. Then there was her personal trainer who put her through a tortuous daily workout to keep her body toned. And the hours spent under bright, hot lights often left her with a migraine. When she and the others went out on the town, it was only to be seen. Not to be real. Not to enjoy real conversation with real people. Not to laugh and talk about books and world affairs.

She missed that. Her father had brought her up to think for herself, to enjoy stretching her mind with the classics, with art and music, to debate politics and world affairs. His dream, especially after her mother died, was for Diane to go to college, to continue to stretch her mind. To practice law.

But in a fit of rebellion, she'd announced that she planned to follow *her* dream—no matter what he said. She was going to New York. Her words had broken his heart. She hadn't cared.

Now Diane looked up at Monica, who frowned as she gestured for Diane to join her on the runway. With a sigh, she took her place beside the artistic coach and struck a ten-point model's pose, pasting on the traditional hollow-cheeked, bored expression. Oh yes, she was almost there. She had almost reached her dream.

Why did she feel so empty?

The music throbbed as she slithered down the runway. *Seven liquid steps, then snap to a turn. Seven more, turn again . . .*

The studio door burst open, and the office manager, Janice Jeffers, a plain but pleasant woman, stepped into the studio. Her heels clicked and echoed like tap-dancing shoes against the polished hardwood floors as she crossed the room.

"Diane, telephone call!" Janice almost shouted to be heard above the runway music.

Diane halted midstep; Monica signaled the engineer to turn off the strobes and music. "Can't it wait?" She shot Diane a glare, then looked back to Janice. "As you can see, we're just beginning the exercise."

"Sorry, Monica," Janice said. "It's an emergency."

"It better be," Monica snapped, then frowned at Diane. "Make it quick, honey."

Diane hurried down the runway steps and jogged to the door, where Janice put her arm around her. "You can take the call in my office." She led Diane down the long hall.

"Who is it?"

"Your father's aide. He said it was urgent." Janice opened the glass door to her office and gestured toward the telephone on her desk.

Diane lifted the receiver to her ear. "Hello?"

"Diane, this is Lieutenant Commander Wilson."

"What's going on, Mitch?"

He hesitated a moment—though it seemed like an eternity—before answering. "Your father's in the hospital. I think you should catch the next flight down here."

Her heart pounded. "What happened?"

"Maybe you should wait until you can talk to his doctor."

"I'm not waiting. Tell me now, Mitch!"

Another hesitation. "Diane . . . the admiral has had a stroke. It's serious . . . I'm sorry."

This isn't happening. This is a bad dream.

"Diane?"

"Is he going to make it?" She blinked back the sting of tears.

"The doctor thinks so, but it'll be touch and go for the next few days."

"Where is he?" She sank into the swivel chair by the desk.

"Portsmouth Naval Hospital. He's getting the very best treatment the Navy can provide. Listen, I've arranged for your plane to fly into Oceana Naval Air Station. I'll meet you there in two hours."

They said their good-byes, then Diane dropped her head into her hands.

"Diane?"

She felt Janice's arm ease across her shoulder.

"I'm sorry . . . Your father's aide didn't want me to tell you. He called us thirty minutes ago to discuss transportation arrangements so you didn't have to worry with them yourself. Mr. Rochembeau is in Paris, but I called him on his cell phone. The company jet will fly you to Virginia Beach."

Two hours later, the *Femme du Monde* Lear jet touched down at the Oceana Naval Air Station in Virginia Beach. Diane put on dark sunglasses to conceal her red-rimmed eyes, long since washed free of makeup by her tears. She stepped from the jet into a sunny Tidewater afternoon.

Her father's aide waited, his expression lined with concern. When she reached him, he took her by the arm and guided her to the admiral's staff car. He returned to the plane for her luggage, placed it in the trunk, and slid into the driver's seat.

Before he turned the key in the ignition, she touched his arm. "How bad is it, Mitch?"

The aide hesitated and then let his hand drop to his lap. "He's paralyzed on the left side of his body. He drifts in and out of consciousness. Both times he regained consciousness, he whispered your mother's name." He met her gaze. "And yours."

"My mother was a wonderful woman. I wish you had known her."

"The admiral has often said you're just like her. Strong, smart, resolute."

"I don't feel so strong and resolute right now." She pulled out a tissue and dabbed her eyes, praying for a dose of the same strength she remembered in her mother. Most of all, she prayed for her father. And tried not to think of her regrets.

U.S. Naval Medical Center
620 John Paul Jones Circle
Portsmouth, Virginia

As the car approached the main gate outside the huge Portsmouth Naval Hospital, Diane still fought to control her tears. A few minutes later, her father's aide steered the car into the flag officers' parking spaces near the front entrance of the hospital.

He came around to the passenger side and opened the door. "Your father is the strongest man I know," he said as Diane swung her legs out of the car. "The sound of your voice will give him strength."

Diane and Mitch got off the elevator at the sixth deck. A slim officer in a khaki uniform, wearing the silver eagle of a Navy captain pinned to one collar and the gold oak leaf and silver acorn of the Navy Medical Corps on the other, stepped forward and greeted them. "I'm Captain Ornsbee. Lead physician in charge of your father's treatment."

"Is he going to be okay, Doctor?"

"It's still early. These next few hours will be crucial. We're worried about the possibility of an aneurysm. We're giving him blood thinners and watching him constantly."

"May I see him?"

"Yes. I'll take you. But be prepared. He's had a massive stroke. The left part of his body is paralyzed. He may not recognize you."

"I want to see him."

He gave her a solemn nod and then led her down the corridor, past the nurses' station, to a hospital room on the other side.

She halted midstep, stunned. The proud body that was once Vice Admiral Stephen Colcernian lay in a helpless form attached to wires and tubes. "Oh, Daddy." She swallowed the tears at the back of her throat, willing herself not to cry.

The doctor's voice was low. "Your father may be able to hear you. I know it's hard, but try to stay strong."

"Okay." She wiped her eyes, took a deep breath, and moved closer to take her father's hand. "I love you, Daddy. You'd better not leave me. Not now. Please. You're so strong. You're going to be fine." *Please, God. Let him hear me.* "I came as soon as I found out. Bob has been great. You'd be so proud of him. He arranged to have a plane take me from New York to Oceana. He's a great admiral's aide, Daddy."

Nothing.

Please, God . . .

"Squeeze my hand if you can hear me, Daddy."

Was it her imagination?

"Daddy, can you squeeze it again?"

It was faint, but this time, definite.

Thank you, Lord.

"Daddy, I'm leaving New York, coming home to be close to you. And when we get you up and on your feet, I'll go to UVA so I can come see you on the weekends."

Another squeeze.

She drew in a shaky breath and cleared her throat. "I know how much it means to you to have someone in the family uphold our Navy legacy. I want it too, Daddy, not just for you, but for me. And I was thinking on the plane coming down here. I'm going to go to UVA, and then I'm going to apply for law school. And then I'll apply for a direct commission in the Navy JAG Corps. And I'm going to be the best JAG officer the Navy's ever seen."

This time, it was different. The squeeze was still faint, but twice as strong as the others.

"I won't let you down, Daddy. I promise."

CHAPTER 1

Headquarters
Commander, U.S. Naval Base
San Diego, California

Seven years later

Lieutenant Zack Brewer, JAGC, USNR, checked his watch. The slow-crawling traffic on Harbor Drive, a six-mile route along San Diego Bay connecting the 32nd Street Naval Station to COMNAVBASE headquarters downtown, was not cooperating with Vice Admiral John F. Ayers's penchant for punctuality.

Brewer checked his watch again. *Twelve minutes.*

When the brake lights on an old rusty Toyota flashed red just inches in front of his Mercedes, Brewer's foot hit the antilock brakes. The sudden jolt thrust him forward, tightening the shoulder harness across his chest, which tempted him to utter a phrase not customarily used in most Sunday school classes. He refrained.

He hit his horn. The shrill blare prompted the Toyota driver, in denim work clothes, to turn around and glare through the window. Zack chuckled and managed a grin as he gave the man a half-wave of apology.

A few minutes later, he wheeled his Mercedes into the parking lot at the corner of Broadway and Harbor Drive. Brewer snatched his leather briefcase off the backseat, slammed the car door, and briskly walked toward the entrance of the building.

Two shore patrol sailors, each flanking the front door of the building and dressed in crisply starched white uniforms with pixie cup hats, came to attention, then flashed sharp salutes.

Zack shot back an equally sharp salute, then passed through the entrance of the building, under a large navy blue and white sign that read "COMNAVBASE SAN DIEGO."

The chief petty officer manning the security station in the main lobby rose to his feet. "May I help you, Lieutenant?"

"Lieutenant Brewer for a meeting with Admiral Ayers and Captain Morrison at ten hundred hours."

"Identification, please, sir."

Brewer handed the chief his armed services identification card, then checked his watch as the chief picked up the telephone. "Lieutenant Brewer for Admiral Ayers."

The chief hung up and glanced at Zack. "They'll be ready in five minutes. You know the drill, Lieutenant. Sixth deck. First door on your right."

Brewer stepped into the elevator and punched the number. A moment later the aluminum doors parted, and he stepped out into a large, antiseptic-smelling hallway. He checked his watch again. Just enough time to stop by the head for a last-minute uniform check. The admiral was a stickler for detail—more than once, officers had been dismissed for the slightest infraction of dress.

He stepped to the mirror and turned for a closer inspection of his short-sleeved summer whites. The black shoulder boards bearing the two full gold stripes and the JAG insignia were in place.

His salad row, the row of ribbons displaying his individual medals and achievements, though not as full as that of a twenty-year sea dog, was impressive for a junior JAG officer. There was a pink and white Meritorious Defense Service Medal, a green and white Navy Commendation Medal, a green and orange Navy Achievement Medal, a multicolored Sea Service Ribbon, and an orange and yellow National Defense Service Medal. The impressive array of colors was pinned perfectly on two rows of bars on the breast of his white shirt just above the pocket.

He checked to see if the right side of his gold belt buckle was aligned with the gig line of his zipper and the line of buttons up the front of his white shirt.

He frowned at his shoes and snatched a paper towel from the dispenser, doused it with water, added a couple of drops of soap, and with one swipe transformed the toe of his right shoe into the same ice-cream white color dominating the rest of his uniform.

Then he stepped back for a final assessment. The U.S. Navy's summer white uniform, resplendent with black and gold shoulder boards, was the second-best-looking military uniform in the world. Only the Navy's formal "choker" white uniform—the one worn with ceremonial swords—looked better. He had one of those too, hanging in his closet at home.

Neither Tom Cruise nor Richard Gere had anything on Zack Brewer today. He mentally pronounced himself shipshape, then headed back to the hallway, turned right, and marched into the reception area of Admiral Ayers's office.

A moment later, a lieutenant in summer whites stepped out of the admiral's inner sanctum and into the reception area. The aide-de-camp's uniform was identical to Zack's except for the gold rope looping around his right shoulder, signifying he was an admiral's aide. "The admiral is ready for you now, Lieutenant."

Zack nodded to his brother-in-arms, then walked through the entrance to the admiral's richly paneled office, came to a halt under the gold chandelier about five feet in front of the officer's desk, and stood at attention. The admiral was sitting behind his large mahogany desk. In strict compliance with Navy protocol, Zack bored his eyes three feet over the admiral's head, finding a spot on the back wall. With his peripheral vision, he noticed two other Navy captains in khaki uniforms in the office. He recognized Captain Tom Morrison, who was standing by the window holding a steaming cup of coffee. The other, whom he did not recognize, bore the insignia of a Navy SEAL on his khaki uniform shirt and sat in a large leather chair just to the left of the admiral's desk.

"Lieutenant Brewer reporting as ordered, sir."

"At ease, Lieutenant," Ayers said. "You know my personal JAG officer, Captain Tom Morrison?"

"Yes, sir, quite well." Zack exchanged a pleasant nod with Morrison, who was sipping his coffee by the window.

"And I'd like you to meet Captain Buck Noble." The admiral gestured toward the captain seated in the leather chair. "Captain Noble is commanding officer of Navy Special Warfare School in Coronado."

"Lieutenant." Noble stood and extended his hand to Brewer.

Two seconds later, Zack almost grimaced as he withdrew his hand from Captain Noble's vicelike grip.

"Please sit. No need to be overly formal here, Counselor." The admiral waved Zack to a chair in front of his desk.

Ayers nodded to Captain Morrison. "Captain, care to brief the lieu-tenant on what we have here?"

"Certainly, Admiral." Morrison took a sip of coffee. "There's been a rape over at the amphibious base." He paused.

"Yes, sir?"

"We'd like you to prosecute."

It sounded routine. So why call him down here to meet with the admiral and Captain "Grip"?

"I've explained to the admiral and the captain that, in my opinion, you're the best man for this. You were awarded the Navy Commendation Medal for the great job you did in that *Jones-O'Leary* rape prosecution involving the dental technician down at the naval station."

"Just doing my job, sir."

"In this case, Lieutenant, your job is complicated by the victim."

"I don't follow you, Captain."

Captains Morrison and Noble exchanged glances as Admiral Ayers rocked back in his chair, folded his arms, and stared at Zack.

"Your victim, Lieutenant, is an officer," Admiral Ayers said. "An Annapolis graduate. Deputy Public Affairs Officer for the Naval Air Station at North Island. The matter is complicated most by her uncle."

"Her uncle?"

"Ensign Marianne Landrieu's uncle is United States Senator Rober-son Fowler."

Zack gulped, then inhaled slowly. "Democrat? Louisiana? Ranking Minority Member? Senate Armed Services Committee? Roberson Fowler?"

"One and the same." The admiral looked at Captain Noble. "Captain, you want to take it from here?"

Noble gave the admiral a brisk nod, then turned to Zack. "The ani-mal that did this is one of ours. A Navy SEAL." His voice reflected his disgust. "We want this maggot nailed, Lieutenant. We want his heart cut out. His head served up on a platter. Understand?"

"Loud and clear, sir." If he didn't deliver, it would be *his* head on the platter in place of the maggot's. "With respect, Captain Noble, the Uni-form Code of Military Justice allows imposition of the death penalty for a rape conviction."

"Really?" Noble's eyebrows rose.

"Yes, sir. Article 120 of the UCMJ technically provides for death or life imprisonment for a convicted rapist. The convening authority would have to request it, and we'd have to notify the defense in advance. I've been waiting for the right case to come along."

A slight smile crept onto the tough SEAL commander's battle-hardened lips. "I think we'll get along just fine, Lieutenant."

"Now hang on a minute." Captain Morrison leaned forward. "Lieutenant Brewer's aggressive reputation precedes him. He's right. The death penalty is technically an option for a rape conviction under military law. But then again, that's true for convictions for murder, mutiny, desertion, and treason. With respect, Admiral, you would be the first Navy convening authority to seek the death penalty for rape since World War II. It may look like political pandering to a powerful senator if we do. Besides, Roberson Fowler opposes capital punishment."

Admiral Ayers lifted his hand, calling for a moment of silence. "I agree with Captain Morrison. I'm not going to be the first Navy convening authority since the war to go capital on a rape charge. But it *is* good to see the Navy JAG Corps is well represented by both the aggressive young tiger *and* the seasoned gray owl."

When the obligatory chuckles subsided, Zack nodded. "May I ask about the status of the Article 32 Investigation, Admiral?"

"By all means, son. That's why you're here. I want our game plan in place before you head back down to 32nd Street," Ayers said, referring to the 32nd Street Naval Station, the largest of all the military installations around San Diego. He gestured to Morrison. "Why don't you take this one, Tom?"

"Yes, sir, Admiral." Morrison turned to Zack. "The Article 32 has been completed, Lieutenant. The investigating officer found probable cause to proceed with a charge of felony rape." He paused. "And I might add, he had his hands full with this investigation."

"Sir?"

"This could be messy, Lieutenant. The perpetrator, a Petty Officer Antonio Blount, is claiming consent."

Zack frowned. "An officer and an enlisted SEAL."

"It gets messier, Zack. This one is interracial."

"How so?"

"Caucasian victim, Filipino-American perpetrator."

"It's not as hard to believe as the officer-enlisted thing," Zack mused. "But an ensign fresh out of the Academy risking captain's mast by romantically fraternizing with an enlisted man? Unbelievable, even if the enlisted man is a SEAL."

"Good point, Lieutenant," Morrison said.

"But there is one positive thing about a consent defense, gentlemen." Zack had their attention. "If the accused claims consent as a defense, that means he must testify. If he testifies, I get to cross-examine him." He paused, looking directly at Captain Noble. "That, Skipper, is where I will cut his heart out for you. And with all due respect, sir, you'd better believe I will."

"Somehow," Ayers said, "I think he means it."

"I like your killer instinct, Brewer." A half grin eased across Noble's features. "Ever think about a cross-designation transfer into the SEALs?"

"The SEALs are the finest special warfare unit in the world, Captain."

"I hate to pour water on this mutual admiration society," Captain Morrison said, "but there's one other thing I think you need to know, Lieutenant. Defense counsel has been appointed." Captain Morrison pursed his lips. "Lieutenant Colcernian is representing the accused."

Zack's smile faded, and a grunt escaped his lips.

Captain Noble eyed him. "You have a problem with that, Lieutenant?"

"My apologies, sir. It's just that Lieutenant Diane Colcernian and I are—how should I say this diplomatically?"

"Out with it, son," Ayers ordered.

"Professional rivals." He weighed his words. "We go way back. We're in for a real war here, gentlemen."

"I hope you're still convinced we can win."

"Captain Noble, I've beaten Colcernian before. I know her game. We will win. It'll be a battle, sir, but at the end of the day, I'll give you your man with a big fat conviction stamped across his head. It doesn't really matter who the defense counsel is, sir."

"Well then," Admiral Ayers said, "on that note, it seems we've covered all relevant information for now, Lieutenant. Unless Captain Morrison has anything else?"

"No, sir." Morrison leaned back. "Lieutenant, I'll have the Blount file couriered to your office at 32nd Street this afternoon."

"Aye, sir."

"Very well then," the admiral said. "That will be all, Lieutenant."

So dismissed, Zack rose from his chair and stood at attention. "By your leave, sir."

"Permission granted, Lieutenant. You are dismissed."

As Zack turned and marched out of the admiral's office, his mind was consumed with the image of fiery, angry green eyes. Diane Colcernian was a beauty. One who'd accused him of stabbing her in the back when he'd beaten her in the final round of the Naval Justice School trial advocacy competition.

Her words still rang in his memory: *"I don't know when or how, Lieutenant, but I'll get you for this. And when I do, the stakes will be even higher. If I were you, I'd watch my back."*

That was two years ago. And though both were stationed in San Diego, and though he was the best prosecutor and she was the best defense counsel in San Diego, they had yet to go head-to-head in court.

Until now.

Now they'd face each other in a high-stakes court-martial that would be scrutinized by the Navy's top brass because of the victim's uncle.

The elevator opened on the first deck of COMNAVBASE headquarters, and Zack stepped out, past the chief who was manning the reception desk and into the warm, arid Southern California sunshine.

Not that he was the least bit intimidated by Diane Colcernian, Zack thought as he returned the simultaneous salutes of the two shore patrolmen guarding the entrance of the building, but this trial was going to be a bloodbath.

A monumental bloodbath.

CHAPTER 2

Saturday afternoon, two weeks later

Anthony Neptune preferred to be called al-Ahmad Neptune, son of Muhammad, devout follower of Islam. It didn't matter that the Navy knew him as Anthony Neptune, a gunner's mate third class, or that his home was Queens, New York, where he'd grown up. He'd found his new identity. *Praise be to Allah!*

His spiritual transformation began when he saw a flyer posted on the 32nd Street Naval Station for a Muslim religious service held at the base chapel on Saturday afternoons. He attended, mainly out of curiosity. There he met Lieutenant Commander Mohammed Olajuwon, Chaplain Corps, United States Navy. The man changed his life.

Saturdays, while on leave from the USS *Tarawa*, became a time of pilgrimage to rekindled faith, to a hope that he would become something larger than life. Like his father before him, and with Commander Olajuwon's encouragement, he was now, in the eyes of Allah, al-Ahmad Neptune, son of Muhammad, devout follower of Islam above all.

The chaplain suggested Neptune use his new Muslim name only in the presence of fellow Muslims. Other sailors might misinterpret his intentions, the commander advised. When the time was right, Allah would reveal his plan for al-Ahmad Neptune. And his true Muslim name would be revealed to the sailors in the fleet and to people of the world.

When Olajuwon spoke, Neptune buried the words deep in his soul, knowing the words were true.

"Islam's enemies are Allah's enemies," Olajuwon preached one Saturday. "We must sacrifice *all* for Islam, if necessary." He held up a newspaper article from the *San Diego Union*. "This, brothers, is a living example of what the prophet means when he speaks of the enemies of Allah. This so-called Bible study."

The Navy chaplain thumped the paper on the pine pulpit. "Listen to the headlines in the religion section of our own *San Diego Union*: 'Local Church Catering to Sailors, Studying Cults.'"

He ripped open the paper, scanned the article, and then looked out at the faithful brothers again. "This so-called church, which takes money from Navy personnel, lies about the Great Faith. It defames the prophet Muhammad, declaring the great prophet of Allah to be a *child molester*!" His voice was low and raw. His dark eyes met Neptune's, as if speaking directly to him. "It declares the great religion of Islam to be a *cult*!

"Blasphemy! I declare this blasphemy against Allah!" This time the Navy chaplain pounded the pulpit with his fist. "How can Allah rest as such venom is spewed forth?" He paused, his swarthy face flushed, blood vessels rising at his temples. "I declare to you, Allah will raise up warriors to vindicate his name!"

Neptune was enraged. Such lies about Islam were an affront, an insult to the memory of his father—to the very blood flowing in his veins.

When the Navy chaplain called them to prayer, Neptune's heart still pounded. They rolled out their prayer mats and bowed toward Mecca as the chaplain raised his hands. "May the name of Allah be vindicated. May the honor of the holy prophet be defended!"

The holy music began, piped in electronically. One by one, his brothers joined the chant that had been recorded in Mecca. It soothed Neptune. It didn't matter that he couldn't understand Arabic—few in the small congregation did—but he could wail, moan, and hum along.

His anger subsided, but his determination to defend Islam grew. When Commander Olajuwon proclaimed the service complete, Neptune rolled up his mat and walked swiftly out to the small used Volkswagen he'd bought just after boot camp. He swung by the Navy Exchange before heading back to Pier 6, where the *Tarawa* was moored.

Two copies of today's newspaper remained in the metal dispenser in front of the Exchange. He dropped in a quarter and took them both.

Back in the Volkswagen, he cranked the windows down and—still sitting in the sunbaked asphalt Navy Exchange parking lot—flipped through the *San Diego Union* to the religion section.

CHURCH ATTRACTS SAILORS TO COURSE ON "CULTS"
By June Moorefield, Faith and Values Editor

Lemon Grove—A San Diego–area church has been attracting a large number of Navy personnel to its services with a twelve-week course it has been teaching on cults.

The controversial course, taught at the ten o'clock Sunday school hour immediately preceding the eleven o'clock worship service, compares and contrasts evangelical Christianity with other religions such as Islam, Buddhism, Mormonism, and the New Age teachings of L. Ron Hubbard, Hare Krishna, Sun Yun Moon, and others. The course teaches that all such religions and beliefs other than evangelical Christianity are "cults," masterminded by the devil to ultimately lead souls into the fires of hell.

"We stand by our teaching," said the Rev. Jeff Spletto, pastor of Community Bible Church of Lemon Grove. "We wanted our members to be savvy to the tactics of our enemy, the devil. Our message is simple. There is but one way to heaven—through the spilled blood of Jesus Christ. All other religions and teachings are 'cults'—which sometimes have a pretty package on the outside, but seek to distract their followers from the powerful truth of the life-giving blood of Christ."

Dozens of sailors and marines from San Diego's nearby military installations have been in attendance.

"We are a medium-sized church, with just a handful of military personnel who regularly attend," Spletto said. "So we are very grateful for the attendance of the sailors."

Spletto said that many were interested in learning about Islam because of the military tension in the Middle East. Others, he said, had been bombarded with "New Age peddlers" and wanted to understand the principles behind such ideas.

The course will last seven more weeks, according to Spletto. It is being taught in the church's fellowship hall.

Neptune threw the paper onto the floorboard of his car. His blood boiled like a witch's brew in a hot cauldron. He checked his watch. *Time to get back to the ship. But soon . . .*

He would pay a visit to this Sunday school class.

CHAPTER 3

Lieutenant Zack Brewer's office
Naval Trial Command
Building 73
32nd Street Naval Station
San Diego

Zack Brewer's office window offered a view across the small canal sepa-rating the northern perimeter of the 32nd Street Naval Station from NASSCO, the National Steel and Shipbuilding Company.

Yesterday, an Aegis class cruiser, the USS *Valley Forge*, was moored across the way, getting minor repair work done. But today the repair dry dock was empty, giving Zack an unimpeded view of the Coronado Bay Bridge spanning the spectacular waters of San Diego Bay, just a mile or so to the north. The inspirational view helped him think.

At the short, shrill buzz of his telephone intercom, Zack rotated his government-issued, black vinyl chair 180 degrees.

"Lieutenant Brewer?" The voice on the telephone loudspeaker was Legalman First Class Amy DeBenedetto, a young petty officer from St. Louis. She served as military paralegal for Zack; his boss, Commander Bob Awe; and three other prosecutors.

"Yes, Amy?"

"Ensign Landrieu is here, sir."

By now he was familiar with the Landrieu file. Captain Morrison, COMNAVBASE's JAG, delivered it two days ago as promised. Zack stud-ied the Naval Criminal Investigative Service's report as soon as it arrived. Now, as he waited for Landrieu, he reviewed the dossier.

Ensign Marianne Landrieu had stopped by the Naval Air Station Offi-cers' Club the evening in question for a cocktail with a girlfriend from the Academy, Ensign Laura Rogerson, an aviator. When Rogerson met a male classmate from flight school in Pensacola, Landrieu decided to leave—alone. It was late, just an hour before midnight. So she excused herself, paid her bill, and headed to her car.

Per the NCIS report, she wore her summer white uniform, complete with white skirt, natural hose, and white shoes. Although her Lexus convertible was parked in the periphery of the lot, she thought she'd be safe. She'd parked under a streetlight.

But when she arrived at her car just before midnight, the streetlight was out. The corner of the parking lot sat in the dark crevices of long shadows—shadows that would blanket even her white uniform from visibility.

The assailant hid behind a hedge. He rushed her from the dark, grabbed her from behind, and squeezed her mouth shut. Then he pulled her behind the hedgerow where he assaulted her. Two shore patrol members walked by and heard a "suspicious rustling" from the bushes.

When their high-beam flashlights pointed in the direction of the sound, the assailant panicked, got up, and ran across the parking lot, wearing only a T-shirt, white boxers, black socks, and shoes. The shore patrolmen gave chase, but the suspect, a well built and muscular SEAL, was too fast for his pursuers. He was unable, however, to evade two U.S. Marine Corps second lieutenants who had just exited their car. Angling from forty-five degrees, they pounced on him.

One lieutenant dove at the suspect's legs as the other corraled him around the neck. Petty Officer Antonio Blount, the Navy SEAL who had just assaulted a female ensign in the United States Navy, was going nowhere.

The ensign was found lying on the grass. Her injuries were assessed before she was rushed to Balboa Naval Hospital. An examination confirmed sexual assault. Subsequent DNA tests proved Blount was the assailant.

At a knock on Zack's office door, he folded the dossier and placed it in his desk drawer. "Come in."

The door opened.

"Lieutenant Brewer, this is Ensign Landrieu," Amy said.

The female officer stepped into his office and came to attention. "Ensign Marianne Landrieu reporting as ordered, sir."

"Stand at ease, Ensign Landrieu. And please, have a seat. I want your time here to be as relaxing as possible."

"Thank you, sir." She settled into one of the two chairs across the desk from him, her smile shaky but grateful.

"You too, Petty Officer DeBenedetto." Zack gestured to Amy, who sat down next to Ensign Landrieu.

Landrieu seemed nervous. Her gaze darted around his office, lingering briefly on the wall that displayed his diplomas, commission, and bar licenses. "You went to Carolina, sir?" Her voice was barely more than a whisper.

"A Tar Heel born and a Tar Heel bred." Hoping to lighten her spirits, he half-mimicked the famous words of the University of North Carolina's fight song. It seemed to work.

"Carolina was my first choice when I graduated from prep school." She sat back, crossed her ankles, and angled her legs to one side of the chair in a modest fashion. She was wearing her summer uniform, and it struck Zack that her uniform was the same one she'd worn the night of the rape. When her watery blue eyes met his, he tried to keep his simmering rage toward her perpetrator from showing.

The woman seemed to have the classic signs of trauma: nervousness in the presence of another male, an expression that said she was fighting to keep from crying. Her hands trembled as she smoothed her skirt.

"But you chose the Naval Academy?" He hoped to put her at ease.

She drew in a deep, trembling breath. "The Academy is a great school. My going there was the dream of my father and my uncle. My father was a naval officer. My uncle, shall we say, has a bit of political pull." Her voice was stronger now, but she nibbled on her bottom lip as she waited for his response.

"You're talking about your Uncle Roberson?"

She brightened somewhat. "Yes, sir. I call him Uncle Pinkie. That's the family name his mother gave him when he was a boy." A trembling smile seemed about to appear. "He and I are close. He doesn't have any daughters. He says I'm his adopted girl. He pushed me to go to the Naval Academy. He nominated me. I guess it doesn't hurt if your uncle is on the Senate Armed Services Committee. But I really wanted to go to Carolina." She glanced at Amy, smiled, and then looked back to Zack.

"You never considered LSU?"

She let her gaze drift to the floor, but did not comment. He wondered if she was going to cry.

"There's one important thing you need to know about us Tar Heels." He gentled his voice.

"What would that be, sir?" Her blue eyes were on his again.

"We're not quite as formal as they are up at the Naval Academy."

"Not too many places are." Finally, another small smile.

"Right. So that means you can drop the 'sir' and start using 'Zack,' at least when we're not in public."

She twisted a strand of her blond hair and tucked it behind her ear. "Thank you. I'd like that."

"Marianne, I hate to change the subject, but you know why we're meeting today."

She let her gaze drift from his face to some distant place beyond his shoulder. Her mouth was set in a hard, thin line. For a moment she simply stared, then she looked back to him, and her eyes filled. "I've been dreading this part."

"We don't have to go into details today. Those can come later. I have a copy of the NCIS report concerning the incident. You need to read it over and tell me if you agree."

Marianne hesitated. "I've been through a lot of therapy. I think I can handle it. I'd like to try."

"Sure?"

"Yes, s—Zack."

"Good." He handed her the report.

She took it, held it in her lap, and drew in a shaky breath.

"Marianne, are you up to this?"

He gave Amy a beseeching look, and she reached for Marianne's hand. "We can do this later, if you'd rather."

Marianne looked grateful, sighed, and seemed to compose herself before she pulled her hand back and reached for a tissue. "I've got to face it sometime. I must be strong." She lifted the report from her lap and pulled back the first page.

Except for her quiet weeping, the room was silent as she read. Five minutes later, she handed the report to Zack and said softly, her voice cracking, "That's pretty much the way it was."

"Any additions or changes?"

"No, I think the NCIS agent got it right." She reached for another tissue. "Could I have a drink of water?"

"Sure." He poured a cup from the pitcher on his desk and handed it to her. "That's all I need for now. Let's call it a day. I'll have Amy call you later on in the week."

"Okay, thanks."

"Petty Officer DeBenedetto, would you please see Ensign Landrieu out and then report back here?"

"Aye, sir," Amy said as she stood and led Marianne out of Zack's office.

When she returned five minutes later, Zack noticed the puzzled look on her face. He'd seen the contorted look dozens of times before—it wasn't his favorite of Amy's expressions.

"Okay, what's the matter?"

She shook her head slowly. "Something doesn't add up, sir. I don't know. It just doesn't seem like she's telling us everything."

"How so?"

She frowned. "I'm not sure what it is, but—"

The phone rang, interrupting her.

"Lieutenant, Admiral Ayers on the phone," said the voice on the loudspeaker.

Zack lifted the receiver, swiveling his chair toward the window as he spoke. A moment later, when he ended the call and turned back, Amy was gone.

CHAPTER 4

Community Bible Church
Lemon Grove, California
East San Diego County

Weekdays brought with them a jam-packed traffic artery for thousands of commuters from the east San Diego communities of El Cajon, La Mesa, and Lemon Grove traveling to the 32nd Street Naval Station. But on Sunday mornings, California Highway 94 was almost deserted. As a result, the old Volkswagen beetle reached the Lemon Grove exit ten minutes early. The church was only about a mile off the freeway, off Lemon Grove Avenue, the main boulevard cutting through the heart of the east San Diego suburb.

Neptune scanned the parking lot. Two sailors, both in their summer white enlisted uniforms, were getting out of their cars. One, a boiler technician third class, was accompanied by his wife and two young daughters. A few others, with military haircuts, walked across the parking lot in civilian clothes.

An elderly white-haired gentleman in khakis and a golf shirt greeted Neptune with a friendly nod at the front door. Neptune took a bulletin from the greeter's extended hand, then stopped to read it before entering the fellowship hall.

Community Bible Church of Lemon Grove Presents:
A Seminar of Comparison and Contrast
Today's Topic: *"Christianity and Islam: What Are the Differences?"*

Neptune stepped into the crowded room and found an empty chair near the back row, just behind an African-American family of three. The couple's little girl, maybe seven years old, gave him a big smile. She reminded him of his sister from Queens all those years ago. He smiled back, then shifted his eyes forward, to the front of the hall, where a pleasant-looking middle-aged man in a blue suit walked to the simple wooden lectern.

"Good morning," the man said.

"Good morning," came a cheery chorus of responses from the audience.

"Welcome to Lemon Grove. My name is Jeffrey Spletto and I'm the pastor here at Community Bible. This morning we're continuing our ongoing discussion of comparing Christianity with other religions. Today's topic is 'Christianity and Islam: What Are the Differences?'

"Today will be a discussion, not a lecture, with questions and answers from the audience. And remember, no question is a bad question. We are here in search of the truth. Nothing more. Nothing less. Before we start, would you bow your heads as I pray?"

Neptune did not bow, but drilled his gaze into Spletto as he spoke.

"Lord, we thank you for this day. As we come before you to study your Word, we pray truth will be revealed and eyes will be opened to you. In Jesus' name. Amen."

A chorus of "amens" followed.

"Let's start today with a game to tell us a little about ourselves. I call it the 'Where Were You When ...' game. Here's what we'll do. I'll give you a date, and if you remember where you were on that date, I want you to raise your hand. Okay?"

There were smiles and affirmative nods.

"Here we go. December 7, 1941."

About a dozen hands shot up. Most of the hand-raisers had white hair and wrinkled skin. A few were bald. Some wore thick bifocals.

Spletto gestured to a man three rows in front of Neptune. "Leonard. Your hand is up. Where were you that day?"

The old man rose from his seat. "That was the day the Japanese bombed Pearl Harbor. I was a sergeant in the Army Air Corps, at the Presidio up in San Francisco waiting to be shipped out. The lieutenant came running into the mess hall and yelling that the war'd started. After they bombed Pearl, we thought they might try to bomb the West Coast. The lieutenant said everybody's leave was canceled."

Spletto smiled. "Thank you, Leonard. Here's another date. November 22, 1963."

About fifty hands shot up.

"Anybody remember where you were that day?"

"I was in biology class in high school," a middle-aged man blurted out. "The principal came over the intercom and announced that the president had been shot and school was being canceled for the day."

"Thank you, Barney," Spletto said. "November 22. The day John F. Kennedy was assassinated. Like December 7, 1941, it was a turning point in American history. Here's one more date. September 11, 2001."

A day of glory.

Except for Neptune, who refused to participate in Spletto's game, almost every hand in the room was raised.

Spletto's gaze rested on a young blond-headed boy in the front row. "Billy, can you tell us what happened that day?"

"That's when the Muslim terrorists crashed the airplanes into the buildings."

The infidels even train their young to refer to Allah's warriors as "terrorists."

"That's right, Billy. And can you tell us how you know that?"

"Because I saw it on television, and we learned about the terrorists in home school."

"Out of the mouths of babes." Spletto smiled and turned to the audience. "Our young friend has hit the issue on the head. Most of us had heard of the religion known as Islam. Islam was something Middle Eastern, but not relevant to America—until September 11. Even still, most Americans don't understand what Islam is about. There are many, for example, who say Islam is a peaceful religion. Anybody have any thoughts on that? Yes?" Spletto pointed to an attractive woman who looked to be in her late forties.

"Jeff, I've often wondered. These Islamic terrorists murdered all those innocent people in the World Trade Center. Right after that, we had a national day of prayer in Washington. There was an Islamic mullah, or whatever they call it, participating in the service. Isn't it sort of a contradiction? I mean, after all, it was *Islamic* terrorism that caused all the murder in the first place."

"That's a very good question," Spletto said. "You make a good point. As you recall, a couple of days after 9/11, President Bush declared a national day of prayer, and there was a multi-denominational service at the National Cathedral in Washington. Everybody remember that?"

There were dozens of nods and murmurs of agreement.

"The service had a Christian clergy. In fact, Billy Graham delivered the principle sermon."

There were a few "amens."

"But there was also a Jewish Rabbi *and* a Muslim cleric officiating at the service. Remember?"

Again, nods of agreement followed.

"I understand what President Bush was trying to do—unite the country in our darkest hour since World War II."

"Amen!" sang out an older man in the second row.

Spletto nodded. "But I have to be honest. The American public was not fully informed about the true nature of Islam."

"What do you mean?" another woman asked.

"The president said that Islam is a peaceful religion and that what these terrorists did violated the Qur'an. And while it may be true that a good number of Islamic-Americans are peaceful, the truth is that murder and bloodshed are basic tenets of that religion. It is also a historical fact that Muhammad tortured, maimed, and murdered many people who were his political opponents. You see, Muhammad first claimed to have a vision from God in the year AD 610. For thirteen years, he preached peacefully in Mecca. Most historians say that he was at first a peaceful and well-meaning man who opposed paganism.

"Then in the year 623, Muhammad moved from the city of Mecca to the city of Medina, where he became a political leader. Unlike Jesus, who is the true Prince of Peace, Muhammad became a slayer with the sword. He began to assassinate political opponents and led at least twenty-seven bloody invasions—maybe as many as sixty. Once, when he attacked a group known as the Quraizi Jews, Muhammad captured hundreds of Jewish men. Then he executed the men—murdering them in cold blood—and sold hundreds of Jewish women and children into slavery. So the historical fact is that Muhammad, the founder of this so-called peaceful religion, was a ruthless killer."

How dare you blaspheme the holy prophet—peace be upon him!

There was a brief moment of silence.

"But, Jeff . . . ?"

"Yes, Andy?" Spletto turned toward a young man, seated with his wife, who rocked a baby gently over her shoulder.

"Even if Muhammad was violent, and although we've all heard about 9/11 and the violence in Israel, do you think most rank-and-file Muslims are violent?"

"Good question, Andy. I don't think most Muslims living in America are violent at all. But then again, many Muslims living in America are relatively new to that religion and don't understand its violent underpinnings. But if you're asking me if Muslims worldwide are violent, then consider these statistics. Muslims routinely persecute Christians in nations like Algeria, Nigeria, Afghanistan, Iran, Egypt, Pakistan, Tajikistan, and Malaysia. Not only is there persecution in Sudan, but there is also slavery of Christians by Muslims.

"Based on reliable statistics complied by several different sources, we know 160,000 Christians each year are murdered because of their faith in Christ. The vast majority of these Christians are killed by Muslims. So are Muslims worldwide violent? Statistics don't lie. Do we need to be concerned about it here in America? You bet. The worldwide statistics *and* 9/11 prove that."

Infidel.

Another man stood and cleared his throat. "Even given the fact that historically Muhammad was violent, what drives these terrorists from a theological standpoint to murder? Does the Qur'an tell them to kill? I remember President Carter, when he addressed the Egyptian Parliament back in 1979, referring to the Qur'an as the *Holy* Qur'an. Is their drive to commit murder from the Qur'an?"

Spletto nodded. "Yes. At least partially. First let me comment on the Qur'an. The principle text of Islam, the Qur'an, is divided into 114 chapters. These chapters are called *Suras*. If you were to go into a bookstore and buy a copy of the Qur'an, you would find that some of the chapters speak of peace. But then others are bellicose. For example, one of the chapters, entitled 'Accessions,' speaks of 'calling the believers to war.'

"But here's the point on which most Americans are ignorant. The Qur'an is not the only doctrinal writing governing Islamic theology. In fact, a second set of writings delves into far greater detail than the Qur'an. It is a set of writings known as the Bukhari Hadiths." He scanned the audience. "Anybody ever heard of them?"

Of course, infidel.

No hands were raised.

Ignorant fools.

"Bear with me." Spletto rolled an overhead projector to the front center of the hall, flipped on the light, and wrote "Bukhari Hadiths" with a blue marker on a plastic transparency.

"The hadiths, pronounced *a-hadiths*, are a writing of the actions and sayings of Muhammad. There are several collections of hadiths, but those compiled by a man named Bukhari are among the most important and were composed about two hundred years after his death.

"Now the hadiths, along with the Qur'an, govern every aspect of Islamic life. For example, one of the hadiths requires that an Islamic person, when answering the call of nature, cannot face Mecca when doing so."

At the ensuing chuckles, Neptune felt his blood boil.

"From this source, Islam embraces murder. Eleven percent of it advocates jihad, or a holy war. This includes killing Jews and infidels. Muslims are taught that those who fight and die in a jihad will have their sins forgiven, that they will be rewarded with sensual and luxurious pleasures in paradise. In fact, Osama bin Laden, in the videotape discovered in Afghanistan after 9/11, said he was 'ordered to fight the people until there is no god but Allah.' He took those words right out of the Qur'an."

"Infidel!" Neptune leapt to his feet. Everyone in the room turned to stare.

A stunned silence followed.

"Did you have a question, sir?"

He glared at the preacher. "You spread *lies* about the prophet— Peace be upon him!"

"Our goal here is only the truth," Spletto said. "If you believe I have said something untruthful, tell me what it is. If you are right, I will admit it."

"You condemn the one true religion, Islam, by trying to fool the people into believing Christianity is superior. Lies! Muhammad was God's only true prophet—Peace be upon him!"

"Jesus Christ, the mighty prophet of God, God's only begotten Son, never killed anyone. He never harmed anyone, nor sold women and children into slavery. He never sinned against God, his Father. He healed, forgave, and when they killed him, he rose from the dead." Spletto's voice was soft but firm. "When Muhammad died, he stayed in his tomb. The tomb of Jesus is empty. He lives. He alone is our eternal hope for the future."

Neptune's fury burned. "Lies! *Lies!*"

"Is this the religion you embrace? A religion of screaming and shouting? Is this an example of the peace that you pray to be upon your prophet?"

Neptune ignored the infidel's rambling. "Denounce!"

"Excuse me?"

"Denounce Christianity. Admit Christianity is a religion of infidels."

The pastor shook his head. "I can't do that. I can only tell the truth: Jesus Christ is the way, the truth, and the life. No one comes to the Father but by him."

"Denounce or die!" Neptune whipped out the hand grenade he'd kept hidden, pulled the pin, and held it over the head of the young black girl who reminded him of his sister. "Cease blaspheming the holy prophet— Peace be upon him—or die with the rest of the infidels. All of you!"

CHAPTER 5

Communications Center
San Diego Police Department
1401 Broadway
San Diego

Normally, Sunday mornings were the slowest time of the week for the San Diego Police Department Emergency Dispatch operators. And so when the watch captain stepped away from his monitor for a late-morning caffeine break, he expected to take at least five to seven minutes to refill his coffee, hit the bathroom, and then return to his post. But just as the freshly brewed, hot coffee was streaming from the big stainless-steel coffeepot into his San Diego Padres mug, the sudden shouts of three dispatchers from the next room forced a change of plans.

The captain turned with a quick jerk, sloshing his coffee onto the floor, and headed back to the dispatch room. "What's up?" He leaned toward a dispatcher's monitor.

The rookie officer, a recent Academy graduate, didn't look up. "Captain, we've got three separate 911 calls from cell phones at the same location in Lemon Grove. The cell phone lines are open, but nobody is saying anything."

"Do we have a ten-twenty?" The captain drained the last drops of coffee from his mug.

"Calls are being placed from—stand by—2910 Lemon Grove Avenue."

"What's there?"

She typed in the address on her terminal. "It's a church, Captain. Community Bible. Sounds like several people have dialed 911, but they aren't talking for some reason."

"Notify Lemon Grove PD to get someone over there . . ."

She held up one hand and frowned. "Sounds like a possible hostage situation. I'm hearing something that sounds like . . ."

"Amplify all three cell calls on the loudspeaker. I want to hear this."

"Two more 911 calls in from the same location," a second dispatcher called out. "Same thing. Callers not speaking. Definitely some sort of hostage situation unfolding in the background."

"Get 'em all on the loudspeakers, now!"

A male voice poured over the loudspeakers. "If anybody moves, I release the grenade. The name of Allah shall be desecrated no more. The name of the holy prophet—May peace be upon him—shall not be blasphemed."

"Great. Sounds like a religious terrorism standoff." The captain slammed the empty Padres mug on the table beside the dispatcher. "Notify the Sheriff's Department, the Fire Department, and call the FBI. Get a hostage negotiation team at that church, ASAP. Also send the SDPD Bomb Unit and SWAT team out there now. Make our choppers available to all agencies."

"Yes, sir. Right away." The rookie dispatcher grabbed her phone.

Another voice came over the loudspeakers. "Sir, if yours is a religion of peace, as you say, then let these innocent people go. I am the one you have a quarrel with. I am the pastor of this church. I am the one who has made these proclamations about Muhammad and Islam. Does your religion mandate killing innocent women and children?"

"Silence! Denounce Christianity! Confess the truth—Islam is supreme. Then maybe Allah will spare you all!"

The captain frowned. "Who's the pastor? I want to know. Now!"

"Already got it, sir," the second dispatcher said. "Jeffrey Carl Spletto. He's been the senior pastor there for twenty years. Married. Three kids living at home. BA from UCLA. Seminary at Southwestern in Dallas. Goes by 'Jeff.'"

"Source?"

"Church website, sir."

"How 'bout the perpetrator?"

"Nothing yet. Not enough info."

Spletto's voice came back over the loudspeakers. "Sir, I appeal to your sense of humanity. Surely you wish no harm to innocent women and children. Look around you, sir. These are Americans. These are your countrymen."

"My loyalty is to Allah. These have laughed at his ways. I heard them with my own ears. All who reject him are infidels."

"Sir, this is a loving church. We are here to demonstrate God's love. And God loves you, just like you are. Tell us what we can do for you and we will."

The captain nodded. "Good job, Pastor. Keep him talking."

"The only name you need to remember is the name of Allah. And you cannot help me. You can only help yourself—by denouncing Christianity!"

A police sergeant rushed into the dispatch room, teletype in hand. "Captain, the Navy reports three missing grenades from the weapons magazine of the USS *Tarawa*."

"God help us. What type, Sergeant?"

"M67s."

"Great." He took the teletype from the sergeant's hand, anger growing as he read. "Some of the most powerful weapons in the military's arsenal." He looked up at the police sergeant. "How'd this happen?"

"The Navy discovered three fake hand grenades." The sergeant spoke rapidly. "Someone molded the fake grenades in some sort of ceramic, painted them the right color, and hid the fakes in with the real things."

Neptune scoured the sea of faces who had participated in this abomination. His rage made his breathing ragged, but the hand holding the grenade was still. Deadly still. Many of the women were shaking. The cries of the frightened children filled the room like a pack of baby wolves howling at a full moon.

His gaze met that of the father of the African-American girl in front of him. The little girl's arms were wrapped around her father's legs. She looked up at Neptune, her eyes big, sweet, innocent—yet terrified. But like a lioness cub, cute and cuddly at first, she would grow into something dangerous. An infidel. She would become a mother of Christian infidels who opposed and desecrated the name of Allah.

"Come on, brother. Have some compassion, man!" The girl's father pled softly, his eyes locked onto Neptune's. "My little girl ain't done nothin' to you. Please, man. I'm beggin' you. Just let her and my wife walk out the back door. Let all the children walk out. Please ... I'm—"

"Shut up!" Neptune stared at Spletto. "Your time is running out. Deny Christianity! You have two minutes."

"Please, Jeff, just tell him whatever he wants to hear!" The young woman was sobbing as she cradled an infant in her arms. "God will forgive you. Just tell him what he wants to hear."

Another woman spoke, her voice low and trembling. "God understands, Jeff. Just say the words."

"Hold your ground, Jeff." This from the middle-aged man who'd spoken up earlier. "You were born for this very moment. Don't deny the faith. No matter what."

With tears showing his weakness, the man at the podium gazed at the woman cradling the infant. Slowly, deliberately, he moved his gaze to the second woman. Then his eyes met those of the man who just told him to keep the faith. For a moment, he didn't move.

Then he looked directly at Neptune. "I'm sorry, sir. I cannot and I will not deny Christianity. To deny Christianity is to deny Christ—the one who died for me. This I cannot do. This I will never do."

"Fool!" Neptune's rage turned white hot. "All of you. *Fools!* Commander Olajuwon warned me of your hard and wicked hearts. He was right. Only purification will rid the world of your sin against Allah."

Neptune opened his right hand. The grenade fell, clanking to the floor, setting off screams and gasps as he pulled the pin on a second and tossed it forward. The first, blinding blast at his feet guaranteed he would not hear the second.

CHAPTER 6

Navy brig
32nd Street Naval Station
San Diego

The ten-minute walk across base from her office to the brig under the warm, blue, arid San Diego sky had put Diane Colcernian in a good mood. Even a brief stroll outdoors in the world-class weather—the Mediterranean climate most people in the U.S. never experience—was like a tonic to her soul.

San Diego was the perfect antidote to losing her father. She'd been told that a change of pace—or, in this case, a change of geography—could help ease the pain caused by the death of a dear family member. There was some truth in the advice.

Diane was led into the counsel waiting room at the Navy brig by a Filipino petty officer named Enrico Magadia. Diane wasn't sure why they called this place a waiting room. With plain battleship-gray paint on the floors and walls, and lighting cast from overhead fluorescent bulbs, this place was more like a detention cell set up for the Navy's defense attorneys to meet their clients.

Despite the warm greetings from the brig staff, the cold, barren atmosphere of the place made her shudder every time she met a client here.

"Wait here, ma'am. We'll bring him out." Magadia disappeared behind a door with steel bars.

Diane set her briefcase on the steel table, unfastened the latches, and opened it. Inside were an assortment of pens, a calculator, a legal pad, today's *San Diego Union*, and a file for the case of *United States v. BT3 (SEAL) Antonio Blount*.

This would be her first meeting with her new client, Boiler Technician Third Class Antonio Blount, the Navy SEAL accused of raping an officer. He was probably guilty. Most of her clients were. She shuddered at the thought of defending a rapist. Easing her breath out, she tried to put aside her prejudice. Blount was her client, innocent until proven guilty, and she would defend him to the best of her abilities.

As she waited for the master-at-arms to return with Blount, Diane sat down in one of two metal folding chairs and took the *San Diego Union* from her briefcase. She went immediately to the front-page story that had the entire Navy base abuzz.

DERANGED SAILOR TURNS TERRORIST ASSAILANT, EIGHT OTHERS KILLED, 25 INJURED IN HAND GRENADE ATTACK AT LOCAL CHURCH

Lemon Grove—A deranged Navy petty officer stole three powerful hand grenades from the weapons magazine of a U.S. Navy warship Sunday morning, then later detonated two of the three in a packed seminar at a local church, leaving eight people dead and twenty-five others seriously injured from shrapnel wounds.

According to witnesses . . .

Magadia, standing at the steel-barred door to the corridor that connected the waiting room to the cell blocks, interrupted her reading. "Lieutenant, we have your client."

She put down the newspaper.

"Send him in."

"Aye, aye, ma'am."

Magadia pushed open the door, and BT3 (SEAL) Antonio Blount, in ankle chains and handcuffs, followed him in. He wore the same uniform his jailor sported. A second master-at-arms, a third-class petty officer, followed the prisoner into the room.

Blount, a well-chiseled physical specimen, came to attention and stared at the opposite wall.

"Well, well, the wayward SEAL." Diane made her tone more sympathetic than sarcastic.

"Ma'am," Blount said, still not making eye contact.

"I've got him now." She nodded to Magadia. "You can unchain him."

"Ma'am?" Magadia hesitated, as if unchaining the prisoner would invite the rape of yet another female naval officer.

"You heard me, Magadia. Unchain the prisoner. That's an order."

"Yes, ma'am." Magadia inserted his master key first into the ankle chains, and then, with the clanking of chains dropping onto the cement floor, he unlocked the handcuffs.

"That will be all, Magadia. I'll let you know when we're done."

"We'll be here if you need us, ma'am."

Diane waited until Magadia and the other master-at-arms were out of hearing range. "I want you to relax and have a seat, please, Petty Officer Blount."

"Thank you, ma'am." Blount pulled out the metal chair opposite her and made eye contact for the first time.

She studied him. "I'm Lieutenant Colcernian, your detailed defense counsel. Have you ever had an attorney before?"

"No, ma'am."

"Good. I assume that means, except for the reason you're here now, you've remained pretty much out of trouble."

"Yes, ma'am."

"Do you know what the 'attorney-client privilege' is, Petty Officer Blount?"

"Yes, ma'am. I think so."

"All right. Why don't you tell me what you think it is?"

"From what I've heard from the guys here in the brig, they say whatever I tell you stays a secret."

"You've got the right idea. Whatever you tell me here is in the strictest confidence. I cannot repeat anything you tell me to anyone without your express permission. Do you understand?"

"Yes, ma'am."

"There's one other thing. Just because I've been detailed as defense counsel to your case, it doesn't mean you're stuck with me. You have the right, should you choose, to request any officer in the Navy JAG Corps to defend you, provided that officer is not currently detailed as a prosecutor. That's called an IMC request." He frowned, so she continued. "IMC means Individual Military Counsel. Do you understand?"

"Yes, ma'am." Blount's gaze drifted away from her.

"You also have the right to hire a civilian defense counsel, at your own expense. If you choose to go that route, I would still be available to assist on your case. Or, if you and your civilian counsel request, I could be relieved. Understand?"

Diane waited for his response.

He cut his eyes back. "I've heard from the guys in the brig that you're pretty good, ma'am. Can you get me off?"

"I don't know. We haven't talked about your case yet."

Blount paused again. "If it's okay with you, I'd like to stick with you for now and see how things go."

"Fine." At least he was decisive. "But before we move on, do you have any other questions about your right to counsel or the attorney-client privilege?"

"No, ma'am."

"Good. Then let's get down to business."

"Yes, ma'am."

"Do you know why you're here, Petty Officer Blount?"

"They say I raped the ensign."

Diane poured ice water into a paper cup from a pitcher sitting on the table. "Right."

"But it's not like that!"

"It's not?" She took a sip of water.

"No, ma'am. I never raped anybody!" It sounded like he meant it.

"Want some water?"

"Yes, ma'am."

Diane poured Blount a cup and slid it across the table. "Okay, Petty Officer Blount. Here's how I want to approach this. Have you read the Naval Criminal Investigative Service's report about the incident?"

"No, ma'am."

"Okay, I've got a copy right here. Why don't you read it over, then I'll ask you some questions, okay?"

"Yes, ma'am."

She handed him the four-page report and watched as his gaze swept the document.

Barely a minute into the reading, he frowned. "It ain't right."

"What's not right?"

"Ma'am, I never pulled the ensign back behind the hedgerow. This is a lie!"

She braced herself. "The NCIS report isn't right?"

"No, ma'am, it *is not*!" His dark eyes glinted with rage.

"All right." Diane spoke softly, in contrast to his tone. "Why don't you just relax and tell me how you think the report is wrong."

"You don't believe me, do you?"

"Petty Officer Blount," she said, her voice firm, "I haven't heard your side of the story yet. Besides, if you decide to testify, it's not whether *I* believe you that matters. It's whether the *jury* believes you. I'm here to help you. Tell me what happened, and if it doesn't sound believable, I'll level with you and shoot it straight. Now, how about shooting it straight with me?"

Blount waited about ten seconds, his black-eyed gaze hard as he started talking. "I was out taking a walk. It was about midnight. I was heading through the parking lot next to the Officers' Club. I could hear the music coming from the club. It was loud, but I was at the far end of the parking lot when the ensign came walking toward her car. When she walked past me, I saluted, like I always do. She sort of saluted back and smiled."

"What do you mean, she sort of saluted back?"

"She gave me one of those backhanded, British salutes. I could tell she'd been drinking."

"How?"

"Just the way she was laughing and giggling. She was acting real silly—not the way an officer would act unless she'd been drinking."

"What about you, Petty Officer Blount. Did you have anything to drink that night?"

"I had two beers at the Enlisted Club earlier that night."

"Go on."

"I said something like, 'Good evening, ma'am,' and then she started talking."

"Saying what?"

"The first thing she said was, 'Hold on a minute, sailor.' So I stopped. When an officer tells you to stop, you stop. Then she asked me where I was from. I told her Mississippi. Actually, I told her Pascagoula, Mississippi. She said she was from New Orleans."

Diane scribbled a note on her legal pad. *Check NASNI E-Club for witnesses. Call manager. Speak to bartender on duty.*

"Did she tell you her name?"

"She said it was Ensign . . ." Blount stopped, rolled his eyes to the ceiling as if he were trying to recall the name. "Landry, I think."

Landry . . . Landrieu. Close enough. She scribbled *Name* on her yellow legal pad. "Did she give you a first name?"

"No, ma'am."

Of course not. "Okay. What happened next?"

"It was like she wanted to talk. She said she'd been to Pascagoula and she liked it. Then she asked if I'd been to New Orleans. I told her I used to hang out there on the weekends. She asked me what my rank was, and I told her I'd been a boiler technician on the USS *Vincennes*, but now I've got my SEAL designation. That got her attention."

"Got her attention? In what way?"

"She said she admired SEALs more than any group in the military. She said we're in better shape and stronger than even the Marines. She's right about that. Then she put her hand on my bicep and said she used to date some SEALs back in New Orleans and at the Naval Academy. Next thing I know, we were standing real close and she was looking in my face."

"Where were your hands?"

"Around the back of her waist."

"Then what?"

"Then we started kissing."

"She was voluntarily participating?"

"Oh yeah." He stopped, looking down. "Excuse me. I mean, yes, ma'am."

"Then what?"

"She said we'd better get out of the parking lot or we might get caught by the shore patrol. So she took my hand and led me back behind the hedgerows. We got down on the grass just on the other side of the shrubs. It was dark. We didn't think anybody from the parking lot would see us. One thing led to another. Next thing I know, there was a flashlight shining through the bushes. I figured it was the shore patrol. I panicked. So I ran."

Diane sat back for a moment in the metal folding chair, thumping her gold Cross pen on her legal pad. "Why did you run?"

"'Cause I knew it wouldn't look good. Plus I knew I could outrun the shore patrol. I just didn't count on the Marines showing up."

"At any time, did the ensign ever tell you to stop?"

"Never. She was the one being aggressive."

"So that's your story? The ensign consented to what you did?"

"Yes, ma'am." He paused, his expression troubled. "I'd say it was her idea."

"Thank you, Petty Officer. I'm going to check into this and get back with you."

"Thank you, ma'am."

Diane gathered her briefcase, settled her cover on her head, and walked out the front door of the brig into the warm San Diego sunshine. The soothing dose of the sun's rays was a stark contrast to the cold cell block from which she had emerged. This was the feel of freedom, a simple pleasure that, unless she did her job to the best of her ability, Petty Officer Blount might not enjoy for many years.

Her instincts told her Blount was telling the truth. Her hunch—Blount was in the wrong place at the wrong time. But zealously defending him would mean attacking the veracity and reputation of the niece of one of the most powerful men in the United States Senate. Even if Diane won, her career as a naval officer might be over. But it would mean beating Zack Brewer . . .

Maybe it was worth the tradeoff.

She plotted a course due west, about three blocks, to The Main Brace. It was almost lunchtime, she was thirsty, and she had some thinking to do.

CHAPTER 7

Shoney's restaurant
Four blocks from the main gate
Oceana Naval Air Station
Virginia Beach, Virginia

A viation Structural Mechanic Second Class Sulayman al-Aziz sat alone in a corner booth in the smoking section of his favorite Shoney's. The smoke brought fond memories of his visits to Saudi Arabia with his grandparents, where smoking was everywhere—even on Islamic airliners. This section of the restaurant also gave him more privacy.

Lieutenant Commander Reska said that his hunger for righteousness was a gift from Allah and that the hand of the Almighty was surely upon him. Perhaps the chaplain could see into his soul, could prophesy his future. Great things were in store, Reska had told him. Allah had a special calling for his life.

Deep down, AMS2 Sulayman al-Aziz knew that Reska was right. After all, how many Muslims were in the position he was in? His was an exhilarating profession: he had the great responsibility of maintaining the most powerful jet fighters in the most powerful navy in the world.

His struggle recently was theological. The Qur'an and the Hadiths seemed at odds with the political and military mission of his employer, the United States Navy.

The papers told of the tension in the Middle East, namely the age-old friction between the Islamic nations and their arch-nemesis, the apostate Jewish government in Israel. America was siding with the apostates. This troubled Sulayman.

He took a swig of juice and perused the headlines of the *Virginian Pilot*.

TENSIONS BUILDING IN MIDDLE EAST PRESIDENT PLEDGES U.S. MILITARY SUPPORT FOR ISRAEL
Nimitz Battle Group to Sail from Hampton Rhodes

Norfolk.—As military tensions build between the government of Israel and the governments of Syria, Jordan, Iraq and Egypt over Israel's refusal to dismantle Jewish settlements in the West Bank and the Gaza Strip, the supercarrier USS Nimitz and its battle group of ten ships is frantically preparing to set sail from Norfolk next Wednesday.

The *Nimitz* is being deployed along with other U.S. Naval forces because of the Syrian and Jordanian troop buildups along those countries' respective borders with Israel. The international crisis has reached a boiling point and appears headed toward a military showdown.

Syrian president Ouday Assad has demanded immediate dismantlement of the settlements, claiming that Israel has "stalled long enough," and military intervention may be the only means of "forcing the issue."

"Peace be unto you, Petty Officer al-Aziz."

Sulayman looked up. Lieutenant Commander Mohammed Reska, Chaplain Corps, United States Navy, stood by his booth. Reska, with an olive complexion and jet-black hair reflecting his Middle Eastern heritage, wore his working khaki uniform.

Aziz stood to acknowledge the officer's presence. "Peace be unto you also, sir."

Reska smiled. "May I join you?"

"Sorry, sir. Please." Sulayman gestured to the seat across from him. "I was distracted."

Reska waited to speak until the waitress had taken their orders; then he said, "Allah wants our minds to be sharp. What is it that so distracts my young brother today?"

Sulayman pushed the newspaper across the table. A minute later, the chaplain's eyes met his. "This has you so distracted?"

"This President Assad—he seems so determined," Sulayman said. "Yes?"

"I've contemplated your teachings about the Jews, sir. The Hadiths teach that the Jews are an apostate people. They have renounced the prophet—Peace be upon him. They control the holy city of Jerusalem, the city from which the prophet—Peace be upon him—ascended to meet Allah, then descended again."

Reska smiled. "Allah is pleased at your attentiveness." He paused as the waitress placed the cantaloupe and oatmeal in front of him. When she was out of earshot, he continued. "What has been written we cannot change. We are privileged, however, to serve as warriors for Allah, in our own way, wherever he has placed us."

"I want to be his warrior," Sulayman said. "Instead, I prepare the weapons of destruction to be used against his people."

Reska craned his neck, looking back toward the door and the empty booths around them. "Allah calls us to wage jihad," he whispered, "wherever and under whatever circumstances he has placed us. If the warplanes you maintain will be used against Allah's people, then perhaps he calls upon you to choose today for which side you will fight. Do you understand that your time has come?"

Sulayman had longed to hear these words. Goose flesh shivered across the back of his neck and on his arms. "I understand, sir."

CHAPTER 8

Base Family Housing Offices
Building 1138
Outside on the parade grounds
United States Marine Corps Base
Camp Pendleton, California

Staff Sergeant Nasser Saidi, United States Marine Corps, closed the office door behind him, moved to the window, and looked down at the parade grounds.

Just at the base of the podium, the United States Marine Corps Band was starting the breakup strain of "Semper Fidelis." Flown in from Washington for this occasion, The President's Own added pomp and pageantry for the event. With their silver trumpets, trombones, and sousaphones glistening in the morning sun, they were an impressive unit.

The entire Eleventh and Thirteenth Marine Expeditionary Units, more than four thousand combat marines, stood at parade rest on the lush green parade grounds in the early morning California sunshine. The leathernecks had formed a giant circular mass of humanity around the podium, awaiting their distinguished visitor.

The Secret Service had enlisted Marine Security to ensure the visitor's stay at Pendleton would be safe. Nasser's proficiency with the sniper rifle, along with his clean record and stable psychological profile, had earned him a berth on the armed security detail in the buildings around the parade grounds. His post was the third floor of the administrative office of Building 1138, headquarters of Base Family Housing.

His job today was to remain vigilant, to report anything at all unusual, and open fire only if necessary to defend the life of the distinguished visitor.

His was a glorious fate.

A squawk from the government-issued walkie-talkie dangling from his belt broke his concentration. A burst of shrill static followed, then the voice of the special agent in charge of security came through loud and clear. "All units—civilian and military. Protectees arriving. Stay alert."

A small motorcade was approaching on Vandergrift Boulevard. Two black luxury sedans crept along, each with flags snapping at the front corners of the hoods. The first car flew the Israeli flag, and the other flew the two-star banner of a major general. They were flanked by half a dozen California Highway Patrol motorcycles. The sedans slowed and then turned from Vandergrift onto the parade grounds, inching across the grass lawn through a cleared pathway between regiments of Marines.

When the cars halted at the base of the platform, a full-bird Marine colonel walked briskly up the stairs and stepped to the podium.

"Attention on deck!" The simple command echoed over the loud-speakers. Four thousand marines snapped to attention. "Ladies and Gentlemen, the Commanding General of Camp Pendleton, and His Excellency, the Ambassador of the State of Israel to the United States of America."

As the trumpet section from The President's Own broke the morning air with "Ruffles and Flourishes," followed by a prolonged drumroll from a row of snare drummers, two Marine corporals in dress blue uniforms opened the back door of each car. Crisp salutes from the corporals followed.

The commanding general and the ambassador stepped up the wooden stairway onto the platform. Another salute followed, this time from the full-bird colonel. End of drumroll.

"Ladies and Gentlemen"—the full-bird was back at the microphone, flanked by the ambassador to his left and the general on the right—"in accordance with diplomatic custom and military courtesy, please remain at attention for the playing of the national anthems of the State of Israel and of the United States of America."

Another drumroll rumbled, followed by the national anthem of the Jewish state.

The four thousand marines snapped salutes, as ordered, at the Star of David flag on the platform. Diplomatic courtesy or not, the sight of Marines saluting the Jewish rag was repulsive to Nasser. The first note of "The Star Spangled Banner" rang out. The nausea lessened; the anger did not.

"Fellow Marines, may I present the Commanding General of Camp Pendleton, Major General Trent Lee Cox."

"At ease, Marines," General Cox thundered at his Marines. "As you know, it's no secret that the State of Israel is an important strategic ally of the United States. Nor is it a secret that tensions in the Med and the Gulf region are at an all-time high. Because you may be deployed at a moment's notice to fight in this region, the president feels it is important that you know more about our ally Israel to better understand why you might be fighting.

"Ambassador Daniel Barak is a warrior's warrior. A former colonel in the Israeli Defense Force, the ambassador has seen combat—real combat—in the war on terrorism and has been involved in commanding troops as part of his military career."

Ordering troops to spray bullets at Allah's people. A real warrior indeed. Nasser worked the bolt action on the rifle, chambering a live round.

"Please join me in presenting a robust Marine welcome to His Excellency, the honorable Daniel Barak, Israeli ambassador to the United States."

The applause gave way to a cascade of "ooh rahs" and then the refrain "Ah *root*! Ah *root*! Ah *root*!"

"What is the barking I hear?" the smiling ambassador called out to his audience. Massive laughter from the Marines followed. "I can't tell if it's a bunch of hound dogs barking, or a family of seals squawking out on a rock in San Diego Bay!"

More laughter followed. Then silence.

"I see that Marines really do obey orders without question. General Cox calls for a robust Marine welcome, and I am *not* disappointed. Ooh *raaah*!"

Cheers erupted from the leathernecks.

"Seriously, the widely recognized sound of a United States Marine barking—or whatever you call it—is to Israel a welcome sound. It is the sound of security. It is the sound of freedom. And to you all we say, *Semper Fidelis*!"

More applause. More Marines cheering.

Zionist propaganda.

"Today I come in friendship, as ours is a great friendship between two great nations—the United States, the most powerful nation in the world, and the State of Israel, a small but stable democracy. We are also your most loyal ally in the most volatile region of the world, the Middle East.

"Our region, the Middle East, as you know, has become the cradle of murderous terrorism in the world today. We in Israel have known this for generations.

"The enemies of freedom hate us because of who we are. They hate us because we are a democracy. They despise us because our religion is different from theirs. They detest us because we believe in equal rights under the law."

May Allah bless me and give me strength for the task at hand.

"Unfortunately, my brave friends, these enemies of freedom hate America for the same reasons they hate Israel. They hate you also because you are a freedom-loving democracy, committed to equal justice under the law."

Zionist liar.

"This became evident on September 11, 2001, the infamous day they murdered thousands of American citizens on American soil. They attack like cowards, out of the night, preying on innocent civilians who are incapable of defending themselves."

Cowards? Hardly.

"They justify murders on the false claim that we *illegally* possess *occupied* territories. This claim is false propaganda. It is revisionist history."

Barak paused, surveying the Marines.

"When our nation was reborn in 1948, there *was* no such country as Palestine. It was a mandate controlled by the British dating back to World War I. Before that, the land had been controlled by Turkey.

"Then in 1917, Britain declared, through a document known as the *Balfour Declaration*, that this land should be set aside for Jewish people, who were scattered throughout the world since the year AD 70. The British had legal authority over the land at that time, and this was *their* declaration.

"Then the United Nations, in 1948, decreed we should have *all* the land they now claim, including the West Bank and Jerusalem. This angered the terrorists, and in 1948, a massive Arab army attacked us and stole part of the land from us, land the UN said was ours. By God's grace, we stopped them before they drove us into the sea. Then in 1967, when they attacked again, by God's grace, we recaptured land the UN mandated was ours to begin with."

Yes, and you Jews murdered innocent Palestinians who lived peacefully in their homes, didn't you? You ran women and children into the

streets and built settlements where their homes had been. You mur-
derous swine. You gunned down my great-grandfather in cold blood,
didn't you? May the blood of Anwar Nasser be avenged this day by his
great-grandson.

"The whole conflict, therefore, has been about an effort to steal, I
regret to say."

Easy . . . bring the crosshair down off the head. Easy on the trigger.

"Beginning in 1948, they have sought to thumb their noses at international law. They have sought, at all costs, to take, to manipulate, to kill ..."

There. On the sternum. Praise be to Allah!

Squeeze!

The reverberation from the rifle sounded like a grenade exploding in
his ears. Nasser chambered another shell.

"Shots fired! Ambassador down." The walkie-talkies squawked like a
flock of chickens being chased by a fox.

Another shot.

"Where's that coming from?" A strident, panic-stricken voice from
the walkie-talkie. "Call in medevac. Now!"

Nasser rechambered a third round. Then squeezed the trigger again.
The smell of fresh gunpowder drifted up his nostrils.

Another squawk from the walkie-talkie. "Shots reported from Base
Housing! All units secure that building. Move it!"

He had been discovered. Now it was a matter of time. There was no
escape.

Praise be to Allah. Soon I will be in paradise.

Nasser chambered another round as tear-gas canisters crashed
through the windows.

His eyes watering profusely from the gas filling the room, he put the
barrel in his mouth and pulled the trigger.

CHAPTER 9

When the phone buzzed on his desk, Lieutenant Zack Brewer was scanning the shocking headlines of the *Union-Tribune*.

"Lieutenant Brewer?"

"Yes, Amy?"

"Sir, Lieutenant Colcernian returning your call on one."

"Thanks, Amy. I'll take it." He punched line one. "Diane." He spoke in a friendly tone, as if greeting a long-lost friend.

"Zack. What's up?" Her voice was cool. *The bad blood from Justice School still drippeth.*

"Just reading the headlines about the Marine shooting the ambassador at Pendleton—"

"You mean *allegedly* shooting the ambassador?"

"Come on, Diane." Zack drummed his fingers on his desk. "They've traced the trajectory of the bullet fired from *his* gun. Nobody else in the area. Case closed."

"Yeah, yeah." Her voice was laced with sarcasm. "Other than the minor principle that in this country, citizens, even *dead* ones, are innocent until proven guilty beyond a reasonable doubt. But you're probably right."

"Do my ears deceive me?" He relished the argumentative banter with his gorgeous, redheaded, green-eyed rival. "The best defense counsel in the Navy, conceding a point?"

"Forget the flattery, Lieutenant. Won't work. Besides, as long as I don't have to concede a point concerning one of *my* cases, it's sort of harmless error, eh?"

"I was afraid you'd say that, Diane." He chuckled. "And I'll bet you didn't call just to discuss the Muslim Marine with the sniper rifle?"

"Cut to the chase, Lieutenant. I've got a date tonight."

"Anyone I know?"

She ignored the question. "What's the real reason for your call?"

He sighed. What did he care who she was seeing?

"Okay. Here's the deal. Blount pleads to rape; the convening authority recommends five years. And, of course, a dishonorable discharge."

He heard papers rustling at the other end of the line. "Fifty-five minutes."

"Excuse me?"

"Now I've got just fifty-five minutes to get to the airport to pick up my date, and here I am, wasting my time listening to your ridiculous proposals. Traffic on Harbor Drive is bad this time of day."

"That's all you're going to say?"

"What do you *want* me to say? I should sell my client up the river for *five* years in Leavenworth without a fight?" More papers rustled on her end.

"It's a lot better than life in prison."

"Hah." Sarcasm dripped. "You know as well as I do that rarely happens in a general court-martial. Tell the convening authority six months, a bad conduct discharge—and a plea to simple assault, and I will consider, let me repeat, *consider*, recommending Petty Officer Blount take the deal. Otherwise, we go to trial."

"Diane, I know you're competitive, and I know you're good." *Not good enough to beat me, but still good.* "But we're talking about the rape of an officer here. By a SEAL. And I know you've not forgotten that two-thirds of the members sitting on the jury will be officers. If we get a conviction in this case, the sentencing phase could get ugly. Your client will wish he'd taken the five years."

"*If* you get the conviction. First, you've got to convince the officers on that jury that it's okay for one of their fellow officers to run around at midnight—sloppy drunk—fraternizing with enlisted guys in the parking lot."

A smile crossed Zack's face. "You've got to be kidding me. You're not seriously going to try the old 'she wanted it' defense with a Naval Academy grad."

"An Academy grad whose uncle just happens to be one of the most powerful men in Washington?"

Great. She knows.

"I don't know what you're talking about. Besides, who her uncle is has nothing to do with her getting raped."

"You know darn well what I'm talking about, Zack. Testimony in a general court-martial that the niece of Senator Roberson Fowler was parading around—drunk—in the middle of the night, with an enlisted SEAL . . . well, you get the picture. Won't look too good for the Navy, will it? And with Fowler on the Armed Services Committee?" She paused. "Are you sure the convening authority wants to go through with this? Tell them six months, BCD, and a plea to assault. Then we talk."

"Diane, think about this—"

"No, *you* think about it, Lieutenant. I'm late. I've gotta run. Ciao."

The phone went dead. He'd just put the receiver down when Amy buzzed. With an impatient sigh, he lifted it again. "Yes?"

"Sir, Ensign Landrieu is here."

"Bring her down, please, Amy."

"Aye, sir."

A few minutes later, LN1 Amy DeBenedetto stood at the door with Ensign Marianne Landrieu, both in summer whites. Zack rose from his chair as Amy stepped back to let Marianne enter the room.

"Would you like me to stay, sir?"

"No thanks, Amy. I'll call you in a few minutes."

"Yes, sir." She closed the door quietly behind her.

Still standing, Zack inclined his head to Ensign Landrieu. "Good to see you, Marianne. Would you like to have a seat?"

"Thank you." She gave him a tremulous smile and sat down on the edge of her chair, ankles crossed.

He settled into his chair, steepling his fingers as he leaned back. "Marianne, I was just on the phone with Lieutenant Colcernian, counsel for the defense. She and I have had some preliminary discussions about your case."

She raised her eyebrows. "What kind of discussions?"

"Plea discussions. The convening authority for the court-martial, Admiral Ayers, ordered me to find out if Petty Officer Blount might be willing to plead guilty for a capped sentence."

"I don't understand."

"COMNAVBASE will recommend a cap of five years' confinement if Blount pleads guilty. That would save the government the expense—and you the trauma—of going through with a trial."

A glint appeared in her eyes. "You mean I won't have to testify?"

"Only if they accept the deal."

"Will they?"

"Are you willing to cap this animal's confinement at five years? After what he did to you?"

She hesitated for a moment, and her face flushed. "Zack, I—really, I just want to get on with my life." Her eyes moistened. "I want to return to my duty station. I miss my work." She met his gaze, her chin trembling, and then she looked away quickly as if embarrassed. "I've been attending my counseling sessions and I'm taking prescribed medication for post-traumatic stress disorder." She blinked rapidly as if trying to control tears.

Zack nodded.

"It's like I'm in a fishbowl." Her gaze was on something distant, over his shoulder, through the window to the bay beyond. Her voice dropped to almost a whisper. "I feel like a lab rat. So yes, I'd trade getting my life back for five years' confinement for this rapist."

Zack passed her a box of tissues and watched her carefully as she dabbed the corners of her eyes, then returned the box to his desk. She gave him a shy smile. "I want that for you too, Marianne. I'd like to personally cut this guy's heart out. Unfortunately, it looks like we are not going to be able to strike a deal."

"He won't plead?"

"Not unless we reduce the cap to six months and let him plead to assault. The convening authority won't buy off on that. Neither will Special Warfare Command. The SEALs want a rape conviction and a multiyear confinement pinned on this guy."

Her eyes, still watery, met his. "So what does all this mean?"

He moved his gaze to the window behind his desk, out to the sparkling waters of San Diego Bay. He knew what he had to say would hurt, possibly even cause great psychological and emotional damage. He wished there was some way to avoid telling her. He turned back to her. "It means they are claiming a consent defense."

"Consent defense?" She frowned. "Can you explain?"

With a heavy sigh, Zack stood, crossed his arms, and stood next to the window, facing her. "The law says a person is not guilty of rape if the victim consented to relations. They are going to say you were drunk and consented to relations with this petty officer."

"Consented to relations? With *him*?" Two bright spots appeared on her cheeks, and she pressed her lips into a straight, angry line.

Her reaction certainly seemed sincere. She was angry, and he didn't blame her. "Marianne, nothing personal. It's a common defense; in fact, it's the *most* common defense lawyers raise in these types of cases. They do it *all* the time. Sometimes they threaten it just to intimidate ... Marianne?" He stopped speaking as she buried her face in her hands. "It's going to be okay." He'd never known what to do when women cried. Not that he'd had much experience with this sort of thing. "I promise. Marianne?"

She wept quietly. "Does this mean she's going to tell the jury I ... ?" She uttered the muffled question into the palms of her hands. "She's going to ruin me."

"Marianne, look at me."

After a moment, she lifted her head. He handed her the box of tissues again. "I promise you, no matter what, I won't let her ruin you. You have my word."

She dabbed her eyes with a wadded tissue. "Sorry. I just feel ... well, like a pariah. Ever since this happened, I've been an outcast. People have been nice, but it's all so superficial. I know they're whispering behind my back. No one wants to get close." She shuddered, her eyes filling again. "And I'm not certain I want them to. Maybe it's better to be alone at a time like this." She shook her head. "And if this defense attorney finds out about my uncle ... It will be all over the national news. Zack, please promise me you won't let her find out about my family."

Maybe he should tell her Colcernian already knew.

Her watery gaze was on him, expectant. "Marianne, may I ask you a question?"

"Sure."

"Do you have any plans for tomorrow?"

"I'm planning to spend my Saturday night barricaded in my house with a novel. Reading takes my mind off things."

"Well, I was wondering ... You really need a friend right now. If you can break yourself away from your novel for an hour or two—maybe you'd like to have coffee? Just to talk?"

"Really?" For the second time, a light appeared in her blue eyes.

"But only if you feel up to it."

She pulled another tissue from the box. "This might be just what the doctor ordered."

He sat back down, suddenly uneasy. What was he thinking? Coffee with a client? Perhaps this wasn't such a good idea after all.

"In fact ..." She dabbed her eyes. "The more I think about it, it might do me good to get out for ... longer. Maybe an evening." Her wide eyes focused on him. "Maybe dinner?"

He tried to hide his surprise. Didn't rape victims usually have a difficult time in the company of males, especially in a social setting? He frowned. "Are you sure you're up to dinner?"

She sipped her bottled water. "I think so. My counselors say I shouldn't just lie around in my misery. I should start going out again with friends." She blinked hard. "It's just that since this ... this happened, I haven't had anyone to call a friend." She swallowed hard. "When you said, 'You need a friend,' well ..." She tilted her face toward his again. "Well ... spending time with you seems like the right step to take ... in the journey to healing."

"Okay." What had he gotten himself into?

They said their good-byes, and he sat for a moment at his desk, tapping a pen on his legal pad and thinking he should pick up the phone and ask Amy to cancel the engagement.

Then he remembered Marianne's loneliness, her fear of being made a spectacle of in the media, her reaction to his offer of friendship. He swiveled his chair toward the window and stared out at the bay.

Something nagged at him about Marianne Landrieu, but he couldn't put a finger on it. Maybe Amy was right and Marianne wasn't telling the whole truth. Here he sat, about to throw the book at the perpetrator ...

But what if the man was innocent?

CHAPTER 10

F/A-18 flight line
Oceana Naval Air Station
Virginia Beach, Virginia

0500 hours (EST)

With the cool, early morning breeze from the Atlantic blowing in his face and the deafening roar of fighter jets vibrating his earphones, Petty Officer Sulayman al-Aziz checked his watch.

Five o'clock.

He turned off his flashlight and, purpose in his step, walked out to the flight line, to the parked F/A-18C Super Hornet of Viper squadron. The ground crew was not due at the plane for another hour, but he still needed to hurry.

Aziz squatted under the fuselage, reached into his pocket, and pulled out the pliable substance he had hidden there earlier. He balled the C-4 plastic explosive into a small cylinder.

He stripped more C-4 off his body and molded the cylinder into a larger, football-sized lump. He held it up, assessing his handiwork. It would provide more than enough firepower to accomplish Allah's mission.

He reached into his left pocket for the other necessary ingredient. The detonator was small and simple. Black and plastic with an electronic diode, it resembled a digital stopwatch. He set the timer for 0815 hours, Lima time, buried the wires deep, and clicked the small switch. The plastic bomb was armed and ticking silently.

Switching on his flashlight, he pointed it back toward the tail of the plane. Moving closer, he carefully positioned the bomb deep into the avionics bay, pushing it into an inconspicuous space behind the data bus. He knew from experience that the avionics bay would not be inspected during preflight. Even if the chief took a quick look, the bomb would be difficult to spot.

He flipped off the flashlight, tucked in his shirttail, and walked back to the hangar. Soon he would be off duty. It was almost time for Shoney's.

Lieutenant Diane Colcernian's townhouse
Near Jimmy Durante Boulevard
Del Mar, California

0240 hours (PST)

Diane flipped on her bedside lamp, jerked off the covers, and felt her feet hit the carpet. She took the large manila envelope from Baton Rouge off her nightstand and headed to the kitchen. Within a few minutes, the appealing scent of a vanilla coffee from Starbucks floated through the air. The gourmet coffee warmed her throat and brought her senses to life. Sitting at her kitchen table, she pulled the private detective's report from the envelope.

She had read it through when it arrived the day before, but the information was so astounding that she had tossed and turned from ten o'clock on, unable to get it off her mind.

She took another sip of coffee as she flipped past the cover letter to the first page. Her breath caught as she read the third paragraph. Then she chuckled. This was dynamite.

Getting it into evidence would be a war.

She took another sip, thinking about Zack. She could almost see his face when she introduced this new evidence.

He would object. Vehemently. Vigorously. Passionately. Dramatically. But this could win her case.

She grinned, took another sip, then put her mug down. She went to the refrigerator, found a cup of blueberry yogurt, and swirled her spoon to bring the fruit to the top.

Surprise was the key. She couldn't give Zack much reaction time. If she disclosed this up front, he would slap her with a rape-shield brief.

And what about the political ramifications? Did she really want to take on the niece of a powerful United States senator, divulging this kind of damaging information?

She swirled the yogurt with her spoon.

Of course the media would have a field day with this one. The information would damage Marianne Landrieu's reputation. It was the kind of thing that would haunt her for the rest of her life. But if the woman had lied about the rape—and Diane was now more convinced than ever that she had—an innocent man's life would be ruined. His career, his family life, his reputation . . .

She popped a blueberry-laden spoonful into her mouth.

And what about her own career? Granted, it would be tough for the Navy to ruin her, at least overtly, once the press caught wind of this. Covertly was another matter. The senator was a powerful man. The Navy might find a way to destroy everything she had worked for.

When it came down to it, though, it wasn't her career that mattered. It was the innocence of a man falsely accused. His life hung in the balance, and she was the only one who could tip the scales of justice—she hoped—in the right direction.

She drained the last drops of Starbucks, flipped to another page of the report, then looked up again, lost in thought. It wasn't about winning or losing for the sake of combat. It was about saving the life of an innocent man.

But it wouldn't hurt to beat Zack while she was at it.

She grinned as she tossed the empty yogurt container in the trashcan. *Two points.*

CHAPTER 11

F/A-18 flight line
Oceana Naval Air Station
Virginia Beach, Virginia

0730 hours (EST)

In his green flight suit and jump boots, Commander Mark Latcher peered through the Hornet's window at the F-14D Tomcat feathering down at the end of the runway. He glanced at the photo of his wife and three children, just as he always did right before takeoff, then slipped it back into his flight-suit pocket.

"One-one-five Alpha. Oceana Tower. You are clear for takeoff on runway one-four."

"Oceana Tower. One-one-five Alpha," he answered. "Acknowledge. Clear for takeoff."

"Clear for takeoff."

Latcher steered the jet to the edge of the runway, then pushed down the throttles. The speed, power, and vibration of the Hornet's twin turbofans shot adrenaline through his body as the warplane accelerated down the long concrete runway.

He pulled back on the stick and the plane climbed sharply, the g-forces pressing him deep into his seat.

He banked into an eastern climb and saw the sun, now a bright ball just over the Atlantic horizon. The jet streaked out over the ocean, away from commercial traffic in the area. After receiving more instructions from air traffic control, he banked the Hornet again, this time to the southwest on a vector toward the bombing range. When he crossed the northeastern end of North Carolina's Outer Banks, just over Duck in Currituck County, the altimeter read five thousand feet.

Descending rapidly for the strafing run, he leveled at one thousand feet over the Albemarle Sound and glanced over his left shoulder. A white obelisk rose over the sand dunes at Kitty Hawk. Latcher shot a quick salute to the Wright Memorial. It was a ritual he followed every time he made this run, his way of saying thank you to Wilbur and Orville.

He switched to channel 113, the bombing range's radio frequency. "Dare County Tower. Navy Victor Foxtrot one-one-five Alpha requests clearance on approach for live fire exercise for target five. Request clearance to proceed."

"One-one-five Alpha. We've got you inbound on scope. Be advised clearance granted, repeat granted, for target five. Turn course one-five-four and go to two hundred feet on approach. Fire at your discretion."

"Roger, Dare County. One-one-five Alpha. Course one-five-four. Going to two hundred feet. Proceeding now."

Latcher pushed down on the stick, pointing the Hornet's nose toward the sound at five hundred knots. With the shoreline and a canopy of pine trees racing by in a blur just two hundred feet below, he spotted the red and white military observation tower. He gave the stick a slight flick to the left. The Hornet shot over the tower, then over an open field.

The three-paneled strafing target rose from the ground. His reaction was almost automatic.

Arm switch.

Fire.

Shaking the nose of the jet, the M61A1 Vulcan twenty-millimeter cannon sprayed a wall of lead, ripping a cloud of dust in a straight line across the ground directly to the target.

Bull's-eye!

"Nice shootin' there, Commander." It was the tower superintendent, speaking in a deadpan North Carolina accent. "Nothin' wrong with that gun."

"Just had her rebuilt." Latcher breathed a sigh of relief.

"Want to bring her around for another round?"

"Dare Tower. One-one-five Alpha. I'd love to stick around, but I'd better boogie. Got a carrier to catch."

"Roger, Commander. See you in six months. Happy hunting."

"Thanks for the hospitality, gentlemen."

Latcher put the war bird into a climb and turned west, where he would loop over Tyrell and Washington counties before turning north for the short trip back to Oceana.

Two miles from Lake Phelps
Eastern Washington County, North Carolina

0814 hours (EST)

The twin silos of the Tyson Farms grain elevators rose 150 feet into clear blue sky above the waving cornfields on either side of the road. Darryl Swain slowed his truck, carefully executing a right turn. His son looked back at the boat trailer they were pulling behind.

"You're good to go, Dad." The twelve-year-old shot him a grin as he settled back in his seat.

The twin elevators marked the gravel road leading down the last two-mile stretch to the boat landing at Lake Phelps. As the truck straightened, Darryl glanced at the digital clock in the console of the pickup. *8:14. Right on time for an 8:30 launch.* He'd spend a few hours on the lake with the boy, maybe catch a few brim, then head home to get ready for the weekend and try not to think about work. His shift at the mill started Sunday at midnight.

The twin-engine jet streaking in over the grain elevators pulled his attention from the dashboard. "Adam, look at the jet!"

An eerie silence followed as the jet outran its sound. A sonic boom shook the truck, quickly followed by a blinding flash. Before Darryl or his son could speak, a fireball of flames and smoke shot from the jet. Wings flew like boomerangs in opposite directions as the plane's fuselage plunged into the lake like a burning meteor. A split-second later, another boom shook the truck, the explosion's echo from across the lake.

Darryl floored it. Ninety seconds later, the truck and trailer rolled into the parking area of the isolated boat landing. No other cars, boats, or trailers were in sight. The flaming mass looked to be about a half mile out on the lake.

He circled the truck, boat trailer still attached, around the gravel parking lot. Then, with his heart racing like a machine gun and his palms sweating, he began backing the dusty trailer down the ramp into the water.

"Adam, stay on the ramp!" Darryl stepped into the boat, primed the pump, and pulled the cord on the old 45-horsepower Mercury outboard motor. Nothing.

Lord, help me get this motor started. Another yank. Still nothing. Another explosion and more flames. *Help me, Lord.* He jerked the cord with a third powerful heave.

The motor coughed, sputtered, then caught hold and spat a cloud of white marine gas in a puff. Darryl worked the throttle, brought the boat around in a circle away from the dock, aimed the bow directly at the smoking wreckage, and threw the throttle wide open.

The bow skimmed across the light swells, bouncing slightly as the smoke and glow of flames drew nearer. Two minutes later, the boat closed in on the crash site, and Darryl felt the heat of burning fuel. He squinted through the flames, looking for survivors. A large circle of jet fuel burned around some floating wreckage.

Another explosion sprayed water into the boat. Too close for comfort. He backed the craft a few yards away and turned into another circle. He slowed to almost a standstill, peering through the smoke, coughing as the acrid fumes filled his lungs.

He brought the boat still closer to the floating firewall, so close the heat stung his eyes. The stench of his own hair singeing filled his nostrils. The flame licked up. His eyes watered, and he couldn't see. Then the smoke cleared for a second.

He blinked, then moved the boat closer. A body in a green flight suit floated near the firewall. He was facedown in the water, a white crash helmet covering his head, his arms and legs outstretched.

A rocking explosion sent the boat in one direction and Darryl overboard. Gagging on a mouthful of water as his head popped above the surface, he saw the stern of his boat speeding away from him, pushed away by the still-running motor. Turning to the left, he looked for the tree line and the dock half a mile in the distance. Nothing was visible but water, smoke, and flames.

He was a decent swimmer, but not a great one. In the rush to get the boat in the lake, he had neglected his life preserver. *Lord, help me.* His boots were flooding, making them feel like bricks strapped to his feet. He struggled to tread water. He gasped for air, then ducked under the surface and fingered the laces he had double-knotted. No luck.

Jesus, let me see my family again.

With his arms aching and the top of his head bobbing just under the surface, his nose was filling with cool lake water. He was sinking deeper when he heard a *thwhock-thwhock-thwhock-thwhock-thwhock-thwhock* chopping through the water from above. He tilted his face to the surface and saw ripples lit by the sun. Mustering what little strength remained, he kicked to the surface and opened his eyes.

Hovering overhead was a large orange helicopter. "United States Coast Guard," a voice boomed. "Hold on! We're gonna get you out!"

With a supernatural strength that could only be from God, he kicked his boots against the water. As muscle cramps knotted the back of his calves, two rubber-suited divers with oxygen tanks plunged in the water, one to his left, the other to his right. They reached him a heartbeat later with a donut-shaped flotation device.

"Hold on to this." The first diver to reach him slid a white life ring over Darryl's neck and helped him lift his arms through.

The second diver instantly inflated a rubber raft and swam with it to Darryl's side. "We're gonna get you in, then hoist you into the chopper."

"There's a man ... a pilot, I think ... a man in the water." Darryl gasped out the words.

"Where?" The first diver treaded water. "Point."

"Over there. Behind ... the flames."

"Stay here with him. I'll go." The diver farthest from the raft disappeared under the water, while the other helped Darryl into the life raft.

The orange Coast Guard chopper moved directly over the flames. Two more divers dropped out of the chopper. From the northeast came the throbbing *thwhock-thwhock-thwhock* sounds of additional helicopters on the move across the lake.

Seconds later, two massive helicopters, gray with "NAVY" painted in black on the tail sections, came to a hovering standstill over the water. The three choppers now stood watch in a triangle, each hovering about fifty feet in the air over the crash site. The Coast Guard chopper rotated, dropped its nose, and moved back into position directly over Darryl.

The wind from the chopper's blades was ferocious. Darryl looked up as a basket slowly moved from the helicopter toward the raft. The diver nearest him reached up to steady the metal, stretcher-like basket.

"Just roll over into it, sir."

Darryl had never received a better invitation.

As the winch hoisted him up, he looked back at the wreckage. The entire fuselage of the plane, broken into several parts, was visible. Two divers swam near an inflated rubber raft just like the one that had saved Darryl's life. The pilot was stretched out inside, his arms hanging limp.

The Navy chopper moved over the downed jet, about three hundred feet east of the Coast Guard chopper, and lowered a basket. Now almost to the cargo bay door, Darryl had an unobstructed view of the U.S. Navy helicopter hoisting its downed flier into the Carolina sky.

For a brief moment, both the USN and USCG helicopters hovered side by side, each dangling a basket holding a man. Then the basket holding Darryl reached the orange chopper, and he was pulled into the cargo bay by a Coast Guard petty officer.

"Are you all right, sir?" The petty officer studied Darryl.

He remembered Adam, and his heart caught. "My boy . . ." He couldn't keep the panic from his hoarse voice. "I left him on the dock!"

"He's okay, sir. The sheriff has him. They'll meet us at the hospital."

"The pilot?" He asked, though he already knew the answer.

"Your actions were heroic, but I'm afraid the pilot didn't survive."

CHAPTER 12

Near Jimmy Durante Boulevard
Del Mar, California

Diane adjusted her black Bollé sunglasses and glanced at her watch as she jogged south down the white sands of Del Mar Beach. She wore orange running shorts, a white T-shirt with "Virginia Cavaliers" stenciled across the front, and orange running shoes. The bright sun all but made the colors she wore glow. She figured her red hair picked up a flame-colored glint in the sunlight. She grinned at the spectacle she was likely creating as she streaked down the packed sand toward the 15th Street cut-through, which she would take back over to Camino Del Mar for the final leg home. She purposely didn't look to see if heads were turning as she ran. Her craving for that kind of attention had stopped the minute she left the superficial life of modeling and enrolled in law school.

As she jogged, her thoughts turned to the arrogant, shoot-it-from-the-hip hotshot named Lieutenant Zack Brewer. And her determination to beat him in the Blount-Landrieu case.

Sure, she had been the valedictorian at the Navy Justice School. But that honor was spoiled by then-Lieutenant (jg) Zachary M. Brewer. Their feud went back to the final round of the Justice School's trial advocacy competition, sponsored by the New York City Bar Association.

It was the most prestigious award in the JAG Corps, and she'd wanted it. She couldn't even remember the name of the case now. But it was a mock trial for murder. She was assigned the role of prosecutor. Brewer was the defense counsel.

It was a case tailor-made for a conviction, and thus for a victory by the prosecution. All she had to do was show the mock jury a series of bloody photographs from the murder scene on an imaginary aircraft carrier. She had a *right* to show those pictures to the jury. They were highly relevant to her case. Get the photos to the jury, and the trophy was hers.

But Brewer pulled some last-minute shenanigans with the military judge to keep the pictures away from the jury. Brewer offered a written stipulation to the court just as she was about to offer the photos into evidence. And he never gave Diane the courtesy of an advanced copy. Slimy.

The military judge—a female Marine officer who seemed to swoon over his silver tongue and the cute dimple in his chin—let him get away with it. There was no time to research any cases in opposition because Justice School graduation was the next day, and Brewer knew it.

The middle-aged judge, whose eyes always seemed to brighten when she watched Brewer, let him *read* his stipulation to the jury—the victim had been cut and there was blood on the floor—rather than just showing them the color photographs.

The jury was fooled by it all, just as Brewer planned, and came back with a not guilty verdict. Brewer had stolen her award. She had to admit it *was* a slick ploy. Dirty, but slick.

But this time she would be the one springing the surprise on the good lieutenant. *We'll see how quick the good lieutenant can think on his feet, won't we?* She almost laughed as she turned north on Camino Del Mar for the final leg of her run.

Thirty minutes later, after she had showered and donned a two-piece bathing suit, she grabbed a Diet Coke, her cell phone, and the Blount file and settled into a lounge chair beside the swimming pool at her townhouse complex. She opened the file to look for the private detective's telephone number from Louisiana.

She powered up her cellular and pressed the number into the key pad.

A voice answered after two rings. "Simon Stone."

"Sir, this is Lieutenant Diane Colcernian. I'm a lawyer in the Navy. You recently prepared a surveillance report for a case I'm working on."

"Oh yeah." Diane heard a note of enthusiasm in the voice. He should be enthusiastic, considering she'd fronted his thousand-dollar fee out of her own paycheck. "Landrieu case, right?"

"That would be the one," she said.

"Thanks for the check, Lieutenant." His voice remained giddy. "Boy, that's gonna be something if the information ever gets out."

Diane sipped her Diet Coke before answering. "Yes, well, that's the reason for my call, Mr. Stone. I wanted to follow up with you, since this case is about to be called to trial."

"Fire away, mama."

"How sure are you about the accuracy of the information?"

"Dead sure." The voice had gone from gruff, to giddy, and now to cocky. "I've got ten witnesses at least. Five she was with personally."

"Any photos?"

"Still working on it."

"Anyone willing to testify?"

"Don't know. She's the niece of a powerful senator, but we're still working on it."

Diane noticed the phrase "still working on it." She knew what that meant.

"Mr. Stone, how's our retainer situation right now?"

"We put a pretty good hurtin' on it with the first report. We could use another thousand or so."

Diane rolled her eyes. "Mr. Stone, with another thousand dollars, you think you could round up some *live* witnesses who can come to California and testify?"

"Yes, ma'am. And I hate to be hitting you up for money, but this stuff takes a lot of time."

I'll bet. "Okay. Based on that assurance, I'm going to get the money together and call you back tomorrow."

"Pleasure talking to you, ma'am."

"You too, Mr. Stone."

The line went dead, and Diane finished her Diet Coke. How would she pay for these private detective expenses? She earned a good paycheck as a Navy lawyer, but she was by no means wealthy. She'd go to the brig later today and tell Blount some of these expenses were his. A third-class petty officer should have at least a thousand lying around. If he didn't have the money, she could always put it on her credit card. Annihilating Zack Brewer in court would be worth it.

The phone signaled an incoming call. She checked the caller ID and, with a smile, flipped open the top. *"Bonjour,"* she said to Pierre.

"Bonjour, ma cher." She could hear the delight in his voice, which raised her spirits.

Pierre always cheered her when she was down, provided a listening ear when she needed a friend, a solid comfort when her world was troubled. Since the day he'd spotted her on campus and recruited her for *Femme du Monde,* he'd watched over her like a surrogate big brother. He teased her about falling so hard for her that she'd ruined his love life forever. He'd asked her to marry him more times than she could count, but it was all in good fun.

In truth, they were friends. Pierre was the best friend she'd ever had ... especially since her father died.

"I know we saw each other last weekend, but I've just flown into town on unexpected business and was wondering if you would honor me with the pleasure of your company at dinner tonight?"

She grinned. "I'd love to." And she meant it. Pierre always provided a good sounding board for issues she struggled with. He probably knew as much about her cases as she did. He knew her history with Zack, the sleazy tactic he'd used to rob her of the award at Justice School. She'd gotten special permission for Pierre to sit in on the trial that day. He'd seen firsthand what the lieutenant had done to her.

That night, Pierre had held her as she cried.

"There's a new French restaurant in La Jolla," he was saying, "overlooking the Pacific. I will pick you up at six. Is this okay?"

"I look forward to it."

"Good-bye, my love," he said, and they both laughed. His declaration of love was a long-standing joke.

CHAPTER 13

Office of the Commander
U.S. Naval Air Forces
Atlantic Fleet
Norfolk, Virginia

But that's impossible!" Rear Admiral Daniel Gibson slammed his fist on his desk. Only one month ago, he had fleeted up to assume the role of commander of all U.S. Naval Air Forces in the Atlantic. This was the first major mishap on his watch in his new job, and he wanted answers. Now.

"Gentlemen, our job—no, *my* job—is to make these planes combat-ready for the Sixth Fleet. We've got seventy squadrons and over fourteen hundred aircraft on six aircraft carriers. We're the shepherd watching over our flock. When one goes down, we all suffer."

Gibson glared at the members of his personal staff, one by one. "I've logged over twenty-five hundred jet hours, made nine hundred carrier landings. Mostly in the F/A-18. And I don't buy that a twenty-million-dollar jet fighter just 'blew up' in the sky over some lake in North Carolina.

"We will get to the bottom of this. Even if we have to fly down there and pick through every screw and interview every man, woman, dog, maggot, or fly that came within five inches of the plane before it took off. We owe it to the widow and to this officer's children. And we owe it to the Navy." Gibson paused and swept his gaze across his staff again. "Do I make myself clear?"

A mixed chorus of "Aye, aye, sir" filled the room.

The admiral turned to his lawyer. "Captain David Guy, give us a brief overview of legal issues and procedures we need to consider."

The staff judge advocate sat up in his chair, pulled a briefcase into his lap, opened it, and extricated a folder. "Admiral, I've prepared a bullet-point memo for you and the staff on basic legal issues. Obviously, we proceed under the JAGMAN—JAG Manual—which governs procedures for determining legal liability by any service members. One of our JAG officers is an ex–F-14 pilot, and I'm requesting that he be appointed as lead investigator for the JAGMAN investigation." Guy stopped and sipped his coffee. "And I have an additional recommendation, Admiral."

Gibson raised his eyebrow at his JAG officer. "Let's hear it, Captain."

"Sir, I have a hunch your suspicions about foul play may have merit. No evidence, but I agree something's not right. I recommend we request a criminal investigation by the Naval Criminal Investigative Service."

"I agree, Captain. Can NCIS handle this sort of thing?"

"With the initial investigation, conducting interviews and so on, the answer is yes, sir."

"Okay, Captain," Gibson said. "Good advice. This needs to happen yesterday. How do I get NCIS involved?"

"Sir, give me the word, and NCIS Norfolk starts detailed interviews of everyone within ten miles of the plane before it took off." Guy sat back, his unblinking gaze on the admiral.

The admiral nodded. "Captain, make it happen. I want a briefing ASAP on the NCIS interviews with the ground crew. I want to know why the plane went down, and I want to know now."

"Aye, aye, sir," Captain Guy said.

"Anything else, gentlemen?"

The staff officers shook their heads.

"Very well then. We are adjourned for now."

CHAPTER 14

Ensign Marianne Landrieu's house
Isabella Avenue
Coronado, California

Zack Brewer drove his silver Mercedes across Coronado Bridge spanning San Diego Bay and wondered how the woman he was about to pick up, an ensign, could afford to live in one of the priciest enclaves in San Diego County. Certainly not on an ensign's pay, he thought as the Mercedes approached the toll booth on the Coronado side.

As he waited in line, he looked out across the bay, breathtaking in the early evening sun. One of the reasons he had chosen the maritime service was that it had the world's best duty stations: Pearl Harbor; Riota, Spain; Sigonella, Sicily.

He inched toward the toll booth.

Indeed, the United States Navy controlled some of the most beautiful and most expensive real estate in the country.

One such place was the Naval Air Station at North Island, located at the tip of Coronado, just across the bay from San Diego. Zack remembered how he had spent his first night in San Diego at the Bachelor Officers' Quarters at NASNI, but was unable to find permanent housing on the base there, and certainly could not afford to locate in the quaint, ritzy Coronado where nothing sold for less than a million dollars.

Exactly where he was headed right now.

He flicked the correct change into the collection bucket and drove through the toll booth. The Landrieu family fortune. Probably some sort of trust set up for the grandchildren. It had come from oil, he had learned in his research. Marianne's great-grandfather had mustered the resources to drill in the Gulf of Mexico. The result: black gold.

He pulled up in front of the upscale address she had given him on Isabella Avenue, just off Ocean Boulevard. He got out of the car and walked through the picket gate, up the brick walkway flanked by two manicured spots of plush lawn, to the portico of the white stucco house. The house wasn't palatial, but it was ritzy. And worth at least a million bucks for this view of the Pacific.

He pressed the doorbell, trying to dispel the feeling of uneasiness that had plagued him since they made the date.

"Hi, Zack." Ensign Marianne Landrieu greeted him from the doorway. She seemed as troubled as he did, and he wondered if she was having second thoughts.

"Ready?" Zack smiled nervously, wrestling with his chivalrous desire to help Marianne and his equally strong determination not to cross the bounds of propriety.

"Very much so," she said. But still, she seemed nervous.

The car moved down Isabella Avenue, directly toward the Pacific, then left down Ocean Boulevard, parallel to the beach, before turning left again, heading east. A moment later, they crested the Coronado Bridge, and the magnificent view of downtown San Diego spread before them in a panoramic display.

They drove north up Interstate 5, passing downtown San Diego and then Mission Bay, before Marianne spoke. "Thanks again for doing this. Just getting out and seeing some scenery is doing me some good." But her actions didn't match her words; she shivered and wrapped her arms around herself.

I'm going to bury the animal who attacked this girl. He fought to keep his voice professional, slightly impersonal. He glanced toward her. "Air conditioner too cold?"

"No," she said softly. "But opening the sunroof might be nice."

Zack pressed a button, which slid back the car's sunroof and lowered the side windows. The warm, early evening Pacific breeze hit his face and lifted Marianne's blond hair from her neck.

Zack steered the Mercedes off the Interstate at the La Jolla exit, then into a parking spot off the street about two hundred yards north of the cliffs overlooking La Jolla cove.

"If we hurry, we can catch the sun setting over the Pacific." He shot her a quizzical look to see if she was up to it. Her smile gave him her answer.

A few minutes later, they walked briskly up the sidewalk along Coast Boulevard toward the Ellen Scripps Browning Park, where people had gathered on the lawn, throwing Frisbees, talking, or playing with their dogs. Behind the park, Zack saw the shops, restaurants, and fashionable homes and condos of downtown La Jolla.

They walked to the edge of the cliff. The ocean was about a hundred feet below, crashing into the rocky crevices at the bottom of the cliffs. To their right, the cliffs extended in a peaceful curve for several miles, above the cove where the water lapped against the rocky shores.

The real beauty of the place lay to the west, toward the sea, where the sun—a big, orange, glowing beach ball—was sinking slowly into the horizon. The lower it sank, the wider it seemed, casting a narrow orange carpet across the grayish-blue water from the horizon to the rocky shores below. They watched for a few minutes, saying nothing. No words could add to its beauty.

"Breathtaking," Marianne said finally. "I've been over here several times, but never at sunset." She drew in a deep breath, her expression unreadable.

"We'd better head across the street," he said after a moment. "I made reservations, but I hear this place can get crowded."

She inclined her head, a smile playing at the corner of her mouth. "I will follow your lead, Lieutenant."

He led her back through the park and then across the street to the new French restaurant called *La Vue de la Mer*.

A middle-aged, dark-haired man with a pencil-thin moustache stood at the entrance. "Reservations, monsieur?" His French accent almost sounded legitimate.

"My name is Brewer. I have reservations for eight o'clock."

"Hmmm." He flipped a couple of pages in his red-bound leather reservations booklet, raising and lowering his thick eyebrows in a studious manner. "Ah, yes. Lieutenant Brewer." He rested his index finger on one of the pages. "While we pride ourselves on punctuality, the manager requests that I convey our apologies." He looked up. "We are running half an hour behind tonight. But as a token of our appreciation for your patronage, he has asked that I escort you to our bar, where you will be served complimentary cocktails of your choice as your table is readied."

Zack glanced at Marianne. "Is that okay with you?"

"I'm starting to like this place already," she said.

Zack nodded to the pseudo Frenchman. "Okay. After you."

"Bien sur, monsieur. Venez avec moi."

Zack took Marianne's arm as they followed the host to the bar, where they were seated at a high, round table for two.

A waiter in a white dinner jacket and black pants appeared almost as they were seated. "Welcome to *La Vue de la Mer*, Lieutenant Brewer. What complimentary cocktail may we offer the lady tonight?"

"Pinot noir, please." Marianne said.

"May I recommend our manager's special for the evening, vintage 1993, imported from our winery in Monte Carlo?"

"Sounds great." Marianne smiled at the waiter, then at Zack.

"Bien sur. And for you, monsieur?"

"Ginger ale," Zack said and adjusted his collar. He was growing uncomfortable with the new Marianne who seemed to be emerging. He thought back to the report, the accusations that she had been drinking the night of the assault.

"You're not going to order a drink?" Marianne's voice seemed to hold a hint of disappointment. Or was it his imagination?

"You go ahead," he said. "But I don't drink and drive—"

"Lieutenant Brewer!" He was interrupted by an all-too-familiar voice from behind.

He turned to see Lieutenant Diane Colcernian striding toward him. She was followed by a sophisticated middle-aged man whom Zack remembered as her friend Pierre Rochembeau.

"Diane. What a surprise to see you here."

She smiled at him, then glanced at the woman at his side. Her eyes widened before she looked back to Zack.

"A pleasure, mademoiselle." Pierre gave Marianne a slight bow and lifted her hand to his lips. Zack noticed she didn't pull back. Quite the contrary. She seemed to enjoy his attention.

"Do you work here?" Marianne asked.

Pierre chuckled. "No, but I really am French. I live in New York and am here visiting my friend Diane. I am Pierre Rochembeau. And you are . . . ?"

"Marianne Landrieu. I'm a naval officer."

Diane's earlier expression of surprise gave way to disapproval. She leaned toward Zack as Pierre and Marianne chatted. "Dating our clients now," she whispered, "are we, Lieutenant?"

"Marianne is not my client," Zack whispered back. "And this is not a date. She needs a friend. That's it." He paused. "Besides, you know as

well as I do that fraternization applies to officer-enlisted relationships."
He shot her a sarcastic grin.

Diane looked pointedly across the table at Marianne and Pierre. For
a moment, she said nothing as Marianne spoke to Pierre, obviously
enjoying herself. Diane then refocused on Zack. "She does seem to have
a way with men," she said, her back now turned to the other couple,
"wouldn't you say?"

"And your meaning is . . . ?"

"Don't get yourself falsely accused tonight, Lieutenant. You may
wind up needing my services."

"I don't think so, Diane. Of that you can be certain."

"Hmmm." She shot him a devilish grin. "Never say never, Lieutenant."

Before he could answer, Pierre's accented voice broke in. "It was a
pleasure meeting you, mademoiselle. But I see that our table is ready."
Pierre met Zack's gaze. "It was good to see you again, Lieutenant Brewer."

"You too, Pierre," Zack said.

"You know them?" Marianne asked as Pierre escorted Diane away
from their table.

"Yes." He nodded, then waited to go on as the waiter brought a tray
with their drinks.

"She's a JAG officer. I've known them both since Justice School."

"She's beautiful. What's her name?"

"Diane." *And she wants to cut your heart out. But I'm not going to
spoil your night by telling you who she is.*

"Lieutenant Brewer, your table is ready, sir."

Zack looked up as the host stepped to their table. He breathed a sigh
of relief as he scooted back his chair and reached for Marianne's hand.
"Shall we?"

Saved by the waiter.

CHAPTER 15

Residential quarters, officers' housing
U.S. Naval Station
Norfolk, Virginia

2330 hours (EST)

Captain David Guy had served in the JAG Corps for twenty-five years. As the new JAG officer for COMNAVAIRLANT, he had expected a low-key final tour in this, his last assignment before retirement. He was one of only a handful of officers with the personal phone number of the commander of all United States Naval Air Forces in the Atlantic Fleet, but he never really expected to have to use that number.

And especially not at 2330 hours.

But when the station branch of the NCIS called him at home thirty minutes earlier, the information passed along was too hot to sit on. The admiral had to be immediately apprised, even at this late hour.

David checked his Palm Pilot, found the admiral's number, and then dialed a code on the phone that would scramble the call in the unlikely event someone was listening in. Then he dialed the home number for COMNAVAIRLANT.

"Hello?" It was a sleepy-sounding woman's voice.

"Mrs. Gibson?"

"Yes?"

"This is Captain David Guy. Is the admiral available?"

"He's asleep."

"Yes, ma'am, and I apologize for the hour. But this is urgent."

"Hang on." In the background he heard her muffled voice. "Danny. There's some captain on the phone for you."

"Admiral Gibson here."

"Sir, this is Captain Guy. I apologize for calling this late, but we've got an urgent situation."

"It better be. What's up, Captain?"

"Sir, it's about the Super Hornet that went down over Lake Phelps."

"What about it?"

"Sir, I just got a call from Harry Kilnap, the SAC—special agent in charge—of our local NCIS office. Sir, they've recovered remnants of plastic explosives in the plane's wreckage."

"C-4?"

"Yes, sir. That's what he thinks."

David heard the admiral swear under his breath.

"You did the right thing by calling, Captain. Listen, I want you to contact my staff. Have them meet me in my office in one hour. See if Mr. Kilnap can come too. See you then."

"Aye, aye, sir."

La Vue de la Mer *restaurant*
Village of La Jolla
San Diego

2145 hours (PST)

Diane sat alone at the window table—the best in the house—that Pierre had reserved for them. A moment ago he had excused himself to make a telephone call. She suspected he had something up his sleeve. All evening he'd had an intriguing gleam in his eye, a lightness in his step, she hadn't seen in years. Telephone call? He usually kept his work and relaxation separate. She wondered what he was up to.

She settled back and took in the casually elegant dining room. The subdued lighting drew attention to the flickering candles sitting atop the burgundy tablecloths. Fresh flowers, soft violin music, and the clinking of crystal goblets: it was a romantic setting indeed.

But it wasn't romance she was considering. Zack and his date were foremost in her mind. She almost laughed as she contemplated the legal skewering she would deliver, with pleasure, in just a few days. A good old-fashioned Carolina barbeque featuring roasted Brewer, topped with Landrieu sauce.

"You seem happy tonight, madam." It was a debonair-looking waiter dressed in black and white. He placed a crystal goblet of white wine to the side of her gold-rimmed plate, then set an identical goblet beside Pierre's plate.

"Champagne?" She wondered again about what Pierre might be celebrating.

The server smiled. "Chardonnay. From our vintage collection."

"My friend knows how to pick the finest." She gestured to the empty chair.

The waiter raised a brow. "It comes with the compliments of your professional colleague. He sends his best wishes to you and your companion for an enjoyable evening."

"My professional colleague?" She lifted the glass to her lips.

"Yes. The Naval officer who is also dining with us tonight. I believe you spoke with him earlier."

Diane almost choked.

"Is everything all right, madam? You are not pleased with the wine?"

She touched her cloth napkin to her lips. "Yes. Yes, the wine is delicious."

"Good. Then shall I deliver a message to the gentleman for you?"

Diane took another sip. It *was* fabulous. She could only imagine the cost of this vintage wine. It had taken her all of a nanosecond to figure out his motive. He was out to distract her. Gain a psychological advantage at trial by feigning friendship.

She smothered a smile. If he wanted to waste his money on the most expensive wine in the house, fine. She wasn't distracted. If anything, she was more determined than ever to beat Zachary Brewer.

She held the goblet to the light, admiring its pale gold color . . . and remembering the lieutenant's penchant for dirty tricks.

"Yes," she said with a grin. "Send the lieutenant my compliments, and tell him that I relish the prospects of our upcoming professional engagement."

"*Bien sur*, madam."

She glanced at her watch, worrying about Pierre. He worked too hard, still as involved as ever with *Femme du Monde*, though at his age, she'd hoped he'd be slowing down. He had stuck by her side all these years, while she was at UVA, then in law school, then at the Justice School, and now in San Diego.

He had been good to her. And she appreciated his friendship. Did he want more? He'd told her jokingly so dozens of times. What if one of these times, he was serious? What about tonight—spring in his step, sparkle in his eye? What if he made her an offer she couldn't refuse? He was wealthy beyond her imagination, handsome in a debonair and sophisticated way, and she loved being with him.

But did she love Pierre?

She checked her watch, sighing. She was letting her imagination run away from her. Pierre probably did have a business call to make.

The light from the table's single candle caught the crystal in her goblet, turning the wine to the color of liquid gold. She picked up the glass and turned it, her thoughts on Zack Brewer.

One thing she found strangely attractive about him, aside from his innate trial skills and his devilishly cute dimple, was that he was not intimidated by her. If not for their bad blood at the Justice School, she might even consider . . .

She caught herself and almost laughed.

She and Brewer? Never.

"Sorry for the delay, my dear." Pierre stood by the table with a dozen roses in his hand. "I noticed a flower vendor across the street as we were walking here. And tonight is the perfect occasion to present these lovely flowers to a lovely lady."

"A perfect occasion?" Her voice came out in a hoarse whisper, and a nagging worry clutched at her insides. She took the bouquet, careful not to prick her fingers with the thorns.

He sat in his chair and, leaning forward expectantly, met her gaze. His affection was clear. "I see you've already ordered wine." He smiled his approval, but before she could explain, he went on. "I propose a toast. May it be a night we always remember." He lifted his glass.

She raised her goblet toward Pierre's, aware that it had been compliments of Zachary Brewer. A moment later, their glasses met with a soft ring.

CHAPTER 16

COMNAVAIRLANT headquarters
U.S. Naval Station
Norfolk, Virginia

0100 hours (EST)

Captain David Guy, along with eight other senior officers in working khaki uniforms, filed into the conference room at COMNAVAIRLANT headquarters. It was just after midnight, eastern time, and David noticed some of the men rubbing their eyes under the fluorescent lights.

David followed the fresh aroma of coffee brewing in the stainless-steel pot in the corner of the room. As he took a swig of the hot, black liquid, Special Agent Harry Kilnap, the gray-haired, gray-mustached special agent in charge of the local branch of the Naval Criminal Investigative Service, walked into the room, nodded to the senior officers on the admiral's staff, and took a seat at the conference table.

The physical readiness requirements that applied to the officers' corps were not applicable to the civilian members of the NCIS. Kilnap's beer gut, accentuated by the white polyester golf shirt stretched over his bulging midsection, was evidence of this.

"Attention on deck!"

Eight senior aviation officers, the senior JAG officer, and Kilnap snapped to their feet.

"At ease, gentlemen. Take your seats." Rear Admiral Dan Gibson walked swiftly into the room with a file in his hand, his personal aide, a lieutenant commander F-14 pilot, in tow. "Sorry to rouse you sleeping beauties at this hour"—obligatory chuckles rippled around the conference table—"but my

JAG officer, Captain Guy, says we have an urgent matter needing our immediate attention." The admiral turned to him. "Captain Guy?"

"Gentlemen," he said as his eyes swept the room. "We have a serious matter on our hands." He paused. "It looks like the F/A-18 that went down over Lake Phelps in North Carolina was sabotaged."

There were murmurs around the table as the officers exchanged glances.

"How sure are we of this?" the chief of staff asked.

"That's a forensics question, Captain Mattox," he said. "Gentlemen, some of you know Special Agent Harry Kilnap. I'm going to let him respond. Harry?"

"Thank you, Captain Guy." Kilnap paused to take a sip of coffee as if pleased to prolong the drama. "This investigation, that is, the examination into possible criminal activity, is in its preliminary stages." Kilnap took another swallow from his mug. "But here's what we know so far. Within two hours of the explosion, a joint emergency task force, consisting of engineers from NAVAIRSYSCOM—Naval Air Systems Command of Pax River, Maryland—the Navy Safety Center, and the Federal Aviation Administration, was on site.

"Fortunately, because Lake Phelps is calm, debris still floated on the surface. There is a large commercial farming operation run by Tyson Farms just about four miles from the crash site."

The staff intelligence officer leaned forward at the end of the table. "Isn't that where the Swain fellow was when he first spotted the jet?"

"Exactly, Commander," Kilnap said. "Swain was driving by the large Tyson grain elevators when the Hornet streaked over. That was the last time anybody saw the jet intact. The joint task force set up a staging area there, and the Navy and Coast Guard choppers have spent all day fishing floating material out of the lake and hauling it to the staging area. Right off the bat, the NAVAIRSYSCOM people noticed an unusual-looking residue on the inside of scrap metal from the plane's avionics bay.

"Light metal parts were flown here for testing. The results showed positive residue for plastic explosives. This, in our opinion, was sabotage."

"Navy personnel planted a bomb on the plane? Is that what you're suggesting?" The staff intelligence officer leaned forward, narrowing his eyes.

"That's not clear. But we don't think the explosive used was a U.S. military-grade product."

"Explain," the admiral ordered.

"Yes, sir. The principle chemical composition we use in the military is a substance called RDX. Commercial plastic explosives use a similar substance called PETN, which is just as explosive but not as stable as RDX. PETN residue has been found in several commercial airliners believed to have been brought down by terrorist explosions. TWA Flight 800, the plane that blew up after taking off for Paris from New York, had traces of PETN found near the seats in one of the rows from the mid-section of the aircraft. Likewise, with the Hornet, we have found traces of PETN, not RDX."

"So you think it might have been a civilian who planted the bomb?" the public affairs officer asked.

"Not necessarily," Kilnap said. "Could've been anyone. Maybe a military member who either did not have access to C-4 military plastic explosives, or didn't want to raise suspicions by snooping around in the Marines' ammunition depot. We're not ruling out anything at this point."

"Thank you, Agent Kilnap," Admiral Gibson said. "Gentlemen, this information clearly changes how we approach this situation. Any comments or questions before we proceed?"

David Guy leaned forward. "It seems, if this information is correct, we have what may amount to an attack on the United States Military. The question is by *whom*."

"Go on, Captain." The admiral raised his eyebrow.

"Yes, sir. If we have an attack that ultimately proves to have been state-sponsored, we may be dealing with an act of war against the United States."

His remark brought several seconds of dead silence.

"Aren't we jumping the gun a bit, Captain Guy?" The chief of staff was playing his customary role of devil's advocate. "Special Agent Kilnap just said, if I understood him correctly, that he has no idea who did this. Shouldn't we let the investigation run its course before we jump to such extreme conclusions?"

"The chief of staff makes a good point, Captain Guy," Admiral Gibson said. "Aren't you jumping the gun a bit with premature speculation? I mean, all we know right now is plastic explosives residue was found on some of the airplane parts."

"Admiral, I agree with the chief of staff in one respect," David said. "We are speculating on the identity of the perpetrator, if that's what we have. It could have been a lone wolf. But this much we do know—a Navy warplane was sabotaged. We also know this: civilians, acting alone, don't often hit military targets. This issue is whether this should remain primarily an AIRLANT-run investigation at this point.

"One of our jets has been attacked, which means someone is intent on striking at our military on the eve of a major battle-group deployment to the Mediterranean, a deployment, I might add, where the possibility of hostility is high. I recommend, Admiral, that we run a flash message to Washington, tonight. If we are wrong, and if we sit on this, our national interests could be compromised. Suppose this is part of something larger that may require a larger, coordinated response?"

"So what you're saying, Captain," the admiral said, "is that we treat this with an elevated level of scrutiny, above and beyond a routine aviation mishap?"

"Yes, sir. I think we have to."

"Gentlemen?" Gibson glanced around the table.

"Admiral, Captain Guy does make a good point," the chief of staff said. "Probably better to run it up the chain out of an abundance of precaution."

"Very well," Gibson said. "We are in consensus. We will reconvene tomorrow morning at 0800 hours."

"Attention on deck!" someone shouted. The staff rose as the admiral headed into his office, trailed by his staff JAG officer, his aide-de-camp, and the command master chief.

CHAPTER 17

La Vue de la Mer *restaurant*
Village of La Jolla
San Diego

2200 hours (PST)

I trust this evening has been as lovely for you as it has been for me," Pierre said.

Under the dim lighting from the brass chandeliers, with melodic strains of the violinist at the opposite side of the room, they were alone in their own corner of the world. Only the distant clangs of silverware touching porcelain plates reminded her that others were around.

It had been a nice evening. With the exception of their run-in with Zack Brewer and his client, an almost perfect evening, come to think of it. The memory of the look on his face when she caught him on a date with his client brought a grin.

"Something funny?"

She reached across the table and patted his hand. "Oh no. The evening was marvelous, Pierre. And the company, especially the company, was superb." She smiled. "It's all been lovely. Thank you."

He smiled at her response, then raised his glass. "To a lovely evening."

"To a lovely evening, Pierre."

Their glasses met over the table. "Diane, I've been thinking," he said, reaching across the table, taking her hand, "about our future."

"About our future?" Her voice came out in a squeak.

He pressed a small velvet box into her palm and gently closed her fingers over it. This he did without his eyes leaving hers. She swallowed hard and looked down.

"Open it," he urged.

"Pierre . . . I . . . I can't." She shook her head, then met his hopeful gaze and melted. She gave him a gentle smile, then flipped open the lid . . . and gaped. Sparkling in the candlelight was the largest diamond she had ever seen. It had to be the size of a quarter, she thought at first glance. She blinked and gazed at it. More realistically, it was the size of a dime. Her heart thudded, which surprised her.

"I had it designed especially for you by my personal jeweler in New York." He took her hand and looked into her eyes. "I have been looking forward to this night for years, Diane."

She was speechless. "I don't know what to say."

"Ah, but that is easy," he said. "Say only that you will marry me, that you are ready to become Mrs. Pierre Rochembeau."

Her mind raced, searching for the right words. She liked Pierre. She enjoyed his company. But was this enough of a reason to spend the rest of her life with him? "Pierre, this is happening too fast."

"Too fast?" His light laughter brimmed with affection. "I have loved you since the day I first saw you. Now tell me what I must do to persuade you to slip the diamond onto your lovely finger."

She considered him. Pierre was always there for her. How could she say no?

"Still thinking it over, are you?" Pierre sighed. "Very well, then I see I must employ phase two of my strategy." He stood, smiling.

"What are you doing?"

Without answering, he walked over to her side of the table, dropped to his knees, and took her hand.

"Pierre, you don't have to do this," she whispered.

"What kind of Frenchman would I be if I proposed from any position other than my knees?"

"But, Pierre . . ."

"And now, Lieutenant Diane Elizabeth Jefferson Colcernian, United States Navy, I, Pierre Rochembeau, of Paris, France, and New York, New York, come to you on my knees, with the utmost humility in every fiber of my being, and do this night ask you the question of questions." He paused, longing in his gaze. "Will you, Diane, become Mrs. Diane Colcernian Rochembeau? Will you marry me?"

She held her breath, and for a moment it seemed everyone in the room held theirs with her. Then the entire restaurant broke into applause in response to Pierre's impassioned plea.

"You go, girl!" called a woman's voice from a few tables over.

"I'll take him if you don't," said a younger-sounding woman.

"You gotta say yes after that!" This was a man's voice in the midst of the applause.

Then silence fell. Diane couldn't see the other patrons, but she felt their stares. It was like being the lone woman left on some reality show. If only she could cut to a commercial and run off. But she couldn't. She had to give some sort of answer. She drew in a deep breath.

Pierre was still kneeling before her, his face so full of affection and expectancy, it nearly broke her heart. How could she say no in front of all these people?

She leaned toward him, so close their foreheads almost touched. "Pierre, I need time . . . please?" She thought she might cry.

With an almost imperceptible nod, he took her hand and squeezed it. Then standing, he looked out at the patrons, barely visible in the dim light. "She said yes!" There was more applause, and the violinist started playing the "Wedding March."

He lowered himself into his chair, smiling at her. "Forgive me, darling. It was the only way to settle them down."

It was so like him to save them both from embarrassment. She reached for his hand, a wave of affection sweeping over her. "But you're still willing to give me time?"

"I will wait forever." He squeezed her fingers.

She had the prickly sense that someone was watching her. From the corner of her eye, she caught sight of two figures in a doorway. She turned her head. Zack stood there, at the entrance to the dining room, his client at his side. Zack's gaze met Diane's; then he turned away, shepherding Marianne Landrieu to the restaurant's front door.

Coronado Bay Bridge
Coronado, California

2215 hours (PST)

Speeding southbound along Interstate 5, with the lights of the residential and business areas just north of downtown San Diego whizzing by to his right, Zack tapped his brakes and clicked his right signal light at the Coronado Bridge exit. A moment later, they reached the base of the huge, curving bridge spanning San Diego Bay.

Along with the summits of Mount Helix and Mount Soledad, and the Cabrillo National Monument, the crest of the Coronado Bay Bridge at night was one of the most spectacular places to take in a panoramic view of San Diego. The reflection of light from the waterfront high-rises glistened against the black waters of the bay.

Unlike Helix, Soledad, and Cabrillo, the glimpse from up here at night was brief. Then it was gone. He always felt cheated. There was never a night that he crossed the bridge and wasn't left wanting more.

Tonight was no exception.

This late at night on a weekend, the traffic was about as light as it would ever get on the bridge. Zack pulled the Mercedes into the far right lane as the car crossed onto the bridge from the San Diego side headed across. When he pulled his foot off the accelerator, he watched the speedometer drop: 55 mph ... 45 ... 35 ... 25. He hit cruise control, then his flasher lights. He hoped he wouldn't get ticketed or rammed from behind.

"Trying to prolong the evening?" Marianne asked as the car slowed and started heading up the slope spanning the bay.

It was the last thing he expected her to say. He glanced across at her. She smiled and gave him a dreamy look while she toyed with a strand of her blond hair draped on her tan shoulder. Her intent was clear.

He pressed the accelerator. The car was about halfway up the bridge. "Look over there," he said, hoping to distract her. He nodded toward the downtown lights as the car crested the top of the span.

She moved closer, gazing up at him. "It is beautiful," she said without looking at the view. "There's nothing in Louisiana like this. I could stay in San Diego forever."

"I've gotta get you home," he said, pressing the accelerator closer to the floor.

Five minutes later, he parked the car on the street beside the curb in front of her house in Coronado. She was still gazing at him.

Zack took a breath. "I'll walk you to the door."

"I thought you'd never offer." She moved to the passenger-side door to wait for him. Zack opened her door and with his hand gently guided her through the gate, which seemed almost florescent under the glow of the full moon. The sound of the gentle swells from the Pacific lapping the beach just down the street, combined with the cool breeze coming off the ocean, made him want to go find a hammock somewhere. Alone.

As they stepped onto the brick walkway, he felt her arm slip around his waist, her body nudge close to his. Her steps toward the house slowed.

She turned, facing him as they approached the front steps, slipping both her hands behind his waist. "Want to come in? I won't tell if you don't," she said, her eyes glowing in the moonlight.

He inhaled deeply, reached for her hands, and gently backed away. "You need a friend right now. Nothing more."

She stared at him, eyes narrowed as if angry at the rebuff. "Okay, I get it," she finally said, nodding slowly. "I've had a great time. Thank you."

"Good night, Marianne," he said.

As Zack drove away, it wasn't Marianne who occupied his thoughts. It was the image of Pierre Rochembeau declaring to the world that Diane had said yes to his proposal of marriage.

CHAPTER 18

Arlington National Cemetery
Arlington, Virginia

It was a long walk, maybe a quarter of a mile up the hill, along the cart way to the grave site. Captain David Guy stayed a few yards behind the family. In front of the family, six horses drew the caisson bearing the flag-draped casket toward the empty grave. There was little noise except for the *clop-clop* of the hooves on the pavement. When they reached the site, just up the hill from the tomb of President John F. Kennedy, a cool breeze rolled from the river, providing a nice respite from the summer heat.

This would be a short ceremony, David knew, as most of the good-byes and the eulogies had been spoken in Norfolk's Grace Episcopal Church yesterday. Still, it was an important ceremony, a privilege afforded Commander Latcher and his family.

"Attention on deck!" The executive officer, now the acting commanding officer of Strike Fighter Squadron 115, called the command from the grassy knoll.

From the direction of the honor guard, David saw the national colors and the Navy flag flapping in the increasing breeze as the family filed into the two rows of aluminum folding chairs and seated themselves.

The Navy chaplain, a lieutenant commander dressed in summer whites, took his place near the casket. "To Mary, Mary Blake, Beth, and Wesley," he said, his gaze on the family. "To the family members and friends of Commander Mark Latcher who are here today, to the members of Strike Fighter Squadron 115 . . ." He paused. ". . . we come here now, in this beautiful setting, on this the most hallowed ground of our great nation, to say good-bye to a husband, to a father, to a leader, to a friend.

"But to those who loved Commander Latcher, to those who served under him, to those who long to see him again, take to heart this irrefutable truth. Mark Latcher not only served his country, but even more importantly, he served his Lord. He made Jesus Christ, the risen, living Son of God, the Lord and Savior of his life.

"Jesus said to the thief on the cross, 'Today you will be with me in paradise.' In addition, the Bible says that when we who know him depart from the body, we are immediately in the presence of the Lord. And we know, based on his assurances, that today Mark Latcher is in the glorious presence of our living Lord.

"And so, in these last few moments on this gorgeous hillside, the resting place of presidents, and supreme court justices, and ambassadors, and thousands of men and women who, like Commander Mark Latcher, have sacrificed their lives for freedom, we take hold of the promises of our Savior. In his promises, there is hope. In his promises, there is truth. For he is the way, and the truth, and the life. Amen."

"Forward march!"

Six white-uniformed petty officers, all members of VFA-115, quietly marched in two columns of three on each side of the casket covered by the American flag. They lifted the casket, positioned it on their shoulders, and carried it, in perfect step, to the steel retractable platform over the grave, where they reverently placed it.

"Present arms!"

Captain Guy and the other uniformed servicemen at the grave snapped a last sharp salute at the casket and held it as three rifle shots from the Navy honor guard, fired at five-second intervals, echoed off the marble grave sites. A trumpeter, standing at the head of the fallen officer's grave, began to play taps.

With the military now in control of the waning moments of Mark Latcher's funeral, David glanced into the tear-streaked face of the widow. A young lieutenant, a naval aviator type, knelt on one knee just in front of her.

"Ma'am, the president of the United States presents this to you on behalf of a grateful nation."

In Mary Latcher's lap, the officer placed the American flag that had draped Mark's coffin.

"Captain?" David felt a tap on his right shoulder board from behind. He turned. It was Harry Kilnap, the NCIS agent, standing behind him. "Beautiful service," Kilnap said.

"It was, considering," David said. "I didn't expect you here."

"Sometimes murderers show up at the grave. Just wanted to check things out. You know. See if any suspicious characters are lingering about."

"Do you see anything suspicious?"

Kilnap turned his head, surveying the receiving line, the casket, and the family members, who were mostly still seated. "Not really. Looks pretty normal."

"Hope it wasn't a wasted trip."

"Captain Guy, we need to talk."

"Now?"

"Soon. Today. How about dinner?"

"I'd planned to grill a steak out in my backyard."

"Skipper, this is real important. I've reviewed the manifest list from VFA-115. I may be on to something here. I need your help, though. Fast. Tell you what, there's a great pub over on Massachusetts Avenue in Georgetown. Good Ole Days, I think it's called. You show; I'll buy."

David sighed as visions of his steak disappeared. "Okay, Harry. See you then."

CHAPTER 19

Captain Richard Reeves, JAGC, USN, was alone inside the senior judge's chambers on the first floor of the building. The afternoon sunlight streamed through the windows, and Reeves was feeling relaxed, having just changed from his summer white uniform into his more comfortable and informal working khakis. Reeves checked the wall clock.

Fifteen hundred hours.

The judge was done with court for the day, and in one hour, he had a tee time at the North Island Naval Golf Course against a four-striper who had taken fifty bucks off him last week when Reeves bogied on the eighteenth.

No bogies today, Reeves thought. He grabbed a putter from the golf bag propped in the corner of the office, dropped three white balls on the putting mat behind his desk, then tapped the first ball into a plastic cup five feet away.

The telephone buzzed as the putter made contact with the second ball, breaking Reeves's concentration and causing it to rim around the outside of the cup before resting on the green carpet.

I knew I should have bolted out of here, Reeves thought as the voice of his command master chief announced that the judge advocate general of the Navy was on the phone from Washington.

"I'll take it." Reeves dropped the putter back in the bag, then picked up the phone and punched line one. "This is Captain Reeves."

"Admiral Stumbaugh here. I know it's almost tee time out there, but we've got a high-profile case I need you to handle."

"Yes, sir." Reeves checked his watch and sat down.

"This case requires special sensitivity. This is a rape, and the victim is an officer. Not just any officer," he continued. "Her uncle is U.S. Senator Roberson Fowler."

Reeves exhaled. "Pinkie Fowler. Armed Services Committee."

"Look, Dickie. I know that with retirement around the corner you've been assigning a lot of your contested general courts-martial to some of the other judges, and that's fine. Those guys are competing for captain. But in this case, I don't want you to assign this one to a commander. I want you to keep this case yourself."

"Aye, sir."

"You're my best, most experienced judge, Captain. Roberson Fowler's money means billions of dollars to the Navy. The secretary of the Navy wants this handled right."

"Yes, sir."

"Good. Then it's settled. The case should be referred over from Trial Command soon." The admiral paused. "You understand its priority?"

"Yes, sir." The judge checked his watch again. So much for his golf game.

Trial counsel offices
32nd Street Naval Station
San Diego

Friday, August 1, trial day

Zack Brewer had been in his office at the Navy Trial Command working all morning on last-minute preparations for trial. Amy DeBenedetto had been working with him since sunrise, helping him organize exhibits and paperwork. Zack, sitting behind his desk, leaned back in his chair and looked at his watch. *Thirty minutes until jury selection.*

"Okay, Amy, let's hit the checklist again." He glanced at the scribbled list on the white legal pad.

"Yes, sir." Her response was cool, detached.

He glanced up, giving her a quizzical look, but she didn't meet his gaze. "Members' questionnaires?"

"In the first folder, sir."

"Chain-of-custody documentation?"

"Documentation for crime-scene evidence taken is in folder two. Docs for evidence taken at Balboa Naval Hospital, including rape kit results, in folder three. DNA test results are in folder four."

"Excellent." He marked blue checks in the left column on the white paper. "Is NCIS on standby?"

"Yes, sir. I confirmed this morning. They will meet us just before 1400 hours in front of Courtroom 1. They've got the physical evidence and photos of Ensign Landrieu taken at the scene. Also, I spoke to the NCIS crime lab. Doctor Purcell is on standby when we need him. He says he'll need about thirty minutes' advance notice."

"Ensign Landrieu on standby?" There was no point in bringing Marianne Landrieu into the courthouse until she was ready to testify, which would probably be tomorrow.

"Yes, sir." Amy let her gaze drift to the window behind his desk. She seemed troubled.

"What is it?"

"Permission to speak freely?"

"Of course."

"It's Ensign Landrieu, sir."

He wasn't surprised. Amy had voiced her concerns before. "Okay. What about her?"

"I've already told you my doubts about the rape, that the ensign doesn't act like any of the other rape victims we've seen." Silence followed. When he didn't respond, she sighed. "You don't seem concerned."

"She's an officer. None of our other victims were officers, let alone Academy grads who happened to be related to powerful members of the U.S. Senate."

She turned, piercing him with those honest blue eyes. The gold cross she always wore caught the light. "Yes, sir. But you know that's not what I mean."

The uneasiness that had nagged at him for days crept into his consciousness again. Just as quickly, he needed to banish it. He had his orders. The evidence was clear. He didn't want to think about a false accusation. Not now. He had to believe Marianne was telling the truth. No matter her personal problems, she had been assaulted. And he planned to see that the perpetrator paid.

He looked at his watch. "We're getting short on time. If there's something about Ensign Landrieu I need to know, you've got tell me now," he said in a calm but firm voice. She seemed reluctant to continue, so he adopted a more encouraging tone. "Look, you've hinted at all this before. What else are you thinking?"

"Her reaction seems so different from the other victims. All the others cried and shook every time they came in our offices, right up to the date of trial. I know Ensign Landrieu has shown *some* emotion about it all. She cried some the first time you asked her about it. But half the time when she arrives here, she seems, well, somehow . . . eager."

He met her troubled gaze. "Have you forgotten about the torn clothing? And the way she was crying when shore patrol found her?"

"I've thought about that. But is it possible things started one way and just got out of hand?" Her cheeks flushed.

"You think she led him on?"

Her tone became bolder. "Just because the military prohibits officer-enlisted relationships, that doesn't always stop the attraction. Maybe she felt an attraction for him and then changed her mind after."

He rocked back in his chair. "Suppose, for the sake of argument, you're correct. What if there was an attraction there? But suppose she changed her mind—said no. But suppose he did not change his mind. That would still be rape, wouldn't it? The law is clear: a woman has the right to say no."

She nodded.

"Look, Amy. Here's what we know. We've got a victim who claims she was raped. Okay, so maybe her demeanor *is* a little different from the others. But consider this: soldiers in combat have often experienced delayed post-traumatic stress disorder. Years, even, after the fact. The same could be true of a rape victim. Maybe Ensign Landrieu hasn't felt the full effects of PTSD yet.

"All I know is that we've got a job to do. We'll put on our case, let Lieutenant Colcernian do her best to raise a defense, and then let the chips fall where they may. Who knows? Maybe Diane the Doberman will finally beat me." He chuckled aloud at the thought. "Anyway, our job is to do our duty and place this in the hands of the members."

"Diane the Doberman?" Amy laughed, then gave a quick fisted jab in the air. "Ready for battle."

Zack stood up and tucked the file folder and legal pad under his arm.

She scooted back her chair and stood with him. "Thank you for the convincing argument about the legalities."

But as they walked through the door, Zack couldn't get away from one annoying thought: *If it's such a good argument, why am I not convinced?*

CHAPTER 20

Good Ole Days Tavern
Massachusetts Avenue
Georgetown, Washington, D.C.

Not much had changed about Georgetown in the last fifteen years. Captain David Guy piloted the Crown Victoria from Arlington across the Francis Scott Key Bridge, only to be slowed by crawling, bumper-to-bumper traffic as the bridge funneled into M Street on the D.C. side of the Potomac.

Rush hour in Washington in the summer. A huge parking lot of horn-honking automobiles and exhaust fumes rising off hot asphalt. David glanced at his watch. Whatever Kilnap had for him had better be worth it.

Thirty minutes later, he arrived at Good Ole Days. It was a dark, smoky, narrow tavern with booths on both sides, separated by a narrow aisle heading to the back. The bar sported a 1950s and 1960s motif, with Elvis Presley's "Love me Tender" playing in the background.

A young hostess in a "Georgetown Hoyas" T-shirt and white shorts met him at the door. "May I help you, sir?"

"I'm meeting a Mr. Kilnap. He may already be here," David said.

She nodded. "Last booth on your right."

As his eyes adjusted to the dim lighting, David found Kilnap, sitting at a wooden booth at the far end of the bar.

"Why in the world did you pick this place?" David sat down opposite the veteran NCIS agent.

"Helps me think. Fifties nostalgia and all that. Plus it's one of the few bars in the district where fine cigar smoking is still allowed."

David saw a freshly lit Macanudo, at least seven inches long, occupying the ashtray in front of Kilnap.

"Beer?"

"No thanks."

"How about a Macanudo? I've got some fifteen-dollar sticks in my briefcase." Kilnap lifted the giant stogie and inhaled, causing the lit end to glow like Rudolph's nose on Christmas Eve.

"Thanks, Harry, but I quit smoking years ago," David said, coughing.

"Captain Guy, surely you can indulge in *some* decadent pleasure with a worn-out, nearly retired NCIS agent." Kilnap chuckled and then took another puff.

"Okay, you got me, Harry. You can order a cheeseburger and pick up the parking tab for a worn-out, almost-retired Navy JAG officer."

Kilnap smirked. "You've got a deal on the cheeseburger anyway." Then he motioned to a waitress.

When she left, David frowned at Kilnap. "So what is it NCIS has that's so important I'm in a smoke-filled tavern on a Friday afternoon instead of grilling a filet mignon on my back deck?"

Kilnap retrieved a three-page stapled document from his briefcase and slid it across the table. "Take a look at this, Captain."

"Looks like a list of names of all personnel assigned to Latcher's squadron."

"Precisely." Kilnap took another draw from the cigar. "So take a look at the list and tell me if anything, or *anyone*, jumps out."

David examined the list again, then looked back up at Kilnap. "What are you driving at, Harry? I don't see anything unusual."

Kilnap's grin was pure self-satisfaction. "Okay, here's the rundown on VFA-115. See anything funny?"

David glanced at the list again. "Harry, Georgetown isn't exactly my favorite place in Washington. I know you didn't bring me all the way over here just to show me a list of names you could have shown me in my office Monday morning."

"Captain, you disappoint me. Now I'll give you a hint." He played the pause for all it was worth. "This is a list of all squadron members with access to Commander Latcher's jet between his last successful landing, at 1600 hours on Wednesday, and his last takeoff Friday morning."

David waited as the waitress slid two plates of cheeseburgers and piping hot French fries on the table in front of them. "The flight manifest seems like a logical place to start." He scanned the list. "I count sixteen names here. It's a start anyway, assuming the device was planted by active-duty personnel."

"Correct, Captain. And I'm not playing games, but I want your feedback here. Check the list again and tell me if you see anything that helps narrow down those names."

David sipped his sweetened tea as he studied the names. "If I were going to narrow the list, I'd start with the two aviation ordinancemen on the theory that they have the expertise in explosives, and given expertise, they have the best technical capabilities to pull something like this off."

"Very good, Captain." Kilnap crossed his arms over his belly and grinned. "And we *will* interview both of them. Problem is, I've checked their psychological profiles, and I'd be shocked if either were involved."

"Why's that?"

"Stable family men." A swig of beer. "Wives. Each with three kids. Solid church members. Both were close to Commander Latcher. No axes to grind. Where would you go next?"

"Okay. Next I would look at the two aviation structural mechanics, again on the theory that they have the greatest knowledge of how to bring the plane down."

"Bingo." Harry chomped a hole from the circumference of the whopping burger. "Anything else jump out?"

David looked again. "Not really. Something I'm missing?" He took a bite of his cheeseburger.

"Remember the nut with the grenades out in San Diego a few weeks back?"

"A boiler tech, wasn't it? Went crazy with some grenades inside the church."

"Actually, it was a gunner's mate," Kilnap said, "but yeah, you've got the right guy."

"So what's that got to do with this?"

"First, another question," Kilnap said.

"Fire." He grabbed a few fries.

Kilnap doused the cigar, pulled out another, clipped the end, then ignited his Zippo lighter. "Think about the Marine that shot the Israeli ambassador at Pendleton." He sat back, narrowed his eyes, and took his first puff from the new stogie.

"What about him?"

"First thing is the timing. The Israeli ambassador was shot within a week of the incident in San Diego."

"So?"

"So you have two major incidents of violence, performed by members of the naval service, and both by Muslim service members."

"Both of whom, if I recall correctly," David added, "committed suicide during the acts."

"Bingo." Kilnap leaned back, almost slumping in his chair, then flicked ashes into the ashtray.

David raised his eyebrow. "Harry, I guess I'm having a slow day."

"Look at the names of the mechanics again."

He glanced down again. *Al-Aziz, Sulayman, El Paso, TX.* "So we have someone with a Muslim name on the ground crew. But you've just pointed out some drastic differences between the West Coast incidents and the downed jet. Both those guys on the West Coast killed themselves. Jihad, or whatever they call it. No suicide here. At least I presume this al-Aziz guy is still around."

"Right," Kilnap said.

"Plus both of those incidents, as you pointed out, were on the West Coast. Not to mention that those attacks were on civilians or foreign dignitaries. This attack was against our own military." David slid the list back across the table.

"All true, Captain. But remember. No two crimes, even when linked, are ever exactly the same. And here we have two factors that in my judgment override the differences you mentioned."

"I'm listening," David said.

"One: timing, as I mentioned before. The attack on our plane was one week after the attack on the ambassador, so there is a close connection in time." He took another draw from the cigar. "Two: religion. Not only are all three suspects Muslim, but the targets of the attacks were, in the eyes of some people at least, anti-Muslim. In San Diego, the pastor at that church was teaching a course advertised in the paper, calling the Muslim religion a cult. At Pendleton, the target was the Israeli ambassador, for heaven's sake."

He flicked more smoldering ashes into the nearly full ashtray, then took a big swig of beer. "Here, everybody knows that the squadron—and that jet—was headed to the Med to defend Israel against Arab forces. And that gets spun by radical Islamic groups to mean the U.S. is once again defending Jewish Israel against Muslim Syria, or Muslim Egypt or Muslim Jordan or whatever Arab state is involved."

David thoughtfully considered the agent's words. "Okay, Harry. I still think it's a stretch based on what we know right now, but I see where you're going with this. What I don't see is why this couldn't have waited until Monday."

"Because I need your help, Captain. And I need it this weekend." He leaned forward.

"Shoot."

"A search warrant."

"Excuse me?"

"Al-Aziz lives off base. I need your connections through the U.S. attorney's office in Norfolk to get me a warrant to search al-Aziz's apartment. Over the weekend. The sooner the better. I want to get in there before evidence disappears."

"What kind of evidence?"

"Obvious stuff. Plastics. Materials used in bomb preparation. Notes. Anything."

"Harry, we don't have enough for a warrant. We'd have to persuade a federal magistrate to issue a search warrant based on probable cause that a crime has been committed. What are you going to do? Ask him to sign an affidavit because the guy is Muslim? I can't go to the U.S. attorney with that."

"What about the coincidences? Captain, we've got to try. I'll sign the affidavit. I'll outline the connections. Who knows, we might get lucky."

"And even if we get a warrant from a magistrate, and find something, and get a conviction, we still run the risk that the evidence, and then the case, gets thrown out by an appeals court for lack of probable cause."

"So what, Captain? If this guy is the bomber, maybe he's planning to attack another plane. Maybe we can save the lives of other American pilots."

David considered the request as images of Mark Latcher's grieving family flashed through his mind. "Okay. We'll try. I'll advise the admiral and call our JAG officer assigned to the U.S. attorney's office. We'll try to see the federal magistrate tomorrow. But I can't promise anything."

"Thanks, Captain." Kilnap nodded and drained his beer.

CHAPTER 21

Friday afternoon, 1630 hours (PST)

Zack watched the Honorable Captain Richard Reeves, dressed in short-sleeve summer whites, take his place on the bench between the respective flags of the United States of America and the United States Navy. The judge tilted his head down toward the prosecutor's table, peering through his wire rims.

"What happened here, Trial Counsel?" Only Judge Reeves could deliver that devastatingly soft, monotone inquiry. That voice, combined with the icy stare, was far worse than any dressing down Zack had ever endured from more vocal judges.

Zack wanted to slam his fist on the table. He'd tried that before with another military judge and was nearly thrown in the brig for contempt. All his diligent preparation for the biggest trial of his career, and now this.

Amy *never* made mistakes. He glanced toward her and saw her hands trembling. She whispered, "Sorry," then looked at the floor.

She'd been far more than a military subordinate to him. He'd sensed she was a Christian. In the well-placed though subtle remarks she made about praying for him. In the gentle, soft spirit she carried with her. She wasn't talkative about her faith around the office, but she kept a small New Testament open on the corner of her small working cubicle at all times.

He'd always figured her faith was part of what made Amy so meticulous in her work. And now . . . this. One of the military jurors, known as a "member" in the military justice system, was absent and unaccounted for. It was the prosecutor's responsibility to make sure all members were present. Zack had delegated the responsibility to Amy. Clearly, something had gone wrong.

"Lieutenant?"

Zack rose to his feet. "Your Honor, my deepest apologies to the court, the counsel, and the members already present. We've had an administrative snafu in my offices for which I take full responsibility. The government requests a brief recess to locate the missing member and have him transported here."

"Lieutenant Colcernian?" Judge Reeves glanced at Diane and raised his eyebrow. She jumped to her feet.

"We object, Your Honor. My client has been incarcerated in the brig and has a constitutional right to a speedy trial. I'm going—"

Reeves raised his hand, then turned back to Brewer.

"You've got one hour, Trial Counsel, to straighten this out. Otherwise, I'll give Lieutenant Colcernian the opportunity to make whatever motion she would like. Including a possible motion to dismiss for failure to prosecute. This court is in recess for one hour." The single *whap* of the captain's gavel sounded like a rifle shot reverberating through the courtroom.

Ninety minutes later, the last missing juror, a lieutenant commander supply officer from the USS *Inchon*, marched into the courthouse and reported for duty.

"All rise!"

"Be seated." Captain Reeves fixed a piercing gaze on Zack. "Lieutenant Brewer, I understand you now have all members accounted for?"

"Yes, Your Honor. Lieutenant Commander Emerson just arrived from the USS *Inchon*. Additionally, all member questionnaires are accounted for. I've supplied copies to Lieutenant Colcernian and to the court."

"And what time did Lieutenant Commander Emerson report for duty?"

"Two minutes ago, Your Honor." This was Diane Colcernian's eager voice.

"Is that time right, Trial Counsel?" Judge Reeves pinned Zack with a look.

"That is correct, Your Honor."

Captain Reeves turned around and ceremoniously glared at the large, gold-laden clock on the wall behind the bench. Then he turned his gaze back to the gallery. "The record should reflect that the last of the members has reported for this case one and one-half hours after the pre-scribed time of 1400 hours.

"Military justice protocol requires that the government, through the convening authority, in this case COMNAVBASE, and through trial coun-sel, in this case Lieutenant Brewer, must have all members present and accounted for at the appropriate time.

"An hour and a half ago, I gave the government one hour to correct its 'snafu,' as I believe trial counsel called it. While the government has corrected its mistake, it has failed to do so within the prescribed time allowed by the court. Therefore, at this time, the court will entertain any motions that the defense may wish to make. Lieutenant Colcernian?"

He's not really going to do this, is he? Zack's heart jackhammered inside his chest as his redheaded opponent jumped to her feet, cut her green eyes at him, threw him a quick smirk, then addressed the court.

"Your Honor, the defense moves to dismiss all charges and specifi-cations against Petty Officer Blount."

The judge frowned. "Grounds?"

"Not only is Petty Officer Blount entitled to a speedy trial under the Constitution, but he's entitled to an even more stringent right to a speedy trial under the Uniform Code of Military Justice." Diane jabbed her right index finger in the air. "The government had plenty of notifi-cation by the court about today's start time. Not only has the delay sub-jected my client to additional incarceration as a result of the government's ineptitude, but now I am at a severe disadvantage because I've just received the questionnaires and haven't been able to study them.

"And at this late hour, unless the court begins this case over the weekend, either I won't have enough time to study the questionnaires, or my client will have to sit another two and a half days in the brig."

Colcernian seemed altogether too pleased with herself. "Your Honor, there's a good reason we don't play around with speedy trial issues in the military. It's called operational readiness. Our forces must be ready for movement at a moment's notice when called on by the president. These other officers who have been selected to serve as members will now be delayed for hours, perhaps a couple of days, from returning to their duties because of the government's inexcusable mess-up here. What if war breaks out over the weekend?"

The question brought the judge's attention back to Zack, with yet another raised eyebrow. "Lieutenant Brewer?"

Zack rose to his feet. "Your Honor, Petty Officer Blount is accused of rape. Lieutenant Colcernian raises a lot of hypotheticals here. What if we go to war over the weekend? Where did that come from? Of course, in the event of a national emergency, it might be necessary to relieve some of the members of their duties here. But there's also a legitimate need—a paramount need—to maintain good order and discipline in the military. We cannot have a military in which an enlisted man commits a crime against an officer then gets away with it because an administrative foul-up causes a ninety-minute delay."

He studied the judge's impatient expression. He took a deep breath. "The technical test under the UCMJ is whether the accused has been confined for more than ninety days. Today is day eighty-nine. Earlier today, Petty Officer Blount was arraigned. He pled not guilty. That stopped the speedy trial clock. The government is ready to go to trial," he said with a finger jab, "and right now."

He glanced at his opponent, whose expression was unreadable, then looked back to the judge. "We can give Lieutenant Colcernian a few hours to study her questionnaires. We've got our witnesses lined up, and we're prepared to try this case over the weekend, since Lieutenant Colcernian is so concerned about operational readiness. We can work tonight, tomorrow, and Sunday, as far as I'm concerned, and have these officers back to their posts early in the week." He was tempted to shoot Colcernian a smug look of triumph, but resisted.

Judge Reeves leaned back in his big, black leather executive rocker, studied his watch, then looked at Diane. "Lieutenant Colcernian, Lieutenant Brewer says he's willing to give you tonight to study those questionnaires and then start this case tomorrow morning. Does your client really want to start this trial on a Saturday morning?"

Zack looked at Diane, reciprocating the smirk she laid on him a few moments ago. "Your Honor, for the record, we object to the process, but no, we are not suggesting the trial begin tomorrow. I'm concerned that Petty Officer Blount may get the blame for taking these members away from whatever weekend activities they may have."

"Very well," Reeves said. "Do you have any other pretrial motions?"

"No, Your Honor, not at this time."

Zack sat up and took notice. *No other pretrial motions?*

"Then we will reconvene at 0900 on Monday morning, when we will swear the members and proceed with opening statements. This court is in recess." He slammed the gavel.

The bailiff again said loudly, "All rise."

As he gathered his files, Zack couldn't resist glancing at Diane. She gave him another haughty, raised-eyebrow smirk and turned away.

Thirty minutes later, Captain Dick Reeves blasted a small white ball off the first tee at the North Island Naval Station Golf Course.

CHAPTER 22

Barnes & Noble
Grossmont Center
La Mesa, California

Three hours later

Zack headed to his favorite off-duty hangout, the Barnes & Noble book-store in La Mesa, near the small, stucco house he had purchased using his VA loan eligibility three years ago.

As he stood in line to order his Starbucks coffee, he thought about his conversation with Amy. She had been such an emotional wreck this afternoon that he had actually felt guilty even though she was the one who messed up.

No, it had not been a good day for Legalman First Class Amy DeBenedetto.

Technically, he could have reprimanded her or even worse, recom-mended captain's mast for the flub. Maybe even busted her a stripe for dereliction of duty. Some bosses would have pressed the issue.

But he couldn't do it. Not for one mistake—albeit a highly embar-rassing one. Not after all she had done for him for the past two years. And especially not after the uncontrollable cascade of tears that started the moment they stepped outside the courthouse.

Besides, he had observed, more than once, her forgiveness of oth-ers, her generous, giving heart, her willingness to go the extra mile . . . her acting out of her faith. Also, more than once, he'd felt guilty that his own faith wasn't very often evident to others. Zack thought of this often, how he had been raised by his grandmother, a sweet woman who had bathed him in prayer from the moment he was born until the day she died. The positive things in his life—his passing two bar exams, winning his law school's moot court championship, then winning the Navy Justice School's trial advocacy competition—were all blessings from God, he knew.

He felt, even years after her death, that God's blessings were on him still, the result in part of the thousands of prayers she had offered on his behalf when she was alive. There were prayers she had rendered even when she was crippled and on her deathbed. Still, in his professional life, he had sometimes slipped away from the faith. How could he have let her down like that? More important, how could he have let down God?

Amy, in one sense, filled the role in his life that his grandmother once had. Her very presence was a check on his conscience, reminding him that Christians can't survive without prayer and daily doses of God's Word. Funny thing was, Amy was able to accomplish this without saying a word about it to Zack. Her prayers and his appointment to this case had stirred him back to daily Scripture study and prayer.

"May I help you, sir?" A young woman behind the coffee counter smiled at him.

"Regular coffee, please."

"Should I leave room for cream?"

"No thanks. Black to the rim." He slid a dollar bill across the counter, fidgeted in his pocket for three quarters, handed them to the girl, then wrapped his fingers around the warm, medium-sized cup, blowing lightly against the hot, roasted brew before taking a sip.

After a couple of sips of the high-octane Brazilian brew, Zack meandered over to the biographies section. One book caught his eye as he walked in the store, and he spotted it again.

Several dozen fresh, glossy hardback editions were prominently displayed. And just behind the slick display, and by no coincidence, a colorful poster had been tacked to the column announcing the most recent *New York Times* best-seller list.

Just as he suspected, the book in front of him was listed as number one in the nonfiction column. It was the author's second book, the most recent memoir to reach the pinnacle of the publishing world's most prestigious list.

Intrigued, Zack reached for a copy. Wells Levinson, pictured on the cover in a pink polo shirt, smiled out at the world, showing off his magnificently capped white teeth. He looked to be in his late fifties, tanned, silver-haired.

Zack opened the book and scanned the inside cover.

He's been called the world's greatest trial lawyer. And after his successful defense of Armani Sirhan, who was accused of gunning down New York Congressman Abraham Jacobs in broad daylight, if Wells Levinson is not the greatest trial lawyer in the world, he is certainly the best known. His first memoir, chronicling his not-guilty verdict in the most-watched trial in world history, became the all-time highest seller of nonfiction on the *New York Times* best-seller list.

Now, after *Not Guilty: The Wellington Levinson Story*, the irrepressible Mr. Levinson is back at the top of the publishing charts with *The King of Defense*, a captivating chronicle of his ten most renowned victories. In this spellbinding book, the man who has never lost a jury trial reveals, for the first time, his secret tricks of the trade that have truly made him "The King of Defense."

Zack turned two more pages, then thumbed through chapter headings, stopping at chapter 14.

THE DEFENSE LAWYER'S BEST ALLY
The Element of Surprise

Lie low. Deflate the prosecutor's guard. Pump his ego like an overinflated beach ball. And then, when he thinks your client's conviction will come easier than a hot knife through cold butter, AMBUSH!

This has been a principle hallmark of my strategy for years. And it works. Boy, does it ever!

I start with the premise that litigation is warfare. And whether we are talking Pearl Harbor, Little Big Horn, or the United States District Court for the Southern District of New York, a surprise attack is your best strategy. Ambush is your staunchest ally. Your bag of litigation tricks should be concealed until the last possible moment. A sudden surprise witness the prosecutor has never heard of, a last-minute motion filed with the court—these are the hallmarks of the most effective defense strategy.

Zack closed the book, Diane Colcernian's face dancing through his mind. *She's up to something. I know she is. The motion to dismiss today was Judge Reeves's suggestion. But other than that . . . eerie silence.*

Why no motions in limine? Why no pretrial motions to suppress evidence? It's not like her. What does she have up her sleeve? I bet she's got a copy of this book on her nightstand. She'll spend the weekend envisioning herself as Diane Colcernian "Levinson."

"Lieutenant?"

Zack turned.

"Is there something I can help you with?"

His heart pounding like a jackhammer, Zack's gaze moved from her smiling face to the name tag affixed on her blouse. He exhaled, almost laughing at himself. At the way he'd nearly mistaken the young woman for someone else. At the momentary wave of disappointment that washed over him. "No thank you. Just looking."

"Let me know if there's anything I can do for you." She looked enough like Diane Colcernian to be her first cousin. He stared at her as she walked away, then exhaled again, trying to get his ticker under control.

He looked down at the book in his hand, studying the face on the cover. But it wasn't Levinson he saw.

It was Diane Colcernian.

CHAPTER 23

Harry Kilnap flashed his badge at the U.S. Marine sentry, then drove the government-issued navy blue Ford Taurus through the Oceana Naval Air Station main gate. A few minutes later, he turned the Taurus into the asphalt parking lot just outside VFA-115 headquarters.

Killing the Taurus's headlamps, he drove slowly, creeping through the parking lot at three miles per hour, circling between the rows of parked cars in search of the subject vehicle. About a quarter of the way up the third row, his foot hit the brake pedal.

The light-green Dodge Neon bore a Virginia license number.

MLL-1961
THE OLD DOMINION

From his glove compartment, Harry extracted an index card, on which he had written al-Aziz's license plate number. He flipped on the Taurus's overhead interior dome light and read the card: Virginia tag no. MLL-1961, green Neon, registered to Sulayman al-Aziz.

He checked the tag number again. *Bingo.*

He backed the Taurus into a parking space about fifty feet to the right of the Neon, parked the car, and cut the engine. He pulled on a pair of latex gloves, got out, then walked to al-Aziz's parked vehicle. At a few minutes after four in the morning, he doubted anyone else was in the parking lot, but he glanced around to make sure.

The first step was to pick the lock without setting off the car's alarm. If it did go off, the roar of the jets doing touch-and-goes on the runway a quarter of a mile away would help buffer the shrill sound. If someone heard the alarm and showed up, so what? Kilnap would flash his Federal Agent–NCIS badge, explain that he was in the process of a federal investigation, and that would be that.

Of course, Harry Kilnap wasn't worried about getting into trouble with the shore patrol. After all, the NCIS was the premiere law enforcement agency serving the Navy.

Neither the shore patrol nor the Virginia Beach Police Department—if they could get on base—could mess with him. Those guys were small potatoes. He was a *federal agent*. How he loved rolling those words off his tongue when presenting his identification badge, or announcing his presence, or making an arrest.

The "little boys" of law enforcement would never understand the awesome responsibility vested in the few agents bearing that mantle. The NCIS, the FBI, the CIA. Federal agents were in a league of their own. Harry Kilnap was one of the few, one of the elite.

As he approached the Neon by foot, dressed in dark blue jeans, a black sweatshirt, and a black windbreaker, he felt in his pockets for the picklock. He flipped on the flashlight and pointed it into the Dodge's interior. Two newspapers were strewn in the backseat, a pair of athletic shoes lay on the front floorboard, and a copy of the Qur'an rested on the passenger's seat.

Kilnap turned off the flashlight, then tried the driver's side door handle. It was unlocked. Quickly flipping off the Neon's dome light, he reached over into the backseat and grabbed the two newspapers, copies of the *Virginian Pilot* from different days.

The headline on one edition read "Navy Hornet Goes Down in North Carolina." On the front page of the second paper, in the lower right corner, the header read "Investigation Underway on Downed Super Hornet."

He snapped several flash photographs and then replaced the papers exactly as they had been. Then he opened the Qur'an. The flashlight beam revealed an inscription, handwritten in blue ink, on the inside of the book:

To Sulayman al-Aziz, Allah's servant and warrior,
From Mohammed Reska, LCDR, CC, USN

Kilnap fished a pen from his pocket and wrote on the back of the index card the chaplain's name, rank, and military occupation specialty. Next he photographed the Qur'an and glanced around to see if anyone might have seen the camera's flash go off. The lot was still empty.

He jogged back to the Taurus to get one other item.

It was a small, black, plastic device, maybe two inches long and a half inch wide. Kilnap slipped it under the driver's seat. He then rechecked everything in the car to make sure it was left as he found it. After another glance around the parking lot, he walked back to the Taurus and waited.

And waited.

And as he waited in the Taurus, his eyes glued to the Neon, he nursed a lukewarm cup of black coffee from McDonald's. And he fumed about the past weekend's events and particularly about that liberal judge who refused to issue the search warrant.

As it turned out, Captain David Guy had been right when he had predicted the federal magistrate would deny the search warrant of al-Aziz's apartment. Some garbage about not having "probable cause."

Probable cause was just another fancy phrase some lawyer invented two hundred years ago, which, along with the other Latin phrases bantered about by the esteemed juris doctors of this world, was invented by juris doctors to separate them from good, ordinary, law-abiding citizens. And to get in the way of federal law enforcement.

Lawyers or no lawyers, Special Agent Harry Kilnap would get to the bottom of this.

Two hours later, when the suspect walked out of the hangar at the end of his morning shift, Kilnap was wolfing down the last few bites of a stale Egg McMuffin. He swallowed a big gulp of cool coffee, washing down the wad in his mouth, then rolled down his window, ditched the coffee onto the asphalt, and brought his binoculars to his eyes.

In the dim light of the early morning dawn, he could see several dozen enlisted airmen pouring out the front doors of the hangars onto the asphalt parking lot as they headed to their cars.

He pulled the binoculars back, squinted, rubbed his eyes, then swept the binoculars to the left until he found the light-green Dodge Neon.

He grinned. A swarthy-complexioned petty officer, dressed in blue dungaree uniform jeans, a windbreaker, and a ball cap, opened the driver's side door of the Neon and got in.

A burst of smoke puffed from the Neon's exhaust pipe, quickly followed by the glow of the car's headlights and taillights. Kilnap quickly cranked the Taurus and clicked on the Norfolk Naval Base dispatcher radio.

Showtime.

"Suspect is on the move," he told the NCIS dispatcher. He pulled the Taurus into a double line of outbound traffic on Tomcat Boulevard, three cars back and to the right of the Neon.

"Acknowledged," the voice on the radio crackled back.

Now in slow-moving traffic down the main artery exiting the air station, Kilnap reached over and flipped a switch on the portable model UHF-AR, UHF receiver/recorder on the passenger's seat. This was not a government-issued device. Kilnap had paid for it out of his own wallet. All fifteen hundred bucks of it. For that matter, the NCIS hierarchy didn't even know he had it.

But so what?

If agents could voluntarily upgrade their sidearms, above and beyond the standard 9mm Glock, at their own expense, then why not upgrade other tools of the trade? If spending a few bucks on some high-tech electronic gadgetry would get the job done, Harry Kilnap was willing to do that. He was, after all, a *federal agent*, a professional in every sense of the word.

After a crackle of static, he heard sounds coming from the Neon: the engine revving as al-Aziz pressed the accelerator, the car radio—tuned to an all-news station—playing, and al-Aziz coughing. The ultrasensitive transmitter, now set on channel A, was doing its job.

Kilnap rode the bumper of the Chevy just in front of him, close enough to keep the Muslim's brake lights in view. In this rush-hour traffic, there was no immediate danger that al-Aziz could break loose, at least not until they had cleared the main gate.

As he watched the Neon's brake lights go on again, ten short, distinctive beeps came through the portable UHF receiver. *Someone dialing?*

"Commander Reska . . ." This was al-Aziz's voice.

"Yes, sir. This is Sulayman . . ."

Reska. The same name written in the copy of the Qur'an.

"Yes, sir. I've just gotten off duty . . ."

Harry pulled the index card from his coat pocket.

Reska. I knew it! Kilnap, you're a genius.

"Sir, we must talk." A pause. "I have many questions, sir." Another pause. "Now, if possible, sir . . . The usual place? Shoney's on Dam Neck Road? . . . See you in fifteen minutes, sir."

Harry's pulse raced. He knew the place.

Fifteen minutes later, the sun crested the eastern horizon, casting an occasional blinding reflection in his rearview mirror. Kilnap followed the Neon into the Shoney's parking lot on Dam Neck Road. He parked the Taurus about seventy-five feet away, keeping the subject car in his line of sight. He switched to his binoculars. A moment later, al-Aziz opened the driver's side door, stood up, and scanned the parking lot. He was obviously nervous. He slammed the car door and quickly strode toward the front door of Shoney's.

Kilnap switched the UHF receiver on the front seat from channel A to channel B, then punched the record button for channel B. Shrill static poured out. He turned the volume down, then got out of the car and opened the trunk. The large briefcase in the trunk contained more spy gadgetry—all purchased by Kilnap.

He pulled out three devices: a pen bug, a small, ultrasensitive directional listening device resembling a ballpoint pen, which when pointed in a certain direction could transmit voices up to 230 feet; a calculator bug, an ultrasensitive device that looked like an electronic handheld calculator, but picked up and transmitted noises, particularly the human voice; and a slightly more conspicuous Model B-E "Orbiter Electronic Listening Device." This one was known as the bionic ear and resembled a small black plastic handgun with a small plastic dish at the tip of the barrel. It could pick up a whisper from a hundred yards away, transmitting it to an off-site receiver.

Kilnap set all three devices to transmit to channel B on his receiver, then closed the briefcase, took it from the trunk and walked quickly toward the restaurant. He would survey the situation inside to determine which, if any, of these gadgets would be useful in Shoney's.

Kilnap gave the restaurant a quick visual sweep. Al-Aziz sat alone in the smoking section, halfway between the reception station and the bathroom.

He smiled benignly at the hostess. "I'll seat myself."

A few patrons shuffled back and forth between their booths and the all-you-can-eat breakfast bar. Other than that, the smoking section was mostly empty.

Kilnap selected a booth twenty feet behind and catercorner to al-Aziz.

"Breakfast bar, sir?" An eager young waitress with a topknot ponytail stood by his table.

Serving himself would keep her out of his hair. "Sure."

"Coffee?"

"Black, please. Just leave a pot."

"Comin' right up."

Kilnap fidgeted with the briefcase on the floor under the booth just to the left of his feet. He lifted the specialty pen and pocket calculator out of the case and placed them on the table.

"Here's your coffee." The waitress tossed her ponytail as she set his cup on the table. The pot followed.

"Thanks. Just leave it there." Kilnap waited until she walked away; then he placed the bionic ear on the seat between his left thigh and the wall.

When he looked up, al-Aziz was gone. A quick glance to the bathroom door showed it just closing.

Harry looked over his shoulder quickly.

No sign of the chaplain.

He got up, the pen bug in his hand, walked toward the restroom, then quickly bent down and slid the pen directly under the table where al-Aziz had been sitting. He returned to his booth, took his clean, empty plate, and headed to the breakfast bar.

With his serving spoon in the scrambled eggs and his eyes on the bathroom door, he saw al-Aziz, his cap now removed, come out of the bathroom and return to the same booth.

Kilnap moved past a bowl of hardboiled eggs to a vat of bacon. He'd just picked out his third strip when a dark-complexioned officer, wearing a khaki windbreaker with the gold oak leaves of a lieutenant commander, strode into the restaurant.

Lieutenant Commander Mohammed Reska, I presume.

He dropped one more bacon strip onto his plate as the officer made a beeline to the enlisted airman, gave him a brief bear hug, then sat in the booth across from him.

Kilnap returned to his table, forked his eggs, and sipped his coffee, all the while glancing periodically toward the Muslim chaplain and his follower. At one point, Reska's eyes briefly caught his, which prompted him to head back to the bar for pancakes. From a less auspicious position behind the pancake grill, he saw the two engaged in what looked like a heated discussion.

As Harry doused his cakes with butter and a healthy squirt of maple syrup, al-Aziz stood up, his face contorted, and strode out the door. The chaplain also stood up, threw a five-dollar bill on the table, and walked out.

The whole encounter had lasted less than fifteen minutes.

Kilnap took his plate to the table. He dropped a ten on the table, then causally walked over to the booth that had been occupied by the Muslim tandem. Nothing, except the five-dollar bill and two glasses of water. He sat down where the chaplain had been seated and reached down to check on his pen.

It was still there.

With a smile, he picked it up and put it in his pocket. Then he grabbed his briefcase and left the restaurant.

CHAPTER 24

Navy-Marine Corps Trial Judiciary
32nd Street Naval Station
San Diego

Monday, August 4, 1100 hours (PST)

The Navy jury members sat attentively in the jury box in Courtroom 1 just a few feet to the left of the prosecutor's table where Zack sat in his black swivel chair.

There were nine jurors altogether, six officers and three enlisted, resplendent in their summer white uniforms. Five sat in the lower row, just behind the oak banister above Zack's left shoulder. The other four, plus an alternate, sat in the second row, elevated about a foot above the first row. Just behind the jury box rose a large double window. A few rays of sunlight streamed through at a shallow angle from the late-morning sun, glinting off the rich mahogany walls.

The members had seemed attentive, Zack thought, during the opening phase of the trial. Their eyes had followed him during his opening statement. Some of them winced when he told them how Ensign Marianne Landrieu was overpowered in the parking lot of the Officers' Club by an enlisted Navy SEAL, thrown behind a hedgerow, and brutally assaulted. A couple of the female members had cast menacing glances at the accused.

Several times during his opening statement, he had turned and gestured toward the accused, earning a vicious glare from Diane Colcernian.

Now, as he concluded his opening statement, he walked dramatically around the courtroom, stopped in front of Blount, and stared at him.

"The government will prove, ladies and gentlemen"—he kept his voice commanding, pacing his delivery—"that this man, a man entrusted with the high and prestigious mantle of the most elite fighting force in the world, the Navy SEALs, did, on the night in question, use his strength, his athleticism, his force, and his training to overpower and subdue Ensign Marianne Landrieu, a Naval Academy graduate and a member of the officer corps of the United States Navy.

"We will show"—he spoke in a measured cadence, surveying the members from left to right—"that on the night in question, shortly before midnight, the accused was lurking in the dark shadows of the Officers' Club parking lot at the North Island Naval Station. When Ensign Landrieu left the club, walking to her parked car"—Zack pointed at Blount—"the accused spotted her from his hiding place. Liking what he saw, and seeking to take what was not his, the accused waited until Ensign Landrieu, who was walking unaccompanied to her car, in a dark corner of the parking lot, was perhaps two hundred yards from the nearest human." He paused. "Then, like a predator springing from the dark, he struck."

As he went on to describe the assault, including every brutal detail, he studied the expressions of the members, refusing to let their attention waver for even a split second. As he drew to a close, he let the thunder come into his voice. "This we will prove, ladies and gentlemen. And we will prove beyond a reasonable doubt. Thank you."

His dramatic display drew a quick objection from Diane Colcernian, who complained the statement was overly argumentative. At this point, all eighteen eyes of the members fell on the defendant, their brows furrowed, some looking angry. One member, a female ensign with aviator's wings, had been staring at the accused from the beginning of Zack's opening statement. Blount did not meet the jury's eyes, but kept his eyes on the floor.

Judge Reeves overruled the objection, which in Zack's opinion made Diane look desperate and made her client look even guiltier.

When Diane declined to make an opening statement but reserved the right until the beginning of the defense's case, it was time to present evidence. Zack turned and nodded to Amy DeBenedetto, seated three feet behind the counsel table in a metal folding chair. She inclined her head slightly in return before leaving the courtroom.

Zack rose to his feet. "Your Honor, the United States calls Ensign Marianne Landrieu to the stand."

"Very well." When Amy returned with Marianne Landrieu at her side, the judge inclined his head. "Ensign Landrieu, take the stand and be sworn, please."

Marianne placed her left hand on the Bible, raised her right hand, and was sworn by the bailiff as Zack studied his notes.

"Your witness, Trial Counsel."

"Thank you, Your Honor," Zack said. He stood and walked to the podium, which was positioned between the prosecution and defense tables. He laid his notes and a clean legal pad on the podium.

"State your name, rank, and duty station, please." He spoke softly, trying to put Marianne at ease.

"Ensign Marianne Lynne Landrieu. I'm currently assigned as Deputy Public Affairs Officer for the United States Naval Air Station, North Island, Coronado, California."

"How were you commissioned, Ensign Landrieu?"

Marianne smiled slightly and turned to the members. "By direct appointment upon my graduation from the Naval Academy last May."

As the statement settled, Zack glanced at the president of the panel, a Navy captain who was also an Academy grad, and noticed a slightly raised eyebrow from the four-striper.

"So you've been on active duty just a little over a year?"

"Yes, sir." Marianne looked back at Zack. "I've been on active duty fifteen months, sir."

"Ensign, tell us a little bit about what led to your decision to join the Navy."

Diane jumped to her feet. "Objection! Relevance."

"Overruled," Judge Reeves said. "I'll allow some limited background information on the witness."

"Thank you, Your Honor." Zack knew they were jockeying for the first appearance of favoritism with the military judge. "Ensign Landrieu, I'd asked about your decision to join the Navy."

Marianne turned toward the jury again. "Yes, sir. Military service is a family thing. My father was a naval officer. My uncle works with the armed services in Congress."

"Objection!" Diane was back on her feet.

"Grounds, Lieutenant Colcernian?"

"Relevance, Your Honor." A bit of a whining, pleading tone. "I don't see what her family has to do with this case."

"Lieutenant Colcernian, as you know, it is customary in most trials, and in trials before this court, to allow a limited amount of background information concerning witnesses." Reeves paused, his voice resonating throughout the courtroom. "You, of course, will be allowed to cross-examine this or any other witness on any such background information. Now having said that"—Judge Reeves turned back to Zack—"how much more background information do you intend to elicit, Trial Counsel?"

"Not much, Your Honor. Just a few more questions."

"Very well. The objection is overruled. Move along, Lieutenant Brewer."

"Thank you, Your Honor." Zack nodded to Judge Reeves, then looked back to Marianne. "Ensign Landrieu, before the objection, you'd mentioned that your father was a naval officer?"

"Yes, sir. My dad is a retired surface warfare officer. He spent six years on active duty, on a frigate, and fourteen in the reserve before retiring."

"And you mentioned your uncle?"

"Yes, sir. Uncle Pinkie spent some time on active duty as an intelligence officer."

She was making him draw it out of her like she wasn't overly anxious to reveal the identity of her famous uncle. It was achieving the objective, but it was almost as if she had over-rehearsed. Zack wondered just how long she had practiced her words, her expressions, in front of the mirror. He quickly pushed the thought from his mind.

"And I believe you mentioned your uncle does some work with the armed forces in Congress?"

"Yes, sir, my uncle is on the Armed Services Committee."

"The *Senate* Armed Services Committee?"

"Yes, sir."

Zack could see the jury with his peripheral vision. With that news, a few eyebrows shot up and heads turned. Some members leaned forward, their attention riveted on the witness.

"Do you mind if I ask your uncle's name?"

"Not at all. His name is Roberson Fowler."

"The United States senator?"

"Yes, sir. My uncle was very helpful when I expressed my interest in joining the Navy. He encouraged me to select a naval career."

Zack let the response settle for a minute.

"Ensign Landrieu, I'm sorry to have to bring this up, but I need to ask you some questions about the evening of May twenty-fifth. Is that okay?"

"Yes, sir. I understand."

Office of the Staff Judge Advocate
Commander, U.S. Naval Air Forces
Atlantic Fleet
Oceana Naval Air Station
Virginia Beach, Virginia

Monday, August 4, 1430 hours (EST)

Harry Kilnap paced back and forth in the reception area outside the office of the Staff Judge Advocate, United States Naval Air Forces, Atlantic Fleet, currently occupied by Captain David A. Guy, JAGC, USN.

"Mr. Kilnap, I'm sure Captain Guy will be right back," the secretary said. "He stepped out for coffee. He's never gone for more than ten minutes."

"Try him again on his mobile phone. It's an urgent federal matter."

The secretary, a petite, gray-haired woman, flashed him a perturbed look. Before Harry could respond, Captain David Guy walked through the front door of the reception area with a large cup of black coffee in his hand.

Captain Guy looked surprised. "Harry, what's up?"

"We need to talk."

Captain Guy raised his eyebrow. "Harry, I've got a report due on the admiral's desk in an hour. Is this the same kind of 'urgent' you had in Georgetown?"

"Captain, I admit it was at least somewhat speculative. But this info is smoking-gun urgent. Trust me."

David hesitated, then said to his secretary, "Hold my calls—unless it's the admiral—until further notice."

"Yes, Captain."

"Come in, Harry. This better be good." David motioned Kilnap into his office and closed the door. "Have a seat." Kilnap sat and reached into his briefcase to retrieve the tape recorder as David continued. "So tell me about this smoking gun of yours."

Kilnap slid the black, standard Sony tape recorder onto the center of the JAG officer's desk. "Captain, this is a recording of a conversation between our suspect, Petty Officer Sulayman al-Aziz, and a Muslim U.S. Navy chaplain, a Lieutenant Commander Mohammed Reska."

"I'm listening."

Harry pushed the play button. "The first voice you will hear is Reska's, followed by al-Aziz."

"So, my friend. What is it that has you so upset?"

"The investigation."

"The investigation?"

"We've had NCIS agents snooping around the hangar. They have been asking questions about who had access to the plane just before it flew. Why would they be snooping around if they did not suspect foul play?"

"Calm down, my son. We are talking about an aircraft incident. Surely such investigations are routine."

"Yes, of course they are routine. But by agencies such as the Navy Safety Center or NAVAIRSYSCOM. Those are the groups that are supposed to investigate when a plane goes down. But the NCIS? That's a criminal investigative agency. Commander, that's a little too close to the situation. Why would Allah allow this?"

"Remember what we discussed going into this, Petty Officer. We are at war. Allah has already given you a glorious result to your mission. You have destroyed an instrument of war that would have been used against many of our Arab brothers. This morning, there are Muslim families who will keep their fathers for a while because of your heroic act. But remember what we discussed earlier. We must be prepared for martyrdom. If Allah will allow you to be of further service, then so be it. But if he allows detection by the enemy and martyrdom, praise be to Allah!"

"But, Commander, this cannot be Allah's will. You yourself said I had a special calling. I had been placed in a unique position among my brothers. Although this mission was a success, I cannot accept such a limited role in this jihad. It makes no sense. None."

"My son, Allah's ways are far above ours. I too hope for more glory for you. But as I said, we must be prepared for martyrdom now."

"This I cannot accept. This is not what we discussed, Commander. I must go!"

"Sulayman, sit down."

"Good-bye, Commander."

"Sulayman . . ."

Static buzzed, and Kilnap turned off the recorder.

Captain Guy leaned back in his chair and crossed his arms. "Wow." He paused, shaking his head slowly. "Tell me exactly *where* and *how* you got this recording, Harry."

"This morning, about 0400, I set up surveillance in the parking lot outside VFA-115. Al-Aziz came off his shift around 0600. I followed him out of the air station, maintaining visual contact, until he turned his vehicle into a Shoney's parking lot off Dam Neck Road.

"I followed him in. Took a booth close by just to see what he was up to. I brought along some electronic recording equipment just in case. You never know. When he went to the head, I planted a small microphone just under the table where he was sitting.

Captain Guy nodded.

"He came back and sat down. Then a few minutes later, this lieutenant commander chaplain type came in and sat down at the al-Aziz booth. They got in a heated conversation. So I got up and went to the head. When I came out, I walked by their booth and saw the chaplain's name tag. I wrote it down, and later I confirmed that Lieutenant Commander Reska is a Muslim chaplain attached to the Norfolk Naval Station.

"The microphone was transmitting to a receiver with a recording device located in my car in the parking lot. I had no idea what they were saying until I went back to the office and played the tape."

David leaned back, and for a moment he didn't speak. "And you had no idea the chaplain was going to show up?"

"I had no clue. Just blind luck. Hey, sometimes you get a lucky break."

"Hmm." David mused. "Interesting." His arms remained crossed.

"So what do you think, Captain?"

"Well, without doing any research on it, I don't think there's a reasonable expectation of privacy in a public restaurant."

"I don't follow you, Captain."

"Just thinking like a defense counsel, Harry."

"So you think this would be of interest to a prosecutor?"

"Harry, if this came down the pike like you said it did, then you may have just busted this case wide open."

Kilnap felt pleased with himself. *Who would ever know how it really came down the pike?*

CHAPTER 25

From her chair at the defense table, Diane glanced at the gold clock on the mahogany wall behind the empty bench. *Fourteen hundred hours on the money.*

She looked at Marianne, who was already sitting in the witness stand, waiting for the judge. The ensign's eyes were swollen from crying before the break. Diane locked eyes momentarily with the government's star witness.

"All rise!"

With a rumble sounding like a brief stampede, the packed gallery stood as Captain Reeves stepped onto the bench of Courtroom 1.

"Court will come to order. Please be seated," Captain Reeves said. "When we recessed, I believe that the government had finished its direct examination of the witness and the defense was about to begin its cross-examination?"

Diane stood. "That's correct, Your Honor."

"Very well, you may proceed."

"Thank you, Your Honor." Diane fired a sarcastic glance at Zack, then focused her attention on Landrieu.

"Good afternoon, Ensign Landrieu."

"Good afternoon, ma'am."

"You claim that on the night in question, my client came up out of nowhere, pulled you into the bushes, and raped you?"

"Something like that."

"*Something* like that," Diane parroted. "And how long did all this take?"

"Excuse me?"

"The assault. How long did it take?"

"I don't know." Marianne sat forward, looking angry and upset, but her tone was laced with sarcasm. "I didn't time it with my stopwatch."

Her comment brought a few snickers from the galley and a laserlike stare from Diane's eyes directly into Marianne's.

"Order." *Whap. Whap.* Captain Reeves's pounding gavel echoed though the courtroom. "Order in the court." Two more gavel raps. "Spectators will refrain from inappropriate public displays of emotion, or will be removed by the master-at-arms." He paused as the courtroom quieted. "Proceed, Lieutenant Colcernian."

"Ever drink alcoholic beverages, Ensign Landrieu?"

"Occasionally."

"The night of May twenty-fifth was one such occasion, was it not?"

Marianne leaned back and let out an audible sigh. "I had a couple."

"A *couple*?" Diane paused, looked at the members, then returned her gaze to Marianne. "In fact, you really didn't go to the Officers' Club for dinner that night, did you?"

"I didn't order dinner."

"That's because you were seated in the bar, weren't you?"

Marianne glared back at her interrogator. Then, as her face flushed a slight reddish color, she spoke slowly, in a soft, deliberate voice of restrained anger. "I met a girlfriend from the Academy, Ensign Rogerson, at the bar."

"You arrived at the O-Club that night at around 2100 hours. Is that right?"

"Approximately."

"And *what* were you drinking?"

Marianne hesitated. The redness in her face had not subsided. She looked at Zack Brewer and raised her eyebrows as if to say, "Help me!" or "What am I to say?" From the corner of her eye, Diane saw Zack give Marianne a slight nod.

"I asked you a question, Ensign!" Diane snapped.

"I ordered a martini."

"A *martini*." Diane let her words resonate for a moment. "A martini is a pretty stiff drink, isn't it, Miss Landrieu?"

"It wasn't a very big glass. And I *wasn't* drunk, if that's what you're asking."

"That's not what I'm asking, Ensign. Not yet, anyway."

Zack stormed to his feet. "Objection!"

"Overruled."

Diane bored in on Marianne and clasped the counsel podium. "What I asked is this: Would you agree that a martini is a pretty stiff drink?"

"Could be, but I *wasn't* drunk."

Diane kept pushing. She fired off a series of questions about the number of drinks and when they were consumed. With each question, Marianne grew even more flustered and sarcastic, insisting she hadn't been keeping count.

Walking from the podium to the defense counsel table, Diane flipped through a file without looking at Marianne. "If your bar tab records showed that you ordered your second martini at the same time you ordered Ensign Rogerson's first martini"—Diane pulled two small bar tabs out of her file, held them up in front of her so the members could see, slipped her glasses on, and ceremoniously pretended to study them—"would you have any reason to doubt that?"

"I guess not." Marianne spoke softly and again looked at Zack Brewer.

"Fact is, you ordered *more* than one martini, didn't you?"

"Yes, ma'am."

"And so you started your *second* glass when Ensign Rogerson was imbibing her first?"

"I suppose I did, ma'am."

"Tell me, Ensign, what is your height and weight?"

"I'm five-six, 125 pounds."

"Not exactly a heavyweight, are you, Ensign?"

"I'm a naval officer. I stay in shape."

"And at some point, Ensign Rogerson had a male visitor?"

"There was a male officer who stopped by, a pilot, Lieutenant Hawley. We were all there for a while."

"And you sensed that Ensign Rogerson and Lieutenant Hawley had a romantic interest in one another?"

"I don't know about romantic. But yeah, there was chemistry."

"Is Lieutenant Hawley a good-looking guy?"

Marianne hesitated a moment. "Sure. He's nice looking. So what?"

"Lieutenant Hawley is a Navy S-3 pilot, isn't he?"

"I think so."

"And so this nice-looking, handsome aviator was paying more attention to your friend than he was to you, wasn't he?"

"So what?" Marianne snapped. "Hey, it's not like I can't get a date."

"Oh, I'm sure it's not. And we'll get to that in a minute," Diane spoke rapidly, jumping to her next question before Zack could object. "Lieutenant Hawley was *so* enraptured with Ensign Rogerson that you got up and left, didn't you?"

"I got up and left. I said that."

"After you drank three martinis. Isn't that true?"

"That's not true!" Marianne snapped again, startling several members.

"Oh, it's not?" Diane shot back. "Well, if the bar tab shows you in fact ordered *five* glasses of martini, would you have a reason to dispute that?" Diane waved a copy of the bar tab in the air as she asked the question.

Marianne looked flustered. "I *did not* drink all of them. Ensign Rogerson shared the tab."

"Right, and you said earlier that Ensign Rogerson had only two drinks, right?"

Marianne hesitated. "I think that's what I said."

"And you also said, did you not, that there's no way Ensign Rogerson had more than two drinks, right?"

Marianne's face turned redder.

"I guess I said that."

"So if there are five drinks on your bar tab, and if Ensign Rogerson only had two, that means you had three. Isn't that true?"

Marianne Landrieu, her face now beet red, turned to Judge Reeves. "Your Honor, can I explain?"

"The witness will answer the question," the judge said.

Marianne stared at Diane.

"The witness will answer the question," Captain Reeves repeated.

"Um, Your Honor, as I was about to explain, I . . . I may have ordered five drinks, that's true. But I ordered the last drink just before Lieutenant Hawley arrived. I left it on the table when I decided to leave. I didn't drink the third martini."

Diane pounced quickly. "As I understand your testimony, you now claim that you ordered, but did not drink, the third martini for yourself?"

"That's right," Marianne said in an angry, clipped tone.

"You will admit, will you not, that when you left Ensign Rogerson and Lieutenant Hawley alone, you were under the influence of alcohol, won't you?"

"Yes, but I wasn't drunk."

"A bit tipsy, perhaps?"

Zack jumped to his feet. "Objection!"

"Sustained."

Diane ignored the objection and changed the subject. "You're a public affairs officer, right?"

"Yes, ma'am." Marianne had returned to her soft, victim-sounding voice again.

"And your duties as a PAO include serving as a reporter for base closed-circuit television?"

"Correct."

"And isn't it true, Ensign, on April fifteenth, just six weeks before you claim you were assaulted, you did a television report for base closed-circuit TV on the SEALs during their training at Hell Week in Coronado?" Diane turned and motioned to her legalman paralegal who pushed a four-wheeled cart stand with a television and VCR player up the center aisle from the back of the courtroom.

"Yes, I recall doing that piece." Marianne's eyes appeared to be on the television set, now sitting just behind the defense counsel's table.

"Okay. And isn't it true, when you filed your report, you looked into the television camera and said, and I quote, 'The rigorous week of training, known as Hell Week, will help turn these trainees—at least those who survive—into the most perfectly sculpted, physically fit fighting men in the world'? Did you say that?"

"I don't remember what I said, Lieutenant."

"Want to see a videotape of the broadcast?" Diane waved a black videotape in the air, drawing the jury's undivided attention. "Well? Shall we play your broadcast to refresh your memory, Ensign?"

"No, that won't be necessary." She shrugged. "I was just doing my job. I was trying to accurately describe the training process," she snapped.

"And so you came up with 'the most perfectly sculpted, physically fit fighting men in the world'?"

Zack jumped to his feet. "Objection, Your Honor. Not only has the question been asked and answered, but now Lieutenant Colcernian is becoming argumentative."

"Sustained. Move along, defense counsel."

Diane laid the videotape on the stand beside the television. "Ensign, did you ever tell Ensign Rogerson that you 'have a thing' for SEALs?"

"No, I did not."

"Nothing like that?"

"That's right."

"Ensign, I remind you that you're under oath."

"Objection." This was Zack again. "Asked and answered. Argumentative."

"Sustained. Lieutenant, that's your last warning about being argumentative with the witness."

"My apologies, Your Honor," Diane said quickly, then focused again on Marianne. "But it's fair to say, is it not, that you personally admire the SEALs, isn't it, Ensign?"

Marianne took a couple of deep breaths, then said slowly, "Lieutenant, yes, it's true. I admire the SEALs." She clamped her lips together angrily.

"And you felt left out, didn't you, when this good-looking aviator cast his affections at your friend and not at you?"

"I wouldn't say that." Marianne's face was turning red again.

"You were feeling lonely and a little dejected that night, weren't you, Ensign?"

"Not really."

"And you stepped out into the parking lot, feeling tipsy and rejected, when you saw this Navy SEAL?"

"I did not see him!"

"And then you struck up a conversation with him, and one thing led to another, isn't that right?"

"No, that's not the way it happened!"

"Isn't it true that you stopped him in the parking lot and said, 'Where are you from, sailor?'"

"I don't remember saying that."

"But you don't deny it."

Marianne narrowed her eyes. "Yes, I deny it. He attacked me, Lieutenant!"

"Of course, with those martinis you were drinking, you don't really remember *what* happened, do you? Yet you're also saying that your memory could not have been affected at all by two and possibly"—Diane made finger quotation marks in the air—"three martinis?"

"I remember what I remember."

"Didn't you ask Petty Officer Blount where he was from?"

"No. I wouldn't have asked him that."

"Didn't you tell him that you were from New Orleans?"

"No!"

"Didn't you tell him that SEALs are more physically fit even than the Marines?"

Marianne's face was redder than before. "No!"

"And didn't you tell him you used to date enlisted Navy SEALs at the Academy?"

"Objection."

"Overruled."

"Of course not."

"Well, did you ever date enlisted Navy SEALs?"

"Objection." Zack was on his feet, waving his hand in the air. "Your Honor, the question violates the rape-shield law."

"Sustained. Move along, Lieutenant Colcernian."

"You were feeling lonely, rejected, and slightly under the influence, and you saw one of these perfect physical specimens, didn't you?"

"No, I didn't see him."

"And the truth is, you voluntarily experimented with this perfectly sculpted physical specimen."

"That's a lie!"

"You didn't scream or call out, did you?"

"He held my mouth closed, Lieutenant!"

"Right. The whole time."

"Objection! Argumentative."

"Sustained."

"The truth is, you didn't scream or call out because you didn't want to get busted for fraternization with an enlisted person, isn't that so?"

"That's ridiculous, Lieutenant."

"I think I'm about finished, here, Your Honor." Diane turned and walked back to the counsel table. She glanced at Judge Reeves. "I'm done with this witness." She paused, and the courtroom fell silent. "For now."

CHAPTER 26

Quarters of LCDR Mohammed Reska
Apartment 123, Princess Anne Apartments
Virginia Beach, Virginia

Tuesday, August 5, 0700 hours (EST)

You said he would do as the others, Reska!" Commander Mohammed Olajuwon's voice thundered through the telephone.

Reska held the phone away from his ear to protect his eardrums. "But, Commander, I have encouraged martyrdom both before and after the event—"

"Speaking of martyrdom is not good enough! Petty Officer Neptune is now a martyr in Allah's cause. So is Staff Sergeant Saidi. In other words, Commander, Chaplain Abdul-Sehen did his part to persuade Saidi. So did I with Neptune. Neptune and I had many talks about martyrdom. He understood his role from the beginning. But this al-Aziz seems liable to erupt like a volcano with a slew of information that must be contained. This is a risk which cannot be allowed."

"He understands that he cannot compromise our position, Commander."

"Does he? And how can we be assured of this?" Olajuwon's voice lowered. "He already seems distraught as a result of this 'investigation.' We never have to worry about Neptune or Saidi speaking. But I fear this al-Aziz, in his present mental state, constitutes a risk to our network."

"I will speak with him again if you think it is best, Commander."

"Lieutenant Commander Reska, consider what is at stake here. Think of all the Council has worked for over the years. Remember the

138

lawsuit to assure our admission into the Chaplain Corps. Then think of the Council's work with the aviators. We cannot afford to have this strategically placed cell of officers compromised by this young man."

Reska took a breath, but did not speak.

"Perhaps I should inform al-Akhma and the Council through our back channels and seek their guidance on what to do in this situation," Olajuwon said.

"No!" Reska's palms broke out in a sweat. "Please, Commander. Do not bother al-Akhma with this. I beg of you, let me try again with the boy. I can assure you, it will not be necessary to bother the Council with this."

"Lieutenant Commander Reska," Olajuwon said in a slow, restrained voice, "I have spoken with Commander Abdul-Sehen about the problem. He agrees the situation is potentially grave, and our entire core network is at risk. Unless the problem is dealt with immediately, we must inform the Council."

Reska wiped sweat beads from his forehead. He wanted to vomit, but he spoke, almost in a pleading whisper. "Please, Commander. I beg of you. Give me until midnight; I will have the problem eradicated."

"Very well, Commander Reska. You have until midnight tonight."

"Thank you, sir."

"Call me when the problem is resolved."

The line went dead.

Reska picked up the receiver and dialed another number. "Sulayman, how are you this morning? . . . Yes . . . You are off your shift now? . . . No, I do not think Shoney's would be good. Because under the circumstances, I believe we need a more private place . . . Little Creek Marina off 17th Bay Street in Norfolk . . . You know where it is? . . . Yes, I have a boat there. Can you meet me in three hours? About ten hundred? . . . Good . . . I will see you then."

Trial counsel offices
32nd Street Naval Station
San Diego
Tuesday, August 5, 0600 hours (PST)

Zack had been in his office for an hour, preparing for the day's upcoming testimony, when there was a knock on his door. He tossed the legal pad on his desk and looked up. "Come in."

"Good morning." Amy stepped inside. "How is San Diego's most famous prosecutor this morning?"

"I don't know about the famous part, but this prosecutor is worn out. Too much work. Not enough time. As much as I hate to say it, I think Diane scored some points yesterday."

"You haven't seen, have you?"

"Seen what?"

She slid the morning edition of the *Union-Tribune* across his desk. "You read that while I get us some coffee."

"Thanks." Zack opened the paper as Amy headed down the hall to the coffee mess.

NAVY PROSECUTES SEAL FOR RAPING ROBERSON FOWLER'S NIECE

By Brenda Cantor, Military Affairs Correspondent

32nd Street Naval Station—A Navy SEAL stationed in Coronado is being prosecuted this week in San Diego for raping the niece of powerful United States Senator Roberson Fowler of Louisiana, the *Union-Tribune* has learned.

According to inside sources, Petty Officer Antonio Blount, a Navy SEAL, is accused of raping Ensign Marianne Landrieu, a Naval Academy graduate, on May 25 in the Officers' Club parking lot at the North Island Naval Air Station.

Landrieu testified yesterday before a military jury, telling the prosecutor, Lieutenant Zack Brewer, that she was abducted by Blount in the parking lot of the Officers' Club at NASNI just before midnight on May 25. Sources report that the defense counsel, Lieutenant Diane Colcernian, spent much of the afternoon cross-examining Landrieu about her alcohol consumption on the night in question. Colcernian also suggested a romantic involvement between Landrieu and Brewer, a charge denied by Landrieu. Brewer could not be reached for comment.

Testimony is set to resume today at the 32nd Street Naval Station.

"Great." Zack tossed the newspaper on the desk just as Amy came back in with two mugs. He was still steamed that Colcernian had made an issue over seeing him having dinner with Marianne, though he probably deserved it. "Looks like somebody called the press."

The smile was gone when Amy sat down across from him. "There's something else bothering you about all this, isn't there?" Her expression said she knew what it was. Sometimes it seemed that Amy was the best friend he had. He appreciated her more than he'd ever been able to say.

"Yeah. Even in light of the legalities we've talked about, it's the not knowing." He sipped his coffee.

"Not knowing about Marianne, you mean?"

"Struggling. Thinking the guy is guilty. But never really knowing for sure. I lose sleep over it."

Her gaze met his, clear and filled with a wisdom and compassion that gave him peace just seeing it. "I pray for you, you know," she said. "And I'll continue to pray for God to grant you wisdom during this trial . . ." She paused. ". . . and that the result will be just."

The tenderness in her words grabbed Zack's heart, and for a moment he couldn't speak. "Thanks. I appreciate your prayers more than you know."

CHAPTER 27

Lieutenant Commander Reska stepped from the dock onto the back deck of the twenty-seven foot Grady-White cabin cruiser. Christened the *River Rat*, the boat was complete with a small sleeping cabin and powered by twin 225-horsepower Mercury outboards. It had been purchased by a Bahamian corporation several months earlier, which also made monthly payments for slip and storage fees directly to the Little Creek Marina in Norfolk. Keys for the boat were provided to Reska, who had negotiated the purchase from the marina and had executed all the paperwork on behalf of the Bahamian corporation as its local agent.

"Good morning, Commander."

Reska, who was bending over in the back of the boat, fiddling in a tackle box, looked up as Petty Officer al-Aziz approached, his green windbreaker snapping in the breeze, his tennis shoes nearly silent.

"Hello, Sulayman. You like fishing?"

"Yes, sir. Though I haven't fished since I was a boy. My father used to take me."

"I will take you to the Gulf Stream, home of king mackerel, if you are up to an adventure." Reska saw a smile flicker on the young petty officer's face and then added, "It will give us a chance to talk. Help get our minds off things."

"This is your boat, Commander?"

"No, but it is loaned for my use whenever I wish. Allah is provident. Come aboard. We have much food, drink, and bait. You will have plenty of time to rest when we are done."

"Thank you. I would be honored to sail with you today, sir." Sulayman saluted the imaginary ensign on the fantail, and then, mimicking the procedure for boarding a real U.S. Navy warship, he saluted Reska. "Permission to come aboard, sir."

Reska forced a smile and saluted back. "Permission granted."

Reska made a one-quarter clockwise turn of the key in the ignition as al-Aziz stepped onto the back deck of the *River Rat*. The twin 225-horsepower Mercury outboards jumped, then purred like twin kittens, spewing a burst of white smoke upon ignition, then with a slight roar, gurgled a modest amount of water around the stern as Reska threw the *River Rat* into a slow reverse out of the slip.

When the cruiser cleared the slip, Reska gently pushed the throttle into the forward position. The *River Rat* lunged forward at five miles per hour through the no-wake zone in Little Creek. After a quarter of a mile, Reska turned left through the channel leading into Hampton Roads.

The wide, expansive waters of Hampton Roads came into view, and al-Aziz took a seat in the first mate's chair, adjacent to the captain's chair. As they cleared the last no-wake buoy, Reska brought the *River Rat* to half throttle. The twin outboard engines revved into cruising speed, lifting the bow slightly.

Reska held a northerly course for a minute, turned right, and headed due east, toward the Atlantic. Now the engines throttled to full power, and the cruiser skimmed across the bay under warm, sunny skies. A few minutes later, they slowed to pass under the southern section of the Chesapeake Bay Bridge. The chaplain brought the throttle back to full.

Sulayman tapped the chaplain on his shoulder and pointed off the bow, slightly to the left. Two U.S. Navy warships, a cruiser and a frigate, were entering the harbor, about a mile to the northeast of the *River Rat*.

Reska nodded. "We will head southeast about forty-five minutes. The fishing is good out that way, plus we will be out of the shipping lanes."

"I trust your judgment, Commander."

"Perhaps you should catch a nap until we arrive. You have had a long night."

One hour later, Reska pulled back on the *River Rat*'s throttles. With the engines shut off, they were now rolling on the open sea. Land had disappeared behind the stern half an hour ago. Reska scanned the horizon and saw a couple of large ships, probably tankers, out on the horizon. Several jet streams trailed in crisscrossing patterns against the deep blue sky. Other than that, there were no signs of human life.

"They say this is a good spot for mackerel and dolphin," Reska said, waking al-Aziz. "Choose your rod. I have live bluefish in the bait well."

Al-Aziz rubbed his eyes. "Where are we?"

"Somewhere near the Gulf Stream, I think. A few miles off the Virginia-Carolina border."

Al-Aziz sat up, squinted, and looked around. "The fishing sounds good, but first there is the call of nature."

"You have your option of going off the stern, or you can go in there." Reska pointed to a small hatch just inside the forward section of the cabin. "It is rather small, but there is at least privacy."

"Which way is Mecca, Commander?"

Reska looked at the compass mounted on the boat's interior dash just left of the steering wheel. "It looks like the wind has swung us around. Mecca is, more or less, off the stern."

"Then I will go to the front of the boat."

"You are a devout member of our faith, my son."

Al-Aziz crouched and stepped down into the forward section, then, bending down, he stepped into the head, closing the fiberglass hatch behind him.

Reska reached under his shirt and retrieved the black, 9mm Beretta from the midsection of his back. He worked the action on the pistol, chambering a hollow-point bullet into the firing position, and flipped the safety off. Then, as a flushing sound came from the cabin, he stuck the Beretta back under his shirt.

"I am ready to fish, Commander." Al-Aziz smiled as he emerged from the cabin. It was the first time in weeks that Reska had seen the young man show any joy.

"Come, let us bait our hooks." The chaplain motioned the petty officer to the back of the boat, then handed him a rod. "You know how to use one of these?"

"It has been awhile, but you never forget."

"Good. I will help you get baited." Reska reached into the well, grabbed a small live bluefish with his left hand, and then with his right hand, pushed a large fishing hook through the bluefish's spine. The fish flapped rapidly as the hook penetrated its dorsal.

"If we get him into the water now, he should live for an hour or so. A perfect target for king mackerel if we are lucky. Why don't you cast off the port, and I will bait up and try the stern."

"Aye, sir." Al-Aziz complied, casting the bait over the side.

May Allah have mercy on your soul, my friend.

In a swift motion, Reska brought the gun to the back of Sulayman's skull and squeezed the trigger. The Beretta jumped, instantly splattering blood all over the port gunwale. The echo of the shot was strangely absent, absorbed by the vastness of the ocean and the whipping wind. Al-Aziz's body fell forward against the port gunwale, facing away from the gunman, but the back of his head, at least what was left of it, resembled a bursted watermelon dropped on concrete.

The young man's heart kept pumping geysers of dark red blood out the entry wound left by the hollow-point, streaming down his neck onto the deck of the *River Rat*.

Reska, a warrior for Allah, wasn't prepared for the sight now before him. He turned away, leaned over the starboard gunwale, and vomited into the Atlantic. When his upchucking turned to dry heaves, he pushed away from the gunwale, knees shaking.

He made two trips into the forward cabin, each time hauling back a cement block. On the third trip he carried a gym bag, which contained several Craftsman locks and chains he had purchased from Wal-Mart on the way to the marina.

Reska chained the blocks tightly around al-Aziz's chest, secured the chain with two steel combination locks, and then pushed the body overboard.

His eyes followed it for a moment, as the remains of Sulayman al-Aziz slipped under the buoyant, murky saltwater of the Atlantic.

Reska stood up, looked at the sky, and screamed out his agony. "Why me, Allah? Why me? Are we not a religion of peace?"

There was no answer.

Nothing but wind and a twenty-seven-foot cruiser rolling gently on the swells of the open sea.

CHAPTER 28

Navy-Marine Corps Trial Judiciary
32nd Street Naval Station
San Diego

Tuesday, August 5, 0900 hours (PST)

When Zack's Mercedes wheeled around the last corner just outside Building 1, a sight he had never witnessed outside the military courthouse greeted him.

Television trucks.

With satellite uplinks.

And smartly dressed, attractive reporters wearing thick makeup standing in front of cameras held by sloppily dressed, blue jean–clad cameramen.

At least a half dozen news vehicles were parked around the building. A large white van, with a multicolored peacock and the call sign KNSD on the side, was in front. Next to it was another sporting the CBS "eye" and the call sign KCBS. Off to one side was a truck bearing the CNN logo.

"Great," Zack muttered to Amy. He wheeled the car into the parking space reserved for JAG officers and cut the engine. "Just walk fast. Make a beeline to the front door. We should be safe inside the courtroom."

Zack opened the car door and stepped out.

"Over there," someone shouted.

"There he is," shouted another.

"Hurry up!" Several newscasters and cameramen stampeded across the asphalt, shouting and holding microphones, booms, and cameras.

Like a pack of charging wolves, they converged on Zack and Amy before they were two steps from his car. A battery of television microphones were thrust in front of Zack's face.

"Bonnie Benson. KNBC-TV Los Angeles. You're the prosecutor in the Landrieu case?"

"That's correct," Zack said, pushing his way through the herd.

"Jan Oberholtz, KNSD San Diego. I understand you represent Ensign Landrieu in this trial?"

Zack stopped, bit his lip, and chuckled inwardly. He recognized the lovely Miss Oberholtz, a San Diego television legend.

"Two NBC affiliates covering the same event?" he asked rhetorically with a slight smile. "No, Miss Oberholtz. I do *not* represent Ensign Landrieu. I represent the United States government in the trial. Ensign Landrieu is one of several witnesses testifying."

"Lieuten—"

"Lieuten—"

"But isn't this case really about Ensign Landrieu?" Jan Oberholtz's velvet-smooth voice rose above the cacophony of the other media vultures surrounding their prey. No wonder she was known as the Barbara Walters of San Diego.

"It is true, Miss Oberholtz, that Ensign Landrieu is a key government witness here."

"But, Lieutenant—"

"Lieuten—"

"Lieutenant Brewer. Bernie Woodson, CNN. Have you been in touch with Senator Fowler?"

"Morning, Bernie," Zack nodded to the well-known CNN legal-affairs correspondent as if he personally knew the distinguished African-American. "By Senator Fowler, I take it you mean United States Senator Roberson Fowler of Louisiana?"

"That is correct, Lieutenant," Woodson said back.

"No, Bernie. The only thing I know of Senator Fowler is what I've learned from the media. I've never met him nor spoken with him. And there's no reason that I *would* speak to him under these circumstances. He's one of many relatives of the victim, but other than that, he has no knowledge of the facts surrounding this case. And to my knowledge, the Navy has not been in contact with him about this case."

"But, Lieutenant Brewer, how do you respond to charges that the Navy is prosecuting this case only because of who the alleged victim's uncle is?" This was an unidentified female voice shouting from the crowd. The reporters pushed their microphones a bit closer to Zack's face.

Zack felt his anger rising, took a breath to regain his composure, and then with a cool demeanor, spoke into the cameras. "My grandmother, who grew up poor on a dirt farm in eastern North Carolina, and who earned a few pennies for Christmas by shelling peanuts, priming tobacco, and slopping waste in the family hog pen, would have a vernacular phrase to describe such a suggestion."

He gave the cameras a tight smile. "Since we are in the presence of mixed company, I won't repeat that phrase. But I will say this. Ensign Landrieu is the victim of a crime that was perpetrated on a United States naval installation. Rape is a serious crime under the Uniform Code of Military Justice. The Navy treats these matters with an even and fair hand. We protect victims. We punish perpetrators. And whether this victim's uncle is a senator or a pauper in no way affects our decision to prosecute this case or the way it will be prosecuted."

"Now if you'll excuse me, ladies and gentlemen"—Zack looked at his watch—"I'm due in front of Judge Reeves in five minutes."

"But, Lieutenant—"

"Lieuten—"

With Amy at his side, Zack pushed through the small media mob and into the front door of Building 1.

Dirksen Senate Office Building
Capitol Hill
Washington, D.C.

Tuesday, August 5, 1205 hours (EST)

Senator Roberson Fowler turned to his Washington office chief of staff. "Turn it off now, Ed." From inside the politician's office on Capitol Hill, they had been watching the CNN live feed from San Diego.

"Seems to be a sharp young man," Ed Brinkley replied, punching the remote control. The big-screen television in the corner of the senator's office went black. "A real feel for the camera. I couldn't have personally scripted that response any better."

"Yes," the senator said. He stood, sauntered over to a walnut and brass coat tree, and grabbed his seersucker jacket. Ed hurried over to hold it as Fowler pushed his arms through the sleeves. "And the thing that impressed me is how the boy watched my backside in the interview."

His young aide narrowed his eyes in thought. "True, Senator. Not the slightest hint of preferential treatment for your niece by the Navy." His smile was sly. "Just as instructed."

Fowler stepped in front of the ornate mirror just beside his desk and straightened his tie, then brushed imaginary lint from his seersucker slacks.

As if reading his mind, Ed walked over to Fowler's humidor, retrieved a Monte Cristo, clipped the small end, and handed it to the senator.

As he offered him a light, Fowler chuckled.

Ed half smiled and shot him a knowing look. The no-smoking rules in federal buildings, imposed by the General Services Administration, did not apply to powerful senators who controlled the GSA's purse strings.

"And you can bet the barn, Ed"—Fowler drew on the cigar, then blew smoke into the room—"Republicans would be on my case right now if the boy hadn't handled that interview just as he did. I really liked the thing about the hog pen." Fowler chuckled again and took another puff. "The boy has some political talent. I can see why my niece raves about him. We'll have to check his party affiliation."

"I already have. He's a Republican."

Fowler grunted and blew a perfect halo of white smoke. It drifted above the mahogany desk, slowly engulfing the gold chandelier hanging from the ornate ceiling.

"We can always persuade him to change his political affiliation"— Ed's voice was a perfect monotone—"should it suit your purposes. You just give me the word."

"And my purposes would be . . . ?" Fowler sat back, smoke drifting above his head, as he watched the wheels turning in his go-getter aide's head.

Ed laughed and shrugged. "Maybe I should say if he—this Zack Brewer—suits your purposes." His smile was wily.

Fowler blew another circle of smoke. "For now, his purpose is to keep the meat out of the sharks' mouths—just as he did in the interview this morning." He leaned back in his chair. "Maybe that's enough."

Another half smile from Ed. "For now."

"Let's keep close tabs on this one. And if Marianne calls again, tell her Uncle Pinkie will have to wait till this trial is over before he can talk to her."

"Yes, Senator."

"Time to go. I've got a vote in ten minutes." He gently tapped the end of the Monte Cristo and slid it into his sterling cigar saver. He headed to the door, then stopped and turned back to his aide, who was three steps behind him.

"I like the way you think, son." He grinned. "You and me—we think alike." He chuckled. "Devious as all get-out." He slapped the young man on the back as they exited his suite of offices. "Devious as all get-out," he repeated, his laughter booming down the hallway.

CHAPTER 29

The cleanup took longer than Reska anticipated.

On his knees, scrubbing the aft section of the *River Rat*'s deck, the chaplain became nauseated from the combination of the slow, rolling waves and the strong fumes of the ammonia floating into his nostrils. Every fifteen minutes or so throughout the four hours, he raised his head to gulp for air, hoping the fresh Atlantic breeze would make him feel better.

Instead, his seasickness worsened. Hanging over the railing, he tried to vomit into the Atlantic. His only accomplishment: dry heaves. Dozens of times.

Still, it was important, for the cause of Allah and the organization, to eliminate all evidence of Sulayman al-Aziz before returning to port. And so Reska, feeling such motion sickness that he more than once thought of using the Beretta on himself to end his misery, kept scrubbing, washing, and tossing waste into the ocean.

By 1500 hours, Reska saw no more evidence that Aviation Structural Mechanic Second Class Sulayman al-Aziz had ever been on board the *River Rat*. The body was dumped far enough out that the Gulf Stream would wash it into the North Atlantic, if the sharks did not first make mincemeat of it. The bloody rags were already in the belly of some hammerhead, and the brain matter would dissolve in the salt water. It had been a tough job, but Reska would perform tough assignments for Allah. He surveyed the clean deck and felt a strange satisfaction now that it was over.

The chaplain smiled when the twin outboards jumped and caught. He checked the GPS and set a course of 275 degrees north-northwest toward Hampton Roads.

Two hours later, he steered the twenty-seven-footer into the no-wake zone in the channel leading into Little Creek Marina.

He picked up the microphone, set the radio frequency for the marina, and announced that he would arrive at slip number 17 in ten minutes. Two deckhands would be waiting to take the boat to storage, he was told. Their services were covered as part of the hefty slip fees paid by the Council.

The Muslim chaplain saw the deckhands waiting at the end of the pier as he gently idled the boat against the rubber tires bolted to the dock.

"We've got it, Commander," one said, stepping onto the bow. He threw a line to the other.

Reska cut the engines as the deckhands tied the *River Rat* to the pier. He hopped over the side of the boat and onto the pier, strolled to the end, and reached into his pants pocket for his car keys.

He halted midstep when he spotted two men standing by his car.

The older of the two, a gray-haired, potbellied man, stepped forward. "Lieutenant Commander Mohammed Reska?"

"Yes?"

"Federal Agent Harry Kilnap." The words seemed to roll off the man's tongue. "NCIS. You're under arrest for murder, conspiracy to commit murder, treason, and rendering aid to the enemy."

With those words, four more agents appeared from behind a nearby vehicle with weapons drawn. Reska felt the cold steel of handcuffs tighten around his wrists and shuddered.

The plump one spoke again. "Lieutenant Commander Mohammed Reska, United States Navy, it is my duty, under Article 31(b) of the Uniform Code of Military Justice, to inform you that you have the right to remain silent. Should you give up your right to remain silent, anything you say can and will be used . . ."

CHAPTER 30

Navy-Marine Corps Trial Judiciary
Building 1
32nd Street Naval Station
San Diego

Ensign Laura Rogerson took her place in the witness chair. She sat up, shoulders straight, looking resplendent in her summer whites. Zack waited until she was sworn in; then he stood and walked toward her.

"Ensign," he said, "you were at the club with Ensign Landrieu the night of the attack?"

"Yes, sir." Rogerson's voice was firm and confident.

"At any time, was she ever drunk?"

"Absolutely not, Lieutenant Brewer," she said in a confident tone. "I would not have allowed her to leave alone if I thought she was intoxicated."

"And one other question," Zack asked. "Did Ensign Landrieu ever say anything to you about having some sort of special attraction to Navy SEALs?"

Rogerson stared at Zack, then at the members, and with a righteously indignant expression, proclaimed, "Absolutely not, Lieutenant. Marianne said no such thing."

"No further questions," Zack said, then watched as Diane approached counsel podium for cross-examination.

"But isn't it true, Ensign Rogerson," Diane demanded, "that you had also been drinking yourself, and after two martinis, you don't remember much about Ensign Landrieu's level of sobriety?"

"She wasn't drunk. I remember that."

"But your infatuation with this handsome pilot distracted you from observing Ensign Landrieu, did it not?"

"I am an aviator, Lieutenant," Rogerson snapped. "With respect, aviators are paid to pay attention to things." This brought a smile from the female aviator on the jury. "I saw Ensign Landrieu that night. I was with her long before the Lieutenant arrived. She was not drunk. If she had been drunk, either I or Lieutenant Hawley would have driven her home."

Next, Zack called Lieutenant (jg) Arthur Hawley, the S-2 pilot and supposed object of Laura Rogerson's attention, to the stand.

"No, sir, Lieutenant Brewer," Hawley said. "Ensign Landrieu wasn't drunk. Her speech wasn't slurred. Her eyes weren't glassy. She definitely didn't stagger when she walked." Hawley looked a bit embarrassed. "I watched her walk out the front door, if you know what I mean. She was walking smoothly."

That drew a few snickers from the jury.

"No further questions."

Next, the first of the two shore patrolmen were called by the prosecution.

"We heard rustling in the leaves behind the hedgerow," said the first in a Midwestern accent. "And then we shined our flashlights toward the sound. The assailant, a muscular white man in a T-shirt and white boxers, ran across the parking lot."

"He ran too fast to catch him on foot," insisted the second man. "But then the Marines came out of nowhere. So we went back over to the hedgerow to check it out."

"What did you find at the hedgerow?" Zack asked.

"That's when we saw the ensign," number two said. "She was crying. Crumpled on the grass, just crying."

"What was she wearing?"

"She was wearing the officer's white uniform with the white skirt. Like the one the Lieutenant there's got on." The shore patrolman pointed to Diane. "Only it was real messed up. Grass stains and all."

"I'll show you what we've marked as Prosecution Exhibit 1, Petty Officer," Zack walked from the counsel table to the witness stand. "Do you recognize this?" He held up Marianne's articles of clothing, one by one, and the shore patrolman identified them.

"Thank you," Zack said and walked back to his chair.

"Lieutenant Colcernian? Cross-exam?" Judge Reeves asked.

Diane stood. "The ensign never actually told you she had been raped, did she, Petty Officer?"

"No, ma'am. She was just crying."

"And it's possible, is it not, that she was crying because she was embarrassed you caught her in a compromising position with an enlisted man?"

Zack shot to his feet. "Objection! Calls for speculation."

"I reckon," the petty officer said before Judge Reeves could speak.

"Sustained," Judge Reeves said.

Diane fixed her gaze on the witness. "You don't know whether Ensign Landrieu consented to relations with Petty Officer Blount or not, do you?"

"No, ma'am."

Zack's last witness was a PhD forensics expert from the NCIS crime lab in San Diego. The technician, professorial and timid-looking in his yellow polyester-blend shirt and wire-rimmed spectacles, said that analysis proved "with a virtual 100 percent certainty" the stains found on the clothing in evidence matched the DNA of BT3 (SEAL) Antonio Blount, United States Navy.

At the end of his testimony, silence filled the courtroom, but the echo of Brewer's footsteps as he crossed the hardwood floor between the witness stand and the jury box was strangely deafening.

Diane declined cross-examination. She gave Zack a smug look as she settled back in her chair, arms crossed. She obviously had something up her sleeve.

"Your Honor, the government rests," Zack said with more confidence than he felt.

Judge Reeves fixed his gaze on Diane. "Lieutenant Colcernian, will the defense be putting on evidence?"

Diane rose. "The defense calls Mr. Willie Garrett of Metairie, Louisiana."

"Objection!" Zack jumped to his feet. "Your Honor, this person is not on the witness list."

Reeves rifled through some papers on the bench, then glanced at Diane. "Lieutenant, I don't see this witness on your list."

"Your Honor, Mr. Garrett will testify—"

"Your Honor," Zack interrupted. "I request an Article 39(a) session outside of the presence of the members."

"Lieutenant Colcernian"—Reeves glared at Diane—"don't say another word until we have sequestered the members in the deliberation room."

"But, Your Honor," Diane persisted, "I was just going to say that Mr. Garrett—"

"Lieutenant!" Reeves snapped. "One more word before the members leave and I'll hold you in contempt and have the master-at-arms escort you to the brig. Is that clear?"

Diane flushed crimson. "Aye, sir."

As the members filed out of the courtroom in silence, Zack smirked across the aisle at his red-faced rival.

Chalk up one for the prosecution.

"Now then," Judge Reeves said as the bailiff closed the door to the jury room. "Lieutenant Colcernian, you're aware of the court's rule that we do not have substantive discussions about prospective testimony from a witness in front of the members, are you not?"

"Yes, sir," Diane said.

"Because to do so may result in them hearing testimony or evidence that I may later deem as inadmissible. You wouldn't want that to happen, would you, Lieutenant?"

Zack snickered as Diane, still rocking from the admonishment, said, "Of course not, Your Honor."

"So there will be no more stunts like that from you during the course of this trial. Understood?"

"Yes, sir. My apologies."

"Tell me about this surprise witness. What's his name?" Reeves looked down at the note he had scribbled on his legal pad. "A Mr. Garrett?"

"Your Honor, Mr. Garrett is a young man from Louisiana that Ensign Landrieu dated when she was in high school and also some while she was at the Naval Academy."

Zack shot to his feet. "Your Honor—"

"Hold on, Lieutenant Brewer," Reeves said, holding up a hand, palm out, in Zack's direction, but keeping his gaze on the defense counsel. "Lieutenant Colcernian, can you explain to me how who Ensign Landrieu may have dated has anything to do with whether your client raped her?"

"Your Honor, we're raising a consent defense. In other words, that Petty Officer Blount is not guilty of rape because Ensign Landrieu consented to relations with him. Now this, as you know, is an alleged rape that not only crosses the officer-enlisted boundary, but also crosses racial boundaries. In this case, the alleged victim is a white officer, and the alleged perpetrator is a Filipino American, a former enlisted man who was a Navy SEAL—and a rather athletic one at that."

"So?" Reeves whipped his wire rims off.

"So just like Petty Officer Blount, Mr. Garrett was an enlisted Navy SEAL."

So this was the surprise stunt he had expected from Diane. "Your Honor, may I address that, please?"

"Very well, Trial Counsel."

"Judge Reeves, despite the fact that the defense withheld notice of this surprise witness—and despite the fact that the witness should be excluded for violation of the rules alone—even if she had given us the requisite notice, this proffered testimony is a violation of the rape-shield statute. You simply can't bring in evidence of a victim's past sexual history, including evidence of who she's dated, for the purposes of proving consent in a rape trial. This is a classic rape-shield situation. Victims are by law entitled to protection in court. You should disallow this testimony."

"Lieutenant Colcernian, Lieutenant Brewer raises a couple of good points. First, you did not comply with the rule requiring you to disclose this witness to the prosecutor. And second, he raises a good point about the rape-shield statute. How do you address that?"

"Your Honor, we did not learn of this witness and others like him until over the weekend, when a private detective we had employed in Louisiana found him. So there wasn't time before trial to disclose his existence. And if I haven't complied in a timely manner, it's unfair to hold my incompetence against my client. He's facing life in prison, and he's entitled to call witnesses to his defense. As you know, the Armed Forces Court of Military Review routinely reverses convictions for ineffective assistance of counsel. So I'd ask you, Judge, please don't hold my incompetence against my client."

She was using the oldest trick in the book: try a dirty trick and blame it on incompetence.

"And the other point I'd like to make is this: we aren't calling this witness to testify about specific promiscuous acts by the ensign. We have no interest in the details. But in a consent defense, Petty Officer Blount is entitled to 'blunt' the notion that the officer-enlisted nature of this alleged offense makes it more likely the act was nonconsensual."

"That's ridiculous, Your Honor." Zack waved his hands in the air. "The rape-shield statute contains no such exception to it. Whether Mr. Garrett is or is not a former SEAL, the law does not allow him to get on the witness stand and talk about his relationship with Marianne Landrieu."

"Maybe not," Diane shot back with that eye-of-the-tiger look she had. "But there *is* a constitutional right to a fair trial. And even though we

are in the twenty-first century, there is still the notion floating around
that a Naval Academy graduate, the daughter of a powerful United States
senator, would never date an enlisted man, especially one in a lower
socioeconomic class. So these witnesses are being called simply to rebut
that notion. That's all."

"Did you say *these* witnesses, Lieutenant?"

"Your Honor, in addition to Mr. Garrett, our investigator has located
two other young men. All witnesses are former Navy SEALs. All will testify to having dated Marianne Landrieu on numerous occasions."

Zack felt the hair rising on the back of his neck. "Your Honor, this
is an outrageous, below-the-belt smear tactic. I hope the court won't
allow any of these witnesses to testify."

Reeves put his glasses back on and stared at Diane. "Any more surprises, Lieutenant?"

"No, sir, Your Honor."

"Very well. Court is in recess while I take this matter under advisement.
I will return with a decision on whether these witnesses may testify once I
have had an opportunity to conduct some research."

"All rise."

The banging gavel echoed throughout the courtroom as press members furiously scribbled notes on their pads.

CHAPTER 31

President Mack Williams leaned back in his chair and crossed his arms. Sunlight streamed through the three bulletproof windows just behind his leather chair, slicing a sharp, diagonal light across his desk. Outside the window, the South Lawn and the Rose Garden made a picturesque backdrop, a peaceful contrast to the heated debate taking place in his office.

The debate was between Attorney General R. Wiley Hutchinson and Secretary of Defense Erwin Manuel Lopez, who sat in wingback chairs in front of his desk. White House chief of staff and the president's chief political advisor, Wally Walsh, sat quietly to one side, more to observe than to contribute. His opinion would be sought later.

Sitting in this room, listening to both of the arguments, President Williams imagined what Franklin Roosevelt must have felt when the Army and the Navy fought over who would be in charge of the war in the Pacific in the early 1940s. Or when J. Edgar Hoover's FBI clashed with Bill Donovan's Office of Strategic Services—later the CIA—over which agency would be responsible for foreign intelligence gathering. Whether it was MacArthur clashing with Nimitz, or Hoover clashing with Donovan, interagency turf wars in Washington were as old as the republic itself. In this case, the turf war was between the attorney general and the secretary of defense.

The president had heard enough sniping between Hutchinson and Lopez. It was time to give each of the parties a last say and then make a decision. "You realize, do you not, Mr. Attorney General, that I began both my legal *and* my military career as a Navy JAG officer?"

Attorney General Hutchinson, slim, silver-haired, and just shy of six feet two inches tall, unfolded himself from the leather wingback chair in front of the president's desk. "Mr. President, with all due respect to the Department of Defense"—his tone was clipped, clearly impatient—"what's happened here is a threat to the national security of the United States."

He hooked his thumbs under his suspenders and walked toward the presidential seal at the center of the Oval Office's navy blue carpet. "I have great admiration for the JAG Corps. Most of our JAG officers *are* the best and the brightest of their law school classes. They are talented young litigators. But with all respect, Mr. President, because they *are* the best and the brightest, they often leave the Navy after a few years when they get recruited by big law firms paying big bucks, or, as you did, sir, they go into politics. The lawyers who stay in the service, the JAG Corps' senior officers, so to speak, migrate into non-litigation areas, such as international law and drafting wills."

He frowned, pacing a few steps. "That means most of the JAG Corps' criminal prosecutors, as you know, sir, are the junior officers with less than five years' experience out of law school. Think about what we would be asking some junior JAG officer to do. Look at what these defendants have done. They ordered the Israeli ambassador to the United States to be shot by a United States Marine. They ordered a sailor to attack and murder innocent civilians in a church service. And they ordered the sabotage of a Navy fighter jet."

Hutchinson removed his thumb from his suspender and, with a courtly dignity, gestured with his right hand. "So it isn't the intelligence of these junior JAG officers that concerns me. It's their inexperience. And I mean no offense to the active-duty military lawyers, Mr. President, but many are relatively inexperienced in trial matters, having graduated from law school and having fewer than five years' trial experience in the best-case scenario. In a case of this magnitude, we need experience. We cannot afford an acquittal for any of these chaplains. An acquittal would be an unacceptable victory for terrorism.

"It is true, as the secretary of defense has said, that this does directly involve active-duty service members, but there's more to it than that." Hutchinson's tone was forceful but respectful. "This type of infiltration of the military poses not only a direct threat to members of our armed forces, but to innocent American civilians. And that's where the Justice Department comes into play. There is concurrent jurisdiction for prosecution here, sir. What we need here, sir, is a conviction.

"Followed by swift punishment." The attorney general had a well-known habit of repeating himself for emphasis. The president waited. Sure enough, Hutchinson said, "Swift punishment."

Hutchinson walked across the presidential seal, seated himself, and leaned forward earnestly. "The Justice Department's well-seasoned career prosecutors are accustomed to dealing with such complex matters, with years of experience under their belts. Why gamble on a conviction here? These defendants could still have military lawyers defending them. I believe they're entitled to that. But let's put this in the hands of the best prosecutors the government has at its disposal. Thank you, sir."

A brief period of silence followed as Mack Williams took a swig of coffee, then set the mug back on the desk and recrossed his arms. He pivoted the big chair about thirty degrees to his left, aiming his gaze in the direction of the forty-eight-year-old Erwin Lopez, secretary of defense. "Mr. Secretary, the attorney general makes a persuasive argument about the need to avoid an acquittal here. Does it really matter to the Defense Department who prosecutes this case?"

Lopez took a sip of ice water from the crystal glass on the silver tray held by the white-jacketed Navy steward. "Mr. President, I congratulate my friend and colleague, the attorney general, for his passionate and cogent argument. He represents the Justice Department with the highest degree of professionalism, and this nation is fortunate to have him, sir.

"But with all respect, I disagree with his assessment of the military's capability to prosecute these cases and also with his view that the national security is best served by having the Justice Department prosecute. To the contrary, sir, the national security is best served by having the Navy prosecute these cases."

The president leaned forward. "All right, let's hear your national security argument first."

"Yes, Mr. President," Lopez said. "As you know, the need to maintain good order and discipline within the military is also essential to national security. Since the days of George Washington, there has been a longstanding tradition that the military takes care of its own, and that the military punishes its own. The court-martial is the process by which the armed forces dispense with discipline. In this case, the alleged offenders, these three chaplains, are active-duty service members, which gives the Navy the primary jurisdiction over the prosecution and defense of these cases. Not only that, but two of the three crimes, shooting the ambassador and planting the bomb on the plane, were committed on United States Military installations.

"The remedies available to a military tribunal are swift and effective. My advisors tell me, for example, that the Uniform Code of Military Justice provides the death penalty for certain offenses, including treason and murder." He narrowed his eyes, his expression intense. "Mr. President, our national security depends in large part on the strength of our military. To have a strong military, we must internally"—Lopez made a karate-chop gesture—"maintain good order and discipline. This is a military matter. That means, sir, we must prosecute our own, without interference by outside agencies. The military's ability to police itself is at stake here."

When the whiz kid paused for another sip of water, the president uncrossed his arms and leaned back. "Secretary Lopez, I agree with everything you say about good order and discipline. And ordinarily, I agree—the military should prosecute its own. But what about the attorney general's concern over the perceived lack of experience of the junior officers in the JAG Corps?"

"Mr. President," Lopez shot back. "You used the right word, in my opinion, when you said 'perceived.' Mr. President, you served in the JAG Corps, and the attorney general, despite his distinguished career, never did. Therefore, the attorney general may not be in a position to fully realize the true level of experience that our JAG officers have. While it's true that in the Navy, most prosecutors are at the junior officer level, it's also true that the sheer number of cases they have prosecuted greatly exceeds that of most DOJ prosecutors.

"In other words, a Navy prosecutor at the senior lieutenant or lieutenant commander level, according to my research, has ordinarily prosecuted hundreds of trials, including dozens of jury trials. Our prosecutors, while generally younger than their DOJ counterparts, have better jury experience than many DOJ attorneys who've been practicing law twice as long."

Mack glanced at the attorney general, still bristling at the Lopez comments, then looked back to Lopez.

"And that's characteristic of military experience in general, sir." Lopez took another sip of ice water. "So, Mr. President, I close by saying the military justice system is more than capable of handling these prosecutions, and I urge you, sir, to let the military justice system do its job." He leaned back and folded his arms.

Hutchinson started to speak, but the president held up his hand and turned to his chief of staff. "Wally, we've gotta wrap this real soon. But first I want to get your thoughts on all this."

Walsh was known by the *Washington Post* and the *New York Times* as the Republican Kingmaker for successfully orchestrating the political campaigns of four U.S. Senate candidates, including that of Mack Williams. He cleared his throat and adjusted his tie. "Mr. President, I'm not a lawyer, so I'm not in a position to comment on which lawyers are better qualified to prosecute this. Both the attorney general and the secretary of defense make outstanding arguments supporting their respective positions." He paused, removed his glasses, and pinched the bridge of his nose. "But we seem to have overlooked the political ramifications." He put his glasses back on.

"Out with it." The president reached for his mug and took a swig of coffee.

"Michigan, sir."

"Michigan?" Mack raised his eyebrow.

"A swing state in next year's election. And a state with the highest concentration of Muslim-Americans."

"So? If you think this shouldn't be prosecuted because the defendants are Muslim, that's not going to happen."

"I'm not suggesting that at all, sir. But my concern is that if the Justice Department prosecutes it, instead of the military, it may come across as looking like the Administration is singling out Muslims and the Muslim faith. That's all. If the military handles it internally, that would be the expected, routine response."

Mack felt the hair standing up on the back of his neck. "Wally, you know I don't give a rat's derriere about political consequences, not in a case like this." His eyes fell on *The Buck Stops Here*, and he thought of Truman. What would "Give 'Em Hell" Harry do? "But your point is well taken, Wally."

Mack turned to Lopez. "Erwin, what was the name of that Navy captain you said was responsible for helping break open this case?"

Lopez thumbed through his notes. "Guy, sir. Captain David Guy."

"Good. I want him in my office within forty-eight hours."

"We are adjourned."

CHAPTER 32

Navy-Marine Corps Trial Judiciary
Building 1
32nd Street Naval Station
San Diego

When Captain Reeves ordered a recess to consider the issue of Diane's proposed witnesses, Zack expected a quick decision. The rape-shield law was clear. Mr. Willie Garrett and company would be on the next plane back to Louisiana. After all, the rules are the rules.

Forty-five minutes later, Reeves announced an overnight recess to "further study the question."

This was not a good sign.

Zack's jaw worked overtime; his blood pressure rose. He stacked his files on the table, refusing to look across at Diane and catch her smile of triumph. He only hoped the Honorable Captain Richard Reeves would develop some backbone overnight and put a stop to Diane's sleazy defense tactics.

Not likely.

Zack needed a break from the circus. He pushed his way through the throng of reporters, answered their questions about Mr. Garrett and company with a generic "No comment," climbed into his Mercedes, and drove off base.

An hour later, he was at the Grossmont Center in La Mesa, where he parked the car and got out. Still in his summer whites, he quick-stepped across the parking lot, darted into his favorite Barnes & Noble, retrieved a copy of *The King of Defense* by Wellington Levinson, and flipped it open to chapter 14, "The Element of Surprise."

The first few paragraphs confirmed his suspicions about the surprise witness tactic. An hour later, he plunked down twenty-five dollars for the best seller, making it the latest addition to his burgeoning personal library, and left the store.

The alarm clock beeped at 0500 the next morning. He rolled out of bed, showered, shaved, and sprayed a shot of Geoffrey Beene under his chin. Then he threw on a fresh summer white uniform, donned the officer's cap, and bolted out the door.

As the Mercedes merged onto California Highway 94, the twelve-mile freeway that spilled out just in front of the 32nd Street Naval Station, he turned the radio on; the AM was tuned to his favorite station, KSDO.

"The court-martial of a Navy SEAL accused of raping a woman naval officer who happens to be the niece of a prominent United States senator is gaining national attention.

"The military judge, Captain Richard Reeves, recessed the court overnight to consider the matter of three former Navy SEALs added to the defense witness list yesterday, who claim they dated Ensign Landrieu when she was in Louisiana. A decision is expected from Reeves this morning on whether they can testify. Both JAG officers declined comment as they left the courtroom yesterday.

"But others are not remaining silent on the issue. The Reverend JamesOn Barbour of SARD, the Society Against Racial Discrimination, held a news conference from their headquarters in Chicago. Here's what the Reverend Barbour had to say last night . . ."

"Oh, please," Zack groaned.

"'We are concerned about the Navy's decision to prosecute a young man, a Navy SEAL, because of who the alleged victim's uncle is. If the Navy is prosecuting this young man to curry favor with a powerful senator who sits on the Armed Services Committee, that's influence peddling. And that is unacceptable. We expect to be in San Diego tomorrow to look further into this.'

"And the prominent religious and civil rights leader, just back from a pro-abortion rally in Washington, arrived at Lindburg Field late last night aboard a private SARD jet. He is expected to hold a news conference sometime today. There has been no comment as of yet from Senator Roberson Fowler's office.

"Meanwhile, the court-martial of Petty Officer Antonio Blount, the Navy SEAL, is scheduled to resume this morning at the 32nd Street Naval Station."

Zack punched off the radio as the car merged into the slow, base-bound traffic just outside the main gate of the naval station. About two dozen protesters stood on each side of the main entrance, waving large signs.

Free Petty Officer Blount!
Navy Justice—An Oxymoron!
Justice Raped!

Zack rolled the window down, inching closer to the main gate. The protesters were chanting something in rhythmic syncopation, alternatively raising and lowering their signs.

"Blount's not guilty! Human rights for all!"

"Blount's not guilty! Human rights for all!"

"Blount's not guil—"

The crisp salute from the United States Marine at the entrance took Zack's gaze from the protesters. He drove through the gate, the signs disappearing in his rearview mirror. A minute later, he wheeled into the reserved parking spot outside Building 1. Like buffalo trampling across the prairie, reporters and cameramen rushed at his car in an all-out blitz before he could open the door.

"Lieutenant—"

"Lieuten—"

This time, they blinded his eyes with bright lights pointed toward the inside of his car. He squinted and heard his name called out over the dissonant rumbling of voices as he opened the door and stepped out.

San Diego's pseudo Barbara Walters was at it again, no doubt having elbowed her way to the front of the herd. "Lieutenant Brewer, what do you think of the defense surprise witness list yesterday, and what do you expect Judge Reeves to do this morning?"

"Miss Oberholtz"—he almost slipped and called her Barbara—"we stated our position in court yesterday afternoon. The testimony should be disallowed."

"But doesn't the delay show that the judge is at least thinking about letting these men testify?"

"I won't speculate on that." Zack grabbed his briefcase and started across the parking lot, engulfed by the media mob that moved with him toward the courthouse.

"Why shouldn't they testify?" The shout came from an attractive African-American woman with a CBS microphone.

"Because it's against the rules of evidence."

"But doesn't the public have a right to know if this officer, who claims that she was raped by an enlisted Navy SEAL, may have dated enlisted Navy SEALs in the past?"

Zack stopped and looked at the CBS reporter and smiled. "I'm sorry, ma'am, I didn't catch your name."

"Leslie Shields, CBS News."

"Ms. Shields, I don't know about the public's right to know. I do know about a jury's right to know. And the rape-shield law was enacted to protect the private lives of victims, to prevent the unfortunate type of public circus under which Ensign Landrieu, regrettably, is now being scrutinized. Rules are rules. I didn't write them. In this case, you'll have to take the law up with Congress and the president."

"Lieutenant Brewer." The distinctive voice of CNN's Bernie Woodson boomed above the others as Zack reached the courthouse steps. "Any comment on the Reverend JamesOn Barbour's involvement in this case?"

"It's a free country, Bernie." Zack met the reporter's gaze. "Reverend Barbour can say whatever he wants."

Woodson jammed the microphone closer. "Reverend Barbour accuses the Navy of prosecuting this case only because Ensign Landrieu is Senator Fowler's niece."

Zack's blood boiled. "Bernie, as I said yesterday, we've heard nothing from Senator Fowler or anyone associated with him suggesting that this case should be prosecuted. And as far as the Reverend Barbour goes, maybe the real question you should be asking is how SARD keeps its tax-exempt status when its leader, the Reverend Barbour, actively campaigns for ultraliberal candidates all over the country. And if you ask me that question, I'll say I have no clue."

"But, Lieutenant," Woodson persisted, "Reverend Barbour also says that this prosecution is politically motivated. How do you respond?"

"Politically motivated?" Zack bit his tongue. "Apparently the Reverend Barbour knows he can raise such reckless allegations that you distinguished members of the media will respond by putting him on television and giving him free publicity, which you have done. His allegations of racism are purely bogus." He paused pointedly. "Now if you'll excuse me, I've got a case to prosecute."

★

"Atta boy." Senator Roberson Fowler grinned as the image of Lieutenant Zack Brewer disappearing into the courthouse faded from his television screen. He kicked his feet on his desk, took a puff from his Churchillian cigar, and turned to his chief of staff. "This kid's good, Ed. And he's watching my backside again."

"Agreed, Senator." The bespectacled aide nodded to his boss. "And he's got an obvious flair for the camera." He chuckled. "I'd say it's a gift."

"I want a full background run on this Lieutenant Brewer. Start with his military file. Then let's send a couple of investigators down to Carolina. Find out about his college and law school activities. Who his girlfriends are. Religious preferences. If he likes MoonPies, I want to know. If he dips snuff, tell me the brand. Got the picture, Ed?"

There was a curious glint in Ed's eyes. As always, this was right down his alley. "Is the senator thinking the same thing I am?"

"Maybe." A victorious puff on the cigar. "Just maybe." Another puff. "But you never know. Anyway, in politics, information is power. Get cracking on it, will you, Ed?"

"I'm already halfway there." His aide chuckled again.

CHAPTER 33

Council of Ishmael temporary headquarters
Rub al-Khali Desert
250 miles southeast of Riyadh, Saudi Arabia

bdur Rahman stood outside his leader's office in the large, ten-thousand-square-foot tent that served as the Council of Ishmael headquarters. He lifted back the doorway flap and peered into the office. A simple message, written in green-stenciled Arabic on white linen, hung behind the leader's desk: "God the Merciful, God the Compassionate."

To the left of the hanging was a large color image of the man for whom the leader was named, the former Iraqi president, Saddam Hussein. To the right, a picture of the man al-Akhma called "the greatest Muslim to walk the earth since the prophet Muhammad himself," the glorious hero of 9/11, Osama bin Laden.

Rahman bowed slightly and cleared his throat to announce his presence.

"Enter." Hussein al-Akhma, speaking in his native tongue, did not look up from where he worked at his desk. He was dressed in white Arabic garb. Though he took pride in his ability to look and speak like a Westerner, he had decreed that turbans be worn within the secretive Council of Ishmael headquarters, now located in the hot Saudi desert.

"Un hum del Allah." Praise be to God. Rahman stepped into al-Akhma's office.

"Un hum del Allah." Hussein al-Akhma still concentrated on the papers in front of him.

"My leader, we have a problem." As soon as the words were out of Abdur Rahman's mouth, al-Akhma looked up, his piercing black eyes now fixed on Abdur.

Abdur had thought often of that summer day in Zurich, seven years ago, when he first met the great Hussein al-Akhma. Hussein had been warm, charismatic. Becoming a part of the chosen Council of Twenty to shake the world for Islam never lost its luster. Abdur's resolve, and the resolve of his fellow council members, at least those who survived, had strengthened over the years.

But as the Council's master plan unfolded during the seven years of planting cells of dedicated Muslims within the United States Navy, al-Akhma's explosiveness grew. Two original Council members received bullets in their brains, courtesy of al-Akhma's Beretta. Their crime? Daring to question their leader in front of the Council. No one knew who would be next.

No established hierarchy existed among the Council, but Abdur Rahman had emerged as the clear first lieutenant to al-Akhma. As such, he shouldered the potentially dangerous responsibility of delivering bad news.

"What is it, my brother?"

"It is the Americans."

"The heathen Americans are always a problem." Al-Akhma switched to English with a hint of impatience in his voice. "What about them?"

Abdur took his cue and also spoke in English. "I am sorry to bring unpleasant news, my leader, but they have arrested three of the imams we planted in their Navy."

"What?" Hussein stood, staring angrily into his subordinate's eyes. "What do you mean, *arrested*? What has happened?"

"The Navy's criminal investigators have arrested Commanders Olajuwon, Reska, and Abdul-Sehen. They are being held in connection with several operations against the Americans."

"Which operations?"

"The shooting of the Zionist dog, Barak. That was Abdul-Sehen's recruit. One of Olajuwon's recruits attacked a Christian meeting when the leader blasphemed Islam. Reska's recruit bombed the American fighter jet bound for use against our Muslim brothers in Syria."

"And how was this discovered?" Hussein switched back to Arabic. "We ordered all recruits enter martyrdom, did we not? I thought our operatives had experienced martyrdom."

"That is the root of our problem, my leader." Abdur kept his voice calm.

"What do you mean?"

"It seems one did not."

"Details. I want details! Now!"

"The Navy petty officer who planted the bomb in the fighter plane did not enter martyrdom. Not at first."

"Explain!" Hussein al-Akhma's voice rose in volume.

"Our chaplain believed the recruit would enter martyrdom as instructed. When the recruit hesitated, the chaplain pressed the matter. The recruit still hesitated, and the chaplain took care of the problem. The recruit's body is on the bottom of the ocean. But the Americans intercepted some information about the bombing before Commander Reska acted. Perhaps it was through a recording device. Their agents arrested the three chaplains all at the same time."

Standing behind his desk, his veins bulging at his temples, al-Akhma closed his eyes, then slowly opened them. A swift, furious movement of his right hand sent a stack of papers flying to the floor. "How could this happen, Abdur?"

Abdur winced from the shrill pitch of Hussein's voice.

"You said our operations were protected by martyrdom!" His hand flew to his white tunic. When it reappeared, it held the familiar, black 9mm Beretta.

Abdur thought about running, but a sudden move might excite Hussein's trigger finger.

"Please, my leader." Abdur shook as Hussein worked the firing pin on the pistol, chambering a live round. He prayed he would not wet himself.

"Why should I not kill the one who is responsible!" Hussein waved the pistol toward the roof of the tent.

Because those responsible for this are in America, Abdur wanted to say. But he held his tongue, searching for the words to calm his leader rather than incite him to further rage. "Because you, Leader, brilliantly planned this in advance and have already created an organization to deal with this very problem."

"And what does this mean?"

"Remember when you first called the Council together?" Abdur lowered his voice to a whisper. This was a technique he had successfully used before to calm Hussein. But never when the man waved a loaded gun toward him. "You shared the vision Allah laid upon your heart—to infiltrate the American military—to then order commencement of Operation Islamic Glory. And the day is coming. The day of glory draws near."

The pistol was now pointed to the floor.

"And you proclaimed, Leader, that we will exploit their corrupt system, using it against them." He attempted a smile. "We will use their own laws to achieve Allah's purposes."

"Yes, I did say those things." The pitch of his voice dropped.

"And even before you called the Council together, you established the Muslim Legal Foundation, and you used the foundation to force the Navy to admit our imams into their Chaplain Corps."

"Yes." An even calmer pitch.

"We funded that organization with millions of their dollars, Leader. Remember the day in Zurich when you spoke of meaningless car bombings by our predecessors, which only inflamed the Western Zionist media?"

"Yes." Hussein slumped back into his chair, laying the pistol on his desk.

"Now is the time to breathe life into your vision, Leader, to use their laws against them to advance our cause."

Hussein raised an eyebrow. "To provide legal representation to the chaplains through the foundation?"

"Precisely. We can pay for the finest lawyers in America. Let us explore that option. It was a vision given you by Allah. It is a vision that will work. And besides, we still have chaplains operating who have not been arrested, and I do not believe that the arrest of these three compromises Islamic Glory. These three were not informed of it. That plan is confined to our aviators, at least for the time being."

"Yes," Hussein said calmly. "Yours is the voice of reason, Abdur. What would I do without you?" Hussein walked around his desk and, placing his hands on Abdur's shoulder's, kissed him on each cheek. "Coordinate this, Abdur. Do it personally. Do not let me down."

"As you wish, Leader. I will leave for Turks and Caicos tomorrow morning."

CHAPTER 34

Navy-Marine Corps Trial Judiciary
Building 1
32nd Street Naval Station
San Diego

"All rise."

Diane's stomach tightened as the packed gallery rose for Captain Reeves.

"Be seated." Judge Reeves hesitated briefly before continuing. "The court finds that the proffer by the defense *does* violate the spirit, if not the letter, of the rape-shield statute. To that extent, the defense proffer to allow the testimony of these three witnesses is denied."

The reaction from the gallery was swift and loud.

Brewer smiled and rose to his feet, almost shouting above the cacophony. "Thank you, Your Honor."

"Order!"

This was not what Diane had expected. The case was over. She slumped in her chair.

"Order in the court." Two raps of the gavel quieted the gallery of spectators.

"However"—Judge Reeves slightly inclined his head to Zack—"the court is also mindful of the defendant's constitutional right to a speedy and fair trial under the Sixth Amendment of the Constitution. Moreover, the court is concerned about ineffective assistance of counsel and having this case reversed on appeal, in light of defense counsel's failure to make timely disclosure of these witnesses to the prosecution.

"Therefore, in an effort to protect the witness's rights to privacy under the rape-shield statute, and to balance those rights against those of the accused to a fair trial, the court will allow the following. Only one of the three witnesses, of the defense's choosing, may testify. The testimony of the other two witnesses, which the court deems cumulative, will not be allowed.

"Furthermore, the defense may ask only general questions to the witness about having dated Ensign Landrieu. No specific acts of promiscuous conduct, if there was any such conduct, shall be allowed. That is the ruling of this court."

More mumbling rose from the gallery.

Two more raps of the gavel followed.

Diane put her hands on the table, leaned forward, and exhaled. A victory. Or was it? Could she damage the prosecution under Judge Reeves's restrictions? Calling only one witness? Asking limited questions? Did this make her gamble even riskier?

She cleared her throat. "Your Honor, the defense requests that the court reconsider its restrictions on the witnesses."

Reeves whipped off his glasses and peered at Diane. "If the court is to reconsider anything, Lieutenant Colcernian, the court might change its mind about letting any of these last-minute witnesses testify at all. Under the circumstances, you're lucky to get one. If you ask me to reconsider, I will. But be forewarned. You might not like the results. Now you can take the court's ruling, or you can leave it."

Diane felt Zack's glare boring into her back. A grin was undoubtedly there too. She knew him all too well. And she would not give him the satisfaction of seeing her flinch. "We call Mr. Willie Garrett as our witness on this issue."

"Very well," Reeves said. "Bailiff, call the witness to the stand and then summon the members."

A few minutes later, the back door of Courtroom 1 swung open and a muscular young man wearing tight blue jeans, Air-Jordan athletic shoes, and an LSU T-shirt walked in. With a slow, bouncing strut, Garrett walked to the witness stand, was sworn in, and sat down.

Diane fixed her attention on the witness, hoping to wipe the grin from Zack's face in short order. "You're Willie Garrett of Metairie, Louisiana?"

"That's me." Garrett's voice was low and whispery. He flicked a piece of lint off his sleeve.

Judge Reeves leaned forward. "Speak up, please."

Diane started again. "Mr. Garrett, do you know Ensign Marianne Landrieu?"

"Oh yeah." A wide grin flashed across Garrett's face.

"Could you tell us how, please?"

"Me and her. We used to go out."

Diane paused, letting his words sink in. "What do you mean, 'go out'?"

"Her family is very big in Louisiana, so we had to keep it quiet. Know what I mean?"

"I'm not sure that I do," Diane said. "Please explain."

"You know. Dating."

"You and Ensign Landrieu dated?"

"When we were in high school and some in college. But yes, we dated."

"Why did you keep it quiet?"

"You know. I was an enlisted Navy SEAL. It might hurt her uncle's political chances."

"I don't understand."

"You know, they were grooming her for someone with better social standing. Not an enlisted guy, a nobody. My family was on food stamps before I joined the Navy. They still live in the projects. It wasn't like her family wanted me showing up at cocktail parties or political functions. That sort of thing."

"What did Ensign Landrieu think about dating an enlisted guy with your background?"

"She had no problem with it. Trust me." He shot her another grin, looking pleased with himself.

"Why do you say that?"

"She always used to say she had a thing for SEALs."

The sustained roar from the gallery brought two raps of Reeves's gavel, and when that didn't quiet the crowd, three more. *Whap. Whap. Whap.*

"Order! Order in the court."

Perfect. Leave it there. The roar faded into a dramatic silence. After a moment, Diane smiled. "No further questions."

"Cross-examination?" Captain Reeves nodded toward Zack.

The trim, tanned prosecutor stepped to the podium and shot her a sarcastic grin that made her want to shove him back down into his seat. "Mr. Garrett, how long ago do you claim you and Ensign Landrieu dated?"

"I don't claim. It happened." He flicked lint off the opposite arm.

"How long, Mr. Garrett?"

"Maybe about five years."

"Five years. And you were both teenagers back then, weren't you?"

"Yeah."

"And she certainly wasn't a naval officer back then, was she?"

"No."

"And you never forced her behind a hedgerow in a cold, dark parking lot, did you?"

"No, sir."

"And you never assaulted her, did you?"

Garrett's dark eyes flashed in anger. "I never assaulted anybody!"

Zack tossed Diane another inconspicuous, sarcastic smile that only she could see. Then he winked at her before turning back to the judge.

"I'm done, Your Honor."

"Very well. Court will be in recess."

"All rise."

CHAPTER 35

Law offices of Wellington Levinson
Wells Fargo Plaza
Century City
Los Angeles, California

Mr. Levinson's office, Terrie Bearden speaking." *Make this fast, buddy.*
It's just about quitting time. Terrie crossed her legs and sipped her
freshly opened bottle of Perrier as the caller, a man, introduced himself.
"Yes, sir," she said when he'd finished. "You're speaking to Mr. Levinson's
lead appointments secretary."

The caller rambled about needing the services of the world's greatest
lawyer as Terrie glanced at the digital clock on her desk: five minutes until
her workday was over, which meant heading to the gym, trading her high
heels for cross trainers, and then commencing a much-needed workout.
She would top off her glorious hour of tension-relieving exercise with a
refreshing shower and an evening of shopping on Rodeo Drive.

The fool still babbled on the other end of the phone. If she let him,
he might ramble right into her personal time at the gym. If the guy could
seriously afford Wells Levinson's services, that would be different. She
would forgo the workout for the 2 percent bonus that Levinson paid her
for booking serious clients. But those with the money had been rare
recently, and the loonies always tended to call right before quitting time.

She would go straight for the closer on this one. That would shut
him up, just as it had all those other fools who thought they had the
biggest case in history.

"Excuse me, sir." She interrupted some point about "religious discrimination." "As you know, Mr. Levinson is the author of two bestselling

books, and his services are in great demand. Therefore, our clients make financial arrangements that reflect Mr. Levinson's unique position in the legal community. We require a seventy-five-thousand-dollar nonrefundable retainer, paid up front, which entitles the client to a one-hour consultation with Mr. Levinson. This does not guarantee that Mr. Levinson will take your case. If he does decide to take your case, an additional, substantial retainer would be required."

Terrie sipped her Perrier, then plucked a Kleenex from the box sitting by the phone and wiped the lipstick from the clear bottle. "I cannot quote what that fee would be. That's between you and Mr. Levinson. Needless to say, it would be substantial. Do you have any questions about the financial arrangements?" She stopped talking. Usually, this was the point in the sales pitch when callers either backed out or simply hung up.

The man on the other end of the line didn't hesitate. "Give us wiring instructions, and the money will be in Mr. Levinson's account within one hour."

Terrie took another sip of Perrier. "And just to repeat, you do understand there's a seventy-five-thousand-dollar nonrefundable fee for one hour?"

"I understood you the first time, Ms. Bearden," the man snapped. "As I said, the money is no problem. Now would you like to discuss wiring instructions? Or should we seek other counsel?"

This guy is serious. Two percent of seventy-five thousand is fifteen hundred bucks. Forget the gym.

"I would be pleased to provide those numbers, sir. Please hold."

CHAPTER 36

Office of the Judge Advocate General of the Navy
The Pentagon
Arlington, Virginia

Captain David Guy, wearing his four-stripe dress blues, carried a thick file as he walked swiftly through the corridor connecting the "E" and "D" rings of the Pentagon. When he got to the "D" ring, he turned left and walked about fifty yards, just past the first concentric bend, and found office number D-S 402 on his right. Above the door, the sign read "Judge Advocate General of the Navy."

The captain stepped through the doors, announced his presence to the lieutenant manning the front desk, and then was immediately escorted into the office of Rear Admiral Joseph Stumbaugh.

Stumbaugh stood to greet him. "David, how was your drive up from Norfolk?"

"Fine, thank you, sir." David stepped forward to shake his hand. "Ginny and the kids send their best to you and Mrs. Stumbaugh."

"Thanks. David, I hate to drag you all the way up here. I know how you hate Washington." He paused. "You prepared for your briefing?"

"Yes, sir. I've got the file. I'm ready when you are, sir."

"Actually, there's been a change of plans."

"Sir?"

"I just got a call from the secretary of the Navy. You and I are due at the White House in one hour."

"The White House?" David's jaw dropped.

"All they've told me is that we are to meet the secretary over there. I don't know anything else, except that you should be prepared to give a briefing, if asked, on the situation with the sabotaged aircraft."

"Any idea who I'm briefing?"

"Possibly someone on the national security staff. Maybe even the president's national security advisor if he's available. That's all I know. Anyway, my car is waiting at the river entrance. We'd better get going."

Stumbaugh pressed a button on his desk. "We're ready, Kurt."

Within seconds, a briefcase-carrying lieutenant commander, the JAG's senior aide, appeared at the door.

"Let's roll." Stumbaugh stepped to the doorway, and then he and Captain Guy followed the aide back through the corridors. They passed the office of the secretary of defense on their way to the river entrance door, and minutes later, they stepped out into the sunny Washington morning.

They were greeted by the deafening roar of an airliner on final approach to Reagan National. The aide led the senior officers down the front steps of the building where the JAG's Lincoln Towncar waited, its hood-mounted, blue and white flags snapping in the breeze.

Captain Guy and Admiral Stumbaugh accepted salutes from the white-uniformed petty officers stationed at each back door of the car. Per protocol, David waited for the admiral to be seated first, in the rear passenger-side seat, then sat next to him, with the aide taking his seat in front beside the driver.

"We've been told it may take a half hour to clear security, gentlemen." The aide wheeled the Lincoln onto George Washington Parkway for the short jaunt to Memorial Bridge and then across the Potomac River into the District of Columbia. They turned left off Constitution Avenue onto 17th Street NW just in front of the Washington Monument and skirted the outside perimeter of the South Lawn.

As they approached the White House, David's stomach knotted. He had rubbed shoulders with high-ranking flag officers in his career, but he had never been inside the White House. The car slowed, turned right, and immediately halted in front of a small contingent of Marines and uniformed Secret Service personnel carrying M-16s.

"Admiral." The Marine captain rendered a sharp salute to the judge advocate general of the Navy. He was wearing a dress blue uniform with white gloves and white cap. "Please accept my apologies, sir, but could you step out of the car, please? Standard security, sir."

They exited the car and moved to the South Lawn of the White House, watching dogs and armed men perform their search. After checking their IDs, the Marine led the JAG, his aide, and Captain Guy to a small, high-tech security shack on the perimeter of the South Lawn, where the trio stepped into an X-ray booth.

When they had been cleared, the Marine stepped toward the JAG. "Admiral, if you and your party will follow me, I'll take you to your meeting, sir."

"Lead the way." Admiral Stumbaugh glanced toward David as they fell in behind the Marine captain.

The Marine captain led the officers back across the lawn into a small inconspicuous-looking door on the west side of the White House, adjacent to 17th Street. A four-striper Navy captain, sporting a surplus of heavy gold cording on his shoulder, stepped out to meet them.

The Marine captain saluted. "Sir, presenting Rear Admiral Stumbaugh, Captain Guy, and Lieutenant Commander Foster."

"Thank you, Captain." The Navy captain retuned the junior officer's salute. "I'll take it from here. You are dismissed."

"Aye, sir." The Marine captain clicked his heels, pivoted 180 degrees, and walked away. The Navy captain turned to Admiral Stumbaugh and flashed a smart salute to the judge advocate general.

"Good morning, sir. I'm Captain Jay Hancock, naval attaché to the president."

"A pleasure, Captain," Stumbaugh said, returning the salute. "Naval attaché to the president?"

"One of the lesser-publicized jobs in the Navy, I suppose." Hancock shot Stumbaugh an embarrassed grin.

"Does that mean we are meeting the president this morning?" the JAG asked.

Hancock nodded. "The president, as you know, is an ex-JAG officer himself, and he is looking forward to meeting you, Admiral. And he is particularly interested in speaking with Captain Guy."

David's heart plunged to the floor. He had barely recovered when Captain Hancock extended his hand. "Jay Hancock. Nice to meet you, Captain Guy."

"A pleasure, Captain Hancock." David swallowed hard and clasped the hand of the naval attaché.

Hancock's friendly gray eyes met David's. "He is really a nice guy. Don't sweat it."

"Reading my mind, Captain?"

"I was a bit starstruck myself the first time. Everybody gets that way." Hancock checked his watch, then looked back to Stumbaugh.

"Please follow me, sir. The commander in chief is running a very tight schedule today."

Hancock led the men down an outer hallway and through a large secretarial office past three smiling women. When they reached a large white door, he opened it, stepped inside, and announced, "Mr. President, presenting the Judge Advocate General of the Navy, Captain David Guy, and Lieutenant Commander Kurt Foster."

David stepped into an expansive office. At the opposite end of the room, the president stood and paused for a moment behind his desk. There was no mistaking his identity. His presence, even from the distance between them, was commanding. David drew in a deep breath. He was about to shake hands with the president of the United States!

David recognized the men on either side of the president: the secretary of defense, the attorney general, and the secretary of the Navy.

"Thank you for coming, gentlemen, and welcome to the White House," said the commander in chief as he walked from behind his desk and shook Joseph Stumbaugh's hand. "I'm Mack Williams."

"Thank you for the invitation, sir." Stumbaugh spoke as senior officer on behalf of the group. "It's a pleasure to be here."

Then the president turned and extended his hand to David. "I've heard a lot of good things about you, Captain. And we appreciate your good work on the sabotage case."

"Thank you, sir." It was all David could muster as the rest of the introductions were made.

"Gentlemen, please be seated." The president gestured to three chairs directly in front of his. "Admiral, one of the reasons I called you here today is to personally thank you for the JAG Corps' involvement in breaking open the case involving the three Muslim chaplains."

"There's ample credit to be spread around, Mr. President. But I appreciate your kind words."

Mack Williams turned to David. "And I understand, Captain, that you made the initial recommendation to open this into a criminal investigation?"

David nodded. "As Admiral Stumbaugh said, I can't claim a lot of credit. The NCIS took the ball and ran with it."

"I appreciate your modesty, Captain, but I shudder to think where we'd be if not for your gut instinct on this one."

"Thank you, Mr. President."

"Admiral, there's a debate that's been raging within this office over how the government should prosecute these three Muslim chaplains. The attorney general here feels the Department of Justice should handle the matter. The secretary of the Navy wants to let the Navy JAG Corps handle it.

"This is no routine court-martial. The potential prosecution of these terrorists posing as military officers is a matter of utmost national security. My worry is that other Islamic terrorists may be planted in our armed forces, which is why I've placed the military on heightened alert until the completion of this trial. Frankly, the national security may depend on the outcome of this trial. I want you to level with me," the president said. "Can the JAG Corps handle this? Or should we let the civvies get involved?"

"Mr. President, I assure you that the Navy JAG Corps is more than capable on this one," Stumbaugh said without hesitation.

The president turned to David. "Captain Guy, what do you think?"

"Sir, I concur with Admiral Stumbaugh."

The president fixed a serious gaze on Stumbaugh. "Admiral, if we leave this in the hands of the Navy, who would you detail to prosecute this matter?"

"Mr. President, the JAG Corps has a stable of experienced and talented trial counsel who could handle this. I would, of course, confer with some of our senior captains before making a recommendation." It was obvious he didn't know who to recommend.

David noticed an almost imperceptible smirk crawl across Attorney General Hutchinson's face.

"Well, we have one of your senior captains right here." The president turned his eyes squarely on David Guy. "What do you think, Captain Guy? You know the JAG Corps. Is there an active-duty JAG officer you'd recommend to prosecute this case?"

"Mr. President, before I came to Norfolk, I was the commanding officer of the Naval Justice School at Newport, Rhode Island."

"Know it well." The president smiled. "Spent about five months there myself."

"Yes, sir. And if you will recall, the Justice School not only provides a very extensive trial advocacy program, but there is also a trial advocacy tournament sponsored by the New York City Bar Association."

"Remember that too." This time the president snorted. "Didn't do too well in it."

184 ★ Don Brown

"Well, sir, in my three years as CO of the Justice School, there was one young officer who had an exceptional flair for trial advocacy. He was the only officer we've ever had win the trial advocacy award when assigned the role of defense counsel. The facts of that case are heavily weighted in favor of the prosecution."

"You mean the Newcombe murder trial? With all those bloody pictures? You guys still using that?"

"Yes, Mr. President." He grinned. "Your memory serves you well, sir."

"Memory, heck. Who can forget all those bloody pictures? I got stuck on the defense side of that one too."

"Yes, sir. The facts are deliberately slanted for the prosecution. The defense challenge is to put on a good enough show in the sentencing phase to avoid the death penalty."

"My guy got fried." The president leaned back in his chair, seeming to enjoy the memory.

"Most do, sir. But we had one officer, a young man from North Carolina, who played the defense role like a maestro and wound up with a not-guilty verdict. It was the first time in twenty years we had seen a clean defense verdict in the final round. I sat in on the trial myself. This kid was unbelievable. And he beat a very good opponent."

"What's this officer's name?"

"Brewer, sir."

"Why's the name familiar?"

"Sir, Lieutenant Brewer is currently stationed in San Diego. You may have heard his name because he is the officer who is prosecuting the rape trial involving Senator Fowler's niece."

"Oh yeah." A hint of recognition crossed the president's face. "The case that's got our good friend Reverend Barbour camped out in San Diego looking for a racist behind every bush." He chuckled. "The guy's enough to make even Roberson Fowler consider switching parties." He laughed again. Obligatory laughter erupted from the secretary of defense and the attorney general.

"Yes, sir. That's the case, Mr. President."

"Admiral, what do you think?"

"Since I've spent the past few years of my career here in Washington, I don't personally know Lieutenant Brewer. But I have spoken to his commanding officer, and he does come highly recommended."

"Mr. Attorney General?" The president turned to Hutchinson.

The attorney general adjusted his bow tie and leaned forward slightly. "I'm sure he's a fine young officer, Mr. President. But I emphasize *young*. I've been following the assault trial with some degree of interest, and it appears that with the Reverend Barbour on the scene, this lieutenant has his hands full. My recommendation, sir, is let's wait and see what happens."

"Fair enough," the president said. "Admiral, Captain, thank you for coming today. It has been a privilege. I will take your thoughts under advisement. Captain Hancock will see you out."

Realizing that they had just been dismissed, David rose, shook hands with President Williams once more, then followed Stumbaugh, his aide, and the naval attaché out of the Oval Office.

CHAPTER 37

Defense counsel's lounge
Navy-Marine Corps Trial Judiciary
Building 1
32nd Street Naval Station
San Diego

Lieutenant Diane Colcernian sat alone in the defense counsel's lounge, sipping a Diet Coke. The chirping inside her purse signaled a phone call. She fished it out and read the caller ID flashing on the screen. She drew in a deep breath, hesitating for a few beats of her heart. "Hi, Pierre."

"How is the most beautiful naval officer in the world?"

"Never met him." Even as she said the words, she pictured Zack.

"The camera loves you," Pierre said. "It always has."

Something sad colored his usually buoyant voice, and Diane softened her tone. "I'm trying to avoid the television these days. Brewer's the star. Not me."

"It's been reported you won your motion." He paused. "I'm proud of you."

She leaned back, picturing her dear friend, the kindness in his handsome face, the affection in his eyes. "Thanks. Honestly, I don't know how much damage we did."

"Is your client going to testify?"

"I can't really say."

Silence fell between them. Finally, Pierre said, "You finish this weekend. I'd like nothing better than to fly out, take you someplace special to celebrate . . . and start working on our wedding plans."

Diane looked down at her bare finger. She couldn't wait any longer to tell him her decision. She squeezed her eyes shut for a moment, gathering her courage. "Pierre . . . I—"

"Dearest," he said, interrupting. "I have another call coming in. May I call you back?"

"And I think the bailiff's calling us. We'll talk later." She hesitated, thinking of all he had meant to her through the years. "It's important."

She thought she heard him swallow hard, and then he sighed. "Of course." He paused again. "I love you."

"Pierre—" Diane began, but the line was already dead. She dropped her head into her hands, aching for this man, her friend, and his broken dreams.

Trial counsel's lounge
Navy-Marine Corps Trial Judiciary
Building 1
32nd Street Naval Station
San Diego

Your cross-examination was magnificent." Amy sat across the table from Zack. "So what did you think about Garrett's testimony?" She scooted her chair forward and rested her elbows on the table, a stack of files on one side, Zack's attaché on the other.

"Hard to say. I felt good about the cross, I guess. But that comment about her liking Navy SEALs seemed to get quite a reaction." He hadn't felt good about it then; he still didn't.

"That was before you put him on the defensive."

"We'll see how well I can cross Blount when he testifies."

"Think he will?"

"If the judge had let all three of those guys testify, then maybe not. But yeah, I don't see how she can avoid putting him on the stand. I don't think she got enough out of Garrett."

"She's good, isn't she?" Amy's little gold cross caught the light as she leaned forward, her gaze meeting his.

"Who, Diane?"

"Yeah." There was a glint of knowing in Amy's eyes. He almost chuckled. *A knowing?* What was he thinking? A knowing of *what*?

"She is," he admitted reluctantly.

Three raps sounded at the door. "Lieutenant Brewer, the judge is ready." The voice from the hallway was that of the legalman chief.

"Right there, Chief."

They gathered their files, and he followed Amy to the door. He swung it open and stepped back to let her pass through. Then he rushed into the hallway, shifted his attaché case to the opposite hand, and glanced at his watch . . . only to look up and halt midstep before running into Diane Colcernian, who had just slammed out of the ladies' room.

"Diane . . ."

She turned toward him and blinked. "Counselor." She was pale, her eyes red-rimmed as if she had been crying. Through the years, he had seldom—if ever—seen such a vulnerable expression on her face. The look was so alien to the Diane he knew, it didn't register at first. But that was exactly what he had seen in the depths of those wide emerald eyes: vulnerability. He had a sudden urge to gather her into his arms.

He shook away the image just as quickly as it appeared. Almost trotting, he caught up with her, matching her stride as they headed to the courtroom. "You okay?"

She shot him a flinty, fiery look and tossed her head. "Never better."

He grinned. The old Diane was back. "Good." He stood back to let her enter the courtroom.

Dirksen Senate Office Building
Office of Senator Roberson Fowler
Washington, D.C.

Excuse me, Senator." Ed rapped lightly then pushed open the door. Senator Fowler, sitting at his desk, looked up as his aide entered the room.

"CNN is back on the air with the court-martial coverage. JamesOn Barbour is about to make a statement."

The Senator frowned and leaned back in his leather chair. "Flip it on."

Ed crossed the room, pressed a button to expose a plasma TV screen from behind a cabinet, and flipped the channel to CNN. Bernie Woodson stood in front of the camera, talking into a handheld microphone.

"I'm standing just outside the main gate of the 32nd Street Naval station in San Diego, where things are developing rapidly in the court-martial of Petty Officer Antonio Blount, the Navy SEAL accused of assaulting a naval officer who is the niece of United States Senator Roberson Fowler. We're waiting for a statement from the Reverend JamesOn Barbour, who's just arrived here at the main gate. We're told that the Reverend Barbour will criticize the Navy for Judge Richard Reeves's decision not to let all three young men testify in the defense of the Navy SEAL."

Woodson fidgeted with his earpiece. "I've just been told that the Reverend Barbour is on the platform at a location just across the street and is about to speak. And now, the Reverend Barbour."

The CNN camera switched to Barbour with two elderly women, standing on a podium with a palm tree and the gated entrance of the naval station behind him.

"Good morning, ladies and gentlemen," Barbour said, wrapping his arms around the two frail-looking, gray-haired women in wire-rimmed glasses. "I'd like to introduce two very special people. To my left is Mrs. Annie Belle Jones. Miss Annie Belle is ninety-two years old, and she is the great-grandmother of Petty Officer Blount.

"And to my right is Mrs. Jamie Perry. Miss Jamie is seventy-three years old, and she is Petty Officer Blount's grandmother."

Barbour gave each woman a kiss on the cheek. The cameras zoomed in on each of them, their eyes beaming and sparkling as though they had been hugged by their guardian angel.

"What a grandstander." Fowler exchanged an irritated glance with Ed.

As if reading Fowler's mind, Ed turned up the volume as the cameras zoomed in on Barbour, who looked appropriately sincere for the camera's sake.

"We are concerned, in this day of modern computers and modern weapons, that the Navy is becoming antiquated in its thought processes. Why is it, in this great nation, a nation that stands for equal justice for all people—not just for the kinfolk of the rich and famous, not just for the kinfolk of powerful United States senators, but for all people . . . why is it there is no justice for three simple young men, former Navy SEALs who wish to tell their story, who deserve their day in court?

"Why must this judge stifle their testimony and refuse to let two even testify? Why must he limit the testimony of the third? And why is it that a young hero of this nation, a Navy SEAL, who saved the life of his shipmate in a rescue operation off Libya, is not allowed to put on a full defense when accused of so serious a crime?

190 ★ Don Brown

"Is it because this young man is so unlucky as to be accused by the niece of such a powerful member of Congress?

"I, as the minister to this family, call for a congressional investigation into the Navy's conduct of this matter."

"Thank you." Barbour walked off the podium, ignoring questions being shouted at him.

"Good luck with the congressional investigation, JamesOn," Fowler snorted as Ed flipped off the television. Ed went to Fowler's humidor, took out a Monte Cristo, and handed it to Fowler. As the senator leaned back in his plush leather chair, circles of smoke rising above his head, he grinned at his right-hand man. "So what's the latest dirt you've dug up on our young *wunderkind*? I want to know where we're heading once he whips the tail off the defense—and gets this officious oaf away from the cameras."

Ed chuckled, leaned back in his chair, and straightened his tie. The young go-getter's eyes glinted, just as they always did when he was given a particularly surreptitious assignment. "Dirt?" he said, still laughing. "Hardly."

CHAPTER 38

Diane turned and nodded to her legalman who was sitting just behind the defense table. At the signal, the legalman pulled a previously concealed manila file from her briefcase. The label affixed to the file read "Direct Examination of Defendant."

Diane took the file, smiled a thank-you, and then stood. "Your Honor, the defense calls Petty Officer Antonio Blount."

The announcement brought a chorus of whispers from the gallery followed by a shuffling of papers as reporters positioned their legal pads for the high drama about to unfold.

Antonio Blount, trim and muscular, walked with a confident stride to the witness stand. He wore the white jumper suit and gleaming black leather shoes of a Navy enlisted man, with his gold, pitch-forked SEAL medallion polished and pinned above the colorful row of thin service ribbons over his pocket. A momentary silence filled the courtroom. Then the witness was sworn in.

"You're Petty Officer Antonio Blount?"

"Yes, ma'am."

"You're a Navy SEAL?"

"Yes, ma'am."

"How long have you been in the Navy?"

"Five years."

"And you are accused of raping Ensign Marianne Landrieu?"

"I didn't do it!"

Diane tried to ignore Zack as he leaned back in his swivel chair, his fingers crossed nonchalantly over his stomach.

She glanced toward the members, trying unsuccessfully to read their expressions, then focused again on Blount. "Are you sure?"

"I'm sure."

"All right, Petty Officer. Tell us what really did happen on the evening of May twenty-fifth."

"Sometimes I take a walk around the base. It helps me get relaxed. You know? That night, I was taking such a walk. I heard some music coming from the Officers' Club, so I cut through the parking lot. You know? To check things out. And while I was walking through the parking lot, that's when I saw her come out."

"By 'her,' who do you mean?"

"You know, the ensign."

"Ensign Landrieu?"

"Yes, ma'am."

"And then what?"

"Well, when she came out, she looked drunk."

"Why do you say that, Petty Officer?"

"She was stumbling around and all."

"And then what?"

"I was worried about her. We SEALs take care of our officers. So I volunteered to help her get to her car, or if she needed help getting home, I was going to help her."

"What happened next?"

"She wanted to know where I was from. I told her I was from Mississippi, and she said she was from Louisiana. And then we started talking, and one thing led to another."

"What do you mean by that?"

"I could tell she liked me. She said she liked Navy SEALs. And then we started kissing, and next thing I know, the shore patrol was pointing flashlights at us."

"This is very important, Petty Officer. Did Ensign Landrieu agree to what happened between you two that night?"

"Absolutely. It was consensual."

"Any doubt in your mind?"

"No doubt, ma'am. On my word as a SEAL."

"No further questions."

"Cross-examination?" Judge Reeves turned to Zack.

Zack stood, taking in a deep breath. "Yes, Your Honor." He stepped to the podium between the counsel tables. "Petty Officer Blount, as I understand your testimony, you claim that Ensign Landrieu allowed you to do what you did?"

"Yes, sir."

"And of course, you went along with her, right?"

"Right."

"Petty Officer, you're not an officer, are you?"

"No, sir."

"You're enlisted, right?"

"Yes, sir."

"Petty Officer, what is fraternization?"

"That's when an officer isn't supposed to socialize with an enlisted person."

"And so, if what you're saying is the truth, that you and the ensign voluntarily did this act, then that makes you guilty of fraternization, doesn't it?"

"Objection." Diane Colcernian sprang to her feet like a red-furred cat. "Relevance!"

"Overruled."

"You're guilty of fraternization, Petty Officer?"

"The witness will answer the question," Judge Reeves said after Blount hesitated.

"If I'm guilty of fraternization, then the ensign is too."

"But you are guilty yourself, aren't you, Petty Officer?"

"I guess."

"And so you admit to violating the Uniform Code of Military Justice because of your attraction to this woman?"

"Objection." Diane slammed her hand down on the table and glared at Zack.

"Overruled."

"Yes, sir." Blount's words came out in a sputter.

"So when you're attracted to a good-looking woman, you're prepared to throw the law out the window?"

Diane jumped to her feet again. "Objection! Argumentative."

"Sustained."

"Petty Officer, you testified that the ensign was drunk, and you just happened to be walking around near the Officers' Club—which, since you're not an officer, you can't enter—when you saw the ensign?"

"Like I said. I like to take a walk sometimes at night." Blount squirmed on the stand.

"And you testified that you were so concerned about the ensign being drunk that you wanted her to make it home safely?"

"Like I said, we SEALs are trained to take care of our officers."

"And this drunk officer, as you have described her, was stumbling around?"

"Yeah."

"So it's fair to say she did not have total control of her faculties?"

"Yeah."

"So you're saying she was so drunk she could not have consented to what you intended, isn't that true?"

"She wasn't that drunk."

"What's it gonna be, Petty Officer? She was so drunk she was stumbling around, or she was lucid enough to have an ongoing conversation about her being from Louisiana and you being from Mississippi?" Zack stood back and crossed his arms.

"Objection!" Diane's face was red as she leaped to her feet again.

"Overruled."

"What's it gonna be, Petty Officer?"

"She was drunk."

"As a Navy SEAL, you're trained to kill with your hands, aren't you?"

"Yes, sir."

"And you're bigger than Ensign Landrieu, aren't you?"

"Yes, sir."

"And stronger?"

"Yes, sir."

"You could easily overpower her, couldn't you?"

"I didn't overpower her." Blount glared at Zack.

"Petty Officer, if you get convicted of raping an officer, you could go to prison for the rest of your life, couldn't you?"

Blount met Diane's eyes for a brief moment; then he shifted his gaze back to Zack.

"The witness will answer the question," Judge Reeves said.

"Yes, sir."

"And you don't want to go to prison for the rest of your life, do you?"

"No, sir."

"Tell the truth, Petty Officer. Wouldn't you tell one little white lie if it kept you out of prison for the rest of your life?"

"Objection!" Diane stormed to her feet.

"What is your objection, Lieutenant Colcernian?" Judge Reeves leaned forward intently.

"That's a trick question." Diane's face matched her hair color.

"Want to explain that, Lieutenant?" The judge sat back and peered at Diane over his glasses.

"It's unfair to require the witness to answer, Your Honor."

"Why?" Reeves persisted.

"Because if he answers 'yes,' Lieutenant Brewer will argue that he will commit perjury to stay out of prison. If he answers 'no,' Lieutenant Brewer will argue that he's lying, that most people will tell a white lie to stay out of prison. This is a trick question and should be disallowed, because under Rule 403 of the Military Rules of Evidence, the danger of unfair prejudice substantially outweighs any probative value."

Judge Reeves whipped his glasses off, wiped them with a handkerchief, carefully repositioned them on his nose, then crossed his arms and leaned back in his chair. "Lieutenant, the defendant was not compelled to testify. But he decided to do so. And aggressive cross-examination in cases such as these is not unexpected. Furthermore, a witness's motivation to tell the truth or to fabricate is always relevant. Your objection is overruled. The witness will answer the question."

Blount slumped. "I forgot the question."

"Repeat your question, Lieutenant Brewer." Reeves adjusted his eyeglasses again and peered at Zack.

"Petty Officer, you said you didn't want to go to prison for the rest of your life. My question is, wouldn't you tell a *little white lie* to keep from going to prison for the rest of your life?"

Blount sat up straight and stared at Diane, whose face was still bright red. Then he glanced back at the judge. Finally, he turned again to Zack. "Yes, sir."

"So you would tell a lie to stay out of prison?" Zack asked this slowly and forcefully, his words echoing through the courtroom.

"Yes, sir."

"No further questions."

Judge Reeves broke the deathly silence. "Court is in recess."

CHAPTER 39

Zack stepped into the empty chapel, moved by the solitude of this quiet place, an inauspicious escape from the bustling activity of the huge naval base all around. In the chancel, a silver chalice and simple gold cross, positioned on the table, sat beneath a bar of sunlight streaming through the stained-glass windows.

He sat down in the first row of pews, bowed his head, and prayed silently for wisdom. When he raised his head, he felt a hand on his shoulder and turned to see a trim, African-American naval officer, wearing working khakis, standing in the aisle just beside him. The officer wore the silver oak leaf pin of a full commander on his right collar and the cross of Jesus Christ on the left. Zack recognized the commander as a member of the United States Navy Chaplain Corps.

"Deep in thought, Lieutenant?" The commander's voice was gentle, his accent slightly Southern.

"Right now, I feel pulled in a thousand different directions."

"So even the famous Lieutenant Brewer is not immune from the mundane struggles of life."

The chaplain's eyes seemed kind. "My face is that recognizable, sir?"

"I guess our friend the Reverend Barbour has seen to that. But I wouldn't let that guy bother you. He's a publicity hound."

"Why do you say that, sir?"

"Barbour calls himself a reverend, but how many times have you ever heard him actually preach the gospel? With him, it's all about politics.

The guy doesn't speak for most African-Americans. He certainly doesn't speak for me. Anyway, I didn't mean to ramble, son. I'll be back in my office if you need anything." The chaplain turned and started walking toward the entrance of the chapel.

Zack watched him go, but before he reached the door, he called out, "Chaplain?"

"Yes, Lieutenant?"

"It's this trial, sir. My job is largely over. We finished yesterday with closing arguments, and now it's in the jury's hands."

"From what I've read in the papers and seen on television, you seem to have done an outstanding job, regardless of the outcome." The chaplain walked toward him again. "You worried about it?"

"What I'm worried about, sir, is the truth. Based on the evidence I've seen, I think the defendant is guilty. But even as the prosecutor, you can never know for sure. I worry about sending an innocent man to jail. That's all."

"You think this man might be innocent?"

"No, sir. I don't think so. But I could be wrong. Only God knows for sure. I came here to pray that the right decision would be reached."

"'Justice is mine, saith the Lord.' And the Lord directs the hearts of kings and judges. I'll join you in a prayer for truth and justice here." The chaplain put his hand on Zack's shoulder. "You're a believer?"

"Without a doubt. I gave my life to the Lord when I was thirteen. But my Bible study and fellowship have not been what they should have been for the last few years." He paused, looking up at the cross, the colors flooding the altar from the stained-glass windows. "There's something missing, though." He moved his gaze to the chaplain's compassionate face. "I suppose it's, well, a sense of unworthiness to come to the Lord. Too often I go off in my own hardheaded direction—with the best of intentions to draw closer to him, to seek time alone with him, study his Word ..." He paused, shaking his head slightly, then shrugged. "Life goes on, gets busier, frantically busier, and before I know it, I'm here where I am today, wondering why God feels so far away. Trying to pray, only to have the words, the thoughts, die inside me."

The chaplain sat down beside him. "You know, son, God hasn't changed. He loves you as much as he did when you gave him your heart as a child. He hasn't moved away from you."

Zack smiled. "Like the old saying, 'If it seems like God is far away, guess who moved?'"

The chaplain didn't smile with him; instead, he nodded solemnly. "He's here, son, with you this minute. Waiting to fellowship with you. Waiting to listen. Waiting to let you know he cares."

Zack felt a sting at the top of his throat and swallowed hard.

"Let me lead us in prayer." The chaplain bowed his head.

Zack studied the cross for a moment, remembering the sacrifice his Lord had made for him. Feeling ashamed, he couldn't look any longer and bowed his head.

As the chaplain began to pray, the timbre of his voice was deep, his soft Southern accent, comforting. "Our Father, who art in heaven, we come to you this day in the almighty name of Jesus Christ our Lord, and your only begotten Son. Forgive us, Father, when we sin against you by allowing our lives to become so busy with the mundane that we forget and neglect our relationship with you. Forgive us for forgetting that you gave your life for us—the ultimate sacrifice one Friend makes for another.

"You have promised us that you will always hear us when we pray. And here, this day, in this, your house, I join this officer, my brother, in asking for wisdom. Thank you that he is seeking justice, even though the flesh would want a victory. Lord, I join him in praying for the jury, even as they deliberate right now, that justice, your justice, would be accomplished in the verdict.

"Draw my brother close to your heart, Father. May he sense your presence this moment, this hour . . . this day. And may he recognize your voice even in the midst of his busy life."

He paused, and Zack swallowed around the lump in his throat.

"Thank you for hearing us, Father. For we trust these things to you in the name of Jesus Christ our Lord, Amen."

"Amen," Zack breathed in response.

"I'm glad I found you here today, Lieutenant." The chaplain stood and gave Zack a friendly squeeze on the shoulder. "You will be in my prayers."

Zack sat in wonder for a moment, listening to the chaplain's footsteps as he walked to the entrance door. He turned, realizing he hadn't even asked his name. But the door had closed, and the man was gone.

His cell phone rang, and he flipped it open. "Lieutenant Brewer."

"It's Amy. The members have a verdict."

CHAPTER 40

he members have a verdict, ma'am." The voice of the legalman chief carried through the closed door followed by a light knock. "Captain Reeves wants the attorneys in the courtroom in fifteen minutes."

Fifteen minutes. Diane took a deep breath. Fifteen minutes until the verdict was announced that would make or break her career as a JAG officer. Had her gamble paid off?

It was hard to say.

Zack ripped her client in his closing argument. It was vintage Brewer: driving his points home with emotion and drama. Raising and lowering his voice to build suspense. Flailing his hands like a maestro conducting an orchestra. Of course, her argument had been effective, too, earning nods from a few members. And that's all she needed to do, really, just plant enough seeds of doubt.

Maybe there was reason for hope.

She grabbed her briefcase, left the counsel lounge, and headed down the stairway to the first deck. Like vultures, reporters swarmed in the hallway; they came at her, microphones and cameras extended.

"No comment." She pushed through the press, entered the back door of the courtroom, and walked confidently up to the defense counsel's table, where the accused sat, waiting for her.

In a moment, Brewer walked in with his paralegal at his side. She bristled when Zack shot her a brief cocksure smile.

"All rise."

The jury entered the courtroom slowly, ceremoniously, each member looking somber and avoiding eye contact with anyone but the judge.

"I understand the members have reached a verdict," Judge Reeves said.

"We have, Your Honor," the president of the panel said.

"Please hand your decision to the bailiff."

Reeves unfolded the paper, studied it for a moment, and then handed it back to the bailiff. "I have examined the verdict, and it appears to be in order. Will the accused and counsel please rise?"

Diane's knees shook as she rose from her chair to stand with Blount.

The judge turned to the clerk. "Madam Clerk, would you publish the verdict of the members?"

"In the case of *United States versus GM3 (SEAL) Antonio Blount, United States Navy*, we the members find the defendant, on the charges and specifications of rape . . ." The clerk paused.

". . . guilty."

A roar rose from the gallery.

Five solid raps of Captain Reeves's gavel echoed through the courtroom. "Order! Order!"

Diane's gaze swept to Brewer, then to the chaos behind him. Reporters and observers shuffled papers, buzzing like bees surrounding a honeycomb.

The gavel pounded harder. "Order in the court, or the bailiff will remove spectators." Judge Reeves looked squarely at Diane. "Does the defense have evidence in mitigation before sentencing?"

Her gamble had failed. Brewer had won. *Again.*

CHAPTER 41

The Oval Office
The White House
Washington, D.C.

The president and the ambassador of France were chatting over tea, served by two white-jacketed Navy stewards, when Wally Walsh, the president's chief of staff, entered the Oval Office.

"Mr. President, Mr. Ambassador, please pardon the interruption, but I need just a moment, Mr. President."

The president was seated in a navy blue wingback chair in front of the marble fireplace just a few feet from his desk. The ambassador sat in an identical chair at an angle from the president. A third chair, making the vortex of a triangle between the president and the ambassador, was occupied by a female translator from the State Department.

"Can you excuse me for a moment, please, Mr. Ambassador?" Mack Williams spoke in French, bypassing the translator.

"Certainment, Monsieur President." The ambassador sipped his tea as the president stood and, with his cup of tea in hand, walked over to Walsh.

"What's up, Wally?" Mack Williams frowned at his chief of staff.

"Sir, a verdict's coming in right now on that SEAL court-martial in San Diego," Walsh said.

"We got a live feed?"

"Yes, sir. In the secretary's office."

"Let's go."

The two men, followed by two dark-suited Secret Service agents, stepped out of the Oval Office, through the anteroom, and into the

202 ★ DON BROWN

secretarial spaces. The president's unannounced presence caused a stir, as it always did.

"Please be seated." Mack smiled and waved nonchalantly. "Wally and I just want to watch a little TV for a minute." Wally picked up the remote and flipped on the television.

". . . about one hour ago, a Navy jury returned with a verdict of guilty against Petty Officer Antonio Blount on the charge of raping Ensign Marianne Landrieu, the niece of Senator Fowler. The trial then went into a sentencing phase in which the only defense witness was the mother of Petty Officer Blount, Mrs. Sophie Jones.

"Mrs. Jones, in tearful testimony, pled for mercy for her son. She portrayed him as a good, respectful boy whose dream as a child was to be a Navy SEAL.

"But the military jury—or 'members' as they call themselves in the military justice system—apparently did not buy Lieutenant Colcernian's arguments. Nor did they buy Mrs. Jones's plea for mercy. After deliberating only fifty-two minutes, the members returned with a sentence against Petty Officer Blount, confining him to thirty years in the Navy brig."

"Wow," the president mumbled. "Thirty years."

"The sentence also reduces Petty Officer Blount to pay grade E-1, which is the lowest enlisted pay grade, and dishonorably discharges him from the Navy.

"Although military law allows for up to life imprisonment for a rape charge, we are told by JAG Corps veterans that the thirty-year sentence is considered to be very heavy for this type of offense.

"The Reverend JamesOn Barbour has been here in San Diego monitoring the trial. He just issued a statement condemning the verdict and the sentence as—and these are his words—'an unfortunate example of racism in the twenty-first century.' We're told that the prosecutor, Lieutenant Zack Brewer, will be leaving the courthouse in just a few seconds and may have a few words for us.

"And now, Lieutenant Brewer is exiting the military courthouse. Let's see what he has to say."

The president saw the image of a young, trim naval officer in smart summer whites step through the familiar-looking front door of Building 1 to a battery of pre-positioned microphones attached to a temporary podium.

"Lieutenant, Jan Oberholtz. KNSD. Your thoughts on the outcome of the trial?"

"Jan. Here are my thoughts," Zack said calmly. "The Navy has today shown that we will not tolerate this kind of conduct, especially when the victim is an officer. At the same time, however, it is a sad day, in that one of our Navy SEALs, now a former Navy SEAL, has fallen. So justice was served. And this is good. But it has been a painful process for all."

"Lieutenant, did Blount get a fair trial, and did the judge's restriction on the testimony of the three defense witnesses influence the jury?"

"Yes, Blount got a fair trial. Judge Reeves's ruling, in my view, was overly generous to the defense. Under the rape-shield statute, none of the witnesses should have been allowed to testify at all. Beyond that, I'm not going to speculate what the members thought or comment any more on the ruling."

"Lieutenant Brewer, could you comment on the Reverend Barbour's calling the trial and the verdict 'an unfortunate example of racism in the twenty-first century'?"

"I've been busy in the courtroom the last couple of days and haven't heard those particular comments. But I have heard similar comments coming out of Mr. Barbour's camp all week."

The president snickered when Brewer called the Reverend Barbour "*Mr.* Barbour."

"Such comments are unhelpful. They come from a man who has no clue about any of the real facts surrounding this case. Mr. Barbour's presence in San Diego has created an unfortunate sideshow obviously designed to promote his own agenda, whatever that might be. Frankly, his presence here and his irresponsible statements have no legal or relevant significance, except to give you good people of the media something to talk about."

The president choked on his tea. When he could speak again, he grinned at Walsh. "Captain Guy is right. This Brewer kid is good." Mack Williams drained the last drop of lukewarm tea from his cup. "I'd better get back to the French ambassador. Before he gets huffy. You know how the French are."

Walsh nodded. "Think we've found our prosecutor, Mr. President?"

"Don't know yet, Wally. We'll see."

CHAPTER 42

During the weekend following the greatest victory of his career, Zack tried to restore some normalcy to his life.

Saturday, he drove into the mountains on Interstate 8 to the little village of Julian, the quaint restored village dating back to California's Gold Rush. Now it was known for its crafts, antiques, and homemade apple pies. He had gone alone, trying to get his thoughts together.

On Sunday, he visited College Avenue Church on University Avenue near San Diego State University. He wore a blazer, khakis, and shades, hoping the large crowds would provide him anonymity. But because the *San Diego Union* had run two wrap-up articles that morning, he was spotted.

"You look familiar."

"Hey, aren't you that JAG officer?"

"I saw you on television."

The questions were not all that bothersome, and a simple "yes" or "thank you" in response was generally enough to satisfy the curiosity seeker. After hearing a thought-provoking message on God's grace, he slipped through the sea of worshipers and out the back doors unnoticed.

As he searched for his car in the parking lot, something stirred his heart. He remembered the sense of peace, the sense of God's presence, he had felt during his conversation with the chaplain the day of the verdict. What was it the chaplain had prayed for? That God would draw Zack closer to his heart.

After the hoopla of the verdict, he had almost forgotten the man's prayer. But he hadn't forgotten that sense of peace he longed for. Or the earnestness of his heart in seeking a renewed commitment to his Lord.

He drove through a Jack-in-the-Box, bought a burger, fries, and a Coke, then drove the short distance to the summit of La Mesa's Mount Helix.

Just a few others were picnicking under the huge, white, thirty-six-foot cross perched on the vista overlooking east San Diego.

Zack walked to the three-foot-high stone ridge wall just a few feet in front of the cross, looking to the west. On this clear, bright Sunday afternoon, his view included all of San Diego, from the San Jacinto Mountains, San Diego Bay, and the sparkling downtown high-rises, to the distinctive outline of Point Loma in the distance, and beyond all that, the Pacific. The breathtaking, panoramic vista reminded him of the awesome creative power of God.

All weekend, he had been plagued by a sense of uneasiness. Was God trying to tell him something? Blount was innocent after all? Zack had sent an innocent man away for thirty years? It was the heaviest sentence for a rape trial out of a San Diego court-martial in recent memory. Surely, Blount was guilty. He'd even prayed for justice with the chaplain just before the verdict.

He dropped his head into his hands. But instead of the peaceful communion he sought with his Lord, images of the trial, his triumphant defeat of the defense, marched into his mind. He had triumphed. Good things were ahead for him. He knew it would be so. He had prayed for the outcome of the trial. Didn't it stand to reason that whatever accolades followed were deserved? Actually, gifts from God himself?

Monday morning came quickly, and it was nice to report to work in a working khaki uniform for a change. With khakis, you didn't have to worry about a splotch of coffee showing up. This very thought occurred to him as he stepped into the coffee mess at 0700 hours for his first caffeine dose of the day. His immediate boss, the senior trial counsel, was already there, sipping his coffee from a San Diego Chargers mug.

"Good morning, Zack."

"Morning, Commander." Zack poured his coffee and walked across the room to where his commander was standing.

"Things seem normal again on the morning after?"

"I hope so, sir. I'm ready for a few simple unauthorized-absence guilty pleas."

"Don't get too excited about things getting simple just yet. The skipper wants you in his office immediately."

Zack took another sip of the hot, black coffee. "Sir, do you know what that's all about?"

"Yes, but I think the skipper wants to talk to you about it personally."

Zack hated secrets, and even more so, he hated being kept in suspense. "Sir, I'm ready whenever you are."

They walked out of the coffee mess, around the corner, and a moment later, Zack and his commander stood just outside the captain's office. The commander rapped lightly.

The middle-aged Texan drawled a friendly response, and they entered. "Commander, Lieutenant, come on in and be seated."

"Congratulations on a job well done." He focused on Zack, who sat down on the sofa beside the commander.

"Thank you, Skipper. But this is a team victory for the whole trial wing, not just me. And I can't underscore how much your support has meant in this whole effort, Captain."

The captain exchanged a wide smile with Zack's commander. "You don't have to butter me up. I'm already putting you in for a Navy Commendation Medal for your good work. You earned it."

"Thank you, Skipper."

"And one other thing, Lieutenant."

"Yes, sir?"

"Have you heard anything from Ensign Landrieu over the weekend?"

The question took Zack by surprise. "I haven't talked to her, sir. She called and left a message on my cell phone, but to be honest with you, I took the weekend off."

"She was probably calling you from South Carolina."

"South Carolina?" Zack frowned.

"It seems like you impressed some high-ranking government official with your performance."

"I don't understand, sir."

"Understand this, Lieutenant. You've been extended an invitation to spend time with the ranking minority member of the Senate Armed Services Committee at his beach home in Hilton Head. A Navy C-9 leaves North Island at 0600 hours tomorrow morning headed to the Marine Corps Air Station in Beaufort, South Carolina, where you will be provided transportation over to Hilton Head to Senator Fowler's compound. Consider this similar to a vacation without having to take leave. Congratulations, Lieutenant. And do the JAG Corps proud."

Zack's stomach tightened, and the uneasiness was back. "Sir, I don't know what to say."

"You say what all good officers say when receiving a direct order from a superior officer," his superior officer said, then grinned.

"Aye, aye, sir."

"Very well." The captain rose to his feet, prompting Zack and his commander to do the same. "You've got some packing to do, son. Go home and get ready. You are dismissed."

CHAPTER 43

Lieutenant Diane Colcernian's townhouse
Near Jimmy Durante Boulevard
Del Mar, California

Diane's boss, the senior defense counsel, suggested she take a few days off after the Blount trial. She got up Monday morning, threw on running shorts and a UVA T-shirt, and took a six-mile run on the beach. Still trying to decide about time off, she jumped in the shower, threw on a bath towel, walked to her closet, and pulled out a pastel pink French terry robe.

She had just finished a cup of peach yogurt and poured herself a cup of black coffee when the telephone rang. She let it go to the machine.

"This is Pierre. Where have you been all weekend? I am sorry about the trial. Call me. We must talk." There was a click, followed by a dial tone.

She didn't think she had the emotional energy to return the call. Coffee mug in hand, she wandered back to her closet. Her attention was drawn to the khaki uniform blouse with the silver railroad tracks of a Navy lieutenant on one collar and the mill rind symbol of a JAG officer on the other. Beside it hung the matching khaki skirt.

Her father had been wearing working khakis the last time she saw him before the stroke. He looked so rugged and handsome. The three silver stars of a Navy vice admiral pinned to his collars, sparkling in the sun. Though he was disappointed in her choice, he wrapped his big arms around her in a lovable, protective, teddy-bear hug as he put her on the plane to New York. She remembered the promise she gave him the next time she saw him that day in the Portsmouth Naval Hospital.

After he died, her heart had ached for days and nights with longing to see him again.

She thought of her father's character, how he never let defeat stop him. It wasn't a word in his vocabulary. Even with his seeming defeat over her choice to become a model, the twinkle in his eye said he knew common sense would win in the end.

She touched the sleeve of her uniform and grinned. Common sense had indeed won. *What would Daddy do if he was in my shoes right now?* She didn't have to think twice to come up with the answer: he would shake off the doldrums and go to work. He wouldn't feel sorry for himself. He wouldn't accept personal defeat.

Neither would she.

Besides, she had made a promise to her father. And she was going to keep it.

And even though the best JAG officer in the Navy might be Zack Brewer, for now, she knew she wasn't far behind. Besides, Brewer was probably a short-timer. He would cash in his chips with a big firm or go into politics. At least, that was the rumor. His natural charisma in front of judges, juries—and TV cameras—told her it was bound to be true.

The thought of Brewer leaving the JAG Corps was somehow discomforting. Why was that? He'd just beaten her on national television in the biggest trial of her life.

Ninety minutes later, dressed in her khaki working uniform, her hair twisted into a bun, she slipped in the back door of the defense wing and headed to her office. Closing the door, she picked up the telephone and buzzed her legalman paralegal.

"This is Lieutenant Colcernian. I'm in. You don't have to broadcast it unless someone asks who's senior to me."

"Yes, ma'am," her paralegal said. "Mr. Rochembeau has called here four times already this morning."

"Thanks, Kim." Diane sighed. She could no longer put off talking to Pierre. But what could she tell him? His friendship had meant everything to her through the years. He had done so much for her—and for her father, even arranging for twenty-four-hour nursing care after his stroke. Thanks to Pierre, the admiral had been comfortable during the final year of his life. The nursing care alone cost Pierre over a hundred thousand dollars.

There was no doubt about the goodness of Pierre's heart. But was it enough to marry him? Even though there was no sizzle? No chemistry?

The diamond engagement ring had been locked in her safe-deposit box since he left for New York. She glanced at her finger, picked up the phone, and buzzed her paralegal. "Kim, please get Mr. Rochembeau on the line for me."

"Yes, ma'am."

CHAPTER 44

Marine Corp Air Station
Beaufort, South Carolina

At 1500 hours, eastern time, the Navy C-9 carrying Lieutenant Zack Brewer touched down on the sunny, humid runway at the Marine Corps Air Station, Beaufort, South Carolina. He received the customary salutes from the USMC ground crew as he descended the ladder to the tarmac, then was met by someone who was definitely not a United States Marine.

A richly tanned brunette, wearing white Bermuda shorts, a pink Izod shirt, designer shades, and white sandals, smiled at him. She sported more makeup than a painted Easter egg.

"I'm Sally Burleson, the senator's administrative assistant. Nice uniform. You look better in person than on TV." Her refined, sophisticated tone held a hint of Southern drawl. "I'm driving you to Hilton Head. Ready?"

Without waiting for an answer, she led him to a brand-new BMW and popped the trunk. After he had stashed his bags in the back and slid into the passenger side, she revved the engine and stepped on the accelerator.

During the ride down the long, desolate roads through the salty swamps of Jasper County, Sally talked nonstop, happily disclosing parts of her life story without expecting a response. She was an LSU cheerleader, he learned, and a Baton Rouge debutante. She and the senator had watched him on television many times, and the senator was impressed. She hoped to have a career in Washington and maybe go into politics.

Forty minutes after leaving the base, Sally's BMW crossed the bridge from Bluffton to Hilton Head, and a few minutes later, she turned left off the William Hilton Parkway to the entrance of Palmetto Dunes Plantation.

Spanish moss trees, green, luscious golf courses with irrigation systems spraying water on the greens, thousands of azaleas blooming, and alligators sunbathing along the lagoons were visible along the eastbound causeway cutting through Palmetto Dunes.

Sally pressed a speed-dial number on her mobile phone. "Senator, we're on the plantation. We'll see you in a minute." She tossed a coquettish smile at Zack as she flipped the phone closed. "He's so looking forward to meeting you."

A moment later, Zack caught a glimpse of the Atlantic behind the hotel as the BMW bore left through a traffic circle full of azaleas just in front of the Hilton Resort. They stopped briefly at a security gate and then followed another moss-lined road, running parallel to the beach, for a half mile or so.

"Here we are." Sally turned up a driveway paved with seashells. The large oceanfront house rose before them, pink stucco with expansive palladium windows across the lower floor, providing a view through the house to the beach on the other side.

Zack exited the car just as the massive front door of the house opened. A silver-haired man in a white tennis outfit stepped out. At his side was an exquisitely trim and beautiful blond in a short, blue and white tennis dress: his star witness in the court-martial of *United States v. BT3 (SEAL) Antonio Blount*.

As the smiling duo stepped toward him, Zack recognized the man as Senator Roberson Fowler. He wore the trademark wide smile Zack had seen on television hundreds of times.

"Roberson Fowler." The senator extended his hand. "Welcome to Hilton Head. I finally meet the man who not only took care of my niece, but shredded the Reverend JamesOn Barbour on national television. You are a credit to the Navy, Lieutenant."

Fowler gave an extra squeeze, and Zack felt warmth radiating from the man's hand. Not what he expected. "Thank you, Senator. Just trying to do my job."

"Well, now . . ." The senator shot Zack a devilish grin, looking like J.R. Ewing on the old *Dallas* reruns. "We should get you out of uniform and into something more comfortable."

"Come on." Marianne smiled up at him. "I'll show you to your room. You can change, and then we'll hit the beach before dinner."

"Alberto!" Fowler summoned a graying Spanish man out of the front door. "Please help the lieutenant with his bags."

"Of course, Senator." Alberto's Latin accent was appropriately sophisticated.

Marianne took Zack's hand and led him into the grand foyer of the large home. Zack caught himself just before his jaw dropped at the sight of the shining marbled floors and soaring ceilings. Fine furniture and gold and brass lamp stands filled the foyer and living room. Floor-to-ceiling windows provided an unobstructed view of the blue Carolina sky, powder-white dunes, and the Atlantic in the background. Marble fountains gushed streams of water both inside and outside this political palace by the sea. And against the soothing sound of trickling and gushing water, an elaborate stereo system flooded every crevice of the mansion with the melodic, opening strains of Zack's favorite classical work, Tchaikovsky's *1812 Overture*.

So this was what political power bought.

For years—tucked someplace almost away from conscious thought—he had dreamed of entering politics. But it was always in the future. Now as he glanced around and thought about the senator's warmth and charismatic personality, the old dream surfaced.

Marianne interrupted his thoughts. "Your room is the third door on the right." She gestured toward a hallway leading out of the foyer. "Meet me here in fifteen. Then I think Uncle Pinkie has dinner reservations in a couple of hours."

When Zack returned to the foyer wearing a Tar Heels T-shirt and swimming trunks, Marianne hadn't yet made her appearance, so he walked into a sunroom and looked out at the ocean.

The houseman appeared, holding a tray with various tropical drinks. "Would you care for something, sir?"

"Do you have a Diet Coke?"

The man looked amused. "Diet Coke? But of course."

The man stepped behind the bar, scooped crushed ice into a glass, filled the glass with Diet Coke, and handed it to Zack. "For you, with pleasure, sir." He bowed slightly as Zack took the Coke. "And now, the ensign has requested you join her on the beach." He gestured toward a glass door leading to a foliage-lined path outdoors. "If you take the path toward the ocean, you will find her there."

Zack donned a pair of aviator sunglasses to dim the late-afternoon sun. The fine white sand felt warm, almost luxurious to his feet as he walked through an opening in the dune ridge between the house and the beach.

Marianne, trim, tanned, and exquisite looking in a white swimsuit, sat in a beach chair under a red and white umbrella, facing the ocean. There was a vacant chair beside her.

"Beautiful afternoon," he called out as he approached.

She looked around, smiling at him. "Have a seat."

"So. What's a nice girl like you doing in a place like this?" He leaned his head back as he sat down, enjoying the ocean breeze on his face.

"I guess you're wondering about this whole thing, huh?"

The sip of Coke was refreshing in the hot afternoon. "I have to admit to more than a hint of curiosity."

She removed her sunglasses. "I know you might not believe me. But this really wasn't my idea." She laughed lightly. "Although I must confess, I don't mind having you here for a few days."

"I don't mind it much myself." He took another sip of Coke, then set the glass in the sand beside his chair. "An all-expense-paid vacation without having to use leave. My own private jet to fly me to Hilton Head. No telling what it cost the taxpayers."

"Ah, yes. The taxpayers." Marianne smiled, adjusting her sunglasses. "Uncle Pinkie said you were probably a conservative."

"How would he know that?"

"He's a powerful guy, Zack. You impressed him with how you handled my trial." She reached over and patted his hand. "That's why a Navy plane brought you all the way across the country." She sipped her piña colada. "In a sense, you earned it." She stared off toward the rolling breakers, then looked back to Zack. "Uncle Pinkie wants to talk to us at dinner."

"*Us* meaning . . . ?"

"Uncle Pinkie, Sally, you, me, and the ever-present bodyguards."

"Sounds exciting."

"It just might be more exciting than you can imagine." She grinned. "Up for a walk on the beach?" She stood up, ducked under the beach umbrella, and offered her hand.

"Why not?"

She shot him a laughing, flirty look, tossing her hair, and pulled him from his chair.

CHAPTER 45

Law offices of Wellington Levinson
Wells Fargo Plaza
Century City
Los Angeles, California

Terrie Bearden stood in the doorway of Wellington Levinson's office, announcing her presence by lightly tapping the doorjamb with her long, red fingernails.

"Yes, Terrie?" Levinson peered at her over the top of his glasses.

"Mr. Rahman is here to see you."

"Help me out. What's his problem again?"

"He claims three Muslim Navy chaplains are being discriminated against by the Navy."

"Really? *Muslim* chaplains. Does he realize I'm Jewish?"

"He must. I saw him thumbing through *Not Guilty* out in the lobby, and he was staring at the picture of you and the Israeli prime minister on the wall."

"Initial retainer?"

"When I spoke with him on the phone yesterday, I made it clear you required the seventy-five grand up front, boss. I didn't know if he was serious or just another crackpot. But I've checked with our banker in Nassau. Mr. Rahman wired every dime into our Bahamian account yesterday afternoon."

"Excellent." Levinson felt a smile creep across his face at the thought of another nonrefundable retainer tucked away in his offshore account. "And he knows there's no guarantee that we'll take his case?"

"Wells Levinson." Terrie put her hands on her hips and shot him a half-affectionate, half-impatient smirk. "How long have we been together?"

"Okay, okay." He grinned and threw his hands up in mock surrender. "Just being anal retentive again. Bring him in. And bring a legal pad. I want you to take notes."

A moment later, she reappeared at the door with an Arab man dressed in a white suit, white shirt, and white tie. "Mr. Rahman, I'd like to introduce Wellington Levinson." Terrie then stepped aside as the two men shook hands.

"This is an honor," Rahman said.

"What can I do for you today, Mr. Rahman?" Levinson motioned the Arab and Terrie Bearden to be seated.

"I represent the Muslim Legal Foundation. We pay legal fees on a case-by-case basis to defend religious liberty in instances where Muslims are being discriminated against because of their faith."

"I see." Levinson sat back and steepled his fingers, elbows resting on the padded arms of his chair. "And you have such a case now?"

"Yes. The Navy has arrested three Muslim chaplains for crimes of which they are innocent."

"What sort of crimes?"

"The murder of the Israeli ambassador. Then there was the bombing of an airplane."

"I knew the Israeli ambassador. Not well, but I spoke with him at several functions. I thought his murderer committed suicide."

"Precisely," Raman said. "His killer was a deranged Marine who called himself a Muslim. He did not represent the millions of peace-loving Muslims around the world. Unfortunately, the killer's suicide was not enough for the U.S. government. Now the Navy searches for a live scapegoat. We believe the government is embarking on a witch hunt."

"The fact that I'm Jewish does not concern your organization?"

"We trust you, Mr. Levinson. We know of your great work in defending Armani Sirhan, who was also Muslim. I have read *Not Guilty* several times in preparation for this meeting."

Levinson stared into the man's black eyes, knowing an agenda somehow existed behind all this. What was it? More importantly, what did it matter? "I am flattered. But if you read the epilogue to *Not Guilty*, you know how difficult that trial was for me personally. Congressman Jacobs was a Jewish brother with a loving wife, children, and grandchildren. I attended his funeral before I was retained by Mr. Sirhan. I am now a persona non grata in the Jacobs family. That pains me."

"I appreciate your candor, Mr. Levinson. We are all part of the brotherhood of man and all have our human struggles. But you also wrote in your epilogue, at the end of the day, you did the right thing. Sirhan was a mentally ill, delusional fanatic who had lost touch with reality. As you pointed out, your conscience would not allow the execution of another human being whose real crime was being delusional."

My conscience plus a two-million-dollar fee, plus the book deal and movie rights that came out of winning the case. "You have done your homework, Mr. Rahman."

"Mr. Levinson, we believe that you, of all people, are best equipped to fight religious persecution against these three defendants."

"Three defendants, you say?" Levinson glanced at Terrie. "I rarely represent more than one client at a time. This could be a drawn-out, expensive proposition for your organization."

"We understand the value of your services, Mr. Levinson. We believe this would be a simple matter for you. We're told the military prosecutors are young, inexperienced, and ill prepared. Against you, there would be no contest."

"True"—Levinson shot a quick smile at Terrie Bearden, who was sitting to one side, taking notes—"but three defendants are still three defendants. And despite the inexperience of the Navy prosecutors, my preparation level is unmatched regardless of who the prosecutor is. I prepare not just to win, but to crush my opposition. That is why I have never lost a trial, sir."

"We understand, Mr. Levinson. And we are prepared, today, to wire to your Bahamian account a nonrefundable retainer in the amount of 3.3 million dollars per defendant."

Levinson raised an eyebrow. "Your organization is prepared to advance a nonrefundable retainer of ten million U.S. dollars for our firm to handle this case?"

Abdur pulled a cell phone from inside his white jacket. "This case is of immense importance for religious liberty around the world. Yes, that's exactly what I'm saying. Give the word and I make the call. You can confirm receipt of the retainer before I leave here today if you'd like."

Wells glanced at Terrie Bearden. She gave him a single nod.

"I do adhere to the principle that all Americans are entitled to a fair trial. And if your organization is prepared to take a stand to defend religious liberty, then our firm is interested in standing with these chaplains."

"Good. Then shall I make the call?"

"By all means."

CHAPTER 46

Fowler compound
Palmetto Dunes Plantation
Hilton Head Island, South Carolina

Zack and Marianne returned from their walk on the beach and parted company at the foyer to shower and dress for dinner. A half hour later, Zack headed back to the foyer, where Senator Fowler, looking as distinguished as ever, waited for him.

The senator extended his hand and flashed a warm smile. "How was your afternoon on the beach with my favorite niece, Lieutenant?"

"Nice and relaxing, sir. We walked down the beach to the Crown Plaza and sat under the palmetto trees and enjoyed the ocean breeze. I never realized Hilton Head was so beautiful. So is your place here, Senator."

"Thank you." Fowler made a sweeping gesture around the foyer and great room. "This place is owned by a family trust. I discovered Hilton Head back when President Clinton spent his 'Renaissance Weekends' here during his first term. There are no decent beaches in Louisiana. And even if there were, you get bothered by constituents. Here, for the most part, you're left alone. Of course, I still travel with security guards."

Fowler pointed through the front window at two muscular men, both in dark blazers, who looked like middle linebackers for the Carolina Panthers.

"I call 'em Mutt and Jeff." Fowler chuckled. "They're good guys, and darn good shots. One's got a nine millimeter, the other totes a forty-four magnum. When I'm here, at least two security guards are always on duty. Mutt and Jeff will be following us to dinner tonight. They probably won't be needed, but you never know."

I can't believe I actually like this guy. "That's probably a good idea, Senator."

"Now, Lieutenant, you're going to have to stop that." Fowler smiled as he slapped Zack on the back.

"Sir?"

"I understand you're a good naval officer and respectful of members of Congress, but behind closed doors, and when we're out on the town, please, my close friends call me Pinkie. I'd be honored if you would do the same. After all, I've got a feeling we're gonna be good friends."

Zack blinked in surprise.

"Woo, doggie!" Fowler howled before Zack could answer. "We got the best-looking dates tonight on the East Coast or what?"

Zack followed his gaze down the hallway. Marianne and Sally walked toward the foyer, sandals clicking on the marble, their sun-bronzed skin a beautiful contrast to their pastel outfits. A moment later, Fowler circled his arm around Sally, and Marianne, smiling up at Zack, took his hand. Fowler gave them both a smile of approval and announced that he was hungry and it was time to go.

"You drive, Sally," Fowler ordered as the burly bodyguards opened the doors of the BMW. Zack got in the backseat with Marianne. The bodyguards jumped in a Suburban and followed the BMW out of Palmetto Dunes.

Ten minutes later, the makeshift motorcade crossed through another traffic circle, exiting onto Greenwood Drive. Sally steered into a small upscale shopping area called The Gallery of Shops and parked. From the exterior, Juleps looked to be a quaint, intimate, upscale restaurant located in the Gallery.

"Good to see you tonight, Senator." The proprietor, a smiling middle-aged man in a sports jacket, greeted the party at the front door. "We've got your room waiting for you. And the chef has already prepared your favorite appetizer."

"Thanks. You're a good man." The senator's smile was effusive.

The owner led the quartet into a small, candlelit dining room, away from the other restaurant patrons. The bodyguards stood just outside the door with their hands clasped over their belt buckles.

A smiling, trim, middle-aged woman with graying hair and a white apron entered the room, holding a steaming tray. "Pecan shrimp with sweet pepper sauce. The senator's favorite. And I took the liberty of bringing two bottles of our finest Argentinean merlot, just for the senator."

"Merlot okay with everybody?" Fowler glanced at his companions.

"Iced tea for me." Zack smiled and braced himself for the chiding remarks that surely would follow. None came.

The server poured the merlot and then returned a few minutes later with Zack's iced tea.

Fowler took a sip from his wine glass, popped a shrimp in his mouth, and focused on Zack. "I understand you're a Republican."

"Yes, Senator. I'm a registered Republican."

"Pinkie."

"Sir?"

"Remember, my friends call me Pinkie. I consider you to be a friend."

Sally and Marianne exchanged wide-eyed looks as Fowler popped another shrimp into his mouth. "So what do you say?"

"Well, sir," Zack said, "if Marianne refers to you as 'Uncle Pinkie,' then I suppose I can do the same."

Fowler bent over with a belly laugh. "I like you, son. Takin' your cue from a good-lookin' woman. You'll go far in life and politics."

"All right, Pinkie."

The first use of "Pinkie" by Zack brought laughter from the senator. Soft chuckles from Sally and Marianne followed.

"To friendship and politics." The senator raised his wineglass. The two women lifted theirs, and Zack raised his iced tea glass. "We'll work on the *sir* thing later." The clink of glass on glass sounded almost musical. "So tell me, Zack, have any political aspirations?"

Zack stifled a smile. "I've thought about it. Maybe down the road."

"I understand you were in the College Republicans at Carolina."

What else does this man know about me? "That's right. I was the membership chairman, which was quite a challenge in Chapel Hill."

"I've heard Chapel Hill called the Berkeley of the East." Fowler chuckled.

"Precisely. Which is why the job was a hard sell."

"Have a shrimp." Fowler passed the plate to Zack, who lifted a prawn by the tail. "Now go ahead and dip it in some of this lip-smackin' sauce. You know, I bet membership chairman for the College Republicans was a volunteer job."

"Right." Zack took another shrimp from Marianne, who held out the plate.

"No point in doing a volunteer job in politics when you can get paid."

"Good point." *Is he offering me a job on his staff?*

Fowler drained his Argentinean merlot, poured another glass, and took another sip. He flashed a smile of satisfaction.

"Are you interested in a congressional seat?"

Whoa. "Given the right opportunity, sure I'm interested."

"Good. Then let me cut to the chase. I've been watching you on television during this court-martial you've just finished. I like the way you've handled yourself, not just winning the case, but with the media. I love the way you handled Reverend Barbour's scurrilous charges that Marianne got some kind of special treatment because of me."

"Thank you, Sen . . . Pinkie. I was just telling the truth."

"Yes, well, I don't have any daughters myself, and my two sons didn't amount to much. So Marianne here is like my daughter." He winked at Marianne. "She's smart, beautiful, and she's a Landrieu."

"Oh, Uncle Pinkie." Marianne let out a bashful giggle.

He focused on Zack again. "This business of politics, I'm pretty good at it."

"I agree with you," Zack said.

"Know what makes a fellow good at politics, Zack?"

Where is he going with this? "Can't say I do."

"Vision."

"Makes sense."

"Yes, vision. And I have this vision of a good-looking, smart, charismatic young Washington power couple." He raised his glass for another toast. "To Zack Brewer and Marianne Landrieu."

Marianne had the grace to look embarrassed.

Why do I feel like I'm being ambushed with a gallon of molasses? Zack smiled. "Pinkie, I think all those adjectives—good-looking, smart, charismatic—definitely apply to Marianne. But me? I'm just a country boy from North Carolina."

"You two, stop it." Marianne blushed. Zack wasn't sure whether it was sincere or contrived.

"Here's what I'm driving at," the senator said. "There's gonna be an opening in Louisiana's Fifth Congressional District. That seat's been held by a Republican for a number of years. Good man. Andy Mulligan. He's retiring this year. Seat's ripe for the pickin' by the right kind of Democrat. I'd like you, with Marianne at your side, and with my full backing and support, to run for that seat."

Zack met the smiling, adoring gazes of Marianne and Sally. *So this is why the taxpayers probably spent $50,000 to give me a personal Navy jet for the weekend.*

"Sen—Pinkie. I don't know what to say."

"Well, that's easy." Fowler chuckled. "Just have a sip of your iced tea there, and tell me what you're thinking."

"I'm stunned." He gulped his tea. "I'm flattered. But I'm obligated to the Navy for a couple of more years, and—"

Fowler raised his hand, interrupting Zack. "Serving on the Armed Services Committee has some privileges. I can have you out of the Navy today and back in tomorrow. Say the word."

Zack sucked in a deep breath, trying to comprehend Fowler's offer. "Okay, but I don't live in Louisiana. I've only been there once, when the Tar Heels won the national championship in the Superdome. And what about my party affiliation? Like you said, I'm a registered Republican."

"What do you remember about Bobby Kennedy and Hillary Clinton before they ran for the Senate from New York?"

"Both moved into the state shortly before running."

"You're catching on, boy." Fowler smiled, drained his second wine glass, popped a shrimp in his mouth, and poured more wine.

"My name is neither Kennedy nor Clinton."

"No, but my niece's name is Landrieu, and mine is Fowler. And in the Bayou, that's a better combo than Kennedy and Clinton put together."

U.S. Congressman Zachary Brewer. It had a nice ring.

"Yes. I'm aware of how the Landrieu name is well respected in Louisiana. But what about party affiliation?"

"Let me call a few names, and you tell me what comes to mind."

"Sure. Why not?"

"Sam Ervin."

"Former North Carolina senator from the mountains. Considered a constitutional law expert. Chaired the Senate Watergate Committee that investigated the cover-up of the burglary at Democratic headquarters which led to the resignation of President Nixon."

"Good." Fowler smiled and took another swig. "Sam Nunn."

"Former U.S. senator from Georgia. Chaired the Senate Armed Services Committee. Considered an expert on defense matters. Passed over by Clinton for secretary of defense, and then blocked Clinton's attempts to integrate homosexuals into the military."

"Very good." Fowler leaned back and smiled. "Now what did Ervin and Nunn have in common?"

"Both Democrats. Both from the South. Both conservative."

"Bingo."

"Are you saying you want me to switch parties and run as a Democrat?"

Another J.R. Ewing grin from Fowler. "Let me put it this way. The Fifth Congressional District is heavily a Democratic district and has been for years. Mulligan won there the last four terms, by the skin of his teeth I might add, by spending millions in family money. The Republicans will run a couple of token candidates in the primary, but nobody with Mulligan's stature or money. Meanwhile, the Democrat candidates are all liberal as the day is long, like me. Now you can bet your last dollar this seat will return to the Democratic Party in the next election. So I ask you this. If the seat is going to go Democrat anyway, wouldn't you, as a conservative Republican, rather see the seat go to a conservative Democrat than a liberal?"

He's serious about this. "I see your point. But what if I don't win? I'd be forgoing a career in the Navy and who knows what else."

"What if you *don't* win?" Fowler took a swig and started cackling again. "Zack, I *guarantee* you'll win. If you don't, I'd resign my senate seat and have the governor appoint you to replace me."

I know he's lying.

"You'll have my full backing and the support of my very wealthy contributors." He shot a proud look to Marianne. "And my lovely niece will be campaigning at your side. You know what? We've quietly done some polling in Louisiana, and your chivalrous defense of Marianne in this court-martial has given you some very positive name recognition."

"That's flattering."

"Flattering? It's a fact. I can have my chief of staff fax down the poll numbers in the morning if you'd like."

Zack put his hand on Fowler's shoulder. "Do you mind if I ask you a question?"

"Mind? That's why I've got you here. Ask away."

"If the Democratic candidates in the field are liberal, and if your philosophy is liberal, then why do you want a candidate to run as a conservative Democrat?"

"Because this ain't about liberal or conservative, boy. This is about family."

"Family?"

"You and Marianne. And me." Fowler leaned forward. "Look, there's only room for one *real* liberal politician in Louisiana. I'll shoot it straight. This is about money. There ain't much of it in Louisiana. These guys are trying to siphon my fund-raising base. If one of them wins, next thing you know, they'll challenge me in the primary. I wanna cut them off now. You know, family's thicker than politics. Schwarzenegger, a Republican, married into the Kennedys. Jim Carville, the Louisiana political genius that got Clinton elected, married Mary Matalan, a Bush-lovin' Republican. Here's the point. I *guarantee* your election. And I won't interfere with your votes. Wanna vote to abolish abortion? Go ahead. Vote against homosexual rights? Fine by me. Just run as a Democrat and stick by my niece. That's all I ask."

Zack sat back, stunned. For a moment he couldn't speak.

"I need some fresh air." Fowler stood. "And you need a few minutes to digest more than your succulent shrimp." He smiled down at Sally and reached for her hand. "Come with me." He put his arm around the young woman and escorted her out of the room.

When they were gone, Marianne met Zack's gaze. "I knew he wanted you." She shook her head slowly. "But I didn't know he was going to make it a package deal. Please believe me."

The flickering candles caught the light in her eyes. He studied her perfectly made-up face, searching for the truth. It eluded him, just as it had done so many times during the trial. "I'll take your word for it." He reached for his iced tea. "So where does this leave us?"

She took another sip of merlot. "You should run for the seat. You'll be a great congressman. I'll support you and campaign with you. No strings attached—except maybe a job on your staff if nothing else materializes. Of course, if something *does* materialize between us, I might be persuaded to examine our options more carefully." She gave her hair a toss and smiled into his eyes.

"You know, your uncle must be a mind reader. It was almost like he knew I'd wanted to run for Congress since I was thirteen."

"Dreams can come true in mysterious ways." There was a longing in her eyes that made him turn away.

"Well, now!" Fowler strode to the table, Sally on his arm. "Have you and my most valuable family asset decided on a strategy?"

Zack chuckled and stood as the two sat down. "Pinkie, I have to say, you've really thrown me for a loop tonight." He took his seat again. "Though I must admit, this proposition is enticing."

"Good. Then we can announce your candidacy this week?"

"I'd like to think about it. Maybe talk it over with Marianne some more." He met the senator's pleased gaze. "Seriously," Zack said, leaning forward, "what's our time frame?"

"We've got thirty days before we publicly announce. But I need an answer before you leave. Otherwise, I've got to recruit another candidate."

"Fair enough." Goose bumps crawled up Zack's neck. This man was offering him his life's ambition.

"Good," Fowler said. "I'll drink to that. Now let's order something to eat."

CHAPTER 47

Fowler compound
Palmetto Dunes Plantation
Hilton Head, South Carolina

The morning sun, masquerading as a large orange ball, slipped above the Atlantic, casting a glowing trail on the water from the horizon to the beach.

Zack lifted his head from the pillow and squinted out the window. A guest room with an ocean view certainly did not allow the guest the luxury of sleeping in. Not that he had slept much even while it was dark. He stared up at the ceiling fan's slow-circling blades and rehashed the proposition that had kept him awake all night.

Roberson Fowler had offered what he had always wanted and aspired for.

A seat in Congress. His professional dream, once a farfetched fantasy, was so close he could taste it.

It was ironic. Roberson Fowler, a man whose public persona he detested, now suddenly wanted to become his political godfather. And surprisingly, he actually liked the man.

But running as a Democrat? Being associated with the party he vehemently disagreed with? Being linked with Roberson Fowler, a powerful ringleader in the Democrat Party?

Of course, not all Democrats followed the liberal party line. Bob Casey, the former Pennsylvania Governor, was a staunch right-to-lifer. There were Christians and non-Christians in both parties. Even his own grandparents, lifelong Democrats, were conservative. Maybe this was his chance to be salt and light, to become a strong political prophet leading the party back to its conservative moorings. Was this his calling?

What about the strings attached to this proposition?

Did Pinkie Fowler really expect him to marry his niece?

He could tick off on one hand the reasons that marrying her wasn't right: She wasn't a believer. He didn't know if he trusted her. He didn't love her.

But Pinkie didn't actually say he expected Zack and Marianne to marry. Even Marianne said she would be content to see where things led. Maybe he could run, using the opportunity to witness to Marianne. Was this why all this was happening? Or was he kidding himself, looking for reasons to say yes?

Then there was Diane Colcernian. Her image floated into his mind, the graceful way she moved, the tilt of her chin when she smiled, the fiery snap of those green eyes when she was angry.

He almost laughed. Talk about a real pipe dream. Forget Congress. Diane had made it abundantly clear how she felt about him; he had a better chance of getting elected president than seeing those emerald eyes look at him with anything other than disdain.

He glanced at the alarm clock on his bedside table: 6:02.

What was Fowler's real motivation in all this?

He got up and sat on the edge of his bed. He had put his Bible on the nightstand last night, but hadn't read it before falling asleep. He picked it up now and thumbed through it, but his thoughts were on Roberson Fowler's offer, and he couldn't concentrate. With a deep sigh, he set it back on the table and stood to walk to the window.

The sun was higher now, and it was turning into a perfect morning, full of God's creative glory. The gulls soared above the glistening water, and shorebirds skittered along the wet sand.

Maybe a jog would clear his mind. He pulled on a T-shirt and navy blue jogging shorts and headed out the back door. The beach was wide this morning, maybe a quarter mile from the dunes down to the surf. He stood, facing the ocean and enjoying the breeze on his face, and tried to pray.

"Zack!" Marianne called to him from somewhere near the compound. He turned as she trotted closer.

"Going for a run?" She swept a strand of windblown blond hair off her forehead and tucked it behind one ear.

"You're up early." He pulled on his Oakleys.

"I couldn't sleep."

"You too?"

"Uncle Pinkie dumped a lot on me too, you know."

"He loves you." He gestured down the beach. "If you don't mind a slow, easy pace this morning, let's go."

"Eight-minute mile okay?"

"I'll give it a shot."

They turned right and jogged toward the Crown Plaza and Coligny Beach. The beach was deserted except for a few other early morning joggers and an occasional surf fisherman.

"So," he puffed after a couple hundred yards, "how do you feel about becoming a Washington power couple?"

"Why do you think I've been awake all night?"

"Yeah, me too. But that doesn't answer the question."

"I think he dumped a lot on you. I agree with his instincts. But I feel bad this has come so suddenly."

"Thanks. But you still didn't answer my question about the power couple."

Marianne pulled a sweatband over her forehead. "I'll be honest. I *do* feel some chemistry. I've felt it since the first day I walked in your office to discuss my case. The night you took me to *La Vue de la Mer* in La Jolla? I've thought about that every day."

It struck him as odd that she had been attracted to him in the middle of the terror and sorrow she should have been feeling after the assault. He stared at her, incredulous. But she didn't notice.

She trotted alongside him, puffing as she talked. "But even if nothing develops on the personal level, I can still be an asset to you. With my background in media relations, like I said last night, I could be your press secretary, for example. The thing is, I want this to be your decision. But I know my uncle. If he says he can get you elected, he can." She chuckled. "So let me ask you the same question. What do you think about the Washington power couple thing?"

"I love the Navy, but I could turn my back on it in order to pursue a lifelong dream. As for the other, I honestly can't say. I don't know you well enough to answer."

"Okay. That's fair." They jogged by a row of catamarans beached in front of the Hilton. "What do you want to know about me?"

He pulled off his Oakleys and wiped them on his T-shirt. "Colcernian brought up the Willie Garrett thing so fast we never got to talk much about it." He put his shades back on.

"What about it?"

"Did you date?"

"We hung out together in high school. He was a great athlete and at first was a gentleman. When I left for the Academy, he became a SEAL. We went out for a while; then I cut off communication. I think it made him mad."

"What about the other two?"

"They were his friends. Colcernian got it all wrong." Her voice quavered. "I'd take a polygraph about Willie, but nobody offered."

"Polygraphs aren't admissible in a court-martial."

They reached the Crown Plaza and turned back, still jogging, their footprints leaving circles from their turn on the wet sand.

"So, Lieutenant Brewer, any other questions you'd like to ask?"

"Are you as liberal as your uncle?"

This brought a chuckle through the huffs and puffs. "I'm a registered Democrat. I have to be for family reasons. But I'm also a naval officer. How many liberal naval officers do you know?"

"Never met one."

"And you still haven't."

"Really?"

"I voted for President Williams in the last presidential election."

"Does your uncle know?"

"No. And don't tell him. He'd kick me out of the family."

"Does he know you're conservative?"

"Are you kidding?" She laughed. "We've debated all the hot buttons. Welfare, abortion, gays in the military, affirmative action. You name it. We disagree on them all."

"Unbelievable."

"And you know what else I think?"

"What?"

"When my uncle says blood is thicker than politics, he means it."

"Explain."

"Remember all the stuff about wanting to avoid liberal competition in Louisiana?"

"Yeah," Zack said. "Sounded fishy to me."

"Fishy? Uncle Pinkie's not afraid of losing to anybody. It was pure malarkey. You know what I think his real motives are?"

"Tell me." They trotted by a row of catamarans in front of the Hilton Resort.

"I think he's recruiting a conservative Democrat because he knows I'd never work for, or marry, a liberal one."

Zack's eyes widened. "Interesting theory."

"More than a theory. His two sons have been arrested on multiple drunk-driving charges. They're playboys who sap off the family fortune. I'm his legacy. He knows I'd never run for office, so he's been waiting for someone like you to come along. He wants to perpetuate the family dynasty, Zack. That's what I think this is about. Who knows? Maybe it could be a win-win situation for everybody."

Zack let her comments sink in for a moment as they jogged. He didn't have long to think; a woman running toward them on the beach broke his concentration. He frowned. "Is that Sally? Looks like she's trying to flag us down."

"If it's her, I'm surprised she's up this early."

"Zack. Marianne!" Sally's voice was barely audible over the sound of the wind and surf.

Marianne kicked her jog into a sprint, prompting Zack to follow. A moment later, they met Sally at the edge of the surf, just a few hundred yards down the beach from the compound.

"Zack, you've got an urgent phone call from San Diego," Sally panted. "Call your commanding officer right away."

"Now?" Zack checked his watch, trying to catch his breath. "It's four in the morning out there."

"He called the compound thirty minutes ago. He said to get back to him as soon as I found you." She handed him her cell phone.

Zack wiped the sweat from his forehead and took another deep breath. He flipped open the phone and punched in the number for Captain Rudy's personal cell phone. After a couple of rings, he heard the voice of his commanding officer answer.

"Mornin', Skipper," Zack said. "Sorry to call so early."

"No problem, Zack." The normally affable Rudy spoke in an urgent, businesslike tone. "Look, Zack. I know we sent you out there for ten days on sort of a diplomatic mission, but something's come up."

"Yes, sir."

"We've got a high-profile case we need you to get back for. The Marines have a C-130 ready to bring you home just as soon as you can make it over to Beaufort. I hate to interrupt your vacation, Zack, but I need you to pack and get over to MCAS Beaufort this morning. Senator

Fowler's already been briefed on your change of plans, and I'll brief you fully this afternoon."

"Aye, aye, Captain. I'm on my way, sir."

"Good. Report to me as soon as you get back to base." The line went dead.

Zack flipped the phone closed and shot a half smile at Marianne and Sally. "Well, ladies, it's been a great fourteen hours, but I've just been ordered back to San Diego."

"What?" Marianne's tone reflected her surprise and disappointment.

"Some sort of high-profile case. That's all I know."

They walked through a shallow dip to the other side of the dunes, breaking into the open in full view of the compound a moment later. Roberson Fowler was sitting on the back patio, wearing a flowered Hawaiian shirt and white trousers, sipping a bloody Mary. "Well, now. Seems I'm not the only Washington politician you've impressed, Lieutenant. I just got a call from Mack Williams."

"Mack Williams, the president?"

"One and the same."

Zack exchanged glances with Marianne. She looked as bewildered as he felt.

"Seems like ol' Mack's been watching you on TV, and he likes what he saw."

"My commanding officer said something about a high-profile case."

"The president briefed me this morning. The Navy arrested three Muslim chaplains and charged them with treason and murder. High-profile stuff. Seems like you're the lucky prosecutor, son."

Zack was too stunned to speak for a moment. Finally, he said, "Senator, I very much appreciate your hospitality—and your kind offer— but unfortunately, I've got to hit the shower and then get back over to Beaufort."

Kind offer? More like life-changing offer. And how could he make such a decision within the next few minutes? His mind was racing. Any rational man would ask for more time. Even the high-profile case paled in comparison. Besides, he wanted this chance so much he could taste it. An opportunity like this might not come his way again.

"I understand why you've got to go. When the commander in chief calls, a good officer must respond." The senator blew a puff of premium cigar smoke into the early morning salt breeze. The scent of sweet tobacco reminded Zack of his grandfather's cigars many years ago.

"It seems the president is bringing your decision about the seat in Congress to a head a few days early." Fowler took another puff, studying Zack's face and seeming pleased with what he saw. "What do you say, Lieutenant? A victory in another high-profile case would be a perfect backdrop for a press conference announcing your candidacy thirty days from now." He paused as another puff of sweet smoke drifted toward Zack. "The prize is yours for the taking, son."

Zack's eyes caught Sally's, then Marianne's. They were both nodding their heads in the bright morning sun. It was now or never. *How can I say no?*

"Okay, Senator. I'm your man."

Fowler's eyebrows rose; his smile widened.

"You've got a deal." Zack grinned. "I'll run."

"Well, now." Fowler rose from his chair. "That's my boy." He extended his hand and took Zack's in a hearty shake.

"Thank you, Senator."

"Congressman Brewer." Fowler reached for his bloody Mary, gave it a stir with the stalk of celery, and took a sip. "Got a nice ring to it!"

"I can drive you to Beaufort, Congressman." Marianne beamed.

Zack chuckled. The weight he'd been carrying since the offer was made suddenly lifted. "Thanks. That would be nice."

"Sally and I have some Senate business to attend to this morning, so this may be the last time I see you for now." Fowler grasped Zack's hand again and gave him another warm shake. "As soon as the trial is over, we formally announce your candidacy."

"Thank you, Senator."

CHAPTER 48

Fifteen minutes' flight time from North Island Naval Air Station
Coronado, California

Lieutenant, we're fifteen minutes from North Island," the first officer, a Marine Corps first lieutenant, called over the roar of the C-130's four big propellers. "Captain says go ahead and strap in."

Zack, sitting in the canvas jump seat behind the cabin, fastened his belt. "Thanks, Lieutenant." He leaned back and closed his eyes in a last-minute attempt to catch a snooze. This proved useless when his ears started popping on descent. Plus his mind was too numb from the last twenty-four hours. A congressional seat? A treason trial? The president watching him on television? What was going on?

The bump of the plane's wheels as they skipped against the long concrete runway at the North Island Naval Air Station brought with it a strange feeling of peace.

He was home, at least, if nothing else.

When the C-130 rolled to a stop, Zack waited for the Navy ground crew to wheel the portable ladder across the tarmac. Then he stepped out into the irresistible, balmy Southern California sunshine and inhaled the glorious Pacific breeze before descending the ladder.

"Welcome home, Lieutenant," he heard as he stepped off the ladder.

He glanced up at the senior trial counsel, Commander Bob Awe, and shot him a salute. "Sorry, I didn't see you there."

"The skipper asked me to drive you to the station—and brief you on the way."

"Thanks, Commander." Zack followed Awe to the white Dodge Reliant with U.S. government plates.

"NCIS has arrested three U.S. Navy chaplains," Awe said as soon as they were in the car. "All three are Muslim. Intercepted communications linking them to the murder of the Israeli ambassador, an attack on a church here in San Diego, and the sabotage of an F/A-18 Super Hornet flying out of Virginia Beach. They've been in custody eight days, which means we may have a speedy-trial problem. To make matters worse, both Naval Intelligence and the CIA report more attacks may be planned, but we don't know when, where, or how. And we're very concerned about more radical Muslim infiltration of the Navy. So this prosecution is crucial to the national security. The president saw you on television during the Blount trial, and you've got the job."

Zack let the information sink in, glancing at the glistening high-rises of downtown San Diego, then at the eighteen piers of the 32nd Naval Station that stretched several miles along the waterfront. "Detailed defense counsel?"

"There's a Lieutenant Sulik out of Norfolk, a Marine captain, Captain Blanzy, out of Pendleton, and Lieutenant Melesky from here in San Diego."

Thank goodness Colcernian's not involved.

The car swung right onto Harbor Drive and headed to the main gate of the naval station.

"And we're prosecuting them all in the same action?"

"Yes, we have to because of speedy-trial considerations and because of the conspiracy charge." Awe returned a salute from the enlisted security guard at the main gate.

"Who's the convening authority?"

"The chief of naval operations."

"I've never heard of the CNO convening a general court-marital."

"I haven't either, and I've been in the JAG Corps twenty-five years. They considered the chief of chaplains, but apparently rejected the idea for political reasons."

"Political reasons?"

"They didn't want the chief of chaplains to come across as looking anti-Muslim."

"What's CNO looking for in this case, sir?"

Awe steered the Reliant into the reserved parking space outside the Trial Command offices. He cut the engine, then turned to look directly at Zack.

"The death penalty."

For a moment, Zack was at a loss for words. When he could speak again, he said, "Commander, we haven't had a death-penalty case in the military since World War II. The execution of Private Slovick, I believe."

"Actually, the last military execution was 1961. The Army continued executing after the war. But it's been so long we're practically on virgin territory here. You've got your work cut out for you. Let's go see the captain."

"Bob, Zack, come on in." Captain Glen Rudy stood as Zack and Awe arrived.

Zack stepped into his office and saw a familiar face from years past. "Zack, you remember Captain Guy?"

"From my Justice School days. Good to see you again, sir."

"You, too, Lieutenant," David Guy said.

"Captain Guy is now the JAG for AIRLANT," Rudy said, "and helped break open this treason case. He's going to brief you and make his files available to you, Zack, to assist in your case preparation. Why don't you gentlemen have a seat?" Rudy took a swig of coffee and looked over at Guy as they sat down. "Dave, want to start with an overview?"

"By all means." David Guy glanced at Zack. "You look bushed, Lieutenant. Want some coffee before we start?"

"Yes, sir. I'm operating on forty-eight hours with no sleep."

Rudy gestured to his legalman chief, who was outside in the secretary's office, to come in. A moment later, the chief brought Zack a mug of steaming black coffee. Just a couple of sips gave Zack the caffeine jolt he needed.

"Several years ago," Captain Guy began, "the Navy, under threat of litigation by a civil rights organization, admitted five Muslim imams into the Chaplain Corps. Now it seems at least three of the five chaplains are of a radical Islamic sect, backed by an international terrorist group known as the Council of Ishmael.

"They've encouraged violence within the service by sailors they've recruited into their faith. The target of their hate is the 'apostate nation of Israel,' which they say is 'an anathema to the great Muslim faith.' In their opinion, nations that aid Israel oppose Allah. Their secondary theme opposes 'religious intolerance' in the Navy, particularly among sailors in Christian Bible studies. They claim these groups tout Christianity as supreme over Islam.

"One convert, a Petty Officer Neptune, launched a grenade attack against sailors and civilians in one such Bible study."

Zack leaned forward. "The grenade attack in Lemon Grove that was all over the news?"

"The same." Captain Rudy nodded.

"Another sailor"—Captain Guy stopped for a swig of coffee—"egged on by a chaplain in Virginia Beach, sabotaged an F/A-18 before their squadron left for the Mediterranean to provide military support to Israel. A third, attached to the Marine base at Camp Pendleton, encouraged one of his converts to open fire on the Israeli ambassador. This was the incident that garnered most of the international attention. And frankly, the international pressure being brought by the Israelis and the possibility of another attack are what make the stakes so high. The Israelis expect a conviction, and the president wants a conviction to show the terrorists we mean business."

"Unbelievable." Zack shook his head, suddenly wondering how he could have secret political aspirations with the national security on the line, and with the president personally tapping him to help defend it. No JAG officer in history had ever been personally requested by the president to prosecute a court-martial.

"The NCIS in Norfolk, working closely with our legal staff at COM-NAVAIRLANT, broke this case open. Since then, a debate has raged in Washington over whether the Navy or the Justice Department should prosecute. Ultimately, the president decided this is a military matter, more specifically a Navy matter.

"The president ordered the judge advocate general of the Navy to find a prosecutor."

Captain Guy paused, meeting Zack's eyes with a piercing gaze. "You are that prosecutor, Lieutenant. Your assignment is to prosecute the three Islamic chaplains for conspiracy to commit treason against the United States and conspiracy to commit murder. And to secure a sentence of death."

Goose bumps crept up Zack's arms and neck as Captain Guy's piercing gaze focused on him.

"I want you to understand," Guy continued, "that anything short of a death sentence could imperil the national security. The president believes, as does the secretary of defense and the director of the CIA, that a successful prosecution, conviction, and execution must be accomplished to send a strong, clear message that the military justice system will prosecute and swiftly punish terrorists, and ours will be a zero-tolerance policy for terrorists in the military."

Captain Guy bore his eyes into Zack. For the first time in years, Zack, who counted on his usual abundance of self-confidence, felt butterflies in his stomach.

"Put another way," Guy said, obviously not finished with his lecture, "if you don't get the death penalty for us, or worse still, if you lose this case, you send the message that the United States Military is a benign playground for murdering terrorists who may seek to get their hands on the most powerful weapons on the face of the earth. Terrorists hijacking airplanes is bad enough. If you think 9/11 was bad for this country, Lieutenant Brewer, you can't imagine the terror that could rain down on America if they infiltrate our military and influence the use of weapons of mass destruction."

Captain Rudy leaned forward, arms on his desk, his expression somber. "Nothing will be spared to you in the planning for this case. Any assistance you want, technical or personnel wise, will be made available to you. This is the most important court-martial in well over a century. I don't mean to put on the pressure, son, but we cannot lose this one. Understand?"

"Yes, sir."

"We've got a speedy-trial problem," Guy added. "These chaplains have been in confinement more than eighty days already. In ninety days they walk. So you have to get ready quickly, effectively prosecute these traitors on a very short notice."

"Understood, sir." The butterflies in Zack's stomach turned into a swarm of hornets.

"Captain Guy will give you the file. Your orders are to take it to your office, thoroughly familiarize yourself with it, and have the case ready for prosecution by the end of the week."

"Aye, Captain."

"You are dismissed, Lieutenant."

CHAPTER 49

Zack leaned back in the government-issued swivel chair behind his desk and thumbed through the photographs of the three U.S. Navy chaplains, now defendants facing a general court-martial.

In the color mug shots wearing their khaki uniforms, they looked normal. Dark complexions with black hair, they could pass for any of the dozens of other naval officers he would see before the end of a day.

Who could pick evil from the crowd when evil looked so ordinary?

He tossed the photos on his desk and picked up the NCIS report for the third time. He tried concentrating, but felt his eyes drooping from fatigue. A huge swig of black coffee remedied that for the moment, and he refocused on the first page again.

On paper, the evidence looked solid. The bust started with the tape-recorded conversations intercepted by Special Agent Harry Kilnap, which led to a search warrant by a federal magistrate and then federal court orders authorizing phone tapping of the private, home telephone lines of all three chaplains.

Reska, Olajuwon, and Abdul-Sehen had all acknowledged their roles in the three attacks. Transcripts of intercepted phone calls showed all three had advance knowledge of the shooting of the Israeli ambassador, the downing of the jet, and the grenade attack at the church in Lemon Grove. All were involved in planning the murder of Petty Officer Sulayman al-Aziz, who was himself a murderer.

NCIS had done its job. The evidence seemed airtight, at least on paper. That, in and of itself, was worrisome.

What was missing?

Zack rubbed his eyes, then dropped the file and pivoted his chair 180 degrees so that he faced the sparkling waters of San Diego Bay.

Congressman Brewer? His dream was about to become a reality. This view of the bay, this naval base, this career in the Navy would soon be behind him. And now he had the opportunity to go out in a blaze of glory. Why did the old sense of uneasiness refuse to leave his heart and mind?

He unraveled his third paper clip of the afternoon, bent it around like a flat tire, and flicked it in the trashcan. *Two points! And the Tar Heels have won the national championship.*

Paper clip number four was now a small, straight, rod, waiting to be shaped into a dramatic piece of fine sculpture for all of posterity, when the hand of the sculptor was interrupted by the buzz of his intercom.

"Yes?"

"Welcome home, Lieutenant." The sweet voice of Amy DeBenedetto greeted him.

"Good to be back, Amy. Thanks."

"I hear we've got another high-profile case on board."

"Word spreads quickly."

"I know you're probably busy, but . . ." There was a hesitation in her voice. "Could I see you for a few minutes?"

Zack twisted the little rod into an imitation fishing hook before answering.

"Sure, come on down."

A moment later, Amy was at his door. "I didn't expect to see you back so soon. It's a nice surprise." She gave him an affectionate smile as she sat down across from him.

"From what I've been told, I guess the president had other ideas."

"There's something we need to talk about," she said, her tone serious.

"Is something wrong, Amy?"

"Well, while you were gone—"

A knock at the door cut her off midsentence.

"Yes?" Zack called.

Commander Bob Awe opened the door. "Sorry to interrupt, Zack," he said, "but the skipper needs to see you immediately. We've had an unexpected development in the case."

★

Zack and Commander Awe walked briskly down the passageway, back to Captain Rudy's office, where the commanding officer, sitting on the burgundy leather sofa in front of his desk, waved them in. CNN was blaring from the television in the corner of his office.

"Our chaplain friends have fired their military lawyers and hired a civilian." Even as he spoke, Captain Rudy kept his eyes glued to the screen.

Zack sat down as the all-too-familiar image of Bernie Woodson appeared. He held a microphone in one hand while adjusting his headset with the other. He stood outside a sunbaked office complex in an urban location.

"This is Bernie Woodson reporting from Los Angeles, where we have just learned the U.S. Navy is about to court-martial three Navy chaplains, all members of the Muslim faith, for treason, murder, and conspiracy to commit murder. The chaplains are being implicated in the murder of Daniel Barak, the Israeli ambassador to the United States. Other deaths include an F-18 pilot, a number of civilian deaths in a San Diego area church bombing, and also an enlisted Navy man who allegedly planted a bomb on the F-18 I just mentioned.

"The Navy has neither confirmed nor denied the arrest of the chaplains. Navy Public Affairs Command did not return our calls this afternoon. The chaplains, however, have issued a press release through their civilian attorney, and he's a good one, internationally acclaimed defense attorney Wellington Levinson of Los Angeles."

Zack's eyes widened.

"We're here in front of Mr. Levinson's Century City law offices, where in just a few minutes, Mr. Levinson will make a statement to this growing horde of reporters you can see just over my shoulder. And we will bring you his press conference, which is expected to begin in just a few minutes. Now back to you."

The commanding officer's civilian secretary interrupted just as the picture on the screen switched back to the CNN anchor desk. "Captain, Admiral Stumbaugh on line one from Washington for you, sir."

"Yes, sir," Rudy said, picking up the receiver on his desk. "We're watching it now . . . Yes, sir, I'll pass that on to Lieutenant Brewer . . . Yes, sir." Captain Rudy's gaze was still on CNN. "Yes, sir. They're starting the press conference now . . . Aye, sir . . . I'll call you back."

Wells Levinson was on the screen, decked out in a gray pinstripe suit and red tie. Levinson took a quick hand swipe through his silver hair.

"Good afternoon, and thank you for coming. As you know, the U.S. Navy has, disturbingly, chosen to prosecute three naval officers, all chaplains who happen to be Muslim, for crimes which they did not commit.

"I submit that they are being prosecuted only because they are Muslim, because that's the popular thing to do in this country.

"Sadly, the Navy is conjuring up a political trial against Islam. This court-martial is the epitome of religious discrimination at its most arrogant level. The Navy is saying, to heck with the First Amendment—tolerance and diversity are not welcome. This is despicable. This is disgraceful. And we will prevail." Levinson again ran his hand through his silver hair.

Captain Rudy clicked off the TV, sat down, and exhaled. "So much for Washington's hopes to keep this under the radar screen." He turned to Zack. "Lieutenant, how do you feel about taking on Wells Levinson?"

"Sir, to he honest, so much has happened in the last twenty-four hours, nothing surprises me at this point."

"That was Admiral Stumbaugh on the phone. He was concerned, frankly, that with Levinson in the case, we might need to detail an assistant prosecutor to help you. The admiral says he will assign any officer in the JAG Corps of your choosing, with the understanding you will be the lead trial counsel, even if you pick an officer of higher rank. He says you should let us know in twenty-four hours."

"Skipper, is the admiral ordering that I select an assistant trial counsel?"

"He suggested it. But just remember, this isn't Lieutenant Colcernian you're facing anymore. This is the best defense attorney in the world."

The best defense attorney in the world.

"Lieutenant. Are you okay?"

"My apologies, sir." Captain Rudy's voice snapped Zack from his daze. "Yes, sir. I'm fine."

"The JAG may not have given you a direct order, but I'm going to." The captain paused, looking at Zack pointedly. "Lieutenant Brewer, I want you to get in your car, drive directly home, jump in the sack, and get some rest. Then report back here only when you've had at least five hours of sleep. You're no good to me or anybody else if you're half asleep. Now that's an order, Lieutenant. Do you understand?"

"Yes, sir."

"Come back in the morning, and let me know what you've decided about an assistant."

"Aye, aye, sir."

CHAPTER 50

Base chapel
32nd Street Naval Station
San Diego

Zack got up at six o'clock the next morning, flipped on the television, then headed into a hot, steamy shower. A few minutes later, he wiped the foggy condensation off the small mirror in his bathroom. He dragged his disposable razor through a layer of shaving cream, across his Adam's apple, and up to his chin. The twelve hours of sleep in his own home in peaceful La Mesa was just what the doctor—in this case the captain— had ordered. For the moment, anyway, Zack felt physically refreshed.

Tapping the last vestiges of beard stubble into the white basin, he washed them down the drain with a blast of hot water, tossed the razor in the trash can, and walked out of the bathroom.

He was in the small hallway between his bathroom and bedroom when he heard a phrase coming from the TV that stopped him dead in his tracks.

"It's already being called the court-martial of the century by legal scholars. Three U.S. Navy chaplains, all Muslim, are being prosecuted for treason and murder in a dramatic legal showdown between internationally acclaimed defense attorney Wellington Levinson and Navy prosecutor Lieutenant Zack Brewer. The selection of Lieutenant Brewer as prosecutor was confirmed by a Navy spokesman yesterday afternoon. Brewer, the young JAG officer who successfully prosecuted Petty Officer Antonio Blount, the Navy SEAL accused of assaulting the niece of Senator Roberson Fowler, is expected to be in a fight for his life against the seasoned and experienced Levinson, who has never—repeat, *never*—

lost a jury trial. CNN has been following this late-breaking story since yesterday, and here's our legal affairs correspondent, Bernie Woodson, in Los Angeles ..."

Wells Levinson? Sure, Zack had prosecuted over one hundred courts-martial and dozens of jury trials. But was he ready for this challenge just three years out of law school? Wells Levinson was not just a man. The man was a legend. A worldwide legend.

The court-martial of the century.

Suddenly, Zack felt as if a cement mixer had dumped a ton of concrete in the bottom of his belly. He turned off the television, picked up the phone, and called Captain Rudy.

"Skipper, about our conversation yesterday ... I've got an idea." He took a moment to explain his plan.

"Are you sure about this?" Captain Rudy asked.

"No, sir. I'm not. Not yet. But if lightning strikes, I just want to make sure the command and the JAG are behind me."

Rudy waited a moment before answering. "The admiral gave you the green light to do what you need to do. Of course, he has the prerogative to change his mind ..." He paused again. "And I must admit, I am very apprehensive about your plan."

"Aye, aye, Skipper." The line went dead.

CHAPTER 51

Sitting alone at her desk in the defense wing, Diane scanned the small list of new cases she had just received from the senior defense counsel. Three unauthorized absences, two drug charges—simple marijuana possessions—and a bar fight at the Enlisted Club. All special courts-martial. All guilty pleas.

Maybe they think I'm incompetent because I lost a case.

Maybe I'm getting blackballed for attacking the senator's niece.
Maybe I should just call the detailer and volunteer for aircraft carrier duty. There's a JAG billet open on the USS Nimitz.

The buzz on the telephone intercom system broke her concentration. "Lieutenant Colcernian?" It was Legalman First Class Kim Benedict.

"Yes, Kim?"

"You have a visitor."

"A visitor?"

"Yes, ma'am. Lieutenant Brewer."

She let out a sigh, then sat unmoving for a moment in stunned silence. Finally, she said, "Okay, bring him down."

"Yes, ma'am."

A moment later, a light tapping sounded at her door.

"Come in," she said, puzzled.

"Hi, Diane," Zack said from the hallway, looking extremely glad to see her.

She blinked with surprise. "The good lieutenant graces us with his presence." She leaned back in her chair, attempting nonchalance.

"May I come in?"

"Are you going to read me my rights and have me arrested?"

"Have you arrested?" Zack flashed a puzzled look.

"I assume your presence here means that I'll be prosecuted for dereliction of duty for my performance in the Blount case, and you, as the JAG's new star, would be prosecuting me."

"Funny." He smiled again. "So are you going to let me in or make me talk to you from out here in the passageway?"

She waved him in.

Zack crossed the room and sat down on the opposite side of her desk. "The Blount case is one of the things I wanted to talk to you about."

"To rub salt in the wound?"

"No," he said. "I think you did a fabulous job representing your client."

"I gambled, and I lost. Case closed."

"Sure, calling Garrett was a gamble. But if our roles were reversed, I'd have tried the same thing. Blount would have been convicted anyway if you hadn't rolled the dice. You had a chance for an acquittal if everything broke right."

"Yes, but if I left Garrett off the stand, my guy wouldn't have gotten such a heavy sentence. I mean, thirty years. Come on."

"But if you hadn't put him on the stand, your guy had no chance at an acquittal. As far as the sentence goes, we'll never know. I think you made the correct decisions, for what it's worth. It was excellent lawyering, Diane."

"What's going on, Zack?" This was the first time she had called him Zack since Justice School. She needed to get ahold of herself. Why did she suddenly feel the urge to get chummy? This was the same guy who stabbed her in the back and stole her trial advocacy award. She frowned. "I know you didn't come all the way over here to rave about my performance in the Blount trial."

He studied her for a moment. "Okay, to be honest, there *is* something I want from you. But the main thing I want is to patch things up between us."

She raised an eyebrow and almost laughed. Whatever it was he wanted must be important. "You've made me curious, Lieutenant. I'm listening, if there's something you want to say."

He crossed his legs and rested his clasped hands in his lap like a State Department diplomat at an arms-control summit. "Above all, I want to apologize for the way I've treated you."

"For the way you've treated me?"

"For my attitude."

She quirked a brow again, becoming amused. The great Zack Brewer ... *apologizing*? To her?

"Diane," he softened his voice, "for whatever reason, the powers that be, in this case our JAG Corps superiors, have placed us on opposite sides of the professional aisle ever since our days at Justice School. Ever since our days in Newport, at the trial advocacy competition, in the championship round. Remember that stipulation I sprang on you?"

"Remember it? I'll never forget it."

"I blindsided you to keep you off balance. You were so good I didn't believe I could win without surprising you at the last minute. I did not extend much professional courtesy in that case. If I could do it over differently, I would. I apologize to you."

"Apologize?" She was beginning to believe him. Maybe it was because of the intensity of emotion somewhere behind those hazel eyes. She stared at him, almost afraid to breathe. "It's not like I didn't try the same thing in the Blount trial."

"I deserved it," he said, studying her face.

She felt a blush begin. "If I had given you time to prepare," she added, "you'd have shredded my Mr. Garrett *and* his two friends." She shrugged. "But you shredded him anyway with your cross." She let the comment stand a moment. "And you still won. Big-time."

"It's easier to win when you're the prosecution," he said.

"Oh yeah?" She leaned back from the desk and crossed her legs. "Like when I was the prosecutor in the Justice School competition— and you still beat me?"

"As I said, my tactics weren't exactly gentlemanly."

She sighed. "At the end of the day, you won. Isn't that all that matters?"

"No. The truth is what matters. I can tell you, I wasn't there when Blount met Ensign Landrieu in the parking lot that night, but I'd far rather lose a trial than send an innocent man to the brig."

"Here's the truth, Lieutenant. Look at you now. You're about to take on the great Wells Levinson in the 'court-martial of the century.'" She mimed quotation marks with her fingers. "And I'm back defending UA dives." She couldn't believe she was baring her soul to this man. What was it about him that made her feel she could trust him ... made her feel he cared?

"You bought his book, didn't you?"

"Whose book?"

"Levinson's *King of Defense*. You bought it and studied chapter 14."

Diane felt another flush start at the roots of her hair. "The Element of Surprise." She didn't dare meet his gaze. "Yeah, okay. I did."

Her admission brought a chuckle, and she looked up at him. He was grinning. "Me too. Good book."

"So where are you going with all this?"

"What do you think of Levinson?" Zack was serious again.

"He's a genius. Very rich. Maybe the brightest trial lawyer in the world."

"Think I can handle him?"

"I'm sure you can. You're the great Lieutenant Brewer."

Zack waited a few seconds. "I'm not sure about that."

Intrigued, she fell silent as he studied her face. Something in his eyes told her his admission of weakness was difficult for him to say aloud. There was also a vulnerability in his expression that surprised her. "Go on."

"I need a slingshot."

"A slingshot? Is that a pick-up line—or something out of your next closing argument?"

The flicker of vulnerability passed as quickly as it had come. He laughed heartily. It was contagious, and she laughed with him.

"I still have no clue what you're talking about."

"Let me ask you a question," he said.

"Get to the point, Lieutenant," she said, fighting a smile. "I've got some very serious unauthorized-absence cases I must get to."

"Okay," he said. "When word broke yesterday that these three chaplains hired Wells Levinson, Admiral Stumbaugh called and suggested we add another trial counsel to the prosecution team." His eyes caught and held hers. "The admiral said that I could request any of the 825 JAG officers in the world, even a commander or a captain, and he'd approve it. But if I request anybody at all, I really want the best JAG officer I know." He paused, seeming to measure her reaction before going on. "If you'll agree," he said, "I'd be honored if you would join me on the prosecution team."

Diane gaped at him. "You want *me* to come on as assistant trial counsel?"

"Yes, I do."

"But the way we've clashed in the past—"

He interrupted her midsentence. "Because we were professional opponents. Look, we're both aggressive in the courtroom and passionate about our work. The sparks between us are inevitable. This time we'd bring everything we have to bear for a cause greater than either of us, working together toward a common goal. Besides, I take all responsibility for our past rocky relationship. I promise to bend over backwards to make it work."

She smiled at him. "Still spinning your persuasive yarn on the jury?"

He smiled back. "Right now, this jury-of-one is my most important to date."

She felt herself blush yet again and glanced down at the small stack of unauthorized-absence cases on her desk. *Why does this guy make me blush when no one else can?* "But who would handle my UAs?" She grinned at him.

"Look. I've been a bit cocky in my career. No attorney has ever intimidated me. But this guy Levinson? I don't know if I can handle him by myself. Frankly, there's no other attorney in the JAG Corps with your natural flair for litigation. If you say no, I'll go it alone. But I need you. More important, the Navy and your country need you."

Zack leaned forward as he continued his plea. "Look, Diane, this case isn't just about Levinson and me. It's bigger than all of us. Our national security is at stake. If we lose this case, it's a major victory for terrorism. If we lose, radical Islamic extremists will think they have a license to infiltrate the U.S. military. We can't let this happen."

She stared at Zack, stunned by what he had just told her. Stunned that he wanted her to work with him. Stunned by the high stakes. She wondered if she had what it took. What if she failed again?

Then she thought of her father, the belief he had in her abilities even when she had rebelled against him. This was her moment. She could almost hear his gravelly voice telling her so. She gave Zack a half smile. "Okay, you've got a deal."

Zack grinned like a kid opening presents under the Christmas tree. "Fabulous!" He stood, extending his hand. "Then we've got a deal?"

"We've got a deal."

She grasped his hand for a lingering handshake as their eyes locked again.

A few heartbeats later, he released her grip.

She felt a flash of disappointment.

And then he was gone.

CHAPTER 52

Lieutenant Diane Colcernian's townhouse
Near Jimmy Durante Boulevard
Del Mar, California

The memory of the brief touch of Zack's hand wrapped around hers kept Diane tossing and turning deep into the night. At three o'clock, a cup of chamomile tea with honey slowed things down some. She was now replaying the handshake in her mind only five times an hour instead of ten.

It was not a businesslike grip appropriate to the consummation of a contract. It was, rather, a touch that caused her heart to skip a beat and almost dance. It was, in reality, the instant their hands met, like being plugged into a live socket.

Definite shock.

Undeniable electricity.

She took a sip of herbal tea to calm her thudding heart. *Control yourself, Diane. Are you going to let one meeting with this smooth-talking guy suddenly erase everything he's taken from you?*

She poured her now lukewarm tea down the sink and padded down the hall to her bedroom again. More tossing and turning followed. Finally, she sat up, exasperated, and flipped on the bedside table light.

She had planned to read, but as she reached for her book, the lamp illumined a photograph of her father. The admiral stood there, smiling at her, in his service dress blue uniform, with the thick gold bands of a three-star admiral on his lower sleeves, his hand cradling a white officer's hat with "scrambled eggs" on its black bill. It was her father's last official photograph as COMNAVSURFLANT, taken just one month before the stroke.

She studied his face for a moment, remembering his fire-and-ice personality, his passion for those he loved, his no-nonsense ways and frustratingly high standards. He was complex, difficult ... but she had loved him with all her heart. Somehow, thinking about him made her feel calm again. She turned out the light, deciding she did not want to read after all.

She was just drifting off when her eyes opened wide in the dark. *That's it! Zack reminds me of Daddy. His personality. His intelligence. Even his eyes. Why haven't I seen it before?*

Three hours later, the staticky sound of her clock radio alarm woke her.

She squinted at the clock: 5:30.

She leaned over and tuned the radio to news station KSDO and the soothing, almost grandfatherly voice of the early morning drive-time radio DJ in San Diego.

"More news today coming out of the Navy about the anticipated court-martial of three Muslim Navy chaplains facing treason charges.

"In a surprise announcement, the Navy released a statement late last night announcing Lieutenant Diane Colcernian will be joining the prosecution team. Now this is somewhat surprising because Lieutenant Colcernian was the defense attorney in the recently completed trial of Petty Officer Antonio Blount, the Navy SEAL convicted of assaulting the niece of powerful U.S. Senator Roberson Fowler.

"Blount received thirty years in a Navy brig. Now Colcernian joins Lieutenant Zack Brewer, her opponent in the Blount trial, who will serve as lead prosecutor against the chaplains. Brewer and Colcernian were heated rivals in the Blount trial, and it will be interesting to see if they can patch their differences and work together against Wellington Levinson, the internationally acclaimed defense attorney who is representing the chaplains.

"In response to the press conference held by Levinson and the Reverend JamesOn Barbour on Monday, the Navy announced that it will hold a press conference today to introduce the prosecution team, and the specifics on that are expected to be released later today.

"In sports, the Padres start today's doubleheader three games behind the Dodgers ..."

Diane flipped off the radio. After showering and pulling on her khaki uniform shirt and skirt, she grabbed an apple and headed south down Interstate 5 from Del Mar to the 32nd Street Naval Station.

When she arrived in her office just before 7:00, the orders transferring her to Navy JAG Trial Services Office were already on her desk.

"I understand I'm losing my best defense counsel."

Diane looked up and saw the senior defense counsel standing at her door.

"This has happened so fast, sir."

"Change is the most constant part of Navy life." He gave her a wink. "We'll miss you, Lieutenant."

"Thank you, sir. I'll miss being here."

"I understand they've got a lot of work for you over in the trial shop. I'll send Petty Officer Benedict over there with your personal items. You've got a huge task in front of you, Diane. Maybe you should get going. Good luck."

"Thank you, sir."

With hands trembling, Lieutenant Diane Colcernian walked out of the defense wing for the last time.

CHAPTER 53

Diane felt a tinge of nervousness when she reported to Captain Glen Rudy's office at the JAG Trial Service Office. She wondered if her jangled nerves were from the trauma of changing jobs, from the prospect of working on another high-profile case, or from the idea of working closely with Zack Brewer. She wasn't sure.

"Mornin', ma'am," Master Chief Legalman Richard Cisco said, rising as she stepped into the reception area.

"Morning, Master Chief," Diane nodded. "I'm Lieutenant Colcernian, reporting for duty."

"Yes, ma'am," Cisco said. "We're expecting you, ma'am. The skipper's not in at the moment. He'll be back soon. We're having a brief ceremony in his office."

Diane smiled, wondering if they were planning a little welcome party for her.

"Coffee, ma'am?"

"No thanks, Master Chief." She handed the legalman her orders. "Is Lieutenant Brewer in by any chance?"

"Oh yes, ma'am," the master chief said. "He's expecting you. He said just come on down to his office. No need to knock, he said. He's busy getting ready for a press conference this afternoon. I think they want you in on that one too."

"Where's the lieutenant's office, Master Chief?"

"Last door, starboard."

"Thanks, Master Chief."

Diane followed the legalman's directions, and a minute later she approached the last door on the right. Just outside it, inserted in a small sleeve was a portable gold nameplate that read "LT Brewer."

Her heart pounded with more intensity when she saw that the door was slightly ajar. The master chief had said to just walk in. Zack was expecting her. She told herself to stop fretting and just be professional.

She pushed open the door. And gaped. Zack stood with his back to her, embracing his paralegal, Amy DeBenedetto.

The moment the door opened, Zack's peripheral vision kicked in. "Diane!" he said, stepping back quickly.

"I'm sorry, I should have knocked. I—"

"It's okay." Zack frowned.

Amy, her eyes as wide as saucers, simply stared at Diane.

"I didn't mean to interrupt anything." Diane's heart felt numb as she backed toward the doorway.

"It's okay." Zack composed himself and smiled as if he had nothing to be ashamed of. Which, in Diane's opinion, made what she had just witnessed even worse. He turned to Amy. "Why don't you show Lieutenant Colcernian what you just showed me."

Amy picked up a single-page document from the corner of Zack's desk and handed it to Diane.

Diane scanned the letter, then met Amy's excited gaze. "You're going to law school?"

Amy nodded, her eyes sparkling. "I just found out." She reached for a second set of papers on Zack's desk, grinned at Zack, and handed it to Diane.

Diane read the orders from NMPC. So maybe the embrace was congratulatory. She took a deep breath. "You've been accepted into the JAG Corps."

"Yes, ma'am."

Diane was still trying to sort out her feelings, especially how her heart twisted at the sight of the two embracing, when Zack's intercom buzzed.

"Lieutenant?" It was the voice of the legalman.

"Yes?"

"Skipper's ready for Lieutenant Colcernian and Miss DeBenedetto."

Miss DeBenedetto?

"Let's go, ladies," Zack said, then escorted them to the executive suite, between the offices of the commanding and executive officers, where soft drinks and cookies were lined up on the conference tables.

Captain Glen Rudy appeared a few minutes later. "Lieutenant Colcernian, Miss DeBenedetto, please step into my office."

Diane followed Amy into the commanding officer's office, and Zack trailed them both, the faint scent of his cologne wafting toward her.

"Lieutenant Colcernian, I'd like to present our XO, Commander Bob Reynolds," Captain Rudy said, referring to the command's executive officer.

"Sir," Diane said.

"And your senior trial counsel, Commander Awe."

"We've had the pleasure." Diane smiled.

Rudy introduced several of the trial counsel lined up around the room. "And I think you already know Lieutenant Brewer."

"Yes, sir."

"We'll have a more formal welcoming ceremony for you later, but the rapid developments of the last few days mean that duty calls first. But before we put you to work, we wanted to say welcome aboard, Lieutenant."

"Thank you, sir."

"And now," Rudy said, turning to Amy, "will Miss DeBenedetto step front and center, please."

Amy stepped forward and came to attention before the commanding officer.

"This moment brings me great pride as a commanding officer." Rudy smiled. "Just one hour ago, you were 'Petty Officer' DeBenedetto, but as of thirty minutes ago, I understand you were discharged from the naval service. Is that right, Miss DeBenedetto?"

"Yes, sir." Amy's eyes watered and she blinked back her tears.

"And I understand that you now wish to return to the naval service?"

"Yes, sir."

"Very well. Raise your right hand and repeat after me."

Amy complied. "I, Amy Joy DeBenedetto, do solemnly swear . . . I will support and defend the Constitution of the United States against all enemies, foreign and domestic . . . I will bear true faith and allegiance to the same . . . I take this obligation freely, without any mental reservation or purpose of evasion . . . and I will faithfully discharge the duties of the office on which I am about to enter . . . So help me God," Amy said, her voice breaking.

"Master Chief?" Cisco stepped forward with an open felt box containing two black shoulder boards with the mill rind insignia of the Navy JAG Corps and a single gold stripe on the end. Rudy lifted the shoulder boards from the box and ceremoniously snapped them on Amy's shoulders.

"Congratulations, *Ensign* DeBenedetto," Rudy said, and the small cadre of witnesses broke into applause.

"Thank you, sir." Amy's voice was barely audible over the applause.

"Lieutenant Brewer, please offer Ensign DeBenedetto a handkerchief so we don't have to send her uniform to the cleaners before her flight."

Zack stepped forward, handed Amy a white handkerchief, and gave her an affectionate hug as the applause died down. The young ensign beamed into his face, and Diane's heart caught.

Rudy looked out at the group in front of him. "Just as the winds shift direction and the tides roll in and out, the duties of a naval officer are always subject to change. As good officers, we do not question the orders of our superiors, but rather, we snap a crisp salute and go wherever duty calls.

"Today the JAG Corps stands ready to begin prosecution of perhaps the most important court-martial in the history of military law. We welcome Lieutenant Colcernian aboard, confident that she and Lieutenant Brewer will forge a dynamic prosecution team, well prepared for the task ahead of them.

"At the same time, we say good-bye to a vital member of our prosecution team. Ensign DeBenedetto, you were the best legalman paralegal in the Navy. For the next three years, as you pursue your law degree at William and Mary, remember the JAG Corps. Work hard, study hard, and when you return to us, the JAG Corps will be better because of it."

Rudy gave Amy a brief hug. "Good-bye, Ensign DeBenedetto. We wish you fair winds and following seas." He turned to Zack. "Lieutenant, please escort the ensign to her car."

"Aye, Captain."

Diane watched as Zack left the office with the newly commissioned ensign, wondering what was between them . . . if anything. Maybe it was fatigue that had caused her imagination to kick into overdrive when she witnessed their embrace.

Then the bigger question filled her mind: Why did it matter so much?

Rudy stepped up beside her. "You and Lieutenant Brewer have a press conference this afternoon. You'll need to change into your whites."

"Yes, sir," Diane said, willing her thoughts away from Zack Brewer. "Master Chief, show Lieutenant Colcernian to her new office."

Diane followed the legalman down the hall, determined once again to see Zack Brewer for exactly who he was: a smooth-talking professional who would stop at nothing to win a case ... or win a heart. Even young Amy DeBenedetto's.

And hers.

CHAPTER 54

Diane had changed into her summer white uniform and was waiting in her new office in the trial wing when Zack returned a half hour later.

When he knocked at her new office door, now also in his summer whites, carrying a modest but attractive arrangement of daisies, she assumed that part of his half hour had been taken up changing clothes and the other part spent at the Navy exchange florist, buying daisies as a good-bye gesture to Amy.

"I'm sorry we didn't have time for a more formal welcome." He leaned against the doorjamb, one ankle hooked over the other. "The thing with Amy was a total surprise to me." She raised an eyebrow, but he didn't seem to notice. "I hope these brighten your office."

"For me?"

"Of course." He walked toward her. "From all the guys in the trial shop."

"How kind." She wondered at her disappointment that the bouquet was by committee.

He glanced at his watch. "The Navy chief of information has a press conference scheduled in ninety minutes at COMNAVBASE. Commander Awe will drive us downtown and brief us on the way."

"What am I supposed to say?"

"You mean about the press conference?"

Why do I sense a double meaning? "Yes, the press conference."

"The PAO—public affairs officer—reads a statement. I make a brief statement. Then we field questions and leave. Part of the purpose of the presser is to introduce you, and if you'd like, you can say that you've just been assigned to the case and want to withhold comment. But the main thing the folks in Washington are concerned about is Levinson getting ahead in the PR war."

"That's it?"

"For now. We'll talk strategy this afternoon. They've demanded a speedy trial, and this thing may start next week."

"Next week?"

He grinned as she stood up. "Come on. Muster up that million-dollar modeling smile and help me make the Navy look good."

Ninety minutes later, Zack, Diane, Commander Awe, and Captain Rudy were escorted into the side entrance of the COMNAVBASE. The idea was to avoid the press gathered at the front entrance. But one of the local reporters spotted the quartet just before they reached the door.

"Lieutenant Brewer! Lieutenant Brewer!" Jan Oberholtz jogged toward them from around the corner of the COMNAVBASE building, her jeans-clad cameraman in tow.

"Hurry. Get the door, Chief," Zack barked.

Reporters raced behind the cameraman, rounding the corner of the building like sprinters in the final kick to the finish line. The chief punched the electric door-code as the sound of Oberholtz's clacking heels grew louder. Zack put his hand against Diane's back, moving her quickly into the elevator, then waited outside as Commander Awe and Captain Rudy entered.

Jan Oberholtz suddenly appeared at his elbow. "Just one word, Lieutenant?"

Without answering, Zack ducked inside, and the door closed. He gave Diane a wink and a half smile before turning to the front of the elevator.

A moment later, the doors slid open again. "Right this way." The chief led the group to a back stairway, then through a double doorway and down a large, antiseptic-looking corridor. They stepped onto a back-stage area draped behind a large black curtain and were met by a salt-and-pepper-haired Navy captain in summer whites.

"I'm Captain James Waters with Navy Public Affairs," the four-striper said. He explained how he wanted to conduct the press conference. "Remember," he concluded, "the main purpose here is to put on a good face for the public. Understood?"

From the corner of her eye, Diane saw Zack give him a crisp nod at the same time she did.

"Good." Waters checked his watch. "Let's go."

He stepped through the curtain onto the stage, followed by Zack and Diane. The blinding spotlights, reflecting off the varnished hardwood floor on the stage, made the audience almost disappear in an illusion of darkness.

Captain Waters stepped to the podium as Zack and Diane sat at a long table on his left. Captain Rudy and Commander Awe seated themselves at another table on the opposite side.

"Good afternoon, ladies and gentlemen. I'm Captain James Waters, Senior Public Affairs Officer for Navy Region Southwest."

Diane, her eyes now adjusting to the light, could make out members of the press and media packed into the first seven or eight rows of the auditorium.

Captain Waters introduced the four officers, then nodded amiably to the audience. "As you know, a general court-martial convening authority has referred charges against three United States Navy chaplains who are charged with treason, murder, and conspiracy to commit murder. Because of the very high degree of public interest in this case, today we wanted to introduce you to the prosecution team. But before I do, I have an announcement to make."

He paused dramatically before continuing in a loud voice. "By order of the president of the United States, the case of *United States versus LCDR Mohammed Olajuwon et al.* will be the first court-martial in history in which television cameras will be allowed."

The announcement brought a flood of murmurs from the audience as Diane met Zack's gaze. "News to me," he whispered, frowning.

"And now, I am pleased to present our prosecution team." Captain Waters glanced toward Zack and Diane. "Lieutenant Zack Brewer is our lead trial counsel," he gestured toward Zack, "and he is joined by Lieutenant Diane Colcernian, our assistant trial counsel."

Diane smiled and nodded toward the sea of lights.

"And now, here's Lieutenant Brewer."

Zack stood and walked to the microphone. "Good afternoon, ladies and gentlemen. To say this court-martial is of immense national importance is an understatement. Let me begin by addressing some of the irresponsible public comments made by our opponent during the last couple of days.

"Despite the grossly irresponsible misinformation being pedaled by Mr. Levinson, this case is *not* about religion. It is, rather, about the inexcusable, deliberate, concerted, and shameful actions by a group of individuals who call themselves naval officers, to undermine the interests of the United States *and* to cause death and destruction to innocent American citizens and innocent American sailors. This, ladies and gentlemen, we will prove beyond a reasonable doubt. And make no mistake, we intend to seek the death penalty in this case."

Diane leaned forward, her attention riveted on Zack. *I can't believe he's going after Levinson like this. He's crazy.*

"The defendants have demanded a speedy trial, and they're going to get a speedy trial. Next week, as a matter of fact. Therefore, Lieutenant Colcernian and I have a very busy agenda ahead of us. But before we get back to base to resume our trial preparation, we'll take a few questions."

"Lieutenant, Bernie Woodson, CNN."

"I had a feeling you'd be here today, Mr. Woodson."

"Lieutenant, you hit Mr. Levinson pretty hard, accusing him of making 'irresponsible' statements. But doesn't he raise a legitimate concern about the sanctity of freedom of religion in the Navy and particularly in the Chaplain Corps?"

Zack sipped ice water from the plastic cup on the podium. "Bernie, I stand by my statement. What we want here is justice. I'm not sure what Mr. Levinson wants. For the last couple of days, the publicity-seeking Mr. Levinson played the national media like a marionette. Verbally dancing around on the national morning talk shows *and* the Sunday shows from Washington, Mr. Levinson seems set on milking the press for all that he can. Frankly, Bernie, I'm not concerned with what points Mr. Levinson makes to the press. I *am* concerned about the cancer of terrorism creeping into the United States Military."

He nodded to a woman in the front row.

"Lieutenant, Jan Oberholtz. Just two weeks ago, you and Lieutenant Colcernian were at each other's throats over the prosecution of Petty Officer Antonio Blount. Isn't it a bit odd that now you are on the same team? Doesn't this underscore charges made by the Reverend Barbour that the Blount trial was rigged by the system?"

"Jan, I'd characterize Barbour's statements as even more reckless than Mr. Levinson's. Let me say first that the Blount trial is over. If you knew Lieutenant Colcernian as I have for the last three years, having been on the opposite side of the aisle from her in court, you would know she doesn't roll over and play dead for anybody. And if you know anything about the JAG Corps, you would know that JAG officers are often reassigned from prosecution to defense roles. As far as having Lieutenant Colcernian on the prosecution team, I am personally delighted. She is one of the best—if not the *very best*—trial lawyer in the Navy."

"Lieutenant, how do you feel about having cameras in a Navy courtroom for the first time?" This question came from an unidentified voice in the dark.

"If that's what the president wants, that's fine with me. Next question."

"Lieutenant Colcernian, as a follow-up to Ms. Oberholtz's question, how would you respond to the earlier question about now being paired with Lieutenant Brewer, especially after your scathing cross-examination of Ensign Landrieu in the Blount trial?"

Zack turned to Diane and motioned her to join him at the podium. She stepped to the microphone as Zack moved aside. "I'm not going to comment on the Blount trial. That case is now on appeal. Lieutenant Brewer and I remain professional opponents in that case, and to the extent I am called on by appellate defense counsel to cooperate, I will do so.

"But this prosecution is a separate matter, and with the same energy that I opposed and continue to oppose Lieutenant Brewer in the Blount matter, I will support him here. As Lieutenant Brewer said, this court-martial is important to the national interest. And as naval officers, we all pledge to defend the Constitution against all enemies, foreign and domestic. And that's what I intend to do."

Captain Waters rose from his seat and headed to the podium, standing between Zack and Diane. "Thank you for your attendance this afternoon." His tone was decisive. The press conference was over.

"Captain, just a few more questions?"

"We are out of time. CHINFO will arrange for periodic briefings, as necessary, during this trial. Thank you." Looking pleased, Waters turned to Zack and Diane. "Nice job. Now let's get out of here."

Amid the flashes and shouts from the press, they slipped behind the curtain.

Law offices of Wellington Levinson
Wells Fargo Plaza
Century City
Los Angeles, California

Turn it off," Levinson barked. "That little twit thinks he can talk about me like that and get away with it? I'll have his hide."

Terrie Bearden chuckled at her boss's temper. "I thought he was kind of cute." She pressed the remote control, turning off the television set. "Besides, you've said that kind of thing a dozen times about your opponents. Who knows, maybe he read your book."

Levinson fumed, his face livid. "I've never seen such brazen arrogance."

"Arrogance or confidence?"

"Whose side are you on anyway?"

"I'm the one who brought the case in, remember? Of course I'm on your side." She laughed. "Cases like this make for great shopping sprees on Rodeo Drive. But you've said yourself there's a fine line between arrogance and confidence. Maybe the kid's actually confident about winning."

Levinson narrowed his eyes. "Sure, as I've written in my books, there is a fine line between arrogance and confidence. But there is an even finer line between confidence and ignorance. And whether this kid is arrogant or confident, if he thinks he's going to get away with talking about me like that, he's ignorant.

"I mean, did you hear this little punk in his vanilla ice-cream suit? He called me a *marionette*. That's a brazen insult."

"Actually," Terrie sat down on the corner of his desk and crossed her legs, "I think he said you're playing the media like they're marionettes. Maybe he was trying to pay you a compliment."

"I know what he was doing. He was throwing down the gauntlet." Levinson rolled up his sleeves and loosened his tie.

"Why, Wellington Levinson. All these years we've been together, I've never seen you so riled about an opponent. If I didn't know you better, I'd think you're just a little intimidated by the kid in the ice-cream suit."

"That's garbage, and you know it, Terri," Levinson snapped, the veins rising in his forehead.

Terrie Bearden lifted a brow at Wells, then swung out of his office, leaving her boss still fuming. She always did love a good show. And this was shaping up to be a good one. She chuckled as she went back to her desk and sat down to examine a chipped nail. Oh yes. There were bound to be fireworks.

Terrie knew well, from firsthand experience, that any attorney who dared cross the great Wells Levinson was in for a bloodbath. Wells often hit below the belt to win at all costs. An attorney in Ohio was arrested when Wells dug up an unpaid traffic ticket from years ago and paid off the cops to execute an all-but-forgotten warrant. The arrest was orchestrated by Levinson—in open court before the jury. In a New York case,

Wells hired a prostitute to lure his opponent into her trap; then, after obtaining photographs of the fellow falling for her wiles, he arranged for vice officers to swoop in and arrest them both. He then leaked the photos to the press and the man's unfortunate wife.

She wondered what would become of the young naval officer in the white ice-cream suit who, on national television, dared impugn the great Wells Levinson.

CHAPTER 55

Navy-Marine Corps Trial Judiciary
Building 1
San Diego
Court-martial of United States v.
LCDR Mohammed Olajuwon et al.

Day 1

During the week following Zack Brewer's proposal that she become a Navy prosecutor, Diane worked six consecutive eighteen-hour days, side by side with a man she never wanted to set eyes on again—especially in a courtroom—just one month ago.

Now she didn't know what to think of him.

In their long, tedious hours of reviewing witness statements, listening to tapes, preparing their witnesses, and divvying up trial assignments, he had flashed an occasional smile and sometimes even brushed his hand against hers.

Inadvertent or not, the touch, when it came, created a temporary relapse of the magnetic paralysis she had suffered after the handshake.

Fortunately, there was too much work to do in too little time to let her surprising fascination with him distract her from their mutual goal of whipping Wells Levinson. When the master chief brought in a front-page article in the *San Diego Union* with her picture at the press conference on the front, proclaiming "Diane Mania" was sweeping the nation, she glanced at the front page, smiled, but left the paper on Zack's conference table without even reading the article.

It was easy to ignore the article: an hour before, Zack had assigned her the responsibility of making the opening statement. She would be the first to go head-to-head against Levinson. That fact, more than anything else, had dominated her every waking moment.

"Ready, Lieutenant?" Zack Brewer stood at her door, handsome in his whites, holding his briefcase. Standing behind him was LN2 "Pete" Peterson, the mustached, less attractive, but professional replacement for LN1 Amy DeBenedetto.

"Do I look ready?" *I think I want to pass out.*

"You look fabulous. Time to go. Let's rock and roll."

Five minutes later, Peterson pulled the white Ford Taurus carrying the two young prosecutors into the reserved parking places just outside Building 1. A cadre of white press trucks with satellite dishes was parked around the courthouse. If the media presence at the Blount trial was a circus, this looked like a lion's den.

As their car pulled into place, a squadron of United States Marines, each carrying M-16s and wearing helmets and fatigues, surrounded it to block the crush of reporters from swamping the two JAG officers.

Zack cracked his window when the squadron leader tapped. The officer shouted above the background of yelping reporters barking questions. "Sir, unless you want to talk to the press, our orders are to get you and Lieutenant Colcernian inside."

"We'll save our talking for the courtroom, Lieutenant," Zack said. "Lead the way."

"Aye, sir." The officer walked around the car to Diane's door.

She stepped out and joined Zack and Peterson inside the moving perimeter of armed men as they cut through the throng of shouting reporters.

Zack gave her a nod and a quick wink. "Just give them a pleasant look and a wave."

She took a deep breath, forced herself to smile, and managed a couple of waves.

Pushing the reporters aside, the Marines led the trio to the entrance. Before they climbed the stairs, Diane noticed a silver Rolls-Royce at the curb, its vanity California license plate declaring "NEVRLOSE."

In an instant, they were up the front steps and through the courthouse doors. The squadron dropped off except for the first lieutenant, who accompanied them into Courtroom 1.

Levinson was already in place, sitting at the defense table without his clients, who had not yet been brought from the brig next door. His gray hair was stylishly combed back, and his blue and white pinstripe suit was meticulously tailored. He was more handsome in person than on television, or even on the cover of his book.

At first, the great Wells Levinson ignored their entrance, his eyes focused instead on a folder on the defense table. But as they approached the prosecutor's table, he peered through the lenses of his gold wire-rimmed glasses, first at Diane, then boring in on Zack with an unblinking, icy stare.

Zack quirked a brow at Diane as if to say, "Watch this." Then he flashed Levinson the same cocky smirk he had used on her a hundred times. The sight almost made Diane giggle as Zack turned back and winked.

"All rise!"

The commotion brought about by Judge Reeves's entrance knotted her stomach. In a moment, she would be on national television. She thought of her father, his pride, his gumption, his never-give-up attitude . . . his confidence in her. Just thinking of him relaxed her enough to breathe again.

"Be seated," Judge Reeves ordered. "Will the bailiff bring the defendants in, please?"

"Aye, sir."

A moment later, three ordinary-looking naval officers, dark haired, swarthy complexioned, and wearing the insignia of the Navy Chaplain Corps, walked into Courtroom 1, accompanied by armed shore patrolmen. They seated themselves at the counsel table with Levinson.

Two of the men stared at Diane for an instant before turning away. The third, Mohammed, kept his eyes straight ahead.

"Any pretrial motions before we proceed?" Reeves looked pointedly at Levinson. "Mr. Levinson?"

"Not at this time, Your Honor. The defense is ready to proceed."

"Lieutenant Brewer?"

"No, sir." Zack's voice was calm. "The government is ready."

"Very well. Summon the members." It took only a few minutes for the nine senior officers serving as members to be seated; then Judge Reeves turned to Zack. "Lieutenant Brewer, is the government ready to proceed?"

"We are, Your Honor. Lieutenant Colcernian will be making the opening statement."

Diane had been in front of cameras as a model, and yes, there had been some television exposure in the Blount trial, but this was different. Her heart pounded.

Spotlights.

National television.

Competing against the greatest lawyer in the world.

The national security of the United States on the line.

This is your moment, my daughter. Don't let it slip away.

She rose from the counsel table, walked past Levinson, ignoring him, and strode with runwaylike confidence to the banister.

"Mr. President," she said, referring to the senior member of the military jury, "distinguished members"—she paused to make sure their attention was riveted on her—"murderous terrorism, or the threat of it, has permeated every fabric of civilized nations. And unfortunately, it has now permeated the most sacred crevices of our own beloved United States Navy."

Diane felt her confidence growing as she walked down the banister, eyeing the officers one by one. "In this case, the government will show that three U.S. naval officers, the defendants"—she gestured toward them and then looked back to the members—"all officers in the Navy Chaplain Corps, used their offices to spread hate and terrorism. That *hate* and *terrorism* have resulted in numerous deaths, including the death of the Israeli ambassador to the United States, a naval aviator, and a dozen innocent civilians attending a Bible study here in San Diego.

"We will show that these three, when one of their disciples did not kill himself as they insisted, conspired to and in fact did take matters into their own hands. Remember the name Sulayman al-Aziz." She paused to let the name sink in. "When Petty Officer al-Aziz, an aviation tech in Virginia Beach who planted a deadly bomb in an F/A-18, did not enter martyrdom"—Diane made quotation marks in the air—"as they insisted, then that man, Lieutenant Commander Reska"—she pointed to Reska—"with the concurrence and encouragement of the other two, blew al-Aziz's head off and dumped his body into the Atlantic Ocean.

"How do we know this?" She walked forward, stopping just in front of the banister rail separating the courtroom well from the members. "We know this because forensic examiners have found microscopic evidence of brain tissue in Reska's boat, and gunpowder residue in the gunwales."

She paused, stepped back, and then resumed speaking in a lower, softer voice. "We will prove all this through tapes and transcripts, through the voices of the defendants themselves. We will prove our case beyond a reasonable doubt. Thank you."

Diane strode confidently back to the prosecutor's table, where Zack gave her a subtle nod of approval.

"Mr. Levinson? Opening statement?"

"Thank you, Your Honor," Levinson said in the trademark patrician accent of his native Massachusetts. He stood, straightened his lapels, and then walked to the jury rail and flashed the members a seemingly genuine, caring, and charismatic look.

"Mr. President, and distinguished members of this military jury, it is an honor for me, as a civilian and as a citizen of the United States, to stand before you today.

"You have all taken a sacred oath to defend our lives"—Levinson's hand swept around the gallery of civilian reporters jammed into the courtroom—"to defend *my* life, against enemies of the United States, and yes, to lay down your own lives in doing so.

"If only I could adequately convey the heartfelt appreciation of the millions of American civilians who have neither the means nor the ability to adequately say thank you."

A pause and a smile.

Diane noticed that a couple of the female officers, both commanders in the Nurse Corps, returned his smile. Levinson was less than a minute into his speech, and already the charisma was oozing.

"You know, when I was asked to defend these officers, at first I was reluctant.

"Was I reluctant because I doubted the innocence of my clients? Absolutely not. I have *never* doubted their innocence. And neither will you when we are through." He gave them another pseudo-sincere nod.

"No, ladies and gentlemen, I was reluctant because, frankly, I don't have that much experience in military law and because, frankly, having never served in the military myself, I felt *inadequate*—to be honest with you, *unworthy*—to stand here, as a civilian, before this noble group of officers."

Levinson raised his head, focusing on each of the members one by one. "But then, as I struggled with what I faced here, I began to do research in the area of military law, and I ran across something that struck me profoundly. Something that struck me, frankly, at my very core." Levinson brought his hands to his heart.

"I discovered, ladies and gentlemen, the naval officer's oath." He stepped back and paused, then started again in a slightly more regal version of his patrician accent. "'That I will support and defend the Constitution of the United States against all enemies, foreign and domestic ...'"

Another pause. Then he resumed in a lower voice. "These words, ladies and gentlemen, these words that each of you swore allegiance to, brought chills up and down my spine.

"And then I realized this very trial is about defending the Constitution. Because this Constitution, which is the very fabric of our noble republic, guarantees freedom of religion. Really, that's why we are here.

"Lieutenant Colcernian says this is about murder."

He actually knows my name.

"But I say the murderers are already dead." Levinson's silver hair glistened in the sunlight now pouring through the windows just behind the members. "These men are being prosecuted *only* because they are Muslim, with the government using tapes with ambiguous language to string together a weak case.

"You know, several years before the Constitution that you swore to defend was enacted, there was in my home state of Massachusetts, in the town of Salem, an outbreak of mass hysteria against a large number of innocent women who were burned at the stake or stoned to death.

"History calls that travesty the Salem Witch Trials.

"A few years ago, in the 1930s in Europe, those of us who are of the Jewish faith were the victims of another such hysterical hate.

"Today, unfortunately, Muslim-Americans are the modern legacy to the innocent victims of the Salem Witch Trials. This case will show that same hysterical hate exists today, unfortunately." He paused dramatically. "We are confident that at the end of the day, you will return with a verdict of not guilty.

"Thank you."

Diane almost forgot to breathe during his riveting performance. The members of the jury looked transfixed as they watched Levinson return to his seat. Diane saw the beginning of a smile on the Nurse Corps commander's face. The other commander nodded approvingly, her gaze riveted on the handsome Levinson.

CHAPTER 56

The Lincoln Bedroom
The White House

2330 hours (EST)

Mack, you need some sleep." The first lady, in a blue silk nightgown, looked up from the king-sized, canopied bed, rumored to have been Abraham Lincoln's. Her husband glanced back with a sheepish smile.

The commander-in-chief, wearing navy blue pajamas with the presidential seal embroidered on the pockets, punched the remote control and found the only news show he watched with any regularity.

The sounds of trumpets, drums, and tympanis accompanied the show's opening graphics, which looked like stars flying through the galaxy from the bridge of the *Starship Enterprise* at warp speed.

As the music faded, the show's host appeared on the screen with the lights of the San Diego skyline, reflecting off the bay, behind him.

"I'm Tom Miller, and this is *NightWatch*.

"All week long, since the Navy's press conference introducing the two young prosecutors who would take on the world's greatest lawyer in the court-martial of the century, America's obsession has turned to this trial and the young officers who will prosecute Wells Levinson's clients. It would be the first court-marital in history to be televised, the Navy announced. Today . . . round one in that trial. How did 'Diane Mania' hold up against Wellington Levinson? . . . We'll find out when *NightWatch* returns, live from San Diego."

More trumpets and tympanis.

More stars flying through the galaxy.

More complaining by the first lady.

"You're obsessed with that trial, *Mr. President*." She spoke with a sarcastic grogginess as she pulled the sheets over her shoulders. "I'm going to sleep."

"I just hope I haven't put too much on those kids." When there was no response, he glanced back toward his wife, who was breathing rhythmically under the covers.

"And welcome back to San Diego, where we've completed day one of the trial of *United States versus Olajuwon, Reska, and Abdul-Sehen*, all Muslim chaplains accused of treason, murder, and conspiracy to commit murder. It was a day in which both parties traded opening statements, and the prosecution began putting on its evidence. And CNN legal affairs correspondents Bernie Woodson and Jeanie Van Horton, who I'm sure are more than ready to provide their expert commentary, join us tonight. And we'll start with you, Jeanie. How did these young officers fare against Wells Levinson?"

The camera switched to a middle-aged blond. The caption at the bottom of the screen read "Jeanie Van Horton, Former Federal Prosecutor."

"Well, Tom, Wells Levinson was vintage Wells Levinson today. Smooth and charismatic. He brilliantly spun this as a constitutional trial involving freedom of religion. And if this were a moot court competition, Tom, Levinson would have won on points alone. But having said all that, as good as Levinson was today in his opening statement, in my view, he did not deliver the knockout blow many expected against the younger and less experienced Lieutenant Diane Colcernian, who came across as poised and confident in the government's case. If she was nervous today, Tom, it did not show."

"Fair enough," Miller said as the CNN cameras switched to a picture of the venerable, tough Bernie Woodson. "Bernie, Jeanie thinks the prosecution was left staggering but standing today. Do you agree?"

"Tom, I agree that the defense is ahead on points at this stage, but I wouldn't say that the prosecution is staggered by any means. But since you brought up the boxing analogy, it's true that Levinson, who has never lost a trial, goes for the knockout early on. He says so in his books. And he does this by being head-and-shoulders above his opposition in the opening statement, followed by quick, effective, and devastating cross-examination. Today was vintage Levinson, but Colcernian was good enough to keep the government in it. The amazing thing about Colcernian's performance, Tom, is that this was the very first opening argument she's made as a prosecutor. You'll recall that until just last week, Diane Colcernian was a defense attorney in the JAG Corps. Very impressive by both attorneys today, Tom."

"Jeanie Van Horton, after the opening statements, what about the quality of the prosecution's evidence? Comment on that, please."

"You bet, Tom." The blond was back on the screen. "They began with the testimony of NCIS Special Agent Harry Kilnap, the criminal investigator from Norfolk credited with busting this case open for the government. Kilnap played a series of tape recordings in which the chaplains seemed to acknowledge participation in the acts they're accused of. In one transcript, Chaplain Abdul-Sehen was overheard pressing Chaplain Reska to 'take care of the Aziz problem.' In another tape, Reska said, 'We are going to take a boat ride, and the problem will be taken care of.' In yet another tape, Olajuwon chastised Reska for failing to lecture al-Aziz on the virtues of martyrdom. Then there was a conversation between Reska and al-Aziz in which Reska invited al-Aziz onto his boat, the *River Rat*. After that, al-Aziz disappeared and is presumed dead. All in all, some pretty dramatic stuff, Tom."

"Dramatic indeed," the *NightWatch* anchor said as the image of Bernie Woodson reappeared. "How did Wells Levinson do in rebutting those tapes?"

"Well, Tom, the defense position is that the tapes are ambiguous and inconclusive, a point Levinson tried ramming home on his cross-examination. And Levinson challenged Kilnap several times to point out any specific admission of murder, which the agent admitted he could not.

"But despite Levinson's cross, perhaps the most damaging of the tapes was a recording, supposedly between Petty Officer al-Aziz and Chaplain Reska at a Shoney's restaurant in Virginia Beach, in which Reska, presumably referring to a bomb planted in an F/A-18, says, 'We are at war. Allah has already given you a glorious result to your mission. You have destroyed an instrument of war that would have been used against many of our Arab brothers.'"

"Sounds like damaging stuff, Bernie," Miller said. "How did Levinson counter?"

"Levinson pointed out in his cross-examination that Reska could've been talking about a previous mission to the Middle East, when the squadron to which he was attached struck terrorist sites, which Levinson suggested saved the lives of moderate Arabs. The 'instrument of war' he said, was a rogue missile platform destroyed by one of the planes in al-Aziz's squadron last year. Plus, Kilnap admitted that there was not a specific reference to the downed F/A-18 in the tape. Kilnap also admitted he was not personally familiar with the voices of any of the chaplains and could not positively identify them. The government is expected to call a voice identification expert later in the trial."

"Think the members bought it, Jeanie?"

"You know, I gave up trying to read juries a long time ago, Tom. Just when you think you've got them figured out, they surprise you. Did Levinson plant some seeds of doubt? Maybe, I don't know.

"I do know this, however, Lieutenant Zack Brewer, who will most likely deliver the government's closing argument in this case day after tomorrow, is going to have to really be on top of his game if the government hopes to secure a conviction."

"Jeanie Van Horton, Bernie Woodson, as always it has been a pleasure. And when we come back . . ."

The president clicked the remote control, then crawled back into the Lincoln bed, wrapped himself around the sleeping first lady, and silently prayed for wisdom for his two young prosecutors.

CHAPTER 57

Levinson headquarters
Hotel del Coronado
Coronado, California

2100 hours (PST)

Yes!" Sitting on the corner of his bed, Wells Levinson thumped the report delivered to his suite moments earlier. "Yes!"

"You okay, Wells?" Terrie Bearden leaned against the doorjamb in a blue workout suit and unscrewed the cap on her bottled water. "I was just going down to the gym for a quick workout."

With a grunt of satisfaction, Levinson handed her the envelope. "Read this."

Terrie opened it and studied the papers. "You are ruthless, Wellington."

"This will teach the punk in the ice-cream suit to call my statements irresponsible."

"Aren't we lucky your investigators never followed us around when we were that age?"

"Terrie, postpone your workout. I want this leaked through our back channels to the *LA Times*, the *San Diego Union*, and every other media outlet in our database. Get moving on it now. I want it shouting from the front page tomorrow morning."

She shot him a look of disapproval. "Wells, do you really want to do this to the kid? I mean, it's not like you need this to win the case."

"You heard what Miller and the two talking heads said on *Night-Watch*, didn't you? They want a knockout punch? They'll get a knockout punch." She looked uncertain, so he added, "Now do you want to get paid or not?"

"Okay, okay, Wells." Terrie draped a white Hotel del Coronado towel over her shoulders. "Give me the papers."

Prosecution headquarters
Navy Trial Command
Building 73
32nd Street Naval Station
San Diego

Day 2, 0415 hours (PST)

After working until midnight, Diane and Zack agreed to go home, get some sleep, and meet again at six in the morning.

For Diane, the adrenaline from yesterday's events, and especially from delivering the government's opening statement against Wells Levinson, made the notion of sleep a fleeting concept. Then, when she arrived at her Del Mar townhouse and plopped down on her sofa, she made the mistake of flipping on the television.

All night long, CNN played sound bites from both opening statements, along with Tom Miller's taped interview of Jeanie Van Horton. At the words "He did not deliver the knockout blow many expected against the younger and less experienced Lieutenant Diane Colcernian, who came across as poised and confident in the government's case," she sat up and took notice.

Heady stuff.

But what if they lost? She imagined the moment of defeat, if and when it arrived, and felt her self-confidence ebb.

"That's it. No more media for me till this trial is over." She flipped off the television and headed to bed.

Her "no media" vow lasted until 4:15 a.m., when dressed in her summer whites and ready for the long day ahead, she grabbed her briefcase and headed out the door. On her front steps, the early morning edition of the *San Diego Union-Tribune* beckoned.

She picked it up and glanced at the headline. "Oh no . . ."

She dropped her briefcase and stepped back into her townhouse for more light. Her heart dropped as she read. *Oh, dear Lord. Please don't let this be true.*

Forty-five minutes later, at 5:00 a.m., when she arrived at her reserved parking space at the one-story Trial Command headquarters on base, Brewer's Mercedes was already there. The rest of the spaces were empty.

She pushed the security code and came in the canal entrance of the trial wing—the entrance just across the narrow waterway separating the 32nd Street Naval Station from the National Steel and Shipbuilding Company.

Lights spilled into the hallway from Zack's office, and the sharp-edged clashing sounded like a fist punching a file cabinet.

"I'll kill him! I'll absolutely ring his neck!" Zack's enraged voiced carried down the empty passageway.

He's seen the article.

"That good-for-nothing, unethical rat!"

She stepped into his doorway. "You okay?"

"Diane?" Zack looked stunned. "Sorry. I wasn't expecting you for another hour."

"I understand why you're upset," she said. "It was a real low blow."

He gave her a puzzled look. "You know?"

She nodded.

"How?"

"I get the early edition of the *Union*."

"The *Union*? What are you talking about?"

"You've *not* seen it?"

"Seen what?"

"Seen this." She laid the newspaper on his desk. There it was, under the lead story about the opening statements.

DID BREWER HAVE AN AFFAIR WITH ENLISTED WOMAN? SOME SAY PROSECUTOR VIOLATED MILITARY LAW

By Dennis Wacker, Military Affairs Correspondent

Did Lieutenant Zack Brewer, the government's lead prosecutor in the case of *United States v. Mohammed Olajuwon et al.*, himself violate military law by having an affair with an enlisted woman?

Some say yes.

Witnesses close to the situation and speaking anonymously suggest Brewer, a Navy JAG officer, may have had a romantic relationship with Amy DeBenedetto, an enlisted paralegal who has since been commissioned as an ensign in the JAG Corps and is now attending law school in Virginia.

Although DeBenedetto is now a commissioned officer, if an affair occurred with Brewer while she was enlisted, several former JAG officers interviewed say such a relationship would violate military law, demanding discipline against Brewer ranging from a private reprimand, to captain's mast, to a general court-martial.

The Reverend JamesOn Barbour, reached at SARD headquarters in Chicago, called for an immediate investigation, and if the charges prove to be true, said Brewer should be prosecuted.

"This is a continued example of the Navy's double standard. They prosecute a young, innocent man for rape, and now it appears the prosecutor should be prosecuted," Barbour said.

Zack tossed the newspaper on his desk, his jaw visibly clenching. "Aside from the fact that this is a bald-faced lie, I can't afford to get distracted by Levinson's garbage. Not now. We've got far bigger problems in this case than this, Diane."

"What are you talking about?"

"It's not what I'm talking about; it's who I'm talking about."

"Okay, *who* are you talking about?"

"Special Agent Harry Kilnap, Navy Criminal Investigative Service. That's who. The guy's a worm." Zack dropped into his chair and motioned Diane to have a seat.

"I thought his testimony went okay yesterday. Sure, Levinson crossed him, but we got the tapes in and scored some points."

"That's the problem, Diane. It went *too* well."

"I don't understand."

"Something didn't add up about how he just 'happened' to be in Shoney's restaurant with his tape recorder."

"What are you saying?"

"What I'm saying is that something didn't sit right. So I called him."

"You called Kilnap?"

"Right. I ran him out of his comfortable government-paid-for nest at the Harborside Marriott at four o'clock in the morning."

"And?"

"After I pressed the matter a few times, he admitted something to me that he hasn't revealed to anybody else."

"Go on."

"An hour or so before he got the recordings at Shoneys, Kilnap found al-Aziz's car parked in the base parking lot at Oceana Naval Air Station. Without a warrant, and without probable cause, he planted a bug in the car and waited for al-Aziz to get off work. When al-Aziz climbed into his car, Kilnap's bug picks up a cell call with Reska. Al-Aziz says they will meet at Shoney's. Kilnap follows them there. *Or* goes there based on information he has learned from bugging al-Aziz's car."

Their eyes locked for a few seconds. "What are we going to do?" she said.

"You were just a defense counsel. Tell me. What's the prosecutor's duty when he or she discovers potentially exculpatory evidence?"

"Oh dear ..." Diane held her hand over her mouth for a moment, then removed it. "You're thinking about disclosing this?"

"I don't know what I'm going to do. But you know as well as I do that a prosecutor, even a military prosecutor, has a duty to disclose exculpatory evidence."

"Zack, you know if you disclose this or if Levinson gets hold of it, our whole case could go down in flames."

"No joke." He stood from his chair, folded his arms, and turned his back on her, gazing out his office window at the dark waters of San Diego Bay. "You know, if Kilnap had just come clean from the beginning, we could have dealt with this. Now I've got a real dilemma."

"You mean *we've* got a real dilemma."

"No." He turned around and looked into her face. "I'm the lead prosecutor. I got you into this, and I'll take the heat either way."

"Have you told Captain Rudy or Commander Awe?"

"I'm not going to tell them." Zack sat back down. His face was pale.

She caught her breath. "Are you crazy? Zack, they're your chain of command, and this case is being tried with the whole world watching. They say that the president has a personal interest in this case. So why wouldn't you tell them?"

Zack leaned back and looked up at the ceiling. "First off, they've detailed me as prosecutor in this case, and they've given me the reins to try the case as I see fit. If I tell them about Kilnap's shenanigans, then what?" His eyes met hers. "What if they order me to conceal the information even though I consider it to be exculpatory? I'd consider that to be an unlawful order, and we'd all be in a predicament."

He slammed his fist against the filing cabinet beside his desk. "Kilnap!"

"Zack, calm down a second." She spoke in a calm, reassuring tone. "Maybe it's not really exculpatory. Maybe you're not required to reveal it. Think about it. First off, is this really exculpatory evidence? I mean, just because Kilnap acted like a cowboy and bugged al-Aziz's car without a warrant doesn't really have anything to do with whether these defendants committed the crimes we've charged them with. It's not like it's evidence of an alibi or mistaken identity. These three guys were in on these crimes, and we both know it. So I don't see how Kilnap's bugging the car has anything to do with whether these guys are murderers."

"A good point, Diane. And one I'd certainly argue to the judge if we decide to disclose. But let me ask you this . . ." Zack's voice was calmer.

"Shoot."

"If you were the defense attorney in this case, would you want to know about the government's lead investigator bugging your client's car without a search warrant?"

She considered the question. "Of course."

"Okay. Tell me why."

"The basis for a possible motion to suppress," she said.

"Bingo."

"I see your point."

"Levinson would argue that because the first search was contaminated, all other evidence gathered, including all the tape recordings at the heart of our case, should be thrown out. Gutting our case. Making a conviction impossible."

"Fruit of the poisonous tree?"

"Precisely."

"But in this case, a large part of the evidence has already been heard by the members." Diane leaned forward. "It would be too late to suppress."

"Right." Zack thumped the dimple on his chin. "So Levinson moves for a mistrial, maybe gets it granted, gets a new trial, and then moves to suppress. And then it's over. Unless, of course, our argument can persuade Judge Reeves that discovery was inevitable."

"*Our* argument? You mean *your* argument." She smiled, trying to lighten the mood.

"Okay. *My* argument. Like I said, I'll take the heat for disclosure if it comes to that."

"But, Zack, think for a moment about the national security implications if these guys get away with this." She stood up. "This case is about *terrorists* infiltrating the officer corps, for goodness sakes. If there's ever an instance to justify an exception to the full-disclosure rule, this is it."

"I've had that very thought already a dozen times this morning, Diane."

"Then why not just let it go?"

"Maybe I will. Maybe I won't. I don't know."

He turned around and gazed out the window again. A faint light was pushing the black night back. "But you know what? Levinson did make one good point yesterday. Oh, I know his argument was perverted and twisted to his own ends. But we *are* naval officers. And we *do* take an oath to defend the Constitution. And if we get to the point that we're more concerned about fighting terrorism than preserving the Bill of Rights, haven't the terrorists already won?"

Oh, dear God. He's going to do it. He's going to disclose this. He actually thinks he can beat Levinson with one hand tied behind his back.

"Whatever you decide, I'll support you."

CHAPTER 58

Navy-Marine Corps Trial Judiciary
Building 1
32nd Street Naval Station
San Diego

Day 2

As the white Ford Taurus carrying the prosecution team rounded the last corner, the yellow stucco building came into view. The media positioned themselves around Brewer's reserved parking space like a human horseshoe. The Marines, again sporting combat fatigues and rifles, guarded the inside perimeter, carving out just enough free space for the car.

"Good thing the Marines are protecting the press from my gas pedal this morning," LN2 Cisco grinned.

Brewer managed a chuckle. "Thank God for the Corps." The levity in his voice was a stark contrast to the heaviness in his heart caused by the Kilnap dilemma.

"I can't imagine what they want to talk about this morning," Diane said from the backseat.

As Cisco eased the car into the parking place and cut the engine, Zack glanced over his shoulder and met her eyes. Her hair wasn't in its customary bun this morning, but was down, resting just above her collar, almost, but not quite, too long for regulation. The stark red against the white uniform was amazing. A nice distraction from the storm waiting outside the car. "Probably about the amazing opening statement you made yesterday." He gave her a reassuring smile.

The Marine first lieutenant tapped on the front passenger's window. Zack read his lips. "Ready, sir?"

"Let's go." Zack opened the car door.

The questions came in rapid fire, like a machine gunner emptying his clip:

"Lieutenant Brewer! Did you have an affair with an enlisted petty officer?"

"Lieutenant Brewer, what about Petty Officer DeBenedetto?"

"The Reverend Barbour says you should be prosecuted. How do you respond to that?"

"They sound like a pack of mad dogs yelping in the pound, sir," the squadron leader muttered to Zack as the Marines surrounded the prosecution team. The questions came so fast the voices all ran together.

"Lieutenant, heads up." Zack nodded to the squadron leader. "I'm going to make one statement before we go inside the building, from the front step of the courthouse."

"Aye, sir. We'll keep it secure."

A moment later, Brewer, Cisco, and Colcernian stood at the top of the courthouse steps, separated from the yelping mob only by a thin, albeit sufficiently armed, line of U.S. Marines. Zack turned into the bright lights and raised his hand. In an instant, the cacophonous barking gave way to the cool Pacific breeze, the sounds of car horns from nearby Harbor Drive and bells ringing announcing the arrivals and departures of dignitaries on Navy warships down at the waterfront.

"I know that you all have questions, and that's part of your job," Zack said. "And we have a job too, and that's to finish prosecuting this case. So I'm going to make a brief statement addressing what I think you may be interested in. Because we are pressed for time, I will take no questions, at least not now."

He let his words sink in as newspaper reporters scribbled furiously on legal pads and as the radio and television types jockeyed to poke their microphones and handheld tape recorders toward his face.

"First, we are pleased with yesterday's court proceedings. I was delighted with the powerful and cogent opening argument made by my colleague, Lieutenant Colcernian. I believe that we scored points with the members, and I am confident that at the end of the day, we will secure a conviction."

Another brief pause.

"Now, based upon the one thousand or so questions I have received in the sixty seconds since I stepped out of my car, I presume you have an interest in the story on the lower left front page of the San Diego paper this morning.

"First let me say that I couldn't care less what you—the respected members of the media—decide to say, or write, or think about me. I do, object, however, when some of you sully the name of another member of the naval service with a story that doesn't even name the sources of the allegation. In this case, the person whose name you have sullied was a dedicated, loyal, enlisted member and is now a fine officer. I have the highest personal regard for this officer, and she has broken no laws of the naval service.

"Anyone, whether you call them 'a witness close to the situation and speaking anonymously' or whatever you call them, who makes such an accusation aimed at harming people, but who doesn't have the guts to give their name, is a spineless coward."

He paused again, watching the newspaper reporters furiously scribbling notes. "And kowtowing to such garbage is spineless journalism. This type of tabloid gossip is yellow journalism in its lowest form. You who report such waste should be ashamed of yourselves. That is all."

Zack turned and nodded to one of the Marines, who opened the front door of the courthouse. He snapped a salute as the two Navy JAG prosecutors passed into the building.

When the prosecution team stepped into the courtroom for the morning session, Levinson was already at the defense table with his clients. A sly smile appeared on his face when he made eye contact with Zack.

"His smirk tells all," Diane whispered to Zack.

"All rise!"

With all that he had endured in the Blount prosecution, and now this, Zack had not felt a tinge of nervousness upon the opening of court.

Until now.

Judge Reeves, holding a file in his hand, walked to the bench.

Maybe Diane was right. Maybe national security justified keeping quiet about Kilnap. What about the victims of this heinous terror? What of Commander Mark Latcher's widow and children? They had names. Beth and Mary Blake. The twin girls in high school. And the little boy. Six-year-old Wesley. Didn't he owe it to them and the families of the other victims to secure a conviction?

"Please be seated."

Zack ignored the order and remained standing.

The moment of decision was at hand.

"Your Honor, before we begin, there is a matter the government feels compelled to bring to the court's attention this morning."

"Very well, Lieutenant Brewer." The affable Reeves peered over his gold wire rims.

From his right, across the five-foot passageway separating the prosecution and defense tables, Zack felt the glare of Wells Levinson.

"Your Honor, while we feel the information we are about to bring before the court, under these circumstances, will not have a significant impact in the disposition of this case, in the interest of full disclosure, I want to reveal the following."

Zack reached for his glass and took a sip of ice water. "After we completed yesterday's session, I was on the telephone with one of the government witnesses, NCIS Special Agent Harry Kilnap, who, as you know, testified yesterday."

Captain Reeves nodded his head and also took a swig of water.

"During the course of my conversation with Special Agent Kilnap, I learned last night, for the first time, certain information about the arrest of Lieutenant Commander Reska which Mr. Kilnap did not testify about yesterday, in part, simply because he was not questioned about it."

"Very well." Judge Reeves nodded.

"I learned, Your Honor, that several hours before Mr. Kilnap recorded the conversation between Lieutenant Commander Reska and Petty Officer al-Aziz in Shoney's restaurant, a public place, Special Agent Kilnap was conducting surveillance of the petty officer's car, which was parked in the parking lot at the Oceana Naval Air Station. Agent Kilnap, in the dark hours of the morning, placed a listening device in al-Aziz's car, which transmitted signals and communications to Kilnap's car.

"When al-Aziz drove out of the parking lot, Mr. Kilnap, in his car, followed, maintaining constant visual surveillance. During that time, the transmission device picked up *part*, but not all, of a conversation between Petty Officer al-Aziz and Commander Reska. Mr. Kilnap, who was already in pursuit, heard al-Aziz say they would meet at Shoney's on Dam Neck Road in Virginia Beach. Kilnap never lost visual contact with al-Aziz's car and followed it to Shoney's, where he recorded the conversations already entered into evidence."

"That is all, Your Honor." Zack sat down, his heart pounding.

There was light mumbling in the gallery. Light because, Zack figured, only a handful of the reporters understood the significance of what he had just said. One rap from the judge's gavel instantly quieted things.

The military judge leaned back in his chair, pulled his glasses off, swiped them quickly with a handkerchief, and looked back to Zack.

"Let me see if I understand you, Lieutenant Brewer. Are you saying the prosecution just learned of this last night?"

Zack stood to address the court. "Correct, Your Honor." He sat down again.

Reeves moved his gaze to Levinson. "Mr. Levinson, do you have anything to say about this?"

Levinson rose slowly with his mouth open, as if aghast, and dramatically turned to the gallery, making eye contact with several prominent media members before turning back to face Captain Reeves. "Your Honor, rarely am I so shocked to be at a loss for words, but I must confess I am on the precipice of such an occasion at this very moment."

"Well, Mr. Levinson," Reeves said, "I suggest you find your words in fairly short order, because if you don't, I've got a panel of members sequestered back there I'm about to call back in here to finish the case. In other words, the ball's in your court. Speak now or forever hold your peace."

Levinson nodded, then seemed to find a miraculous cure for his speechlessness.

"First off, Your Honor, I have a hard time believing the prosecution, in a case of this magnitude, discovered this information just last night."

"Mr. Levinson," Reeves said, "I've known Lieutenant Brewer for several years, and if he represents to the court that he was not aware of this until last night, unless you have evidence to the contrary, I have no reason to disbelieve him. Now if you have any motions to make, I will entertain them. If not, we're moving forward."

Levinson displayed a bit of a scowl, as if irritated that Judge Reeves wouldn't tolerate his grandstanding. "Your Honor, the defense moves to dismiss all charges and specifications against my clients at this time. In the alternative, we move for a mistrial."

"Very well." Captain Reeves turned to the court reporter. "Madam Court Reporter, let the record reflect that the defense has moved to dismiss, or in the alternative, for a mistrial at 0905 hours, local time." Reeves looked back to Levinson. "Mr. Levinson, would you care to state your grounds?"

"Yes, Your Honor." Levinson flattened his tie and buttoned his suit jacket. "As the court is aware, the United States Supreme Court has held, in the landmark case of *Brady versus Maryland*, that the right to a fair trial means the government has a responsibility to provide discovery to an accused, and must reveal exculpatory evidence which may lead to an acquittal. In this case, we served discovery on the government demanding all such information, and we did so prior to trial." Levinson scowled.

"And while I'm no expert in military law, I do know military courts are subject to the United States Supreme Court, and the full-disclosure and discovery principles of *Brady versus Maryland* apply to cases tried under the Uniform Code of Military Justice."

"You are correct about that, sir," Reeves said.

"Having said all that—even if there is no prosecutorial misconduct in this case"—Levinson stared at Brewer as if he was lying about the belated discovery—"this information was clearly in the government's control. It was in the control of a government agent and was hidden, *illegally*, by a government agent. It isn't the fault of my clients that this Mr. Kilnap chose to *kidnap* his information and not make it available—"

"Mr. Levinson," Judge Reeves interrupted, "even if you had this information before trial, how would it have helped your clients?"

"Fruit of the poisonous tree. Kilnap bugged my client's car without a warrant. Without probable cause. He learned of the meeting at Shoney's as a result of this illegal search. Therefore, because the first search was illegal, the tape-recorded conversations at Shoney's were illegal, and everything else from that point should be thrown out of court. We wouldn't be here today without those tape recordings, Your Honor, and they all stem from this illegal search. You should throw the government's case out. Alternatively, you should grant a mistrial. But even if you do that, my clients' right to a speedy trial would be violated, and you should still dismiss."

Reeves turned to Zack, who felt a cold sweat beading in the palms of his hands.

"Lieutenant Brewer, I must confess that I am troubled by Mr. Kilnap's actions. Tell me, why should I not grant Mr. Levinson's motions?"

Zack rose to his feet. "Two words, Your Honor. Inevitable discovery."

"Want to be heard, briefly, on that?"

Lord, help me.

"Yes, Your Honor. As you know, the United States Supreme Court has also held that even if certain evidence is tainted, the fruit of the poisonous tree doctrine will not apply if there would have been inevitable discovery of the evidence."

"And you're saying that's the case here?"

"Yes, Your Honor. Because the undisputed evidence shows that Kilnap started following al-Aziz *before* he intercepted the phone calls and that he kept al-Aziz in his sight the entire time. From the time he left base till the time he arrived as Shoney's. Kilnap would have followed al-Aziz into the restaurant, a public place, and would have conducted surveillance whether or not he overheard the first telephone call. In other words, discovery of the conversation at Shoney's, where Reska acknowledged this glorious mission for Allah, would have occurred even without first interception."

Reeves leaned back and crossed his arms. "So by arguing inevitable discovery, are you in essence conceding this initial search was illegal, Lieutenant Brewer?"

Zack stood behind the counsel table and carefully weighed his response. "Your Honor, we do not concede. Whether the search was illegal or not is for the court to decide, not us. What we are saying is given the posture of this case, even if the court finds a problem with Mr. Kilnap's initial activities, the tape recording at Shoney's would have been made anyway. And Shoney's is a public place, where there is no reasonable expectation of privacy, and where a warrant is not required."

Captain Reeves, his arms still crossed, turned to the window for a moment, his expression showing deep contemplation. He seemed unaware that his image was being beamed all over the world via satellite. After thirty seconds or so, he turned back. "Here's what I am going to do, gentlemen. First, we are going to bring Mr. Kilnap back in here, and I am going to question him about what happened, outside of the presence of the members. Then Mr. Levinson will be allowed to ask questions, followed by Lieutenant Brewer."

Zack and Diane locked gazes.

"Then, unless the defense objects, I will require that the government recall Mr. Kilnap in the presence of the members. Questions will be limited to the subject we have just been made aware of, namely the search of al-Aziz's car and his following al-Aziz to Shoney's. Mr. Levinson may cross-examine Mr. Kilnap on the subject if he so desires. If the defense objects, I will not require that Mr. Kilnap be called for more testimony in the presence of the members. In other words, Mr. Levinson"—Reeves looked directly at the famous defense counsel—"it will be your choice

288 ★ DON BROWN

as to whether Mr. Kilnap will be recalled for more testimony in the presence of the members. Finally, I will let the government proceed with its case and finish its case today if that is possible."

Zack heard reporters and spectators whispering behind him as the captain continued. "I am going to hold Mr. Levinson's motion in abeyance overnight and render a decision in the morning.

"If I grant the motion, this case will be over." Louder mumbling rose from the gallery. "If I do *not* grant the motion, we will proceed. In any event, be prepared for closing arguments tomorrow. Any questions?"

"No, sir, Your Honor," Zack said.

"No, Your Honor," Levinson said.

"Very well, court is in recess." Two *whaps* of the gavel followed.

"All rise."

CHAPTER 59

Council of Ishmael headquarters
Rub al-Khali Desert
250 miles southeast of Riyadh, Saudi Arabia

Fourteen hours later

Abdur Rahman stepped into the intelligence room at the Council of Ishmael headquarters. There were no windows in the huge tent. Fluorescent bulbs were lit by a portable, solar-powered generator. The compound's powerful air-conditioning system was most effective here, making the room chilly most of the time. About a dozen or so turban-clad Arab brothers, functioning as council intelligence officers, manned their monitors, collecting data on Council operations around the world. Others fed classified paperwork into shredders and burn bags.

Abdur watched as the laser printer spat out the Internet report he had come for. He waited for the final page to land in the printer bin, then grabbed a stapler and attached the three pages in the upper right corner with a single squeeze, transforming the pages into a single document. A moment later, he stood in the doorway of the leader of the Council of Ishmael.

"Brother Abdur." Hussein al-Akhma spoke in Arabic, looking up from behind his desk. "You bring news of the legal and religious persecution of our brothers in America?"

"Leader," Abdur said giddily, "our Jew lawyer has them twisting in the wind. Now the American Navy judge speaks of dismissing the case. Read this, my leader." Abdur slid the Internet news report across Hussein's desk. His leader read the report, smiled, and burst into hearty laughter.

"Who can understand these foolish Americans?" Al-Akhma chuckled. "Even their military justice system is rife with confusion."

"Perhaps Allah throws confusion into their system, leader. Your vision of beating them with their own rules seems at hand."

"I cannot take all the credit, Brother Abdur. After all, *you* suggested hiring the Jew lawyer. You personally negotiated our contract with him. We appear, as the Americans say, to be 'getting our money's worth.'"

The rare compliment made Abdur's heart swell with pride. "The moment of victory is close at hand, my leader. All credit given to me is bestowed on Allah."

"Spoken as a true Muslim." Hussein al-Akhma looked at his watch. "Isn't it about time for that American nightly news show?"

Abdur motioned his leader into the Council's communications hub, where several dozen computer monitors were logged on to Internet sites from around the world. He typed in the Web address for the show. A moment later, the face of the American anchorman appeared on the screen.

"I'm Tom Miller reporting from San Diego, and this is *NightWatch*.

"A double whammy was delivered today in the Navy court-martial of three Muslim chaplains accused of treason, murder, and conspiracy to commit murder, and the whammy was delivered against the government.

"First, newspaper reports surfaced disclosing that the Navy's lead prosecutor, Lieutenant Zack Brewer, may have had an affair with an enlisted woman, which if true, is in violation of the military's prohibition against officer-enlisted fraternization.

"But the big bomb, delivered by Lieutenant Brewer himself, revealed information that the government's lead investigator, Special Agent Harry Kilnap of the Naval Criminal Investigative Service, may have illegally bugged a car, which was not revealed to the defense until yesterday. The government finished its case today. But tonight, Captain Richard Reeves, the Navy judge overseeing the trial, is seriously considering a motion to dismiss all charges against the chaplains. When we come back, our two legal experts, Jeanie Van Horton and Bernie Woodson, will help us make sense of the new developments."

"Praise be to Allah," Abdur said as the commercial break started.

"Blessed be the prophet," said a voice from over Abdur's shoulder.

"Peace be upon him," said another.

Abdur looked around at the dozen or so Council operatives, wearing white turbans and desert garb, who had gathered behind him, their eyes on the monitor. Several other monitors were logging on to the broadcast as the operatives took their place in front of the screens.

Tom Miller's face reappeared.

"Will Navy Captain Richard Reeves, the military judge in this case, dismiss all charges against three Navy chaplains in the most publicized court-martial in history? That is the question hanging over America tonight, and that is the question we pose to our two legal experts, Jeanie Van Horton and Bernie Woodson.

"And we'll start with you, Bernie. Will Judge Reeves really throw this case out?"

The screen switched to an African-American correspondent, who adjusted his earpiece and, with his characteristic stone face, looked into the camera.

"Good question, Tom. The United States Supreme Court has held that a right to a fair trial is a fundamental right to our system of government. A fair trial means the government cannot hide information from the defense that may exonerate the defendant. This whole business of bugging the car was concealed from the defense until the middle of the trial. And the government just can't do that.

"This is where the prosecution's case, at least in my judgment, is vulnerable, Tom. Judge Reeves appeared visibly upset by the revelation that Kilnap planted a bug and didn't reveal it, although he let evidence progress and will make his ruling in the morning. Mr. Levinson is arguing 'fruit of the poisonous tree,' a doctrine upheld by the Supreme Court which says evidence discovered because of tainted evidence—in this case, the audiotapes we've heard so much about—should be thrown out."

The picture on the screen split with the blond former federal prosecutor on the left and the wise-looking, stone-faced African-American journalist on the right.

"Jeanie Van Horton, can the prosecution counter this fruit of the poisonous tree argument?"

"Tom, the prosecution counters that with another Supreme Court doctrine, the 'inevitable discovery doctrine,' which says even if you have some evidence that has been illegally obtained, you don't have to throw out the baby with the bathwater, for lack of a better term."

The screen switched to Miller. "Jeanie, is the Navy upset Brewer revealed this information?"

The blond reporter reappeared. "Tom, the Navy issued a statement late this afternoon expressing its confidence in Lieutenant Brewer. If high Navy officials are upset that Brewer revealed this, they're not saying. I'm sure they're not happy about it, but he did have this duty as prosecutor."

"Bernie, assume the judge denies the defense motion. Based on the quality of today's evidence, how's the government doing?"

Another head shot of Woodson appeared. "Fairly well, Tom, although perhaps not well enough to secure a conviction. Today the prosecution called a parade of witnesses, but perhaps the most significant was a voice recognition expert who gave his opinion that all the voices on the tapes were those of the three defendants.

"Of course, Levinson was effective on cross-examination when he got the expert to admit he couldn't say with '100 percent certainty' the voices were those of the defendants. And, of course, Levinson scored a direct hit when Agent Kilnap was recalled to the stand. Levinson pounded him repeatedly, suggesting Kilnap had lied out of his zeal to secure a conviction."

"Jeanie, does this case remind you of any other high-profile cases we've ever seen?"

The screen switched to a smiling, nodding Jeanie Van Horton. "The one coming to mind is the Simpson murder trial, where the lead government investigator in the case, Detective Mark Fuhrman, was pummeled in the middle of the trial when allegations of racism suddenly surfaced. The defense in that case successfully turned the trial into a referendum on Fuhrman's credibility. If Judge Reeves does not throw this case out, you can bet that Wells Levinson may try a similar tactic with Kilnap."

"All right," Miller said, "we've got to take a break. When we come back, we'll look at official reaction from Washington about today's events."

"On your knees, oh brothers of the Council of Ishmael!"

Abdur turned. Hussein al-Akhma stood in the middle of the room, holding his arms in the air.

"To your prayer mats! On your knees to Allah! Let us praise him for his beneficence! Let us plead with him for justice!"

Computer monitors shut down as prayer mats were rolled out all over the floor. Moaning wails, the sweet sound of Arabic prayers, soon filled the Council of Ishmael headquarters.

CHAPTER 60

Navy-Marine Corps Trial Judiciary
Building 1
32nd Street Naval Station
San Diego

Day 3, 0915 hours (PST)

The ticking from the ornate nautical clock, hanging on the wall behind the still-empty bench, echoed through the courtroom. From his chair at the counsel table, Zack passed the time exchanging an occasional "What's going on here?" glance with Diane and jotting notes on his legal pad for his closing argument. If there was one.

Captain Reeves had already kept the crowded gallery waiting forty-five minutes beyond the announced start time for this morning's session. Thirty minutes ago, the courtroom bailiff sent word to the attorneys and the press that Reeves was in the building, in his chambers working on his order. After that, nothing.

Zack's command had been eerily silent about the Kilnap disclosure. As well they should. No point in raising allegations of unlawful command influence. Still, it would be nice to get a "You did the right thing, Lieutenant" from somebody. Commander Awe. Captain Rudy. Anybody.

"All rise."

Zack inhaled deeply as Reeves walked in.

"Please be seated and come to order."

I don't mean to put pressure on you, son, but we cannot lose this one. Understand? Captain Rudy's words raced through Zack's mind for the hundredth time since yesterday morning.

Diane gave his hand a warm squeeze, shot him a smile, then quickly let go.

"The record should reflect that the court has made a decision with regard to the defense motions to dismiss, or in the alternative, for a mistrial." Reeves spoke slowly, without emotion. "Before I announce my decision"—Reeves paused and removed his glasses—"I remind our guests and members of the media that this is a court of law, and whether you agree or disagree with my ruling, I caution spectators against any type of verbal or physical reactions or displays in the courtroom. The time and place to react, if you feel compelled to do so, is outside. United States Marines will remove anyone disrupting the court. Enough said."

This did not bode well. Zack leaned forward in anticipation.

"Very well." Reeves put his glasses on and tilted a legal pad slightly upward. Zack knew it contained the handwritten order he was about to read.

"Madam Court Reporter, in the general court-martial of *United States versus LCDR Mohammed Olajuwon et al.*, the defense has made a motion to dismiss, or in the alternative, for a mistrial based upon certain actions of the government's principal investigator in first planting a recording device in the car of a naval member, receiving and taping transmissions from that car, and then failing to inform the defense in a timely manner.

"Defense counsel points out, correctly, the premise set forth by our Supreme Court in the landmark case of *Brady versus Maryland* that law enforcement officials and prosecutors must divulge exculpatory information to the defense, and must do so in a timely manner.

"In the military justice system, there is an even broader right to discovery available to defendants than in civilian federal courts under the *Brady* decision. The Court of Military Appeals has reaffirmed this principle in several decisions, including *United States versus Eshalomi*, *United States versus Dancy*, and *United States versus Simmons*.

"Article 46 of the Uniform Code of Military Justice allows the trial counsel and the defense counsel to have equal access to obtain witnesses and other evidence. This requirement is also found in the Rules for Court Martial, and Rule 701(a)(6) requires the trial counsel to disclose any evidence that would negate the guilt of the accused, reduce the guilt of the accused, or reduce the punishment.

"The court notes several articles, editorials, and commentaries in this morning's papers criticizing Lieutenant Brewer for disclosing this information yesterday morning. Yet Lieutenant Brower did exactly what he was supposed to do, under military regulations and under law, in bringing this matter to the court's attention, and the court commends him for it."

Zack felt Diane's foot nudge his.

Reeves stopped for a swig of water.

"Unfortunately, this brings us to the actions of NCIS Special Agent Harry Kilnap."

Zack braced himself.

"It is my duty to first determine whether Special Agent Kilnap's actions in placing a certain listening device in the car of the late Petty Officer Sulayman al-Aziz were legal or proper.

"On a military installation, such as the Oceana Naval Air Station, a base commander, upon a showing of probable cause, may issue what is known in the military as a 'search authorization.' This is the military equivalent of what is referred to in the civilian legal system as a search warrant.

"For a search authorization to be issued, however, military law enforcement officials or members of a command must show probable cause to believe there has been a violation of the Uniform Code of Military Justice.

"I find that in this case, no probable cause existed at the time to believe a crime had been committed, and I note that a civilian federal magistrate in Norfolk, Virginia, also failed to find probable cause just days earlier based on the same factual presentation at the time.

"I find, therefore, that Mr. Kilnap's search of the car of Petty Officer al-Aziz was illegal, in violation of the Fourth Amendment of the United States Constitution and of military law."

Zack bowed his head slightly. *Jesus, please help me.*

"If the defense were making a motion to suppress the tape recording from inside al-Aziz's vehicle, this court would allow that motion and suppress that evidence. This is not the motion before the court, however.

"The defense claims the tainted search should extend to other evidence in the case and should lead to the exclusion of other evidence, including all other tape recordings in which all three of the defendants allegedly make statements which the government has called incriminating.

"The government argues that Kilnap's illegal search does not contaminate other subsequent evidence because of inevitable discovery.

"This concept of 'inevitable discovery' is recognized Rule 311(b)(2) of the Military Rules of Evidence, which is based on the Supreme Court's recognition of the 'inevitable discovery exception' in the landmark case of *Nix versus Williams*, a 1984 Supreme Court case.

"In this case, I must determine whether the subsequent evidence, especially the tape recordings, was discovered not because of, but rather in spite of, the illegal search of the car."

Reeves paused and took a sip of water.

I don't mean to put pressure on you, son . . .

Zack's mind raced with what would follow if this case was thrown out. His focus was not on what winning meant for his future political career. Neither did it have anything to do with beating the world's greatest attorney—and the publicity it would bring him.

It had to do with justice. It had to do with his nation's security. Images of 9/11 filled his mind . . . and the horror of what might come if terrorists, such as these sitting in the courtroom, were allowed to continue their infiltration of the military.

Reeves put the water glass down. "The limited evidence before the court at this point is Special Agent Kilnap's testimony, that he kept al-Aziz's car in view the whole time he was following, and the evidence of geographic proximity between the base and the restaurant. The court takes judicial notice that the physical distance between the main gate entrance of the Oceana Naval Air Station and the Shoney's restaurant in question is a distance of approximately 1.8 miles."

. . . but we cannot lose this one . . .

"The court is convinced the greater the distance between these two points, the less likely Special Agent Kilnap could have maintained visual surveillance, and vice versa."

. . . understand?

"The court finds that because of the relatively short distance between the main gate of the base . . ."

Yes! Zack resisted the urge to punch the air.

". . . and the entrance to the Shoney's parking lot, and because the route requires very few turns, it would be a fairly easy task for an experienced law enforcement officer to follow a vehicle a short distance under normal traffic conditions and maintain visual contact the entire time."

Thank you, Lord.

A scowl crawled across Levinson's face.

"And while the court notes that it would otherwise have credibility problems with certain aspects of Mr. Kilnap's testimony, the court does find that portion of his testimony—that he followed the al-Aziz car from the main gate of the base to the Shoney's parking lot—to be credible."

Another nudge from Diane's foot touched his, and from the corner of his eye, he caught her beautiful smile.

"Having found, therefore, that Kilnap followed al-Aziz the entire distance from the Oceana Naval Air Station to the Shoney's parking lot on Dam Neck Road in Virginia Beach; and having found that he maintained eye contact with it the entire time, I find the electronically intercepted tape recording of the conversation between Petty Officer al-Aziz and Commander Reska inside the Shoney's restaurant occurred in spite of and not because of the illegal bugging of al-Aziz's car.

"The court finds all tape recordings offered by the government in its case-in-chief fall within the inevitable discovery exception to the exclusionary rule, and the defense motion is denied."

Amen.

"The court will take a fifteen-minute recess."

"All rise."

The Oval Office
The White House
Washington, D.C.

Thirty minutes later

The president of the United States stood in front of his desk congratulating fifteen smiling finalists of the National Spelling Bee, this year sponsored by the Smithsonian Institution.

The White House chief of staff stepped to the doorway and signaled him. "Mr. President, could I see you for a moment?"

"Excuse me, ladies and gentlemen." The president gave the finalists a smile, then walked into the anteroom just outside the Oval Office.

"What's up, Wally?"

"Good news from San Diego, sir. Captain Reeves just denied the defense motion to dismiss."

"Great. What's next?"

"Levinson's just announced that he's resting his case without putting on evidence. He must think he can win based on his argument alone. Closing arguments start in about fifteen minutes."

"Wally, have someone take these kids on a tour or something. See if the first lady is available to show them around. Then clear my schedule for the next hour or so. I've got to see this."

"Yes, Mr. President."

CHAPTER 61

This wasn't Diane's show anymore.

The prosecution dodged a bullet when Judge Reeves bought Zack's argument and denied the defense motion to dismiss. But was the damage too great? Levinson, even though he didn't get the case thrown out, had pounded Kilnap, their star witness, relentlessly.

Now the case was in Zack Brewer's hands. Everything depended on his closing argument.

She glanced to her right. Zack was deep in thought, scribbling notes on a legal pad. The raw strength evident in his profile took her breath away, his jaw line, the high cheekbone, the crisp sweep of hair above his forehead. She forced herself to turn her eyes, and her thoughts, away from him. But in the split second before she did, Zack glanced up, and their eyes locked. He grinned and winked, then looked down at the legal pad again. And her heart skipped a beat.

"All rise."

Zack dropped the pad on their table and stood at attention. She joined him. At the defense table, Levinson rose.

"Are counsel ready for closing argument?"

"The government is ready, Your Honor." Zack's tone exuded confidence.

"The defense is ready," Levinson said with a hint of arrogance.

"Very well. Bailiff, summon the members."

The weight of the case was now on Zack's shoulders, not hers. Yet her stomach twisted tighter than it had two days ago, while making the most important opening statement in JAG Corps history.

"The record should reflect that the members are now in place," Captain Reeves said, then turned to the jury. "Mr. President, Ladies and Gentlemen, we've reached that point in the court-martial where both parties have rested their cases and are ready for closing arguments. Remember, the closing argument is not evidence, but rather is the opinion of the attorneys as to how the evidence was presented, and how you should act based upon that evidence. In other words, closing arguments are the last and best opportunity for these attorneys to advocate their respective positions to you. The evidence, however, is what you have heard and seen from the witness stand during these last few days."

Reeves took a swig of water and then turned his gaze to the counsel. "Counsel, before we proceed, does either party have anything else for the court's consideration?"

Zack stood. "Nothing from the government, Your Honor."

"Nothing from the defense," Levinson said without standing. "The defense is ready for argument."

"Very well. The members are with the defense."

"Mr. Levinson?"

Diane felt her heart pounding as the famous defense counsel rose to his feet. Levinson pulled down the lapels of his gray suit and walked slowly to the banister separating the jury box from the well of the courtroom.

"Mr. President." Levinson made eye contact with the senior officers, then swept his gaze across the other members. "Distinguished members of this court-martial." He paused again. "First, let me say that the sympathies of my clients, as imams of the peaceful religion of Islam, are with all those who lost their lives." Levinson was now in the center of the banister, about ten feet from the railing, holding his palms up and speaking quietly. His emotion-laden voice was about to crack.

"To the families of Commander Latcher, to the families of the Israeli ambassador, and to those who lost their lives in the unfortunate and inexcusable act of terrorism at the church here in San Diego, my clients wish to impart upon them sympathy, and peace, and love, and mercy."

Levinson held his outstretched palm toward the three Chaplain Corps officers, all dressed in white uniforms with black and gold shoulder boards. He gave them an affectionate look as if he were their greatest admirer. "Look at my clients." He pulled a handkerchief from his pocket.

"Men of peace." He dabbed the corner of his eye.

"Men of the cloth.

"Maybe not of the same religion as you or I, but nonetheless, from a great religion of peace.

"All religions—whether Christianity, Judaism, or Islam—speak of justice. And in this case, justice cries out for the defense, ladies and gentlemen.

"Justice screams that two wrongs don't make a right. The government, feeling the need to lash out at somebody in this case, and with the real killers all dead, accuses my clients only because they are ministers of the same faith practiced by the real killers.

"The government's case began as a house of cards. Oh, it was a nice-looking house of cards. Fresh out of the box. A cardboard pyramid propped on the mountaintop by two dynamic and vibrant young prosecutors." He waved his hand grandly toward Zack and Diane. "But do not, I implore you, do not confuse the attractive appearance of this dynamic young prosecution team with the very poor quality of the government's evidence.

"I remind each of you, ladies and gentlemen, not only of your sacred oath as naval officers, but of the sacred promise you made during jury selection, the promise I asked each and every one of you to make about reasonable doubt."

He paused again, dramatically, his eyes searching those of the jury. "I asked you during the jury selection process—the process we call *voir dire*—if the government failed to prove each and every element of its case beyond a reasonable doubt, I asked if you would return a verdict of not guilty.

"And each and every one of you raised your hand in response to my question, promising me that you would."

Diane saw a few nods from the members.

"Now the rubber meets the road. Either the government has proven its case—beyond a reasonable doubt—or it has failed.

"And even if you believe my clients did something improper, but you are not convinced of it beyond a reasonable doubt, the judge will tell you that you must return with a verdict of not guilty." Levinson paused at the center of the banister, again making eye contact with every member.

"I submit to you, ladies and gentlemen, that the government has failed, and it has failed miserably.

"Let us review why this is so.

"I ask you." Levinson's voice grew louder. "Where are the real killers responsible for these crimes? Where is Petty Officer Anthony Neptune, the terrorist who attacked innocent churchgoers?" He raised his palms. "Where is Staff Sergeant Nasser Saidi, the deranged United States Marine who shot the Israeli ambassador?

"I'll tell you where they are. Dead and gone." He jabbed the air with one finger for emphasis. "That's where they are. But they are the criminals responsible for these murders, not my clients"—he walked behind the defendants and rested his hands on Olajuwon and Reska's shoulders—"not your fellow officers.

"And who really planted that bomb in Commander Latcher's aircraft?" Levinson was now walking back toward the banister rail. "The government claims it was Petty Officer Sulayman al-Aziz. Obviously, it must have been al-Aziz, because he was a *Muslim*." Levinson delivered this line with a sarcastic tone. "And Commander Reska must be guilty because he met al-Aziz in a Shoney's." His voice was laced with sarcasm. "And Reska is, of course, *Muslim*.

"But I ask you this. Where is al-Aziz? The government says he is dead. Then where is the body? In the Atlantic, they say. But how do we really know that? The Coast Guard hasn't fished a body out of the ocean, has it? How do we really know that al-Aziz isn't AWOL? How do we know he hasn't high-tailed it to Mexico to avoid this court-martial?

"Al-Aziz must have planted the bomb, the government thinks, because he is a *Muslim*, and all Muslims are killers, aren't they? All Muslims drive airplanes into skyscrapers. And al-Aziz is a Muslim who happens to work around airplanes.

"Case closed.

"Right?"

Only the *tick-tock* of the nautical clock hanging over the judge's bench punctuated his perfectly timed silence.

"Wrong.

"Even if al-Aziz planted the bomb, I can guarantee you one thing: Commander Reska did not." Levinson turned and pointed to Reska. "This peaceful man of the cloth may be an expert in his religion, but he knows nothing of airplanes, and he knows nothing about bombs.

"Guilt by association. That's what the government's flimsy house of cards is built on.

"The government has no killers. The killers are either dead or missing. So what do they have? Tape recordings. Ambiguous tape recordings with no admissions of guilt and with uncertainty even about whose voices are on them."

Levinson stepped to the counsel table and took a sip of water. "Let's start with the infamous Shoney's conversation between Lieutenant Commander Reska and our missing man, Petty Officer al-Aziz.

"The government wants you to believe that this is their so-called 'smoking gun.' But when you get back to the jury room for deliberations, I challenge you to listen to that tape. Listen repeatedly, if you must. Will you hear anyone say that Commander Reska ordered or suggested to al-Aziz that he plant a bomb?

"No.

"What is it, exactly, that Lieutenant Brewer"—Levinson turned and pointed to Zack—"will harp on when he stands before you in a few minutes?" He looked back at the members. "Language taken out of context. That's what.

"Listen carefully to the words they attribute to Reska." He stepped to his table and picked up his notes. "'You have destroyed an instrument of war that would have been used against many of our Arab brothers.'

"Think carefully about this statement." Levinson gently squeezed his chin between his thumb and his forefinger as if in deep thought. "Assume, for the moment, this is actually Commander Reska's voice making this statement—something we are *not* certain of, by the way. But if so, does Reska say anything about bombing an F/A-18? Does he define 'instrument of war'?"

"No.

"The phrase 'instrument of war' could mean anything. It could mean a rifle, a shotgun, or a cannon. It could mean propaganda." Levinson paused, lowering his voice to nearly a whisper. "It could even mean— that's right—a rogue missile platform used by terrorists in the Middle East."

Another pause.

"We heard the government's own witnesses, members of al-Aziz's squadron, testify that last year, as part of Operation Vigilant Freedom, the squadron was awarded a unit commendation. That award was given when Commander Latcher's plane, a plane al-Aziz worked on, swooped

low over the Syrian Mountains and attacked a missile platform that had
been used not only against Israel, but against moderate Arab political
forces in the area.

"And this, I submit to you, is the instrument of war referred to. And
this fact alone should give you more than a reasonable doubt about what
the statement means.

"And speaking of reasonable doubt, how can we convict these officers, and possibly subject them to the death penalty, when the government's star witness is none other than Special Agent Harry Kilnap?

"Think about it, ladies and gentlemen. Harry Kilnap, secret agent
extraordinaire"—his tone was heavily sarcastic—"marches in here the
first time he testifies, and gives a by-the-book rendition of the facts.
Remember what he said? That he conducted visual and electronic surveillance on the *person* of the defendant?

"The *person* of the defendant?" Levinson chuckled. "Come on, ladies
and gentlemen. Who talks like that?

"And he wraps up his testimony after admitting that none of these
tapes contain any direct admission of a crime, and pulls himself to his
fullest height, sits down . . . and then what?

"Then we learn, to our shock and dismay, that Mr. Kilnap has concealed some very important information. That he happened to break the
law by bugging a service member's car without a search warrant.

"No biggie. Just a violation of the Constitution of the United States
and the search-and-seizure laws of the naval service. That's all.

"His explanation for breaking the law? He says nobody asked him.
Until Lieutenant Brewer finally asked him the night after his testimony.

"Just conveniently escaped his mind, did it? Come on. Kilnap has
been in the NCIS for more than twenty years. He's no rookie. He's savvy.
We all know he was fully aware of his duty to disclose. And for him to
suggest that he just didn't think about it until Lieutenant Brewer asked
him is not credible. We all know it's a lie. And this is the testimony over
which the government seeks a conviction and the death penalty?

"Put it this way: If your dearest loved one were charged with a crime
based on the word of Special Agent Harry Kilnap, would you believe
they'd had a fair trial?"

Levinson let the comment hang as several members winced.

"Proof beyond a reasonable doubt means that you can go to bed
tonight with no doubt that these officers committed all the elements of
all the crimes they've been charged with.

"Can you really do that based on the testimony of Harry Kilnap?" He stopped, letting the question resonate through the courtroom.

Diane glanced at Zack, but his attention was riveted on Levinson.

"As I said," Levinson continued, "the government's case, flimsy from the beginning, was built on a precarious house of cards.

"And then along came the wind.

"No, not the wind.

"Along came the hurricane.

"In this case, Hurricane Harry Kilnap blew the remnants of the government's case to the four corners of the earth."

Levinson paused. The air in the courtroom seemed supercharged, electric. The gleam in the attorney's eyes told Diane he recognized it too, and he was playing it for all it was worth.

He lowered his voice, slowed his cadence, and dramatically resumed his delivery. "This case was fraught with prejudice from the beginning. By this prosecution, the government encroaches on the very Constitution we all have sworn to defend by putting the great faith of Islam on trial, based on faulty evidence and a dirty investigator.

"Islam is on trial here today," he said. "This trial is about whether the First Amendment means anything, whether freedom of religion is important to the military. It is not, I submit, just Islam that is on trial. Freedom is being prosecuted. The very freedom that you, as officers are sworn to protect, you are now being asked to condemn.

"Do what's right, ladies and gentlemen.

"Return with a verdict of not guilty.

"I thank you."

The dramatic silence in the courtroom was almost hypnotic, punctuated only by the clock and the sounds of Levinson's shoes clicking against the floor as he made his way back to the defense counsel table.

Diane again glanced at Zack, who was sitting with his hands folded on his lap, smiling slightly as if he were the only one in the packed courtroom who had not fallen under Levinson's swoon.

"Lieutenant Brewer?" Judge Reeves peered down at him. "Would you like a recess before proceeding?"

Zack gave Diane one of his trademark quick winks and rose to his feet. "Your Honor, unless the court or the members want a recess, the government is ready to proceed." Zack's whole demeanor exuded confidence, from his crisp summer whites with the black and gold shoulder boards to the thrust of his chin, the set of his shoulders. Who ever said

Levinson was the greatest trial lawyer in the world? The brightest and the best stood beside her.

"Very well," Reeves said. "Then the members are with the prosecution. Lieutenant Brewer?"

With a pleasant smile on his face, he strode confidently, without notes, and turned to the members.

No notes? How is he going to do this?

"Mr. President, distinguished members, they say great lawyers have the ability to draw on real-life experiences and even borrow from the techniques of professionals in other disciplines." He paused, letting his words settle as he met the gaze of each member before proceeding.

"Ladies and gentlemen, I'm no great lawyer. I am a naval officer, first and foremost. It is the profession I have chosen, and it is the profession of which I am most proud. I am a naval officer who just happens also to be a lawyer.

"We have witnessed today, and during the course of this trial, a textbook performance by one who is undeniably a great lawyer." Zack looked at Levinson, then held his hand toward the defense counsel as he turned back to the members. "One who is recognized as perhaps the world's greatest trial lawyer.

"And I want you to understand that this great lawyer has employed one of the most subtle, yet one of the most effective, techniques that defense lawyers often use to obfuscate the true facts and thwart justice.

"It is a technique borrowed from magicians." He looked into the eyes of the jury, his expression intense. "It is a technique called sleight of hand."

He paused for a moment, and when he continued, his diction was deliberate. "Sleight of hand—the use of skillful tricks and deceptions to produce entertaining and baffling effects."

Zack lowered his voice as he approached the banister rail. "Here's what this means. The illusionist takes an object in his hand, which is in reality a decoy, holds it out to the audience, and proclaims to the audience that what is before their eyes will suddenly disappear. The audience, with its eyes transfixed on the object of the trick," Zack balled his right fist and held it over his head, "does not see the true object of the trick, which is carefully tucked away in the illusionist's other hand, behind his back, out of the audience's view." He moved his left hand behind his back, imitating an illusionist.

306 ★ Don Brown

"At the end of the trick, the object hidden behind the magician's back is suddenly gone. Disposed of in a trap door or taken by an assistant while the audience was distracted.

"Suddenly gone. And the audience is amazed, wondering what happened to the object. That's sleight-of-hand trickery. The truth is suddenly gone, disappearing while our eyes are distracted by a red herring."

Another pause as Zack rested his hands on the banister rail.

"If Harry Houdini were in this courtroom today, he'd be proud . . . proud to see the world's greatest lawyer borrow the most fundamental technique of trickery from the world's greatest magician and bring it into the courtroom."

Zack stepped back to the center of the well and raised his voice. "Mr. Levinson seeks to hold out Harry Kilnap as the visual distraction while hiding behind his back the cold, stark truth of cold-blooded murder!

"Mr. Levinson says that in this case, the killers are dead.

"He's only got that *partially* right.

"You don't have to answer this question, but does anybody here play chess?" Three of the Navy captains on the panel nodded their heads.

"It may be true that the pawns in this case are dead, but the knights and rooks and bishops that are a part of this plot are very much alive and sitting over at the defense counsel table, right beside Mr. Levinson." Zack pointed an accusing finger at the defendants as the gazes of the jury shot toward them.

"The kings and queens—the financial masterminds behind all this who are enemies of the United States—this Council of Ishmael, this Hussein al-Akhma—are somewhere overseas, temporarily out of the reach of this and other U.S. courts."

Zack stepped in front of Judge Reeve's bench, his gaze never leaving the members. "But their day of justice will also arrive," he thundered. "And this is to serve notice on those criminals beyond our borders but who may be listening to the words of my voice—the day of vengeance draweth nigh."

Zack stepped back, his words reverberating throughout the corners of the courtroom. "Mr. Levinson claims, ladies and gentlemen, that our case is built on *a house of cards*.

"Tell that, Mr. Levinson, to Beth and Mary Blake Latcher. Tell them their daddy's airplane was blown out of the sky by a deck of cards." His voice choked as he turned away from the members, his eyes tearing. He paused as if to regain his composure; then he turned back to the members and resumed, his voice softer, lower.

"Tell that, Mr. Levinson, to Naomi Barak, the grief-stricken widow of the Israeli ambassador. Tell her that her husband was shot in the heart, not by a sniper's bullet, but by a house of cards.

"Tell that, Mr. Levinson, to Reverend Jeffrey Spletto, who saw members of his congregation, men, women, and children, murdered by a deranged Muslim sailor. Tell him that the murderous hand grenade, bought and paid for by the United States government, was constructed with a house of cards.

"Let's take a look at this house of cards, and when we do, what we see behind Mr. Levinson's back is hard evidence of cold-blooded murder." The choking tone was gone. Anger had replaced it.

"We start with a routine training flight by a naval aviator whose squadron was about to deploy to the eastern Mediterranean on the USS *Nimitz*. The squadron's role—to provide firepower in supporting Israel, a United States ally and the only true democracy in the region. Israel, as we know, is in a period of heightened international tensions with its Arab neighbors over the issue of settlements in so-called occupied territories.

"About thirty minutes into the flight, after Latcher successfully tests his canon on a strafing run in North Carolina, he banks his plane to the west, following a flight plan that would shortly turn him to the north and then back home to Oceana Naval Air Station.

"Just a few minutes after banking to the west, with the plane over Lake Phelps, the F/A-18 explodes into a fireball, and Latcher's body plunges into the shallow waters below.

"Despite Darryl Swain's heroic efforts to swim through the burning AVJET fuel floating on the water, Latcher is already dead. Military aviation experts from Pax River, Maryland, arrive on the scene and discover the residue of plastic explosives in the jet's avionics bay.

"The existence of the plastic explosives that brought the plane down is uncontroverted. Not even Mr. Levinson has challenged that.

"Somebody, ladies and gentlemen, sabotaged that plane.

"The question is, who?" Zack walked to the prosecution table, took a sip of water. His eyes caught Diane's; then he looked back at the members.

"First of all, not every Tom, Dick, and Harry can just walk through a heavily guarded military installation like Oceana and get their hands on an F/A-18. Access to that plane was *extremely* limited. Limited, in fact, to those aviation electronics and aviation structural mechanics *from that squadron*.

"This bomb was strategically placed in the avionics bay. Thus, the bomber had to know something about the airplane to find that compartment, and had to be experienced enough to hide the plastic explosives device in just the right place at just the right time.

"So of the nearly 300 million people in the United States, you're looking at no more than a dozen men who even might, and I repeat *might*, have access.

"Now let's fast-forward the first recorded conversation we have between Petty Officer al-Aziz and Lieutenant Commander Reska. Mr. Levinson wants you to believe the reference to destroying 'an instrument of war that would be used against many of our Arab brothers' is a reference to some missile platform the squadron attacked on a Med cruise last year.

"But Mr. Levinson is conveniently selective in picking and choosing what he wants you to hear. He conveniently ignores Reska's next statement. And what was that statement? Listen, ladies and gentlemen."

Zack walked to a pre-positioned tape recorder on the prosecutor's table and punched a button to start the tape.

"This morning, there are Muslim families who will keep their fathers for a while because of your heroic act."

"'This morning'? Why would Reska say 'this morning' if he were referring to something that happened over a year ago? He is obviously referring to something that happened very recently.

"And calling it 'your heroic act'?

"The attack last year against the missile platform in Syria was from an air-to-surface missile fired by Commander Latcher, not al-Aziz. Petty Officer al-Aziz was out in the Mediterranean, on board the *Nimitz*, when that missile was fired. Certainly no act of heroism.

"Reska is referring to something that *al-Aziz* did, calling it a heroic act—this destruction of an instrument of war.

"And here's the real kicker. Listen to this, ladies and gentlemen." Zack punched the recorder button again.

"But remember what we discussed earlier. We must be prepared for martyrdom. If Allah will allow you to be of further service, then so be it. But if he allows detection by the enemy and martyrdom, praise be to Allah!"

"'Remember what we discussed earlier'? Here, Reska is talking about something he and the late Petty Officer al-Aziz previously discussed. And what is that something?

"Martyrdom.

"The code word for glorified Islamic suicide, where certain radicals within the faith think they can kill, maim, and murder, and then kill themselves and float off to paradise in the company of a thousand maidens.

"Reska, this peaceful man of the cloth as his lawyer calls him, is encouraging his disciple to take his own life.

"Sounds real peaceful, huh?

"And under what circumstances is Reska encouraging suicide?" Another pause. Diane saw him eyeing the members. Their gazes were locked on him.

"Detection by the enemy."

Zack stopped, walked up and down the banister rail, and in a softer voice repeated, "And what *enemy* is Lieutenant Commander Reska worried about?

"The Naval Criminal Investigative Service. United States Military investigators who were—as al-Aziz said—snooping around the hangar. That's what brought about this whole conversation to begin with.

"Commander Reska calls his own military the enemy." Zack let his comment sink in for a moment. "This criminal network doesn't end with the meeting at Shoney's.

"Afterwards, Reska gets nervous because a witness is alive—al-Aziz—who might link this terrorist network of chaplains into the bombing of the plane. So he gets on the telephone, and he calls the defendant Commander Mohammed Olajuwon, and tells him about his problems with al-Aziz.

"And what is Olajuwon's reaction to all this? He gets upset that al-Aziz hasn't entered martyrdom. And he reminds him of how Neptune, the San Diego church killer, and Saidia, the assassin of the Israeli ambassador, both understood their roles to commit martyrdom after committing murder. Listen again, ladies and gentlemen. This is the voice of Commander Olajuwon, speaking first, recorded from our wiretap of his apartment here in San Diego."

Zack punched the recorder.

"*Speaking of martyrdom is not good enough! Petty Officer Neptune is now a martyr in Allah's cause. So is Staff Sergeant Saidi. In other words, Commander, Chaplain Abdul-Sehen did his part to persuade Saidi. So did I with Neptune. Neptune and I had many talks about martyrdom. He*

310 ★ Don Brown

understood his role from the beginning. But this al-Aziz seems liable to
erupt like a volcano with a slew of information that must be kept con-
tained. This is a risk which cannot be allowed."

"*He understands he cannot compromise our position, Commander,*"
said a second voice.

"*Does he? And how can we be assured of this? He already seems dis-*
traught as a result of this 'investigation.' We never have to worry about
Neptune or Saidi speaking. But I fear this al-Aziz, in his present men-
tal state, constitutes a risk to our network."

Zack pressed the pause button on the recorder. "Ladies and gentlemen, Olajuwon, in this recording, specifically mentions the names of
Neptune, Saidi, *and* al-Aziz. He is speaking of the killers in all three of
these crimes. He is saying the chaplains had specific conversations with
the killers about the murders both before, and in the case of al-Aziz, after
the events. The chaplains worry about having their network compromised. They knew about the murders in advance. They encouraged them.
They helped plan them. They condoned them. They tried in advance to
cover their murderous tracks by encouraging martyrdom, and they
almost succeeded. They never have to worry about Neptune or Saidi
speaking, Olajuwon says.

"But al-Aziz did not have the guts to stick a gun in his mouth and
pull the trigger. And at this point, they hatched the plot to make sure
they didn't have to worry about al-Aziz either.

"The plot thickens, ladies and gentlemen. When Reska offers to
again speak with al-Aziz, to persuade him to commit suicide, Olajuwon
becomes more adamant, threatening to inform someone named al-
Akhma about al-Aziz still being alive. Reska is not happy about this
prospect. Listen again to this . . ."

"*I will speak with him again if you think it is best, Commander.*"

"*Lieutenant Commander Reska, consider what is at stake here.*
Think of all the Council has worked for over the years. Remember the
lawsuit to assure our admission into the Chaplain Corps. Then think of
the Council's work with the aviators. We cannot afford to have this
strategically placed cell of officers compromised by this young man.

"*Perhaps I should inform al-Akhma and the Council through our*
back channels and seek their guidance on what to do in this situation."

"*No! Please, Commander. Do not bother al-Akhma with this. I beg*
of you, let me try again with the boy. I can assure you, it will not be
necessary to bother the Council with this."

Zack remained silent for a moment, letting the condemning words speak for themselves. To Diane, it seemed the members were almost afraid to breathe, so intense were their expressions. "Later, we hear Olajuwon has spoken with Commander Abdul-Sehen, who approves of the murderous plan. And when Olajuwon presses his threat to inform this al-Akhma character, Reska begs for time. Listen again."

"Perhaps I should inform al-Akhma and the Council through our back channels and seek their guidance on what to do in this situation."

"No! Please, Commander. Do not bother al-Akhma with this. I beg of you, let me try again with the boy. I can assure you, it will not be necessary to bother the Council with this."

"Lieutenant Commander Reska, I have spoken with Commander Sehen about the problem. He agrees the situation is potentially grave, our entire core network is at risk. Unless the problem is dealt with immediately, we must inform the Council."

"Please, Commander. I beg of you. Give me until midnight; I will have the problem eradicated."

"Very well, Commander Reska. You have until midnight tonight."

"Thank you, sir."

"Reska says he will have the problem *eradicated*." Zack made quotation marks with his fingers. "He certainly did that, to say the least."

Zack stared, unblinking, at the defense attorney. "No, Mr. Levinson, we don't have a body. Maybe Petty Officer al-Aziz just went for a long swim." He turned back to the members.

"Magic might be great for the stage, Mr. Levinson, but it won't work in a court of law. Not in this court anyway. Not when the cold, hard evidence against the defendants is so compelling, so condemning.

"You know, Reska referred to the NCIS as the enemy. He's right about one thing. The Navy is his enemy, and he is ours. He is an enemy agent." Zack pointed accusingly at Reska, who simply looked down. "They are all enemy agents. And Reska and his cohorts are guilty of *treason*. And *murder*. And *conspiracy to commit murder*.

"Let me close by briefly responding to a couple of accusations made by my opponent.

"Mr. Levinson claims that we are asking you to condemn freedom. That we are putting religion on trial.

"Yes, ladies and gentlemen. We do ask you to condemn freedom." He paused and walked down the banister separating him from the jury. "We do place religion on trial here today."

He paused, meeting the gaze of every member of the jury. "But not freedom as we in America know it. And not the religion we practice. No, the freedom we ask you to condemn is the perverse and inexcusable freedom to commit murder.

"And the religion we condemn is nothing more than a perverted philosophy that seeks to maim, kill, terrorize, and intimidate as means of advancing its goals. A perverted philosophy—in the name of religion—the defendants have adopted and put into practice by taking the lives of American servicemen and innocent civilians.

"Send a strong message that murder, terrorism, and treason will not be tolerated. Not in my Navy.

"Return with a verdict of guilty.

"Thank you."

Zack turned, walked back to the counsel table, pulled out his chair, and sat down.

Judge Reeve's voice thundered through the courtroom. "Court will be in recess for thirty minutes."

"All rise."

CHAPTER 62

The Oval Office, The White House
Washington, D.C.

Twenty-six hours later

What's his calendar?" Wally Walsh, slightly out of breath, stood in front of the president's appointments secretary.

The graying, middle-aged woman looked up, adjusted her glasses, and flashed him a no-nonsense smile. "Right now he's working on tonight's speech to the Teamsters Union, and then he is to see the British ambassador. Shall I tell him you're here?"

"Yes. Please do."

She pressed a button on the intercom. "Mr. President, Mr. Walsh is here."

"Send him in." The president's voice boomed through the intercom speaker.

Walsh rushed into the Oval Office, surprising two Secret Service agents who instinctively reached for their weapons. "Mr. President, we have a verdict."

The president looked up from his desk. "Has it been announced yet?"

"No, sir. The networks just now reported that the members have sent word to Judge Reeves. They're calling in the lawyers now."

Navy-Marine Corps Trial Judiciary
Building 1
32nd Street Naval Station
San Diego

Day 4, 1315 hours (PST)

Diane watched the jury file in. The members were stone-faced as they sat down in the jury box, making no eye contact with anyone. They were focused, it seemed, on the empty chair on the bench, waiting for the occupant of that chair, Captain Richard E. Reeves, to arrive. This jury had been out twenty-six hours.

"All rise."

"Please be seated." Reeves looked at the senior officer of the panel. "Mr. President, I understand the members have reached a verdict?"

"We have, Your Honor."

"Very well. Bailiff, will you please take the verdict sheet from the president of the members and hand it to the court for my examination?"

"Aye, aye, sir."

Reeves unfolded the sheet and studied it. "The verdict appears to be in order." He handed it to the bailiff and then turned to Levinson and the defendants. "Will the accused and counsel please rise?"

As the chaplains rose to face the members, Diane's heart pounded, and she thought she might pass out. Briefly, she thought about grabbing Zack's hand; then she chided herself for considering it.

"Mr. President, you may publish the verdict."

The president, a Navy captain wearing the insignia of a surface warfare officer, stood from his chair on the first row of the jury box and stared down at the verdict sheet.

"In the case of *United States versus Commander Mohammed Olajuwon, Chaplain Corps, United States Navy; Commander Charles Abdul-Sehen, Chaplain Corps, United States Navy; and Lieutenant Commander Mohammed Reska, Chaplain Corps, United States Navy*, on the charges of murder, conspiracy to commit murder, and treason, this court finds you . . ."

The president stopped reading and looked up, staring for a moment into the eyes of the defendants. "Guilty."

Pandemonium broke out in the back of the courtroom. Captain Reeves banged his gavel. Marines, shore patrolmen, and masters-at-arms stood watch around the inside perimeter, but Captain Reeves made no effort to call them into action to quell the uproar.

Diane reached over and gave Zack a quick hug. From the corner of her eye, she saw Levinson. Defeated for the first time in his career, he was standing off to one side with a stunned look on his face. He seemed oblivious to the commotion in the courtroom.

"Don't get too excited," Zack whispered to Diane. "We've still got sentencing to do. And *you're* going to ask for the death penalty."

The Oval Office, The White House
Washington, D.C.

"Thank you, Lord!" The president of the United States, a wide grin on his face, pumped his fist into the air. "And God bless America!"

"Congratulations, Mr. President." Wally Walsh grinned and stepped forward to shake the president's hand. "It looks like you made the right call."

"I had my doubts for a while there, but these young officers were incredible."

"Yes, they were, sir."

"Look, Wally, when sentencing is announced, I want you to issue a statement that the White House is pleased with the results and that we especially commend the professionalism of Lieutenants Brewer and Colcernian."

"Yes, Mr. President. Anything else, sir?"

"Yes, as a matter of fact. Check my schedule. I want you to invite Brewer and Colcernian to the White House. I want to personally thank them for what they've done."

"I've already started working on that one, sir."

Dirksen Senate Office Building
Capitol Hill
Washington, D.C.

Four hours later

From the moment the closing arguments had begun, Senator Roberson Fowler had canceled all of his constituency appointments for two days to watch coverage of his handpicked political protégé at work on television. He said it was because the court-martial was highly relevant to his work on the Armed Services Committee.

Those close to the senator knew better: Life was about politics. The world revolved around it.

The opportunity to bring the hero of the court-martial of the century on board as the newest recruit in the Fowler-Landrieu machine was a salivating thought that the senator could not put aside.

His favorite niece had been less than enthusiastic about the presence of Lieutenant Diane Colcernian on the prosecution team, but she'd get over it. The magnificent political drama and political capital now generated by this conviction couldn't be ignored.

Besides, when Brewer got out of the Navy and moved to Louisiana, then Washington, Colcernian would be left behind in San Diego. Or he could arrange for her transfer to Adak, Alaska. His niece's prosecutor and possible rival for this man would be out of the picture.

The trial couldn't have gone better if he'd scripted it himself. He couldn't stop grinning—or toasting his protégé's success—with clinks against the wineglasses of Ed, his aide, and Sally, his special assistant. During a commercial break, Fowler sent Sally to the staff kitchen for more merlot. The toasts had only just begun.

She returned minutes later with the wine, sat down, and crossed her legs primly on the red leather sofa beside him. The screen switched from the commercial to CNN's Tom Miller, standing in front of the San Diego skyline.

"I'm Tom Miller, as we continue our wrap-up of today's dramatic conclusion of the court-martial of *United States versus Mohammed Olajuwon, Mohammed Reska, and Charles Abdul-Sehen.*

"Now to recap, just about four hours ago, Pacific time, a Navy jury returned with a verdict of guilty on all charges and specifications, convicting all three chaplains for murder, conspiracy to commit murder, and treason. It was the first jury defeat, ever, for the internationally acclaimed defense attorney representing the chaplains, Wells Levinson.

"From that point, things moved from bad to worse for the defense. With Levinson looking stunned, the trial went into the sentencing phase, with Lieutenant Diane Colcernian arguing that the Navy must send a message to terrorists who would seek to infiltrate its officer corps by imposing the death penalty. Levinson, who had the last word, claimed it was an overreaction and the death penalty would only fuel more terrorism. 'Stop the killing now,' Levinson said, pleading for life in prison or an even lesser sentence for his clients.

"But the jury didn't buy it. And just one hour ago, the military jury—the members, as they are known in the military justice system— came back with a sentence which reduced the defendants to pay grade E-1, the lowest rank in the military, gave them a dishonorable discharge from the naval service, and ordered them to be executed for the crimes they had committed.

"Reaction coming in from around the world has been sharply divided along political and religious lines. In the Arab capitals of Riyadh,

Amman, Teheran, and Damascus, massive protests have started erupting on the streets. In London, the British government issued a strong statement of support for the United States, although reactions from Paris and Moscow were less enthusiastic. We will cover international reaction in more detail tonight on *NightWatch* and in the days ahead."

The screen switched, one last time, to the former federal prosecutor Jeanie Van Horton.

"Wow, Tom, what can I say? Four days ago, during opening statements, I commented that the prosecution might have won a moral victory because Levinson did not blow Lieutenant Colcernian out of the water. But to be honest with you, I expected a defense verdict on this case.

"But yesterday, Tom, I've got to tell you, I've never seen a prosecutor handle Wells Levinson like Zack Brewer did. I mean, Brewer gives him a gift on a silver platter with the whole Kilnap thing, then turns around and literally bloodies Levinson's nose in closing argument. A twenty-seven-year-old prosecutor coming in here and whipping the world's greatest trial lawyer.

"Tom, this is the stuff legends are made of."

The camera switched back to a nodding, smiling Tom Miller.

"Bernie Woodson, if you believe Jeanie, we just watched David beat Goliath all over again. What are your thoughts on all this?"

A nodding, almost smiling Bernie Woodson took Miller's place on the screen.

"Tom, Jeanie and I have been your guests in high-profile cases for a number of years, and you know that we don't always see eye to eye. This time, though, I have to agree with my colleague. David versus Goliath? I don't know about that. But certainly a stunning and impressive performance by both these young officers."

"So, Bernie, what does the future hold for them?"

"Good question, Tom. Of course, they are both on active duty in the Navy JAG Corps. But to be honest with you, we're already hearing leaks out of Washington that Brewer has been approached by some very powerful people around the Beltway about running for political office, and we'll just have to wait and see in the next few weeks how it pans out."

"Thanks, Bernie. We've got to take a break now. But when we come back, we'll take a look at the death penalty in the military. When and how might it be imposed in this case?"

"Good job with the leak, Ed." Senator Fowler lifted his wineglass to his chief of staff, took a sip, then clicked off the television set.

"Think he's still coming, Senator?"

Fowler draped his arm around Sally's shoulders. "I would just about stake my life on it. When he said yes to my offer, the gleam in his eyes told me I'd just offered him his life's goal." He chuckled. "The boy's smitten with a flair for politics. Reminds me of me when I was his age." The senator sighed, smiling, and reached for the corkscrew. "And he's smart. He knows now's the time to act." The cork popped, and he poured another round of merlot. "You know what they say. Strike while the iron's hot. Right now the boy could get elected president of the United States if he wanted. I believe he knows it. He also knows how to capitalize on his moment of glory. Oh yes. He's still coming."

He lifted his wineglass. Sally and Ed did the same. "To Congressman and Mrs. Zack Brewer."

CHAPTER 63

Mount Helix
East San Diego County

The large, thirty-six-foot white cross on the top of the mountain took on an orange glow as the sun started its downward trek toward the Pacific. Dressed in blue jeans, a white golf shirt, and sunglasses, Zack sat on the stone wall at the base of the cross and looked to the west.

The ocean, just eleven miles away, was magnificently blue, and the Pacific breeze, cool against his face, was the perfect catharsis to the high-stakes courtroom drama he had finished just three hours ago. He needed to get away, to think, to chill out. And if there was one place in San Diego County that would provide him the best opportunity, Zack figured it would be Mount Helix.

He was right. Not a soul was up here this late afternoon. That might change. In fact, he hoped it would. But for a few minutes anyway, he could reflect on what just happened.

The media said he had just beaten the world's greatest lawyer. Okay. Great. So why wasn't he feeling giddy about it?

The courtroom, in a sense, had been like a grand, four-day, intellectual chess match against Wells Levinson. But when he saw those Marines escorting those three convicted officers out at gunpoint, the hard realization struck him that three men were going to die as a direct result of his professional abilities.

Did they deserve it? Sure. He tried consoling himself by remembering the children and families who were victims of the murderous acts. It gave him little solace. He felt no vengeance in his heart toward the Muslim chaplains, only pity. They had missed out on the truth, and now, they were going to pay.

He turned his eyes away from the ocean and looked up at the cross. *If my actions have been sinful in any way, forgive me.*

His thoughts returned to a simpler time, long ago, when he was a boy in Plymouth, North Carolina. He had been blessed by a grandmother who was a mighty prayer warrior. When he was a baby, she had dedicated his life to God. Her prayers for him were manifold—hundreds, perhaps thousands over his lifetime.

She had written her prayers in notebooks, on the back of church bulletins, on napkins, and on plain white typing paper. She wrote them when he was sick, when he was taking tests in school, when he was starting to date—asking God to bring him the right kind of Christian girlfriend and a Christian wife someday. Her notebooks were discovered in her bedroom and kitchen when she finally died after a long, losing bout with osteoporosis.

"Use my grandson for your glory," she had written, hundreds of times, "and protect him from the temptations of this world."

Zack's eyes watered as he considered how his grandmother's faithful prayers were still being answered. Even this day, they had given him the strength and fortitude to fight for justice and, in some small way, to perhaps stem the tide of terrorism in the United States Navy.

What had happened here was something larger than life. It was a divine appointment, he now realized. Like the prodigal son, Zack had wandered from his roots and sought the things of the world. No more. He may have wandered from the Father, but the Son had never left him nor forsaken him. Just as he promised. And now, Lieutenant Zack Brewer was coming home.

"Hi."

The familiar voice turned his attention to the empty outdoor amphitheatre just under the cross. She was wearing a denim skirt, a green blouse, and large, almost camouflaging sunglasses. If it weren't for her trademark red hair, he might not have recognized her.

"You came."

"You thought I wouldn't?"

"I was hoping you would," he said, smiling. "Come, have a seat." He patted the stone wall beside him.

She walked toward him with the poise of a model. Then with the grace of a gymnast, she hopped up on the wall and sat down, much closer than in the courtroom.

"I've often noticed this place from the highway," she said, "but I've never been up here."

"That's one of the reasons I love it. Most people see the cross from down below but never try to approach it."

She removed her sunglasses and looked up. "It's beautiful."

"And inspiring," he added.

"I read somewhere that they tried to remove it."

"They can never remove or defeat the cross. If they remove this one, ten others will appear on those mountains over there." He pointed to the brown mountain ridges to the south and east, toward Casa de Oro, Rancho San Diego, and across the border into Mexico.

"So why did you do it?" She looked up at him, her hair blowing slightly in the breeze.

"Do what?" His eyes met hers; then for the first time, he noticed Diane was wearing a small gold cross around her neck, much like the one Amy used to wear. The sight of it brought a sting to the back of his throat.

"Kilnap. You didn't have to call him that morning and ask the question. Nobody else even pressed him on the point. It might never have seen the light of day."

"I don't know," he said. "I came up here after we finished the Blount trial. I had a premonition that something was about to happen. It made me uneasy, but I didn't know why. When the thing with Kilnap came up, I knew it could cost us the trial. But . . ."

"But what?"

"I kept thinking about this verse from the Bible my grandmother taught me. *The truth will set you free.* And I felt like the truth had to come out, and if it did, we'd be okay." He couldn't take his eyes from her face.

"Amazing," she said, "isn't it?"

"Not it. *You.*"

She smiled, looking pleased. "Can I ask another question?"

"What? Didn't get enough practice against Levinson?" He quirked a brow.

"Sorry. I don't mean to pry."

"No, go ahead," he said.

"The thing with you and Amy DeBenedetto. Is it true?"

"I knew you'd make a great prosecutor. Go straight for the jugular, don't you?"

"Only because I care." A slight blush colored her cheeks.

"You do?"

"I guess it's kind of hard to go through what we just did and not care a little bit." She let her gaze drift away from him and looked out toward the ocean.

"You realize, don't you, that if the articles in the papers are true, then you could be asking me to incriminate myself."

For a moment she didn't speak; then she turned to him again. "Tell you what." She pushed away a lock of hair that had blown across her face. "How about if you tell me within the context of the attorney-client privilege? That way, what you tell me is confidential, and I'm sworn to secrecy."

They exchanged smiles.

"You never miss a beat, do you?"

"I try not to."

"Okay. Here's the truth. Amy and I were close. She prayed for me even when I couldn't pray for myself. We spent hours discussing cases. She had a way of getting at the truth, seeing things—and people— clearly. Our relationship never moved beyond friendship. Did we commit any acts that made our relationship one of fraternization? No. Never."

She met his eyes, looking surprisingly vulnerable. "So why is it that even her friendship makes me feel . . . a little bit jealous right now?"

He raised his eyebrow. "Let me think. Post-traumatic stress syndrome?"

She laughed and popped him on the knee again. "I'm trying to be serious."

"Serious? I thought you were only serious when it comes to Pierre." His heart seemed to miss a beat as he awaited her answer.

Her gaze drifted away from him again. "Pierre has been good to me. And he was good to my father. He did ask me to marry him—that night we saw you at the restaurant. But I don't love him. There's no future for us in that way."

He looked out toward the ocean. "Speaking of that night at the restaurant, there's something else I should tell you."

"Or someone else?" Her voice dropped to a whisper. "Marianne Landrieu?"

"Not exactly. But it has to do with her uncle."

"The senator?"

He nodded. "When I was in Hilton Head, he approached me with a very tempting proposition."

They sat silently for a moment, with the breeze blowing in their faces.

"Want to tell me about it?"

Zack suddenly felt queasy. "I don't know why, but I feel bad telling you this."

"Attorney-client privilege." She winked, then smiled at him with a teasing glint in her green eyes.

"Senator Fowler wants me to get out of the Navy and move to Louisiana and run for Congress."

The sparkle in her eyes faded. "When?"

"In the next month or so."

"Really?"

"Really. He is guaranteeing my election. And I believe him. The only stipulation is that I'd have to switch parties and run as a Democrat."

"Any other stipulations?"

"Like what?"

"Like Marianne Landrieu is part of the package?"

He dropped his head and stared at the gravel beside the stone wall. "Yes, I think she is part of the package."

She touched his arm, and he raised his head. Their eyes met again. "And you think this congressional race might be tied to the premonition you had?"

"Maybe."

"Maybe?"

"Maybe something else."

"Oh yeah? Like what?"

He looked down again and took a deep breath. "I don't know. I told the senator I would run, but I'm feeling uneasy about it. I'm worried I was pressured into saying yes for the wrong reasons." He looked out at the horizon. "On the one hand, all the power of being in Congress is so attractive." He thought a moment. "On the other hand, all that power doesn't sit well with me somehow."

"Know what?"

"What?" He turned and met her eyes.

"I've been praying for you too," she said, her voice low. "Especially in this trial."

"You have?"

"Yes." She smiled gently.

"I noticed the cross you're wearing"—his gaze fell on it again—"but we've never discussed our faith."

Her eyes watered. "I was in a lot of grief after my father died. I felt guilty about the way I'd headed off on my own, turned my back on him, after all he had done for me. Through it all he was my rock. When I lost him, I didn't know what to do. One of the chaplains told me how I could have a personal relationship with God through accepting his Son." She wiped away a tear with her fingertips. "I've still got a long way to go. Sometimes I get discouraged; then he reminds me I don't have to be perfect to come to him." She laughed lightly. "But he's still working on those rough edges."

He smiled at her as the breeze ruffled her hair.

Their eyes met, and when she spoke again, her voice was softer. "My arrogant attitude toward you before this trial was wrong. I'm sorry." She brushed a strand of hair away from her face.

He reached for her hand and gave it a squeeze. They were silent a moment, dangling their legs off the rock wall and enjoying the late afternoon breeze rushing in from the ocean. Then, standing, he pulled her to her feet. "I've been meaning to ask you something for a long time— probably since Justice School." He drew her closer, and she smiled as if knowing what he was going to say. "Would you like to go out sometime?"

She grinned up at him, the light in her eyes catching the sun. He let go of one hand and touched her face, letting his fingertips trail along the side of her cheek. She stepped into his arms, and they stood there, listening to the sounds of the distant surf and the calls of the seagulls wheeling above them. Zack closed his eyes and buried his face in her hair, thinking that this moment, with Diane in his arms, was one he would remember forever.

After a few minutes, she pulled back and gently touched his jaw. Her eyes seemed luminous with affection, and his heart swelled. "I thought you'd never ask," she said.

"Is that a yes?"

She chuckled. "Of course that's a yes."

Suddenly, he couldn't wait. "How about tonight?"

"Tonight would be great," she said.

"Thank you, Lord," he said, looking heavenward.

"My name's Diane." She laughed lightly.

"No, but your answer just now is a miracle from him." He hugged her again. "Got a cell phone?"

"Sure." She reached into her purse and handed him her phone.

"I just have to make a quick call and clear my schedule for the evening."

"Okay," she said as he punched in the number.

"Sally . . . This is Zack . . . Thank you. Is he in? . . . Yes, I'll hold . . . Senator? . . . Yes, sir. Thank you, sir . . . Senator, about your very kind offer . . . Yes, sir, I've made a decision . . . I've decided to stay in the Navy."

Zack met Diane's gaze and smiled.

"Yes, sir. I'm absolutely sure. Some things have come up"—he squeezed her shoulder—"and I feel like I need to stay in the JAG Corps . . . Maybe one day, sir . . . And, Senator, thank you again for your offer. Good-bye."

"Just like that," she said, her eyes sparkling, "you passed up a political career?"

He took her hand as they sat down again. "Just like that."

"What did he say?"

"He said the Navy was getting a good man."

"Know what?" She grinned at him.

"What?"

"He's wrong. The Navy is *keeping* a good man." She leaned over and kissed him.

He put his arm around her shoulder, and they sat on the stone wall, dangling their legs over the side, and watched the sun set over the Pacific.

ACKNOWLEDGMENTS

The inspiration for this series comes from many sources. I thank my friend and fellow Christian author Robert Whitlow, who lives not far from me in my adopted hometown of Charlotte, North Carolina, and who encouraged me and inspired me to write. Thanks also to my friend and literary agent Chip MacGregor of Alive Communications, who gave me some great advice at a writers' conference several years ago and has continued to be an invaluable sounding board. I am especially indebted to my friend, mentor, and fellow Zondervan author Alton Gansky, whose hands-on encouragement has made this series a reality. I am also grateful to my editor and fellow author Diane Noble, whose unmatched expertise in romance writing helped breathe life into this work, and to Karen Ball, herself a distinguished author, whose recommendation to Zondervan brought this series to life. And finally, I thank my wife, Rhonda, and many others who started reading and editing this work while it was still a work in progress.

We want to hear from you. Please send your comments about this book to us in care of zreview@zondervan.com. Thank you.

GRAND RAPIDS, MICHIGAN 49530 USA

WWW.ZONDERVAN.COM